Jan 9th 20

Best wishes fo

John Meikle

CW01666804

Daughters of the Outback

and from your Vero Beach

Rectory Home hosts.

Come back soon!

Paul & Jackie

John B. Meikle
johnnymeikle@gmail.com

For more information, Please visit: www.johnnymeikle.com

Copyright @ 2011 by John Meikle

Daughters of the Outback

All rights reserved. No part of this book may be reproduced or transmitted in any form or by any means, electronic, or mechanical, including photocopying, recording or by any information storage and retrieval system, without permission in writing from the publisher. No abridgement or changes to the text are authorized by the publisher.

Cover Design:
Allen Spikol, Spikol Pictures Worldwide, Inc.
Melinda Meikle, HeartSong Communications, Inc.

ISBN Number: 978-1-59712-477-5

Printed in the United States of America by:

A&A Printing, Inc.
6103 Johns Road, Suite 5
Tampa, Florida 33634
813-886-0065

DEDICATION

In honor of the memory of David Watson, Ken Skedden and Gavin Wren.

For over 40 years these good men were loyal mates. Hardly a day goes by when thoughts of, at least one of them, brings a smile to my heart.

To write of deep relationships, one must draw from his own valued friendships and, for these, I have been blessed.

To Jim Holley, my friend and neighbor, never too busy to hear an idea, never too tired to encourage.

To my family Alec, Sarah, Brad and my lovely wife Melinda, for the interest they showed in my passion for writing over the years. I also wholeheartedly thank Theakston III, our 14-year old Jack Russell, who did nothing but boss us around!

Poet " Henry Lawson"

Born in a tent in Australia's Weddin Mountains alluvial goldfields in 1867.

Poet of Australian Tradition:

Best known poem, "Faces in the Street"

"On The Night Train"

Have you seen the Bush by moonlight from the train go running by,
Here a patch of glassy water, there a glimpse of mystic sky?
Have you heard the still voice calling, yet so warm and yet so cold:
"I'm the Mother-Bush that bore you! Come to me when you are old?"

Did you see the Bush below you sweeping darkly to the range,
All unchanged and all unchanging, yet so very old and strange!
Did you hear the Bush a-calling, when your heart was young and bold:
"I'm the Mother-Bush that nursed you!
Come to me when you are old?"

Through the long, vociferous cutting as the night train swiftly sped,
Did you hear the grey Bush calling from the pine-ridge overhead:
"You have seen the seas and the cities; all seems done,
and all seems told;
I'm the Mother -Bush that loves you! Come to me, now you are old?"

....

* In those days and today, the Bush and the Outback, are considered the same in the Aussie vernacular.

As It Is Known

To those who have learned to live by her rules, it is a land of desolate beauty and of singular appeal. For those who defy those rules, only torment and certain defeat remain.

As the power of the oceans cannot be challenged, neither can her tantrums of raging fire, floods, and scorching heat. These perils are thrust upon all, man or reptile, who put their survival skills to the ultimate test.

Bleached, windblown skeletons, lying in a place where the last breath was "fought for and taken," serve as the only scorecard for that ultimate test.

Few men seek this place, as most find it their last resort. For the successful, the reward is pride; for others, a realization of a failed life and agonizing death.

If there is a mother nature, she favors neither man nor beast in this harsh place known as the great Australian outback.

Chapter 1

In the vast wilderness of Australia, farms or homesteads are called "stations," and the country's largest station, Naringa, is situated in western Australia, with its fenceless boundaries running for two hundred square miles. This landmass is larger than some countries and has its own weather patterns, causing the grazing herds to constantly follow the seasonal rains in search of food.

Anna Willis sat on the steps of Naringa's beautiful Queenslander homestead, watching the manager's daughters, Peggy and Emma Ellis, play hopscotch on the fine gravel driveway. Anna was the first to spot an approaching vehicle, but before she could warn the girls, they, too, noticed a cloud of dust on the horizon and came running.

"Anna, Anna, look! Someone is coming!" they yelled.

"Yes, I see. Come on, come inside and wash up, and we'll wait for their arrival."

The event of having a visitor was of great excitement to the girls, who complained bitterly about having to go inside.

"Why do we have to go inside?" Emma whined.

Anna ushered them through the doorway. "Number one, there are no visitors expected today," she explained, "so we have no idea who this could be. Number two, only a stranger would come calling this late in the day."

Not giving up, Peggy insisted, "That makes it more exciting!"

"Girls, we might be in the back blocks, but we're not backward. We don't want to show our excitement by running about the place when a stranger drives up our driveway. It could be a stockman looking for work, or just somebody who is lost. How would we appear by jumping up and down at their arrival?" She answered her own question. "Firstly, we would look undignified, and, secondly, we would look pretty silly. You can watch with your little noses pressed hard against the window."

"Okay," said Emma, "but the car won't be here for another twenty minutes."

Anna smiled. "That's good. It will give you time to make yourselves presentable."

~~~

Twenty-six-year-old Paul Bishop was on the biggest adventure of his life, certainly the biggest gamble of his life. He had been driving on the straight, dusty road for the last four hours. In some places, the road was more like a track. Nearly an hour ago, he had passed a bullet-ridden sign saying, *Welcome to Naringa.* Six days ago, when he had left Sydney, he was nervous about getting to Naringa and facing the owner, the famous Mrs. Abernathy, and asking her for the story of Naringa. Now, he was more nervous about making it to Naringa.

Trying to maintain a speed of forty miles per hour, Paul looked back with amazement at the rising dust trail behind him. There was no wind, and the dust hung in the air for miles.

He wiped the sweat from his forehead and muttered, "I couldn't have passed the place, and there hasn't been a turn off. God, no one in the world has a drive this long!" He remembered his mission. "Thank God it's hard to get to, or else I wouldn't be the only one out here asking for the story."

Paul knew that the matriarch, Mrs. Abernathy, had turned down all requests for the story, but that had been in Sydney or London. *Surely she can't turn me down without at least seeing me. That's if I ever find the place.*

Five minutes later, Paul spotted some trees on the horizon. Just as he was doubting his eyes, he made out the familiar shape of a
~~~

windmill. *That's Naringa. It has to be. Boy, I think I love windmills.*

Twenty minutes later, he pulled his dusty, dilapidated car, with two tires and a gas can roped to the roof rack, into an open yard.

After the trailing dust cloud had settled, he emerged from the car and stood in place, stretching. He walked around the car to check the tires. Taking a towel from the front seat, he set it on the hot hood and unhooked the water bag from the front bumper. He folded back the collar of his open-necked shirt and splashed the ice-cold water on his face and wet his hair. As he re-hung the water bag, he squinted into the sun, studying the homestead and the verandas surrounding the great building.

Everything was so quiet, Paul felt like he had entered another world. *Strange*, he thought. *A large building in the middle of nowhere, with nothing out of place and not a soul in sight.* Running a comb through his dust-matted hair proved to be quite a task, for the dust had turned to glue when water was introduced into the equation. The wrinkled cotton sports coat that he pulled from the back seat supported his complete disregard for fashion.

After a slight problem with the front gate, he climbed the stairs to the huge front door and banged the highly-polished brass doorknocker three times.

The door opened on the echo of the third bang. Taken by surprise, he found himself looking into the deep blue eyes of a beautiful woman, causing him to stumble hopelessly for words.

She smiled graciously, and Paul sensed that she could see he was completely out of his depth. In a calming voice, slightly deeper than expected, she greeted him. "Hello. How may I help you?"

"H-Hello . . . My name is Paul Bishop, and I'm from *The Sydney Herald*. Are you Mrs. Abernathy?"

"No, my name is Anna Willis. I'm Mrs. Abernathy's personal

secretary." She reached for his hand. "How do you do, Mr. Bishop."

"Oh, good, thanks. But I'm here to see Mrs. Abernathy."

"I don't think you have an appointment, do you, Mr. Bishop?"

"Well, no, I don't. I was just in the neighborhood and thought I would take a chance she would be about."

Anna appeared to be trying not to laugh. Then she gave him a stern look. "Really, Mr. Bishop? Our nearest neighbor is one hundred twenty-five miles away, and that's as the crow flies, so you could hardly call that a neighborhood."

Paul felt glued to the floor as Anna's clear blue eyes gazed into his, as though anticipating the next word he would utter. Paul didn't want to turn away; it made him feel important to have her full attention.

"Uh, yes, you're right," he conceded. "I did notice there weren't too many houses about." He took a deep breath and let his shoulders slump as he made his confession. "Actually, I haven't been in the country much, and I was getting a bit scared. Silly, isn't it?"

"To the contrary, I think you had good cause to be frightened."

Thinking that he sounded childish, Paul quickly added, "I didn't mean *frightened*, I meant scared. You know, scared I had missed the turn or something."

"Mr. Bishop, this is very dangerous country, and many men have died traveling far shorter distances than you have traveled today." Seeing the shock in his eyes, she gave him another warm, reassuring smile.

Anna invited him to sit, turning to an inviting setting of high-backed natural cane furniture with upholstery in bold prints. "Why don't you make yourself comfortable, and I'll tell Mrs. Abernathy that you're here. Don't get your hopes up, though, as she really doesn't receive anyone these days." Anna waited for Paul to be seated before closing the door behind her.

When she left, Paul lowered his head into the palms of his hands and let his inner voice race. *God, I've got to do better than this immature nervous act. She sure is pretty. A "miss," too. I bet there's a story there, like the French Foreign Legion sort of thing. Hide away to escape the past, I bet. How old would she be? Hard to tell, because she looks so young for an older woman. Now there it is again – "looks so young for an older woman" – another immature thought. Maybe I should have stuck to music.*

~~~

Anna entered the veranda on the other side of the house, shielding her eyes from the blazing setting sun as she entered. She could see Mrs. Abernathy's white hair as she sat in a large upholstered chair. Her shaggy dog, wearing the white face of age, slept at her feet.

Not wanting to startle her, Anna asked quietly, "Mrs. Abernathy, are you awake?"

The woman stirred. "Yes, Anna, I'm awake. I had a little nap earlier and woke to see the sun leaving on its course to another part of the world. What is it? It's a little early for dinner, isn't it?"

"No, it's not dinner. You have a visitor from *The Sydney Herald*."

"Anna, you of all people know how many reporters want to come here, and we have turned them all down."

"Yes, I do know how many. And for every one of those you know of, I have said no to three more, at least."

"Then why on earth are you coming to me about this one? Really, Anna!"

"This one is different. He's just a kid and looks like the dog's breakfast. But there's something there that made me want you to say hello to him, at least. Don't ask me what it is, though. I think it must be his innocence."
~~~

Mrs. Abernathy shaded her eyes from the sun as she looked up at Anna. “If that’s how you feel, I will see him, but don’t think for a minute that I’ll change my mind about giving anyone a story. Another thing – look at the time! This is no time to come calling without an invitation.”

“I think that’s it,” Anna replied. “He’s so far out of his depth, he just doesn’t know what it takes to make a call out here. If he did, I’m quite sure he wouldn’t have tried it in that old rattletrap of a car.”

Mrs. Abernathy sighed. “All right, send him in, and let me take a look at this character of yours.”

~~~

Standing before the aging matriarch, Paul waited for Anna to make the introductions. They shook hands, and at Mrs. Abernathy’s touch, Paul felt his awkward shyness slide away. This new confidence level didn’t help him with his opening statement, however.

“Well, Mr. Bishop?” said the old woman.

As Paul was about to answer, the white-faced dog caught his eye, and without thinking, he blurted out, “That’s an old dog!”

“We are both old dogs, Mr. Bishop. Which one did you come to see?”

Anna coaxed him. “Why don’t you tell Mrs. Abernathy why you came all this way, Mr. Bishop? I’m sure we would both like to know.”

Paul gathered his thoughts and took a deep breath. “Well, Mrs. Abernathy, I saw in my office that you had given the entire Naringa station to the people who work here and the heirs of the families who worked here in the past.”

“Yes, that is correct. Go on.”

“Well, I’m not a communist or anything, but I thought this was the greatest thing I’d ever heard of, and I want to write about it.”
~~~

Both ladies laughed heartily at the communist disclaimer.

Mrs. Abernathy fell quiet for a minute. “But, Paul – may I call you Paul? I think I can. Well, Paul, do you have any idea how many newspaper men and journalists we have turned away? They all wanted to write the same story, and mind you, a lot of these men and women were better known than yourself.”

Paul frowned. He couldn’t believe his ears. “Ma’am, I . . . I’m not well-known at all. As a matter of fact, no one knows me. But I have to start somewhere.”

“Paul, if no one knows you, why? Who sent you out here, and why? Keep in mind that I know a lot of people in your business.”

Paul hesitated again, trying to field the question. “Well, nobody really sent me, ma’am,” he said with a little chuckle. “I got my holiday pay for last year and just took off on an unpaid leave. I know that I really didn’t do enough research, because I had no idea just how far everything is out here. Actually, I never thought of there being so much space.” Thinking that sounded a little dumb, he quickly added, “You know, I did know there was a lot of space, but what I meant was that I’ve never been part of so much space.”

Not saying a word, Anna seemed quite happy. Paul’s genuine openness seemed to answer the question as to why Anna was pulling for him.

Mrs. Abernathy sat up in her seat as she addressed him. “Yes, Paul, they are not the words I would use, but I do understand how hard the vastness of the outback is to put into words.” She looked up at him sharply. “How much would you be willing to pay for the story of Naringa?”

Paul’s voice rose a couple of octaves. “Pay, ma’am? I don’t have any money. I’ll be lucky to make it back to work in Sydney.”

“That might be so, Paul. But, please, if you got this story, you could make a lot of money. Surely you have counted on that?"

"Yes, now that I think about that end of it, there could be money, Mrs. Abernathy, but I hadn't thought about that before. You see, I know I can write, but I can only write about things I believe in. I've been waiting for something that puts a lump in my heart. I just want to write this story. If any money comes from it, I could give it back to Naringa, minus my expenses, of course." Taking in a full breath of air and letting it out slowly, he added, "I just want to let my heart write the story."

Mrs. Abernathy rose slowly to her feet, which signaled that the meeting was over. "That's a pretty tall request, and it's getting late, so I will tell you what to do. You go with Anna, and she will give you a bed and some dinner. Maybe we will talk more in the morning. Anna, please tell the cook I think I will take a dinner tray in my room."

Not waiting for a reply, she turned and left the room, followed by the old dog, which struggled to keep up.

Paul turned to Anna as though they were a team and said, "Well, she didn't say no."

"You're right, and believe me, Mrs. Abernathy has no trouble saying no when she wants to. She's not only one of the best women I've ever met, she's also one of the strongest. Come on, I'll show you where you can put your head down for the night."

Paul followed Anna across the house onto yet another veranda. "Here we are. The bathroom is two doors down the hall, and dinner is at seven." With a warm smile, Anna finished with a last piece of advice: "Wear a tie."

The room was sparse but neat. Paul recognized the Candlewick bedcover that decorated the high, white iron bed. The look and touch of the fabric brought Paul back to his childhood, when his Candlewick bedcover had been his mother's pride and joy. As a kid, he knew he could do anything in his room, but it would be more than his life was worth to harm the Candlewick bedspread.

He sat on the bed and felt quite proud of himself. *Not bad for a day's work – dealing with the owner and sleeping in the main house.* It was then that he realized what he liked so much: the smell, rich and homey, of polished floors and old leather. *How can a smell make you feel at home and give you confidence? But it does.* Checking his watch, he noted that he had only thirty-five minutes before dinner. *Better not lie down,* he thought. *Sleeping through dinner wouldn't go down too well, I'm sure.*

At seven o'clock, Paul made his way to the main hall, led by the sound of a radio broadcasting the news. The four people listening all rose from their chairs to meet Paul as he entered.

A young girl with pigtails ran up to him with her hand extended. "Hello, my name is Peggy Austin, and I am eleven." Pulling her sister in front of her, she added, "And this is my sister, Emma, and she is nine. Our dad is the station manager, and we know your name is Mr. Paul Bishop."

Almost feeling challenged, Paul laughed. "That's right, and I am pleased to meet you two charming and very pretty young ladies."

That did it. Both girls blushed a bright red and retreated, not knowing how to treat the grown-up compliment.

Stan Austin, the station manager, spoke firmly but kindly. "Well, Mr. Bishop, I see you've met our welcoming team. I'm their father, Stan Austin, and this is my wife, Mary. Nice to have you here. Welcome to Naringa."

Their eyes met as they shook hands.

"Thank you very much," said Paul, "and let me be sure to tell you how happy I feel to be here. On the drive out here, I never would have bet on being invited to dinner in this lovely home."

Stan let out a small laugh. "Outback faith, I call it. It seems nothing happens out here, and then, when you try to do something, something else happens. I know what it's like to travel in the outback, seeing nothing except the horizon no matter which way you turn."

Mary Austin was not just good-looking, she was beautiful, with wide, deep brown eyes and shiny black hair that glowed with good health. She wore her hair in a ponytail and could have passed for an eighteen-year-old. As Paul let the numbers go through his head, he knew she had to be in her thirties to have an eleven-year-old. However, he couldn't finish his math before Anna entered the room.

From the moment she appeared, Anna set the tone for the evening with her elegance.

"Ah, Paul, I see that you've met everybody," she said. "Shall we all go in to dinner? I'm sure Mr. Bishop is hungry after his long day of adventure. If you could sit between the girls, Mr. Bishop, it would give them an equal chance to talk you to death."

Paul blushed slightly. "I'd better be careful what I say out here about being hungry, but at home we say, 'I could eat a horse and still find room for the saddle.' And would everybody please call me Paul?"

In unison, both girls chimed in, "Does that mean us, too?"

"Well, of course, if you'll let me call you by your first names and not 'Miss Austin.'"

Giggling at the sound of it, Peggy managed to say, "We wouldn't know who you were talking to, if you called us that."

"Okay, it's a deal, then." Paul had to pinch himself. This was like being famous, compared to being home alone in his boarding house room, trying to make it through the week without starving. *How did this happen? It must be right. But don't let any of your crazy ideas ruin it,* he warned himself.

~~~
~~~

11

Anna could feel the excitement in the room as she entered and admitted to herself that she had taken a little extra care in dressing tonight. While she was dressing, she realized how vain the presence of a stranger could make her. Even though Paul could never be a romantic presence in her life, his presence did, somehow, arouse her womanhood. She was thirty-four and guessed she was ten years older than Paul.

Will there ever be another man in my life? she wondered. Eric had been dead to her for nearly five years. The thought of what had happened, and the loss of Eric's love, made her pause. The lipstick dropped from her hand as faces from the past flashed through her mind, all having one thing in common: the mask of hate.

Anna knew that she would feel that hatred for the rest of her life, no matter how far she ran. The intensity of the feelings were branded with a hot iron into her soul, and only tonight did she realize it had been five years. Those years had allowed her self-image to revive, but not flourish. Elegance and truth had once been her nature. The elegance was natural, and she was truthful to a fault, but the false accusations and slander of others had been so vicious that she had almost believed them to be true. She had become convinced that people always believed the worst of others. Only later did she realize that those same people were so eager to hear the worst about the next person, that she was long forgotten. She had hoped that time alone would heal the wounds from that hateful slander.

No one in the room could possibly be aware of her thoughts as her natural charm took charge of the evening. Anna delighted the girls by clapping her hands in mock delight at their stories.

Leading the way, Anna addressed the group, "Well, everyone seems to be in jolly good spirits tonight. It must be the arrival of the soon-to-be-famous writer from Sydney, Mr. Paul Bishop."

Everybody joined in and applauded heartily for Paul.

In a deep blush, he hurried to say, "Ms. Willis is putting you on. I do work for *The Sydney Herald*, but I've never had a story under my own name. I do really like the sound of that famous writer bit, though."

Anna looked at Paul, not knowing what she was feeling about this young stranger, but she did know that it gave her insides a glow of happiness she hadn't felt for a long time. Chiming in, she added, "It will only be a short while before we'll all say, 'Let's clink our glasses to Paul Bishop, who we are proud to say we knew before he was famous.'"

The girls laughed so heartily that Anna thought she might have overdone it.

~~~

Paul had never eaten so well or felt so special in his life. The girls talked mainly about their one trip to Sydney, where they had spent every hour of daylight at the beach. Conquering Everest would have paled compared to being at the beach, so far as the girls were concerned.

The dinner was served by Jawa, a young Aborigine girl from a tribe that passed through the station every other year. Stan explained that during their last visit, the tribe had come to pick up Jawa. She would have none of it, so they set up camp and negotiated. It took some food supplies, three bottles of grog, and some of Mary's make-up before they finally agreed to let Jawa stay. The negotiations had taken about four days.

Paul had never seen anyone with such black skin. Paul found it most beautiful, as though he were admiring a fine painting.

The cook, Mrs. Martin, took the trouble to bring out the roast leg of Hogget and placed it before Stan to carve. Paul suspected that
~~~

she had come out only to get a look at the house guest. Not only was he pleased to be the center of attention, he felt satisfaction in being the star attraction. *That's the sort of thing good writers know. Now just don't ruin this with some of your naïve comments.*

Anna asked, "If you have had enough, Paul, I think we should all move out to the veranda for coffee. What do you say, Mary?"

Mary stood in apparent agreement. "Yes, that would be lovely, and you two girls can get to your music lessons."

Paul also rose from the table. "I'll say it was the best meal I've ever had in my life, and I will never forget it. I couldn't eat another bite. Thank you."

Sitting on the veranda with his coffee in hand, Paul tried to analyze his feelings at the present moment. *Celebrity* or *VIP* came to mind. It also occurred to him that he would be neither if he fell asleep, which he was very close to doing. To avoid appearing bored, he stood up and went to help the girls with their piano lessons. Peggy was murdering a practice piece as Paul leaned over to ask if he could help.

Peggy was delighted, and in no time, Paul had her playing the piece from beginning to end with only the occasional falter.

"I've never heard her play anywhere near as well before," Mary said with tears in her eyes. "Well done, Paul. You must have a musical background to teach that well."

Pleased to be asked, he said, "Yes, I attended Sydney Classical for three years."

"My goodness, that's fantastic. To be chosen is an achievement beyond the reach of most. Really, Paul, that is fantastic. I'm impressed. How is it that music is not your career path?"

"I would have liked it to be, believe me, but three years was enough to know deep down that I didn't have the creative depth for music to be my life's work." He had her attention and didn't want to lose it, as he could never remember having such a beautiful woman as a captive audience.

"You must have been very disappointed to give up that dream."

"Yes, it took a while, but eating also became a habit that was easy to get used to. But seriously, you get to the place where you know you're not much different from the other talented students. You may know this early on, but admitting it takes time. Then, the more you know, the more you realize that it takes more than just talent. I'm okay with it, actually, as I'm a good writer, but I know music will always be a part of me."

"Yes, it will, but in the meantime, you're going to have to play for this culture-starved group."

"Certainly, it would be my pleasure, and how could I say no after being treated like royalty?"

Paul couldn't see his audience from the piano, so he didn't see Mrs. Abernathy join the others on the veranda. To the delight of the girls, he played their practice pieces in four-four time with all the classical frills. Their laughter filled the air, as they couldn't believe their pieces could sound so good. Anna came over to ask the girls to let Paul have the bench to him. They obediently took their places on the veranda with the others. Paul's choice was Debussy's "Clare de Lune."

As Paul played, stillness came over the night. The silence was not broken until Mrs. Abernathy spoke through her tears. "That was my husband's favorite piece. He wasn't a bad pianist, but certainly couldn't play as well as Mr. Bishop. Those nights that he played on that piano were so long ago, before we were married or had any idea what life had in store for us."

Mrs. Abernathy left the porch before the piece was completed, and as she passed Anna, she bent down to say something the others could not hear.

By the time Paul had finished, both girls were sleeping on the floor. Mary and Stan quietly whispered, “Good night,” and picked up the girls, trying not to wake them.

“You have done very well tonight, Paul,” Anna said. “Your playing was superb. You have introduced yourself in a way I could not have done for you.”

Feeling on top of the world, Paul gave an open-hands gesture. “What on earth could that be?”

“Mrs. Abernathy said she would see you tomorrow.”

Paul had been so caught up with everyone paying so much attention to him; he had nearly forgotten why he was there. “Oh, that’s great. What time?”

“She has her breakfast at seven and will probably see you around nine, I would think. You can have breakfast at seven-thirty, and I will come for you when she is ready. I wouldn’t be too expectant, but there is a chance. Otherwise, I’m sure she would have bid you farewell tonight.”

Paul shook Anna’s hand and thanked her for all the help.

~~~

The next morning, after he had finished his steak and eggs breakfast, Paul waited on the veranda for Anna to come and get him.

Anna greeted him cheerily. “Good morning, Mr. Bishop. I hope you slept well. Mrs. Abernathy will see you now. Could you please follow me?”

Paul smiled but thought Anna sounded a little too formal, which probably meant, *It was nice of you to come all this way, but . . .*

He followed Anna to the veranda, where Mrs. Abernathy sat in the same chair, but somehow seemed more relaxed. Maybe it was the cool shade or the fact that they had already met, but Paul noted her ease.
~~~

She waved Paul to a seat. "Well, Paul, after your beautiful piano playing last night, I lay awake, letting images of the past flood my mind – words and conversations around that very piano repeated word for word, as though they were spoken yesterday. Those images showed me how many people and lives have been connected to Naringa over all those years.

"I must say, those fond memories gave me a warm feeling, but I haven't changed my mind about telling the story of Naringa. However, as you are the first to make it this far, I think we should hear what you have to say. Go ahead, if you would like to try and convince us."

With total confidence, Paul let the words flow through him. "Mrs. Abernathy, it's not me who deserves the story, but the people of Australia. And even more important, Australia's children of tomorrow deserve to know about the Naringas of their country, and the outback. They deserve to know the people who run these stations, and the wonders of their lives in the outback, as well as all of their tragedies. Life changes every day, and none of us sees these historical changes until we look back on the past. I think it is your duty to tell the world about the lives so many people have given to Maringa.

"The duty is to place value on their endeavors. In such a vast terrain, important stories of triumph and failure go without recognition, and become nothing more than the blowing sands of these deserts. No soul on this earth should have their treasured time and efforts totally forgotten." Paul paused, surprised at his own fervor. Quietly, he concluded, "That's what I think, Mrs. Abernathy."

She gazed at him for a moment. "Tell me, Paul, did you rehearse those lines?"

"No, Mrs. Abernathy, they just seemed to burst forth." He added quickly, "But I really believe every word."

Mrs. Abernathy smiled and turned to Anna. "Well, I'm not sure

I like being told what my duties are, but I can see Paul's view, and I must say I have never looked at Naringa and the outback in that manner. What do you think, Anna?"

"Actually, I am pleasantly surprised, as I hadn't really thought about Naringa in those terms, either. But I do think Paul is right about paying respect to the efforts of all those who fought for this place over the years. I also agree that this is Aussie history, and it certainly should be recorded. I also think that if Paul can describe his vision so well to us, as he has done, then he could write the story. I would love to see him get the chance."

Ms. Abernathy turned back to him, "Paul, if I did give you the story, how would you record it?"

"Well, before I left the office, I signed out a recorder and ten hours of tape, hoping for the best, you know?"

With a slight smile, Mrs. Abernathy sighed. "I guess I could fill at least half of those tapes. If you go and get them and set up, I will go over things with Anna. To my amazement, I am willing to start right after lunch. You know, Paul, I have considered doing this before, and the only way it will make sense is if I fill in a lot things that I know now but may not have known then – reenacting them, in a way." She looked up at him. "Do you know what I mean?"

"I think so. You now know the outcome, so you can fill in the unknowns of the time."

Delighted, she said to Paul with a spark in her eye, "You want to shake on it, mate?"

Anna openly clapped with joy. "Oh, Mrs. Abernathy, I'm sure you have made the right decision."

It took Paul several seconds to realize that Anna's joy was for him. He thought he felt himself grow a couple of inches, as this was his first true first success at selling himself and his beliefs. He didn't feel overwhelmed – at least, not yet. He just wanted to get started.

Chapter 2

It was October 1953, and the Pan Am Viscount bound for Sydney, Australia, had just initiated its descent. The monotonous drone of the engines was harshly interrupted by the captain's voice announcing that Pan Am Flight 714 would be landing in Sydney in approximately thirty minutes. A loud round of applause rang throughout the plane from the tired but eager passengers, as if additional oxygen had just been pumped into the cabin.

Slowly rising to a sitting position, Miss Lindsay Graeme realized she felt absolutely terrible, with none of the thrill of independence and adventure that she had anticipated feeling at this moment. She was exhausted and a little apprehensive about the immediate future. *This is nonsense*, she thought. *Once I feel my freedom, this doubt will surely disappear for good.*

The stewardess had now taken over the intercom, giving instructions on filling out the immigration cards and visitor visas. Wide awake, Lindsay began packing up her papers and books. A tattered picture fell from her diary and landed face-up at her feet. As she bent to pick it up, her hand froze, and her mind flashed back to the night her father had proudly presented this picture to her. Already it seemed like a lifetime ago, but in fact, it had been only five short days.

The picture was of her father and his Australian war buddy, Mr. Ralph Abernathy, standing on the wing of an English Spitfire. Lindsay had grown up knowing the name Ralph Abernathy. The stories didn't vary much; in each one, Ralph saved her father's life, or he saved Ralph's life. When she was small, she used to thank Mr. Abernathy in her prayers for saving her daddy. As she grew older, she hated the sound of his name, because for the first fifteen years of her life, her father never stopped talking about the war. Maybe that was it: Had Jack Graeme found real life to be an anti-climax? Maybe not, but something had caused her father to stop enjoying life. Whatever it was, it had happened during that time period, and now all he cared about was having total control. No longer merely a quirk, it had become a sickness.

Lindsay's parents, Jack and Rosemary Graeme, were like many couples whose romantic life had died long ago and been replaced by individual self-doubt and fear of change. Rosemary didn't really care, as Jack's controlling nature had completely taken over and become the classic case of a personality disorder. As the years went by, Jack's obsession grew worse, and neither Lindsay nor her mother could oppose him. Instead, they both constantly made allowances for him in the name of peace. Night after night, Lindsay rehearsed plans to leave home, and, more importantly, how she would break it to them. Instead, she always lost her nerve and remained silent. She would lie in bed cursing for being so spineless. She felt such guilt when designing her freedom plans, knowing that her father did love her. *God, imagine if someone really had it in for me. I would be an absolute gutless wonder.*

As she gazed at the picture of her father and Ralph Abernathy, she tried to reconstruct the exact time when she had finally gathered the courage to speak up.

She had been gazing at herself in the mirror, asking why she had such fear of her father. Looking at her pretty golden hair and hazel eyes, she promised the image in the mirror that she would finally stand up for herself.

She entered the living room, where her father sat perusing the paper and her mother read an ever-present library book. Without planning her approach, Lindsay strode into the middle of the room and announced, “I am leaving for Sydney, Australia, in two days.”

With her eyes closed, she stood facing away from her father, waiting for his expected wrath. Silence reigned. The ticking of the clock seemed to get louder and louder, until her father’s soft voice finally broke the silence. “Does it have to be Australia?”

Taken aback, she said, “Does what have to be Australia?”

He continued in a controlled, monotone pitch: “The place you have chosen, of course.”

She replied with the same tempered voice, “Yes, Australia is the place I have chosen.”

The constant silence caused Lindsay to slump back in her chair, feeling both exhilaration and confusion, not knowing what to say next. She felt as if someone else were in her body, doing the talking. She knew it was difficult for her parents. She was an only child, which made it difficult for them to cope with her independence. *But I’m twenty-eight years old, for god’s sake!* she protested.

Oh, they had tried. Her father had bought her a studio apartment in Manhattan in order to give her space, but that gesture had come with many strings attached. The straw that broke the camel’s back was his rule for her to come home on weekends. Now here she was, waiting expectantly for more rules.

He surprised Lindsay by standing and pacing the floor. A million thoughts raced through her head. *He has never hit me, so why do I feel so scared? He never walks the floor. This is going to be it.*

Jack Graeme’s words were not loud, but Lindsay jumped as he spoke. “Lindsay, both your mother and I acknowledge that we have never known how to handle your independence, out of our love for you, of course. So, let us first say that we understand. However, I ask again, does it have to be Australia?"

Her courage was waning like the outgoing tide. The overwhelming fear of opposing her father both shamed and paralyzed her. An inner voice reminded her that this was her last chance, and every fiber of her body knew that voice was right. Suddenly, a strong voice of conviction blurted out, "Yes, it has to be Australia."

That was that. There was hugging and promises of understanding, but essentially that was it.

Three days later, at the airport, her father gave her the famous photograph. "I haven't heard from him in fifteen years, but in a time of need, all you have to do is introduce yourself. Your name is all you will need, but I want you to have this photo. His last address is on the back." He turned the photo over and read the address aloud: "Wombra Stunt Club, Wombra, New South Wales."

She now picked up the photo from the airplane floor and mockingly exclaimed, "Yes, 'in a time of need' strikes directly in the face of independence, don't you think, Mr. Graeme?" She stuffed the photo into the seat pocket in front of her. "There now, Mr. Abernathy, that's independence nothing personal, by the way my father sends his regards."

A sudden moment of doubt deflated Lindsay's bravado. Her intentions were to stay in Australia for at least two years, but she hadn't told her father that, in case she couldn't do it. She knew that he would sell her apartment if he knew her intentions. She also knew that the apartment would soften her fall, should she fail.

"Excuse me, miss. Miss, excuse me," came the stewardess's request as she stood impatiently at Lindsay's side.

With a start, Lindsay looked up at the expectant stewardess and exclaimed, "I'm sorry, I must have been daydreaming."

The stewardess was unmoved. "I need your entry card, please," she pressed.

Lindsay obliged and handed her the card with a smile.

Thirty minutes later, almost through customs, Lindsay thought it was just like any other American airport, except for the marvelous accents. The Aussie accent was music to her ears, the main indicator that she now stood in a foreign country. *Continent*, she corrected herself. *Yes, Australia is the only continent in the world that is inhabited by one nationality. Got to know these things,* she thought as she followed the bell cap to the bus stop.

As she tipped the porter, he removed his cap to thank her. "The bus leaves every fifteen minutes," he said, "and the second stop is the Excelsior Hotel, miss."

At that moment, an older lady dressed in a rumpled, polished-cotton dress came running up to Lindsay. "Hang on a minute, love. You forgot your photo." She produced the photo that Lindsay had just thrown away.

Surprised, but not wanting to disappoint the thoughtful fellow passenger, she mustered up some enthusiasm. "Oh, thank you for the kind effort."

Proud that she had done a good deed, the lady shrugged off the thanks and looked shyly at the ground. "You're right, love, no trouble at all," and went on her merry way.

With a faint chuckle, Lindsay reluctantly tucked the damned photo into her bag again.

It was warmer than she had expected outside. As she looked at her watch, she was surprised to see how late it was. *Okay, 11:15 p.m., February third, Nineteen Fifty-Three. Independent spirit arrives from New York to take Sydney by storm!*

This feeling didn't linger, because, by the time she reached her room, she felt too tired to do anything other than go straight to bed. *Some adventurer, indeed.* Despite her tiredness, she realized that she was very happy, an experience she hadn't felt for a long time. Happiness brought on an overwhelming sense of reward.

~~~

Lindsay didn't stir until 8:30 the next morning. The sun was trapped behind the blind, managing to squeeze enough light into the room to give evidence of its brilliance outside. After dressing, she gathered her brochures and hurried down to the dining room for breakfast. She couldn't help but notice the two main items listed on the menu: Fish and eggs with chips, and steak and eggs with chips. *That would set you up for the day, and perhaps the night, too*, she thought. Intent on planning her first day of adventure, she looked up from the brochures and noticed a man at the next table trying to get her attention.

"Is this your first visit?" he asked.

Not welcoming the idle chatter of a stranger, but not wanting to be rude, Lindsay reluctantly answered, "Yes, does it show?"

"No, not at all, although I wouldn't have any trouble knowing you were from the States. I would be the first to admit that I'm no detective, but besides your accent, the eggs were a dead giveaway, as eggs-over-easy is strictly American." He raised his hands in mock self-defense. "Please don't mind my chatter. I mean no offense."

Forgetting her earlier annoyance, she replied without hesitation, "No, I don't really mind. I guess I'll have to get used to being the one with the accent."

Swinging his legs from under the table, he turned to face her. "My name is John Swanson, and I'm actually English, but I've been living in New Zealand for eight years. My business brings me to Sydney about three times a year." He extended his hand, and they shook.
~~~

"How do you do? My name is Lindsay Graeme, and I'm on vacation from New York. Do you like it over here, Mr. Swanson?"

"Yes! Actually, my wife is Australian. She couldn't make it this trip, although we will spend a couple of days with her family out in Wombra."

"Wombra?" she echoed in surprise.

"Yes, do you know it?"

"No, but I do have an address from there which, incidentally, I have no intention of using." *Little do you know, mister, but that's the last place I would ever visit.*

"Pity," he said, shaking his head. "It's really a nice little town about thirty-five miles from here. There's a train in the mornings and afternoons. It's most convenient. I think you would like it."

Lindsay yawned as she looked around the room, indicating that she was no longer interested in his idle conversation, and buried her head back in the travel brochures. *Harmless enough, I suppose, but he sounds a bit too much like my father. How does he know what I would like? Plus, that's what my father wants. That's the past. Now it's what I decide.*

Getting the message, he finally bid her good-bye and wished her luck.

It was set. Her choices for the day were strictly to be outdoors. *Keep the museums, etcetera, for when the weather is not so nice. Ha! That's how experienced travelers plan their days.* She knew the famous attraction in Sydney was the harbor, so she decided to spend the entire day taking boat excursions to out-of-the-way places. *What a plan!* She felt very pleased with herself and her new independent spirit.

Thirty minutes later, she was out on her adventure, attractively dressed in white shorts, black tank top, and a large straw sun hat with red ribbon trim.

Chapter 3

As Father Gavin Abernathy entered St. Joseph's Hospital in Rose Bay, one of the most beautiful suburbs of Sydney, the brilliant sun made the hospital garden look like a painter's pallet. However, for Father Gavin, Australia's celebrity priest, God's magnificent artwork did nothing to make this hospital hospitable. The smell of disinfectant made his stomach turn.

His visits to the Rose Bay Sanatorium had become more intimate over the past year, and he now visited three times a week to see his twenty-five-year-old sister, Peggy.

The sanatorium was a separate building inside the St. Joseph's complex, and as Father Gavin approached the reception desk, two young nuns rushed over with cheerful greetings.

Always quick with a smile, he beat the sisters to a greeting. "Good morning, Sisters, how are you on this glorious day?"

With a slight curtsy, both sisters answered, "Good, Father, thank you."

"That's good. How is my willful sister behaving today?"

Once again, both answered in unison, "Good." Sister Ann, the taller of the two, blushed girlishly. "Perhaps we should let Father hear the good news from just one of us. Please, Sister Beth, go ahead."

Sister Beth smiled as she received the honor. "Well, Father, Miss Peggy seems to have had an epiphany, or at least, a huge breakthrough."

"Oh? That sounds great, but what do you mean?"

"Well, we both feel that she has abandoned all the hostility that seemed to possess her. We both noticed it." Then, glancing at the other nun for support she asked, “Didn’t we, Sister Ann?”

Sister Ann took a deep breath and smiled before she cautiously answered, “Yes, Father, there is a definite difference in her attitude.” She quickly added, “Keep in mind, I have been fooled plenty of times with excuses just to get out of here.”

Gavin mulled this over. “Well, thank you, Sisters. I will go and see what she has in store for her poor old unsuspecting brother. And Sister, I wouldn’t worry about being fooled in the past, as it is only a closed heart that does not take a chance on being wrong.”

With a slight curtsy, Sister Ann quietly replied, “Thank you, Father. I will always remember your kind words.”

A moment later, Father Gavin’s tap on Peggy’s door was answered by her loud, commanding voice. “Come in.” She sat by the window, dressed attractively, and refrained from looking around as her brother entered the room.

Gavin was thirty-three years old, eight years Peggy’s senior. It had been a year since he had greeted his sister with a kiss. As he had learned, it was best to first test her mood.

“Gee, Peg, you look well dressed and chipper this morning.”

Still not turning, she replied, “Yeah, I feel good, even though I hardly slept last night.”

“That’s not like you. You normally sleep like a log, and a loud one at that.”

“Gavin, I have decided to stop fighting.”

He paused. “Oh, fighting what, exactly?”

“Fighting the fact that I love you and I hate you. Sometimes love more than hate, and the other way around, too, and sometimes both feelings at the same time. I’m not going to fight the fact that I am an alcoholic anymore. I’ve had enough of this childish bullshit.” Her voice grew louder as she turned to face him. “To hell with this. I’m out of here, and you can't stop me. I'm going around the world on a painting trip. This stuff is behind me forever!"

Taking a seat opposite her, Gavin spoke softly, "This sounds really positive Peggy." But if it evokes such anger to tell me this good news, I don't think you've dealt with the problem. You've merely found a solution that is more appealing than being here."

"Jesus Christ, Gavin, you may be the savior priest to half of Aussie, but you just piss me off with that holier-than-thou quiet talk. I am your sister, remember. I saw you bash up Billy Hearder so bad he had to go to the hospital. I saw you screwing Heather Hadley and getting so drunk you couldn't even clean yourself off. And that's only without even thinking back. So be real."

He sighed. "That's all true. I also know you could dredge up plenty of other not-so-honorable things about me, and I wouldn't deny them. The important question is, why do you hold me responsible for what happened to you in the past?"

Calming down, she turned her back on him and gazed out the window. "I thought about that, too. More than anything else, I think I was bitterly jealous of you – the fact that you took control of my estate, the fact that my life was going steadily downhill while you became famous . . . and the church took you away from me. These thoughts are from a little sister and a grown woman, who both feel sorry for themselves. Anyway, I came to the conclusion that there are only two outcomes to this story. I can continue to come in and out of places like this, or I can cross a bridge and never come back."

Before Gavin could answer, his mind flooded with memories of the countless times he had been called to pick her up from some drinking binge. Every time when the bottom looked so close, she told the same story. More often than not, she would be covered in vomit and crying that this would be the last time. Of course, he wanted to believe her, but he knew it could never be. Could this be any different?

"Sounds good to me, Peg, but don't you think the drinking was the stem of the problem more than me? If you don't sort that out, you'll just be back here, hating me more."

Turning to face him, she cut in. "For once, I agree with you. I realized that crossing that bridge with regard to drinking is not hard for me."

Gavin opened his hands in a gesture of appeal. "Peg, isn't that a little too easy to say when you've been in three rehabs in the last two years?"

In a shrill but even voice, she replied, "Let me paint you a picture, brother dear. A young girl goes out drinking and partying in Sydney's so-called society and all is great, except that she wakes up nude on a bed, covered in her own vaginal blood with six hours missing out of her life. At least six hours missing out of her life! I was saving myself, remember? That's the self-loathing that has kept me here, and that's also why I could no longer paint. Whenever I met a guy, I would think maybe he was there that night . . . maybe he had already had me and was now silently mocking me." She stared at Gavin with profound misery reflected in her bulging, tearful eyes.

Gavin tried to hide the shock from his expression. "Peggy, being a priest does not make this easy to hear, but as your brother who loves you more than ever, I assure you that I am by your side."

With tears in his eyes, he put both arms around her, ignoring the rejection her rigid body conveyed. "I'm really sorry, but I still love you. Don't you know that?"

Her body went limp, and she cried like she had never cried before. They remained in a firm embrace until the heat pushed them apart. Facing each other, they wiped away the tears, in order to enjoy the feeling of unity.

Peggy was the first to break the silence. "I'm glad I was finally able to tell you, Gav. Actually, I can't believe how glad I am that I told you. Maybe there is something to this confessional rubbish."

With a soft laugh, Gavin agreed. "I think there is. It's good to get it out. But just telling me isn't going to make a difference, is it?"

"No, not just telling you. I didn't tell you of my simple breakthrough. The image of that night has kept me drinking and in places like this. Well, a flash just hit me. If it can keep me here, it can also keep me out of here. Gav, you're not going to believe this, but until now, I never actually thought about stopping drinking, even after hundreds of hours of lectures, step meetings, and every other bloody thing. Can you believe it never really occurred to me? But last night it did occur to me that I can stop if I want. I never wanted to because I was living in that blood-covered bed. That bed was just as strong keeping me out of here as it was keeping me in. I feel, at last, I have a choice."

Gavin stood and looked at Peggy as they both tried to suppress their tears. Gavin held her for a long time, and for the first time, he felt no resistance or tension in Peggy's body. "I think a painting trip would be just the thing to get you up and going, but I want you to spend some time at Naringa before you go. There's no hurry, is there?"

"No, there's no rush. But you must promise me that you won't try to stop me from making this trip."

Gavin stood back to display his open hands. "No, Peg, I will not stand in your way, because I have the greatest faith in you. Today may go down as one of the happiest days in my life. I wouldn't spoil that for either of us. As soon as I leave this room, I promise I will start the ball rolling to get you out of here, which will take no more than two days. I promise."

~~~
~~~

Ian Abernathy, Gavin's younger brother by six years, left the city traffic and cruised into the picturesque foothills of the mighty Snowy Mountains. Maybe it was because the terrain was so un-Australian that Ian believed everything was different in this part of the world. This terrain held the soul of Banjo Paterson, author of one of Australia's best-known folk stories, a poem called "The Man from Snowy River." Ian wondered, *Did the land make him famous, or did he make it famous?* Ian couldn't think of the poem's title without realizing the ironic unfairness. He knew it wouldn't sound the same, but thought it should have been called "The Man and the Horse from Snowy River." Neither could have made history without the other.

These thoughts had been with Ian since childhood, for his father must have read the story to him a thousand times. As a kid, he believed 100% that the only reason for the man's fame was because the horse couldn't talk. Even today he chuckled at his childhood logic. No matter what, the famous ride of the man from Snowy River lived on and still carried the reader away with its heartfelt story of true heroism. Without conscious recall, the verses came into Ian's head, and he found himself reciting the words out loud as he drove through the mountains on the beautiful country road.

He sent the flint stones flying, but the pony kept his feet,
He cleared the fallen timbers in his stride,
And the man from Snowy River never shifted in his seat —
It was grand to see that mountain horseman ride.
Through the stringy barks and saplings, on the rough and broken ground,
Down the hillside at a racing pace he went;
And he never drew the bridle till he landed safe and sound,
At the bottom of that terrible descent.

It was definitely Banjo Paterson who had introduced Ian to the Timor pony, in the verse which read,

And one was there, a stripling on a small and weedy beast,
He was something like a racehorse undersized,
With a touch of Timor pony – three parts thoroughbred at least –
And such as are by mountain horsemen prized.

The idea had stayed with him for years, and now he was on his way to initiate the first part of his dream. The family station was in Western Queensland, where the harshest conditions made living a learned task, and farming an affair of the soul. Horses were still man's best friend, and Ian now wanted to take the hardiest of the Timor strain to breed with the hardened Aussie brumby. The brumby was a self-bred horse from the wild and could live in the extreme heat, but lacked the heart and the pluck of the mighty Timor pony.

Ian was familiar with the route to Polmera, as this was his second trip in two days. Polmera was the farm owned by Derrick McCalldy, and that was where Ian had first met Mr. Pango and made an offer for him on the spot.

McCalldy's acceptance of his offer was the highlight of the whole deal, for Ian proudly had beaten McCalldy at negotiations. McCalldy was ready to haggle and act tough, but Ian simply listened and wrote his bid on a piece of paper. Sitting in his car with the car in reverse, ready to leave, he reached out the window and handed McCalldy a folded piece of paper. "I'll only be in town until tomorrow afternoon," he said. "Call me if you want to sell Pango at this price."

He started down the long driveway before McCalldy could

open the note. His offer was fair, but well below the price that had been discussed, so Ian felt great satisfaction when he received McCalldy's call of acceptance. Ian had learned from his brother the important "wisdom of worth." Gavin had cautioned that the biggest danger of being the richest family in the nation was to lose respect for money. Ian knew that if he overpaid for Pango, he wouldn't have less respect for the horse itself.

Several years ago, when the Abernathy family had become the richest in the land because of his father's mining claims, his brother Gavin had spent a large amount of money researching the history of descendants of the world's wealthiest families. He continuously impressed his findings upon Ian and his sister Peggy: "When respect for money is lost, it is followed by generations of destruction, sadness, and utter ruin."

Gavin was convinced that the loss of respect for money caused a disconnection with the common man and his life challenges. The pride that Ian now felt about Pango supported everything in Gavin's research. Ian shook his head in admiration as he praised his brother: "Got a good head on him, that brother of mine."

As he stood with McCalldy, watching Mr. Pango graze, Ian noticed for the first time that there were stallions in the paddock with Pango, along with three other Timor mares that Ian had purchased. Turning to McCalldy, he asked, "Don't you worry about having stallions in with Pango and his mares?"

McCalldy laughed, putting his hand on Ian's shoulder. "That's why he's called Mr. Pango. Those stallions wouldn't go within ten feet of those mares, even if they were in season. Check his papers, and you'll find that his registered name is only 'Pango.' He earned the title 'Mister.' Our boy Pango can take care of any of them, or even if he can't, he has them believing that he can."

After serious business was completed, McCalldy was back on familiar ground and most pleasant to Ian. Out of the blue, McCalldy asked Ian, "I suppose you know who Andrew Barton Paterson is?"

Almost jumping in delight at the question, Ian answered in a casual tone. "I think so. Born in New South Whales in 1864 . . . lawyer, journalist, war correspondent, soldier, noted horseman, and the writer of 'The Man From Snowy River' and 'Waltzing Matilda.' He's my personal hero, Mr. Banjo Paterson." Neither man could hold their shared delight as they laughed together.

"Well," said McCalldy, "that was obviously not much of a trap I set for you, was it?"

"No, as you can see, I've been close to visions of Banjo Paterson since I was a small boy. As a matter of a fact, our whole family has, and always will be."

"I'm glad to see Mr. Pango is going where he will be well appreciated. Do you know the history of the Timor as well as you know Banjo Paterson?"

Ian moved forward in his seat with interest. "No, I guess I really only know of their great will and grit through Banjo's stories. But I would love to know more, if you would tell me."

It was obviously McCalldy's true bailiwick to tell of his life's adoration for this gallant beast. "Back in 1820," he began, "they introduced the very best of the English breeds. But Aussie got the best of them, and they did very poorly in the heat and the dryness. It took them about twenty years to find the Timor breed, up in Scotland, of all places. No one knew much about them then, but in time, they proved to be the best-natured, most loyal animal God put on this earth. There are countless stories of how they stayed with their fallen rider or went up or down hills that man could hardly climb. Did you know that the mare will abort her own foal to survive if the season is too harsh?"

Ian's attention hung on every word, and he delighted McCalldy by asking him to continue.

"Well, they were first brought to Aussie by the Whitcomb family here in the mountains. And for the next eighty years they were man's right arm and the main strain in today's best Aussie breeds, like the waler, for instance. This was true until about fifteen years ago, when every farm got better tractors and nobody wanted horses anymore. They became free range over the years, and large herds roamed the mountains. Not only did no one want them, they didn't want them grazing on the open hilltops, consuming all the cattle feed. These horses eat the grass far closer to the roots than cattle, so it takes twice as long for the grass to regenerate. In the last five years, twenty thousand head have been rounded up and killed, and their hooves harvested."

Ian was transfixed. "Not much of a destiny for one so brave. Hopefully Mr. Pango can restart the cycle in the outback."

McCalldy nodded. "It's a sad thing, indeed, and that's why I've put so much time into trying to save the breed. Ian, you might think you got a good deal because I wanted to sell Pango. But more to the point, I want your experiment to work. I will tell you this, Pango is as good a stallion as I have ever seen. So if your plan is going to work, it will definitely work with him."

Just as Ian sensed that their meeting was over, a tall, dark-haired, handsome young man entered the room. The first thing Ian noticed about the man was the way he wore his shirt, tied in a knot at his waist. It gave him a theatrical appearance.

With a scowl, Mr. McCalldy turned away from the young man and said, "This is my son, Wilson. Thank you for coming, Ian, and good luck." He quickly left the room.

After a brief attention to his father's abrupt departure, Wilson walked straight to Ian with his hand outstretched. "Yes, I am the son who breaks his father's heart by not loving this god-forsaken farm. I have heard of you. You are Ian Abernathy, and you have an even bigger god-forsaken place in some desert. How do you stand it?"

Ian shook his hand and tried not to show his embarrassment at Wilson's lack of tact. He tried not to stare at the way his tied shirt displayed his flat, tanned stomach. "Yes, we have a family station in the back blocks of Aussie. Certainly more remote than this lovely acreage."

Wilson suddenly stood directly in front of Ian and stared into his face, as though he were about to discover something.

A chill ran up Ian's spine. He found the lingering look disturbing.

Backing off, Wilson waved his hand toward the door. Referring to his father, he said, "Don't worry about him. He never approved of me, and I have never approved of him, either."

Ian quietly asked, "Is that because you don't like the farm life?"

A flash of sadness crossed Wilson's smile. "It wouldn't be so bad if that was the only reason. He doesn't approve of *me*. I think he hates me."

"If you're convinced of that, why do you keep coming back here?"

Wilson cocked his head to the side. "Don't you think I've asked myself that?"

Curious, Ian daringly asked, "Well, what answers did you get?"

"It hurts to admit it, but I just hope one day he'll know me and approve of me."

Ian began to sense that Wilson was gay, but he didn't even want to think about it. "Wilson, I'm sure your father doesn't feel that way, and if you give him time, I'm also sure your feelings will change." Feeling oddly uncomfortable and wanting to get away from this situation, Ian turned for the door. "But now, I really must go. I have to get back to Sydney tonight."

Letting out a long sigh, Wilson said quietly, "Okay, then, I will walk you to the car. I envy you, having a passion for what you want to do with the horses. It means you've been thinking about it for a long time, and now you're doing it. I don't have anything like that, but who knows, I might fall in love or something."

Not wanting to continue the conversation, Ian climbed into the car. "Don't worry, you'll find your life's interest, we all do." Now, I must be off. Good-bye." He turned the ignition.

Wilson put his head in the window. "Good-bye, Ian, but remember, you don't know it all. You don't even know you are just like me."

Another chill went up Ian's spine. *This guy's crazy. He doesn't know what he's talking about. He doesn't know anything about me.*

"You'll see that our road is already set," Wilson added. "And there is nothing you can do to alter it."

To escape Wilson's lingering stare, Ian threw the car into gear and started to back down the driveway.

Wilson shouted after him, "Remember, you have to drive carefully down both roads."

Relieved to be back on the road, Ian refused to give thought to Wilson's disjointed, angry ramblings. He did, however, feel for Mr. McCalldy. He briefly reflected on how McCalldy had lost his joy and pride when Wilson had entered the room.

Wanting to forget the whole uncomfortable situation, Ian turned his thoughts to the satisfaction he felt over the purchase of Mr. Pango and his mares. He also looked forward to seeing Gavin and to swimming for the club at the carnival.

Chapter 4

Arriving back at the hotel around five, Lindsay was quite pleased with herself and, for sure, she was very tired. That night while waiting for dinner, she was approached by a good-looking man who looked to be in his early twenties. She couldn't help thinking that, though he was manly, his even, dark tan and white teeth made him look beautiful rather than just good-looking.

In a soft Australian accent that knocked her off her feet, he asked, "Excuse me, ma'am. May I have a few words with you?"

Taken aback, Lindsay said, "Of course," and extended her hand to introduce herself.

He grasped her hand and gushed, "That's jolly good of you. I'm Pat Andrews, and this is my little brother, Chris." He pulled the little guy forward to acknowledge his presence.

So intrigued with Pat, she hadn't noticed the younger brother.

Pat continued, "Please excuse me for approaching you like this, but I'm in a bit of a bind. You see, in about fifteen minutes, my mother and sister should be arriving at the William Street Bus Depot just around the corner. Because our sister is paralyzed and in a chair, I have to be there to bring them back here on foot. It's too difficult to get her into a cab, you see. Anyway, I'm sorry I'm so long-winded, but could you look after Chris for me for just about twenty minutes? He has a game of checkers and a book with him, and I assure you he won't be any bother. They won't be opening the dining room for another thirty minutes, so hopefully it won't inconvenience you."

Taking Chris's hand and crouching down to his level, she asked, "How old are you, Chris?" In a thick Australian accent, he answered,

"Six and a half, miss."

"If I say yes to your brother, what do you want to do while he's gone?"

With real excitement, he answered, "Do you know how to play checkers, miss?"

"Yes, I do. And you can call me Lindsay."

With a puzzled look and a shrug of his shoulders, he protested, "Okay, miss, but isn't that a boy's name?"

Without a smile on his face, Pat broke in before Lindsay could answer. "Don't be cheeky, Chris."

Lindsay took over. "Yes, it can be a name for boys and, yes, I do know how to play checkers. So it will be my pleasure to play while Pat picks up your sister."

Looking at his watch, Pat sat down beside his young brother. "I still have a few minutes before I have to go." Turning to Lindsay, he asked, "What did you think of last night's party?"

Puzzled, she replied, "I didn't go to any party last night."

"Oh, I didn't mean that you were there. I meant, how could you sleep through what happened? You know, the police took them away."

Wide-eyed, Lindsay put her hand to her mouth. "No, what happened?"

"Not that much, really, but about 2:30 a.m., after the party had really warmed up, a couple of jokers turned the fire hose on. We're in Room 422, and there were water marks on our ceiling this morning. So I guess we were right below them."

Taking a minute to remember her room number, Lindsay replied, "It's no wonder I didn't hear anything. I'm way over in Room 604. Sorry I missed the fun."

Standing to leave, he quipped, "I'll bet a few quid that they would have rather missed it with you. The cops don't like you to cut-up too rough. Anyway, just give me twenty minutes. I think you're great to help me out like this."

"Not at all. We'll have a great time, won't we, Chris?"

Pat cut in. "We're in Room 422, but unless he needs something, keep him down here, away from the damn TV." With a big smile and a quick, shy gesture, he turned and left the room.

Chris took over, asking Lindsay questions about the Wild West and if she'd ever seen an Indian.

Finally, Lindsay asked in as tender a voice as she could muster, "What's the matter with your sister, Chris?"

Without looking up, Chris surprised her by announcing matter-of-factly, "She's got multy-scrowsis, and they don't think she'll live long, so that's why they all came to the city." Looking straight at Lindsay, he added, "I would like to be in the city, too, if I was going to die, wouldn't you?"

Red-faced, Lindsay quietly confirmed, "Yes, I would."

Almost afraid to bring up any further subjects, Lindsay kept her head down on the game.

In no time at all, it seemed, Pat was back. Seeing he was alone, Lindsay questioned, "Where's your mother and sister? Is everything all right?"

"Yeah, no sweat. They said the bus would be thirty minutes late, but that could also mean an hour. I came back so we didn't interfere with your dinner plans. Pick up the game, Chris, and we'll both go and wait at the depot."

"It was no trouble, really," Lindsay protested.

Taking her hand and making such direct eye contact that it made her blush, he said, "You know, that was a beaut of you to chip in like that. If you're around after dinner, maybe you would let me thank you and have a drink with me?"

Without thinking, she said, "Sure, I would be delighted."

"Come and see," he said, gesturing for her to follow him. "When I came in, the sky was completely red. We're famous for vibrant painted skies this time of the year."

As they reached the front door, it was evident that the sun had already set and the dark night was upon them. "Never mind. I'm sure you'll see lots of sunsets while you're here. And hopefully, we'll meet after dinner. Right?"

"Right," confirmed Lindsay, as she casually waved good-bye.

Chris returned her wave and yelled above the noise of the traffic, "Thanks for the game, miss." With a smile on her lips, and feeling lightheaded, Lindsay decided to return to her room for her shawl, as the air conditioning was quite chilly.

In the elevator, the thought occurred to her that she should change into something more glamorous, but then decided against it, for fear of appearing too obvious to Pat.

When she opened the door, the room was dark, but the light from the hallway indicated that something was wrong. Flicking on the light, she saw clothes everywhere, drawers tipped upside down, the bed stripped, and mattress and box spring separated. She screamed uncontrollably.

In a panic for her valuables, she hurled clothes aside, crying and frantically searching for her suitcase, which appeared to be missing. To her relief, she saw it halfway covered by the box spring. In a fever, she threw the lid open. The secret pocket was gone. The whole lining had been slashed to threads; even the unlined lid had gashes.

Not believing her eyes, she collapsed on the floor, sobbing hysterically and rocking as though she had a baby in her arms. The suitcase lay open beside her. She cried, not only for the loss of money and goods, but because she felt violated. She might as well have been physically attacked. In shock, she continued to rock back and forth.

The door opened, and she jumped in terror.

A man in uniform put his hand gently on her shoulder. "Miss . . . miss, my name is Hugh Adams, and I'm here to help you," he said in a firm, even voice. "Do you hear me?"

Sobbing, Lindsay nodded.

"I'm going to take you down to the office, away from this room, so we can sort things out. Will you come with me, please?"

She slowly rose to her feet and left the room with him. He gave instructions to his assistant to close and lock the door so no one could enter without his permission.

~~~

Lindsay and Officer Adams sat with Mr. Fendler, the hotel manager, in his office. He was a balding man with piercing blue eyes, and Lindsay guessed him to be in his fifties. Though not a big man, he gave an air of authority and strength.

"Well, Miss Graeme, shall we get on with your story?" The hotel manager put emphasis on the word "story," making it seem as if he didn't believe her. Her suspicion was confirmed when he took a long, deep breath and added without looking at her, "Shall we get this over with, Miss Graeme?"

Defensively, Lindsay replied, "You sound as though you don't believe my story."

Mr. Fendler closed his eyes as though to gather his patience, and then responded in a smug tone, "Really, Miss Graeme, it's hard for me to think that, since I haven't heard one word of your story. Why don't you just get on with it?"

She was about to start with an explanation about the secret pocket and the money, but before she could speak, Fendler impatiently waved his hands in warning. "I must first caution you, Miss Graeme,
~~~

it's extremely hard to understand how anyone in this day and age could travel with cash."

Lindsay heaved a sigh and began her story cautiously. "You see, my whole reason for leaving the U.S. was to exert independence from my father. For this reason, when my father tried to arrange for my traveler's checks and insisted that I should meet him at the bank, I made a quick excuse that I had gotten them myself. Yes, I lied. But, I didn't want him to have control over my trip. He was very impressed by my forethought and independence and pressed to know the details. I stressed again that the matter was taken care of and there was nothing to worry about. The responsible attitude that I displayed to my father was awfully new, you see, because until that point, I had never dared to speak up to him. It was part of building our new understanding, you see."

Mr. Fendler rudely broke in, "Yes, yes, yes. Please stay to the point. Did you or didn't you get the traveler's checks?"

"No, I didn't. I went to the bank on Friday, and there were so many people waiting, the teller told me to come back after closing in order to issue the amount I needed. So, I simply withdrew the money and was going to make a deposit here as soon as I arrived."

"You had all day today to do so, didn't you?"

"I meant to, but I got carried away with the excitement of my adventure, so I put it off until tomorrow. Besides, I didn't see where anyone would think I had any money with me."

"Did you have anyone in your room? Don't be afraid to say 'yes' if you have."

Feeling extremely diminished, her anger growing, she defiantly replied, "No, I didn't have anyone in my room, and if I had three men in my room, I wouldn't be afraid to tell you. Just because I tried to be more explicit about my relationship with my father, please don't treat me like a child."

"Miss Graeme," he continued in a quiet monotone, "this is a well-run hotel with round-the-clock security – a quiet hotel, a hands-on hotel, and you expect me to believe that somehow you were singled out from over four hundred and thirty guests? If you don't mind my saying, many look far more prosperous than you." His expression conveyed the attitude, *Please don't put me through this.* He closed his eyes. "Please, Miss Graeme, I didn't just come down in the last shower."

Adopting the same monotone voice, she mocked, "Hum, quiet hotel, hands-on hotel. What about the fight last night, the fire hoses and the police? I suppose that comes under the heading of well-run? Ha!"

"I really have no idea what you're talking about, Miss Graeme."

"You have a convenient one-sided memory, Mr. Fendler, but I'm sure that the police records would refresh your memory."

Turning to Adams, he queried, "What the bloody hell is she talking about? Are there some reports that weren't brought to my attention?"

Showing no concern, the policeman handed Fendler an open-ring binder. "See for yourself."

After scanning the report sheet, he turned back to Lindsay, searching for the right words. He stared at her while drawing a deep breath. "You know, I'm not getting a very good feeling about all of this."

Lindsay crossed arms in frustration. "If you think I am, Mr. Fendler, you're not only very rude, but stupid to boot."

Not reacting to her remark, he continued, "Where did you get this information about the fight? Or did you just make that up to muddy the waters? You know, Miss Graeme, what I can't figure out is a motive. You have lost no tangible goods, and even you must know that insurance companies don't cover lost cash. Now, where did you hear about this big fight?"

Pleased to answer, she said, "From Mr. Andrews in Room 422, and for your added information, the water had started to come through the ceiling this morning."

Anticipating his next order, Adams left to check the register for Mr. Andrews. Upon his return, he read from his notes. "Nobody by the name of Andrews has been in the house in the last two weeks. Mr. and Mrs. Spurr have been in Room 422 for three days and are not leaving until the day after tomorrow."

Lindsay couldn't believe her ears. "There must be some mistake!" she protested.

Enjoying the role of the victor, Fendler's upper lip curled as he started to grin. With squinted eyes, he said, "Please, Miss Graeme. Why don't we start at the beginning with this invisible Mr. Andrews?"

Now feeling vulnerable and completely unsure of herself, she told them how she had met Pat. They did not interrupt.

Mr. Fendler spoke first, in a more friendly tone. "First, Miss Graeme, I owe you an apology. I thought you were trying to set up the hotel for some sort to insurance claim or the like. Secondly, you have been truly set up by what appears to be a highly professional con-man, which is no consolation, I'm sure."

The image that returned to Lindsay was the way the little kid had shut her up with the "multy-scrowsis" line. Then the thought of getting dressed up for Pat. Not to mention that she had even walked them to the front door to see them off.

"Oh, what an absolute gullible fool I was," she moaned. Tears of self-pity and embarrassment streamed down her cheeks.

Fendler handed her a tissue. "I'm sorry, but I must approach this in a strictly business-like manner, so I will give you three days to work out your problems. There will be no charge, but should you wish to stay longer, you must pay in advance. Is that clear? Do you understand why?"

Trying not to sniffle, she bit her tongue and remorsefully thanked him.

"Just for the record, miss," Adams asked, "how much money did you have in the case?"

Not wanting pity, she dried her eyes and mustered a pleasant smile in the hope of hiding her feeling of stupidity. "Ten thousand U.S. dollars, less the two hundred and fifty that I took in my purse today." She left the room quickly before she could see their reactions.

Back in her room, while reassembling her things, she couldn't stop hearing the voices of Pat and his brother. Remembering every single word distinctly, she wondered if she would ever rid herself of those haunting voices.

Thanks to Adams, the housekeeper had straightened her room and neatly made her bed. Lindsay sat on its edge and lamented, "What on earth am I going to do now?"

With a start, she realized that she was looking directly at the damn photograph her father had so proudly given her. Picking the picture up from the floor, she held it at arm's length and cursed. "God darn you, Ralph what's-your-face!"

Turning the picture over, she repeated his name out loud. "Abernathy. That's right, Scouse Abernathy," she said, as her dad always called him. The thought occurred to her that she had repeatedly tried to get rid of Mr. Abernathy and her father, but they were still both vividly present. She shook her head in resignation. "Maybe this is fate."

Looking at the address, *Wombra Stunt Club*, she noted that there certainly couldn't be too many stunt clubs in Wombra. *Too late now*, she thought, *but tomorrow I'll see if you really are my father's best friend,*

Mr. Ralph Scouse Abernathy. And if not, I will go back to nursing or get a job typing. So don't think I'm dependant on you, Ralph old boy. But we shall see.

Chapter 5

Thanks to the chatty man at the breakfast table, Lindsay knew all about getting to Wombra. The man had been right; it was indeed a nice town, with planned city buildings such as a town hall, courthouse, and a church that all shared the same architecture theme. Lindsay realized that she hadn't actually taken notice of such a thing before, but once she saw it, images of towns that looked like they had just evolved sprung to mind. *Yes, it's very nice.*

Once there, however, things weren't quite that easy. Nobody at the town hall knew anything of a Wombra Stunt Club.

"The last brothel in Wombra was closed two years ago," the male clerk quietly whispered to her.

Red-faced, she demanded in a whisper, "What on earth does that have to do with it?"

It was the clerk's turn to turn red. "A 'stunt club' is Aussie slang for a brothel."

"Well, in that case, I shall now inquire about the Wombra Flying Stunt Club. Thank you."

The library was her next best bet, but it wasn't open on Monday or Tuesday. Her only other thought was to go to the airport, as it at least had something to do with flying. She walked to a gas station to ask where she could catch a bus, and noticed a very old man sitting on a chair, resting his head on his hands, supported by a thick walking stick. She stood in front of him until he finally looked up.

"G'day, what can I do for you?" he asked.

Lindsay wasn't expecting the man to speak first, and she was a little taken aback. Her greeting came out like a question: “I wonder if you might be able to help me?”

“So would I wonder.”

For some silly reason, Lindsay felt herself beginning to blush. “Nice of you to say so, but if you’ve lived here a long time, you may know of a flying club that was here years ago, called the Wombra Stunt Club.”

“Can’t say I really remember it, but I know where it would have been.” His eyes took on a far-away look. “Maybe I’m talking myself into this, but I do remember something. If it’s what I’m thinking of, it only lasted a year, mostly for the Flyer Boys who came back from the war. Most of ‘em had enough flying by the time they got home and were pleased to keep their feet on the ground.”

“Yes, that’s the time, all right. You wouldn’t have heard of a man by the name of Ralph Abernathy, would you?”

He shook his gray head slowly. “I don’t know anyone by that name. The place I’m thinking about is an air club that has its own instructor. I don’t know this fella, but I knew the chap before him. He’s dead now. I used to deliver milk out there to him. I stopped going out there after he died. Dunno what the place is like now.”

“Do you have any suggestion as to how I can get out there?”

“If you want to give my grandson a quid, he’ll take you out there.”

Feeling encouraged, Lindsay replied, “That would be just great.”

“You’ll have to keep the reins on him, though. Don’t let him go too fast. He’s a mad little bugger if you don’t watch him. And make him wait to bring you back, as a quid should cover both ways.”

The grandson had to be fifteen years old to drive, but Lindsay thought he looked more like twelve. He was a great-looking kid with bright red hair and a double cowlick in the front, making his hair look like it was standing on end. He was very polite and happy to drive a car, no matter where he had to go.

Sensing the boy felt shy, Lindsay introduced herself. "Hi, I'm Lindsay."

"G'day. My name is Mike Baker. Nice to meet ya."

He didn't say much during the short trip. After ten minutes of driving on a dusty, stony road, they pulled off and started through a paddock with no road. The boy pointed to a tiny tin building in the distance.

"There she is over there, miss." Moments later, he pulled up beside a lone car parked behind a red corrugated iron building.

Lindsay waited for the dust to settle before she got out of the car. A yellow sign above the door read, *Wombra Aero Club, Captain J. McKenna Instructor & Club Captain.* Still staring at the sign, she almost bumped into an older lady who was just leaving.

Turning to Lindsay, the lady said, "No lessons today, love."

"I don't want any lessons, thanks," Lindsay replied, trying to sound sweet. "Just looking for some information about this place and when it started, etcetera."

"Sorry, miss, I'm not even from around here. You can wait for Kenny, if you want."

"Where is he?"

She gestured upward to the sky. "He's up there now, clearing his head after last night, I'd betcha."

"Thank you. I'll sit outside and wait."

"You'll probably have plenty to watch, because he's working on some new stunts for one of them film studios."

Never having seen aerobatics before, Lindsay didn't like what she was watching, but she couldn't take her eyes off the little red and yellow plane that seemed able to do anything it wanted. *Clear his head?* she thought. *It's a wonder it doesn't come off!*

While watching the dives and spins against the bright blue sky, she realized for the first time that she had known about this type of acrobatic flying before. Both her father and Abernathy must have been highly skilled to survive the war in a Spitfire Squadron. Obviously, Abernathy must have been good, as he had started the stunt club, unlike her father, who had never flown again after the war.

Finally, the small, bi-winged machine touched down so softly that the wheels didn't even bump. The pilot pulled the plane right in front of Lindsay. She had to turn her head to avoid the dust as he swung into the wind before shutting the engine down.

The way the tall, skinny pilot uncoiled himself to get out of the cockpit made the plane look even smaller. As he walked toward her, she guessed him to be mid-thirties, well over six feet tall, and definitely in love with himself.

"Afternoon," he said. "You must be from *The Sydney Herald.* I did a couple of extra loops for you. Did you notice?" Not letting Lindsay get a word in edgewise, he continued boastfully, "No two men in Aussie today can triple-loop from a spin to finish in a signal. Still, I guess that's why you're here."

Somewhat embarrassed for him, she answered, "Well, no, not actually. My name is Lindsay Graeme, and I'm here from New York—"

He broke in, "So they've heard about me even in the States, have they now? Well, I'm open to offers, but let me tell you, I'm not cheap, and you just saw why."

"Please, Mr. McKenna, I'm not with any paper or anything like that. I just want to ask if you know a Ralph Abernathy who started a stunt club years ago on this very site." She handed him the picture.

Apparently embarrassed by his blunder, he became belligerent and thrust the photo back at her with only a quick glance. “No, I’ve never heard of him, even though I’ve heard of them all, the good ones and the dead ones, too. Now, if you’ll excuse me, I must change.”

Lindsay persisted, “Perhaps there are records I could see?”

“There are no bloody records, so if you will excuse me?” He turned abruptly and stormed into the building as though Lindsay were not present.

Amazed by his rudeness, Lindsay yelled after him, “If I were with the papers, you would talk all day!”

He yelled from inside, “And tomorrow, too, so please bugger off!”

“I’m leaving. Thanks for the help. Always nice to meet a gentleman.” Tearing out the page of her notebook where she had written her name and phone number, she crumpled it up and threw it at the door in rage. Then she stomped off to the car.

Almost in tears, she stared out the window, not knowing what to do next. She let the feeling of hopelessness sweep over her. One thing she did know, she would never tell her father any of this, and she wouldn’t ask him for help, no matter what. What she needed now was a long nap.

~~~

Back in her hotel room in Sydney, she lay on the bed and tried not to think about it all. She was on the verge of a sound sleep when the ringing of the phone startled her. Fearing that it might be the horrible hotel management, she was afraid to answer. She fumbled for the receiver, only to hear a booming voice say, “Miss Graeme, this is Jack McKenna.”

She tried to gather her wits. “Uh, yes, Mr. McKenna. What is this? Do you wish to speak to me in case I get a newspaper job in the
~~~

next ten years?"

"No, Miss Graeme. I wish to apologize for my attitude, and I have good news for you."

"Really, hearing from you is a shock enough. To hear good news from anyone would be more than I could handle. Please go on."

"I must first start with an apology for my rudeness. You see, I've been rehearsing to myself all morning about what I would say to the press so I wouldn't show my shyness. I'm afraid it came out all wrong, and unfortunately you got it all. So, I'm sorry."

She paused to let his apology hang in the air. "Well, I forgive you. I guess we both had a bad start. Now, what is the good news?"

"Even though I only looked at the photo for a few seconds," he said, "I knew they were both wearing Battle of Britain fight gear, and 'Aussie' was painted on the fuselage, which I presume was a Spitfire."

"You are correct. That was my father and Ralph Abernathy. They flew bomber escort and flew as many missions as any team in the war. My dad returned to America and never flew again, and according to my father, Ralph Abernathy came here and started the Wombra Stunt Club."

"Well, here's the good news. I felt bad after the fool I made of myself this afternoon, so I went to the local newspaper office for you. I didn't find any Stunt Club, but I found out plenty about this Abernathy dude. It seems that he's one of Aussie's most decorated flyers, not only here but in Britain as well."

Lindsay felt rising excitement. "What else did it say? Do you know where he is now?"

"No, there was nothing current, though there was a photo of him with the Flying Doctor Service, alongside a picture and an article about his son. Gavin is his name. He's a priest, and he was made head priest at St. Barnabas in Bondi. The article is about four years old, so you might start your search there."

"Mr. McKenna, you have certainly earned a reprieve from my heart. I'm very grateful to you. Is Bondi far away from Sydney?"

McKenna laughed heartily. "Yar bloody near in it. Bondi is Sydney. It's Sydney's finest beach, and it's just over the back of Kings Cross. If you don't want to take a cab, you can catch the number nine tram."

"I don't know how your day went, but you just made mine go a lot better. Did the newspaper people show up?"

"No, but they left a message in town that they'll come out tomorrow. Good-bye, and good luck."

"Thanks, and the same to you."

Exhilarated by the news, Lindsay jumped out of bed, threw on her clothes, and headed downstairs to the front desk. The clerk efficiently supplied her with the number for the St. Barnabus Rectory. After making sure she could call from her room, she hurried back upstairs. When she checked her watch, she was surprised that it was only 3:30 in the afternoon.

The phone rang and rang, and because she didn't know what else to do, she just let it ring.

"Surely there must be someone there during the day," she thought.

At last, a voice answered on the other end. "Hello, this is St. Barnabus Rectory."

The woman sounded Irish. *An Irish rectory housekeeper?* Lindsay thought. *That's so typical. I can even picture what she looks like.* "Hello," she said. "I wonder if you could tell me if Father Abernathy is there?"

"Yes, Father Abernathy is the resident priest. Who wants to know, may I ask?"

"My name is Lindsay Graeme from America, and I would like to see Father Abernathy as soon as possible. Can I come over?"

The reply came in a distant fashion. "Of course you can come over, to be sure, but I can't speak for the Father. I am his housekeeper, not his secretary."

"But he's there now, right?"

The woman raised her voice slightly. "Didn't I just say that now?"

Not wanting to challenge her further, Lindsay said, "Oh, yes you did." The phone clicked dead, but Lindsay spoke into the phone anyway. "And thank you very much for your concern and thoughtfulness, I must say."

Within an hour, she was outside St. Barnabus, which looked like a run-of-the-mill church. *Gothic architecture*, she supposed. It also had a matching rectory. Walking up the front steps of the rectory, Lindsay wondered how long it would take the lady to come to the door, seeing as it had taken her so long to answer the phone.

When the door did open, Lindsay found it hard to believe that she could have been so right, for she had pictured the housekeeper to a tee. *Do these people go to rectory housekeeper's school, or what?* she wondered.

Petite, with a slim, wiry build, the woman stood there dressed in her full-length gingham apron, ready to defend. "Yes?" she offered.

"Hello, my name is Lindsay Graeme. I rang an hour ago and wish to see Father Abernathy."

"He's out in the back." With that, she closed the door.

Wishing to make a point, Lindsay deliberately spoke to the closed door. "Thank you, it was nice of you to go to such a trouble"

As Lindsay made her way around the building, she couldn't resist stopping to admire the beautiful roses. *It must be the Aussie sun,* she thought, as she had never seen such large blossoms. Surveying the yard, which was rather small, the only thing Lindsay could see was an open garage with an old car. As she turned to leave, she heard a metal tool hitting the ground, followed by a curse tinged by an Australian accent: "Bloody hell!"

Walking to the other side of the vintage car, Lindsay spotted a suntanned pair of sandal-clad feet protruding from under the running board.

Not thinking for one moment that the feet belonged to a priest, she demanded in a rather loud voice, "Excuse me. Could you tell me where I could find Father Abernathy?"

"You have found him," came the matter-of-fact reply.

Watching the grease-covered man emerge from under the car, Lindsay asked in a challenging tone, "Are you sure?"

"Yes, quite sure. Father Gavin Abernathy at your service. And who might you be, may I ask?"

She guessed Father Gavin to be about thirty-five years old, not very tall, and at first glance he appeared to be overweight, giving him a round, teddy-bear look. Upon closer scrutiny, she could see that the bulk was well-formed muscle. It appeared that he had been a well-trained athlete not too long ago.

After a moment, Lindsay found her voice. "Hello, Father, my name is Lindsay Graeme. I'm from America, and I've been looking for you all day."

His eyebrows rose. "I find that very intriguing. Please tell me why a beautiful young lady, all the way from America, would find her way into my backyard and fish me out from under a car."

The words alone may have sounded harsh, but he smiled as he said them. All her life, Lindsay had never seen such a wonderful smile. Its magnanimous warmth lit up the surroundings and gave her a sense of self-assurance.

Taking the photo from her bag and handing it to the priest, she explained, "Our fathers flew together in the war, and my father made me promise to meet your family while I'm over here."

Paying little notice to the photo, Father Gavin invited her in for tea. "Please join me in a cup of tea, and if we're lucky, we may get some of Mrs. Sweeny's scones. I assure you, what Mrs. Sweeny lacks in outgoing chit-chat, she certainly makes up for in her scones." Putting his arm around Lindsay, he encouraged, "Come on, I promise you."

As he escorted her back inside the rectory, Father Gavin was light on his feet and made Lindsay feel as if she were the most exciting thing to come into his life.

True to his word, he managed to order afternoon tea from the very un-delightful Mrs. Sweeny.

"Thank you for the tea, Mrs. Sweeny," he said. "I'll take it from here. If you would just set it down on the table there." His voice was gentle, yet commanding. It was like nothing Lindsay had ever heard before. She felt an immediate sense of déjà vu, as if she had known Gavin before. It was mysterious and unexplainable. He was relaxed and friendly, but the overwhelming sense of familiarity remained.

"Before you begin, Lindsay, I should warn you that I have had others claim to be relatives or had contracts with my parents." He added with a charming wink, "But so far, none of them have been as pretty as you."

Not believing her ears, Lindsay didn't know how to react and concluded that she must have been completely misunderstood. Putting her hand to her chin, Lindsay replied, "I'm not sure what you mean, Father, but I don't even really know your family, let alone claim to be a relative. Actually, I would like to take this opportunity to put you at ease. While I'm sure there are people who would lie and cheat to have a priest as a brother, let me assure you that I am not of that persuasion."

He laughed out loud. "Quite, quite." Seeing she had no idea what he was talking about, he added, "Yes, yes, you're quite right to be a little angry at my provocative opening. It is certainly no way to begin a friendship."

Lindsay, still not understanding his comments, wanted to start over again. "Then I, too, will apologize for my reaction, and hopefully we can start again."

He handed Lindsay a plate of blueberry scones. "Mrs. Sweeny's scones will save the day again. I'm sure she uses holy water in these divine things. Now, please, why are you are seated before me after coming all the way from the U.S.A.?"

Father Gavin did not interrupt as Lindsay described the events that had led up to their meeting.

His first question was, "If your father loves you, why not simply ask him for some more money?"

"But, Father, don't you understand? The whole reason I left home was to establish my independence. If I went back to him now, I would be proving him right, and I would be sunk in his eyes forever. I think it would break my heart to fail now, since I know I'm not a dunce."

"Now, now. We can't have any broken hearts here. What would you like me to do for you today?"

"Well, Father, I haven't worked out a solution yet. My first thought was to find someone who knew me or knew about me. If you were willing to help me, I would ask you to help me with some accommodation, and I will get a job to survive. I still have enough money for a week or so."

Shaking his head, he replied, "I'm not sure I can go along with that idea, Lindsay."

Lindsay felt her heart sink and her face flush. She could feel her eyes starting to tear.

"You know," he continued, "we Australians are pretty proud of Aussie and our ways. One of our biggest beliefs is 'the fair go.' That means everyone should get a fair go. If they mess up, that's life. But everyone should have at least one good chance." For a moment, his gaze turned wistful, and he excused himself politely, saying he would seek another order of Mrs. Sweeny's delicious scones.

A moment later, he returned to the veranda with an inspired suggestion. "I have a great idea. If you will allow me, I'd like to plan something else for you. Tomorrow, my younger brother Ian is coming to town for a surf carnival, and if you like the looks of him, you could join us to fly back to the cattle station with him the next day. That way, you get to see the heart of Aussie. I know you'll love her. What do you think? Oh, one other thing. My sister Peggy is at the station for the next three weeks before taking off on her world painting trip. You'll love her."

At this point, Lindsay sensed that she would become close friends with Father Gavin. She trusted him, and believed that he felt the same about her.

"Sounds great," she said, "but I'll need to earn money."

"Now, why don't you let me worry about that? I assure you, money is a mere incidental in life. Besides, my father would be furious if I didn't treat you like royalty. After all, you're the daughter of his true friend. No, it's a done deal. I'm obligated to repay a debt on behalf of my dad."

"Father Gavin, I know my father would expect me to visit your parents, especially since I've heard so much about them during my life."

His gaze fell. "I'm sorry to tell you this, Lindsay, but that would be a little tough. Unfortunately, Mom and Dad were killed three years ago in a mining cave-in."

"Oh, I'm very sorry to hear that."

He nodded. "It's quite all right. God works in strange ways."

As the conversation unfolded, Lindsay felt strangely confident that she was embarking upon a predestined journey of awakening. She knew that she should just take it easy and join in with her newfound family.

Chapter 6

The next morning, Lindsay was up early and packed and very excited about leaving the hotel. She had been sitting in the lobby since 10:15, trying to spot Ian Abernathy before he reached the front desk, as he was scheduled to pick her up at eleven o'clock. Realizing how excited she was to finally meet him, she cautioned herself to suppress her enthusiasm.

Finally, she heard the front desk paging her. However, as she approached the front desk, a tall, golden-haired man in his early twenties introduced himself with an outstretched hand.

"Miss Graeme, I'm Ian Abernathy, and I'm very pleased to meet you."

Lindsay was overcome by his overall presence, whether it was his handsome good looks or pleasant manners. "Yes, I'm Lindsay, and I'm also quite pleased to meet you, Ian."

They both blushed when their eyes met. Lindsay thought, *Oh, my! This is the Australia I expected to meet.*

"I wouldn't want to rush you," he said, "but if you have bags, I'll fetch them so we can get going, even though I expect my brother will keep us waiting. Actually, I'm not sure what time the carnival begins, so let's get a quick start."

"Lead the way," she encouraged.

"Gavin called last night to say he had invited you to spend some time with us at Naringa."

"Gavin spoke of my meeting the true Aussie, but I didn't hear him mention Naringa."

"That's the name of our station – a station being a large ranch in the outback. It's in the middle of Queensland, about six hours' flying time from here. What do you think about that?"

"I didn't realize that your brother had extended such an amazing invitation. I thought the farm was just a couple of hours outside the city, not across the continent!"

"You would still like to come, wouldn't you?" asked Ian.

"Absolutely. I'm just trying to say how flattered I am to be invited." She may have imagined it, but Lindsay thought she saw a look of relief in Ian's face upon hearing her reply.

It seemed only minutes before they were pulling into the driveway behind the church. Lindsay smiled as she spotted Gavin ducking under the hood of the disassembled vintage car.

Turning off the ignition, Ian threw both hands down on the steering wheel in mock frustration. "Can you believe it? We hurry here, and he's casually working on that bloody old bomb! I'm surprised God doesn't give him marching orders from that church of his, as he's never been ready on time in his life." Despite Ian's genuine concern for time, Lindsay still heard love and respect in his voice.

Father Gavin immediately put down his tools and threw his arms around Ian, powerfully embracing him with pats on his back that sounded painful.

"Welcome, my brother. How the hell are you?"

"Great, Gav, great. Peg says g'day."

"Good. How is she doin'? Painting again, I hope."

"Yeah, she's doin' great."

As if noticing Lindsay's presence for the first time, Father Gavin reached over and took her hands in his, heartily welcoming her. "Welcome, welcome, to the first day of your love affair with Australia."

Distracted by the sensuous touch of his hands, Lindsay thought, *My God, what is this man doing to me? And he's a priest, too. I must restrain these irreverent thoughts!* Hoping that her blush wasn't obvious, she quickly bent forward to kiss Gavin's cheek. "G'day," she said cheerfully.

"Very nice, Gav," Ian cut in, "but come on, it's nearly twelve o'clock. When does the carni start?"

"Not until one. I have to splash some water on a poor unsuspecting child at a twelve-fifteen christening. So why don't you finish installing this carburetor, and we'll shove off after the service?"

The news of the christening seemed to hit Ian like a smack in the chest. With a loud exhalation, he let his eyes fall to the ground, as if trying to keep his cool. "Bloody hell, Gav. Just once, couldn't we be, bloody on time?"

Hearing nothing but good fellowship, Gavin gave him another smile. "You're right, mate. The quicker you get the carb on, the quicker we can get going."

Ian stared at the dilapidated car. "We're not going in that bloody old tin can, are we?"

Fully in control of the situation, Gavin replied in a steady, even tone, "Ian, I'm going to have to take you to church to learn not to hurt people. I've been working on the resurrection of that worthy machine for the last three months and looking forward to this very day."

Without the slightest hint of a smile, Ian held up his hands in surrender. "Okay, give me the bloody spanners, and we'll be ready as soon as you come from the church, okay?"

Cheerfully, Gavin gave Ian the wrench. "There, that's the spirit." He hurried off to church.

Lindsay hadn't said a word during the confrontational exchange, and she still didn't know if she had witnessed an actual argument or not. Ian's mumbling from under the hood gave her reason to ask, “Are you all right, Ian?”

“Yeah, good as gold, thanks.”

“Oh. I thought maybe you and Gavin just had an argument.”

“No, not at all. Don’t let that brother of mine fool you, though. Do you know what this is all about?”

“His plans were to have the car ready for today, I suspect.”

“You’re partly right, but really it’s to get me to fix it without having to ask me directly, because he doesn’t know how it goes.”

“How do you know?”

“I can tell by the parts. He has already had them on several times, and it still never worked because the carburetor was mounted upside down. He’s a bloody character, this guy. He doesn’t have a prayer when it comes to mechanics.” He added with a look of respect, “Do you know what makes him so lovable? In spite of being one of the most successful priests in Australia and loved by thousands, truly thousands, what do you think he aspires to?” Without waiting for an answer, he exclaimed, “A bloody mechanic! Can you believe that? It’s true love, I tell you.”

Lindsay couldn’t help laughing at Ian’s animated portrayal. This made Ian laugh, too, as he admitted to his own heightened drama.

“You’re not going to tell him that he had a part back-to-front, are you?” she asked.

“Gosh, no. I never do.”

“How old is this car, anyway?”

“She’s an oldie. Nineteen twenty-three Austin, I think.”

Just as Ian was putting the tools away, Father Gavin came rushing across the courtyard, struggling to remove his clerical collar.

“There you go, mate. No worries. Did you get the old girl started?” he asked as he jumped into the driver’s seat.

“Not yet, but she’s all primed. If you set everything up right, she'll take her first breath of new life. Come on, Gav, give it to her, will you? We only have fifteen minutes."

As he turned the key in the ignition, Gavin closed his eyes and blessed himself. They waited with anticipation as a ticking sound came from under the hood, followed by a slow groan. To everyone's relief, the motor sprang to life with a roar.

Gavin let out a yelp of joy. "You bloody old beauty, no worries. Come, Lindsay, sit next to me in the seat of honor." He raised his hand with a forward motion. "Tally ho! Off to Bondi we go!"

Lindsay waited for the loud bang of backfire that usually accompanied an old car, but it didn't come. The car crawled along slowly, but with a smooth drive. Caught up in the excitement and feeling completely at ease with her new friends, Lindsay leaned over to give Gavin a congratulatory pat on the back. It was of no consequence that she had virtually just met Gavin, and his priesthood was taken for granted.

"What do you call her, Gavin?" she asked.

"Well, I haven't thought of that. How would you like that honor?"

"I'd love it. What did they call the baby you christened this morning?"

"Jennifer Agnes Webber."

"So, Jennifer Agnes it is!"

Ian protested. "Come off it. It's bad enough they give a kid the burden of that name. You don't have to label the bloody car with it, too."

"I don't know about that, Ian. I like the name," challenged Lindsay.

"It really doesn't matter what you call her," said Ian, "because if you don't get her moving, we won't be swimming today."

“She’s right, boy. No dignity in haste. We’ll make it.”

Without warning, they were suddenly at the top of a hill, looking down on a breathtaking scene. Lindsay had never seen such brilliant colors and doubted that she could have imagined such a vivid, flawless picture. The bay formed into a perfect half-circle, with slow, rolling swells entering from the sea, breaking into neat rows before lapping onto the white beach.

Pointing at the panoramic view, Ian shouted from the back seat, “Lindsay, look, you can see the carni colors. Each one of those flags represents a team from another club. Come on, Gav, we only have about five minutes!”

As they pulled close to the beach, the traffic was bumper-to-bumper. “We’ll never get to park in this rubbish. Quick, hand me my collar,” commanded Gavin. He attached his collar as he pulled up to the policeman on point duty and signaled for him to come over to their car.

Hesitantly, and with a look that could kill, the officer took the few steps that brought him face-to-face with Father Gavin. “Have you got a problem with your car, mate?”

“No, not actually. But I have a problem with the parking of it, and I hoped you would let me double-park over there.”

The officer reached for his back pocket and started to pull out his ticket book, but before the officer could utter a word, Gavin continued, “I must start the carnival with a prayer. You don’t look like the kind of chap who has something against prayer. You’re not, are you?”

Confused and flushed by the accusation, the policeman said apologetically, “No, no, not at all. Of course, just pull the bloody thing over there.”

Thanking him profusely, they all ran to the clubhouse. Music was playing, and all the teams were standing in groups. The brothers were immediately greeted by a huge, well-suntanned man clearly upset by their tardiness.

"Where the hell have you two mugs been?" he yelled. "We were going to scratch one of the teams. Come on, pull a finger, and let's go. We start in one minute."

Gavin grabbed the man's arm. "Lindsay, this excited gentleman is Brian, the team captain. Brian, this is Lindsay, our guest from the States. If Kay is here, can she look after Lindsay?"

"G'day, Lindsay," Brian greeted her. "Just come with me, and I'll set you up with my old lady. Then maybe these two galahs could get ready."

Kay was certainly no old lady. She was tall and slender, with beautiful blue eyes. Her voice was warm and friendly, and she welcomed Lindsay as though they were already good friends. Brian sped off after the introductions.

With immediate acceptance, Kay put her arm around Lindsay and said, "G'day, Lindsay, nice to meet you. Come with me and meet a few of the girls."

Kay's friends all had husbands or boyfriends competing, and they seemed to be the most personable women Lindsay had ever met. Before long, they started ragging on a girl named June. Apparently June had gone out with Father Gavin for three years with the hopes that they would marry. Lindsay's eyes widened as she heard of this unexpected romance. Lindsay found Gavin extremely attractive, but it never occurred to her that priests might have past relationships like everyone else.

Wide-eyed, Lindsay asked, "Was he fun?"

"God, yes," June replied. "He was hell on wheels. I think he was pretty faithful, too, but every woman in the area was after him."

"It must have been a shock! What happened to make him turn

to the cloth?"

A couple of the girls were now listening in.

"Jesus," June exclaimed, "you old girls all look like you're about to hear something real meaty."

"Well, are we?"

"No, nothing that you haven't heard before."

Seeing that Lindsay was hanging on her every word, June addressed her directly. "It was as much of a shock to Gavin as it was to me, I think. It was after a carnival at Bradman Bay – do you girls remember that fight? God, what a fight. I thought Gavin did really well, actually. Took care of about three of them and only got knocked a couple times, hardly any blood. Well, we took some beer and went off to our spot and did the usual. We went home, and everything was hunky-dory. The next day, he rang to meet at the beach, and there he told me of his plans. "Going to the seminary in Queensland to be a priest," he says, and he left that afternoon.

"June hasn't been able to get a steady since," one of the girls mocked.

"Don't listen to these old hags. They get like that when they get married, you know, Lindsay?"

"What a lot of rubbish," Kay answered. "Tell the truth. It did take you a while to get back into the swing of things, didn't it?"

Now all the fun and ragging had gone from the conversation.

"All right . . . If you all must know, God and Gavin broke my heart, and even though I love Johnny, I will never be able to love anyone like I loved Gav. Even now, four years later, he makes my heart cry when I see him. But I do love Johnny, too."

Elizabeth, a beautiful blonde who hadn't said anything to this point, patted June on the knee, "Never mind, love. Maybe God is gay and wanted Gavin for himself."

Everyone laughed out loud, including June, and happiness filled the air once again.

"Enough of this please," said June. "But one last thing that I reckon, if he is gay, its okay with me, but he should get his own guys and not mine."

They all clapped in approval, and for the first time turned their attention to the races.

The lead men were already in the water swimming to the buoys. June explained to Lindsay, "As soon as the swimmer touches the buoy and puts his hand up, the belt swimmer can leave the beach to rescue him. The belt swimmer wears a harness and pulls the line all the way out to the buoy. He holds up the rope to indicate he has reached the swimmer, then takes hold of the swimmer at the buoy, and they are pulled back to the beach. The rescued swimmer receives CPR and the team gets back into the original formation ready for the march past. Each team gets points for where they place in the race, plus points for precision.

"There they go now – the three of them are off! It looks like the New Zealand team is leading, with Ian second and Gav in fourth place." June reflected aloud, "He still looks beautiful in the water, but in his heyday, there wasn't a bloke who could touch him."

Lindsay watched in awe as Gavin's foam-covered body reappeared from under the breaking waves, and the sun reflected on his strong, brown shoulders. She held her breath in anticipation each time he dove under the oncoming wave, and she exhaled in relief when he reappeared and made a full sprint for the distance before the next crashing wave. As Lindsay turned back to June, she noticed the swell of tears in her eyes.

June almost jumped as Lindsay touched her hand and apologized. "I'm sorry, I feel responsible for bringing back all those memories and having you talk about it in front of the girls, as well."

"Oh, don't worry, love, it's okay. As for these girls, even though they look interested or surprised, there isn't a shoulder amongst them that I haven't cried on. Don't worry. No worries there mate."

Turning back to the competition on the beach, Lindsay couldn't imagine a scene that could be more colorful, with the pure blue sky and the aqua green sea pitching with white foam caps, and breaking waves creating beautiful patterns. On the beach, the competing teams with their vivid club colors contrasted brilliantly against the shining white sand. *God, what a magnificent sight*, she thought.

The teams were now out of the water and being judged on their final march past the finish line.

Kay remarked, "I think the New Zealanders have won both categories, bloody Kiwis. Degrading really."

"Don't the Australians like the kiwis?" asked Lindsay.

"Oh yes, we do. But don't let anyone hear you admit it. The feeling is mutual. We love to resent each other, but we are close. Besides, some of my best jokes are about New Zealanders."

At Kay's encouragement, they all rushed to meet the boys as they broke from their teams.

Ian and Gavin made a bee-line to Lindsay to see if she had been welcomed properly.

"Yes, I caught up on all the gossip and won two hundred dollars betting on the Kiwis," she said.

The official results were announced, and prize-giving was a pretty serious affair. It was official; the Kiwis had won both divisions and placed third in the first division.

There was great fun and laughter, but there was no beer-drinking on the beach, and everyone soon left to get ready for the Surf Club dance later that night.

When they returned to the car, the policeman came over to address Gavin. "That was a bloody long prayer, mate," he said. "I thought you might have drowned." Suspecting that he had been tricked earlier by Gavin, he clearly intended no humor in his comment.

Not acknowledging the officer's anger, Gavin looked up to smile and reached to shake his hand. "Thank heavens, Officer, there was no parking today. I think you should be thanked for that. You understand that prayers do make all the difference. Thanks again." At that precise moment, he threw his old sports car into reverse and sped away, before the bewildered officer could mutter another word. Lindsay and Ian bowed their heads, trying to control their laughter at the cop's reaction.

Back at the rectory, Mrs. Sweeny frowned with displeasure when she learned she would be having Lindsay as a house guest. Ian showed Lindsay to her room and informed her that they would be leaving for the dance at eight o'clock, adding, "Just wear something cool. It'll be hot as blazes down there tonight."

By the time the three of them arrived, the rock band was in full swing. In the entry hall, several kegs of beer had been turned on their sides, and large splash buckets placed under each tap. The intense smell permeated the small room.

"Ah," said Gavin with an exaggerated inhalation, "smells like heaven, doesn't it?"

"Is that how you describe heaven to your followers?" Ian ribbed.

"Pretty much, And then they also understand hell, which comes the next morning." They all laughed.

In spite of the great music and dancing, the most impressive part of the evening for Lindsay was the friendliness of everyone around her. The Aussies seemed to go to great lengths to make fun of one another. It was as if severe ribbing were a sign, or test, of friendship. She had never had such fun. Gavin and Ian seemed to be the most popular men in the room, with both women and men.

Well past midnight, Ian reminded Gavin that he and Lindsay were flying out at 6:00 a.m. for Naringa. Reluctantly, Ian and Lindsay bid their farewells and returned to the vicarage. Despite her giddy anticipation over the upcoming trip, the excitement of the day had taken its toll, and Lindsay dropped into her bed and fell instantly asleep.

Chapter 7

The next morning, Gavin drove them in his regular car to the airport. On the plane to Naringa, Lindsay related many of her father's famous flying stories about Ian's father. Ian laughed, as he knew the end of most of the stories; he had heard them all, too. Lindsay also explained how she had tracked Gavin down from Wombra to Bondi.

Though reluctant to bring up a sensitive subject, she finally said, "I'm very sorry to hear about your parents' death."

Ian blushed and shifted in his seat, seemingly uncomfortable with the sad memory. "They were both killed in a cave in the opal fields four years ago," he said. "Did you know that?"

"Yes, Gavin told me."

"It was some kind of fluke condition that hadn't been seen before. I don't suppose you know, but there are hundreds of people who live underground in the opal fields, and cave-ins just don't happen."

Not knowing what to say, but feeling compelled to say something, Lindsay asked, "Were they mining opals?"

"No, they were staying a few days with one of Dad's mates who had been mining up there for years. The place is called Couberpedi, and it's in the hottest part of Australia, so everyone lives underground in the cool. I'm not talking about living in a hole. These places are like fine homes underground. The opals are in sand, so they don't need big equipment to dig, and their homes just get bigger and bigger as they search. All in all, it's a very safe place."

Eager to change the subject, Lindsay said, "The man at the

airport told me that your dad started the Flying Doctor Service."

Ian smiled. "Yeah, he was one of the first. But it was a group effort to really get started."

"Was he still flying for the service at the time of the accident?

"No, he retired after the claim."

"I'm sorry, I must sound like a schoolgirl with nothing but questions. What was the claim?"

Ian teased her a little more. "Mount Tura is only the largest bauxite deposit in the world."

"Okay, mister, you're definitely the one causing this. What's bauxite?"

"It's a mineral used to strengthen steel, or in the production of steel. It was a fluke, a phenomenon, as Dad was flying back from a doctor drop-off at the Springs Station. It was late afternoon, and the setting sun seemed to shine through the windscreen, causing a shield of glare. This is his explanation. He changed the angle of the plane, and somehow there was a distinct outline in the topography. It wasn't fleeting; Dad said he could see the definite outline for at least five minutes of flying. He noted the location and packed into the area a week or so later. Without knowing what he was searching for, he pegged a claim. A year later, after a bill for test bores, he found out that he had discovered the largest bauxite deposit in the world to date."

Now sitting on the edge of her seat, Lindsay asked, "Is bauxite valuable?"

"Is it! Just the mining rights without the percentages were sold for over a hundred million."

Lindsay couldn't hold back her gasp. "My God so much money." Suddenly, she remembered Gavin being suspicious when they first met. "Is that why Gavin was cool to me at first?"

"Probably, because a lot of con jobs came out of the woodwork with false IOUs and contracts that they supposedly had with Dad. They all fell by the wayside once they discovered that Gavin was no pushover."

"Tell me, did Gavin go into the seminary after, or before, the discovery?"

"Before about a year before. Why?"

"I don't know why I asked. I guess I'll always wonder why a guy like Gavin would enter the priesthood."

"Yeah, everyone thinks there must have been some big happening in his life, and they're all waiting to know what it was. I used to wonder, too, but now I believe it really was a calling. Though, you know, it hasn't changed Gav much. Not quite the boy with the ladies, but that's about all."

Ian settled back in his seat, as though he didn't want to talk further. Lindsay's mind raced as she tried to recall all that had happened to her in the last few days, and how it was that she was now flying over God knows where, with a man who had been a stranger until yesterday. She reminded herself that their father knew her father, and they all seemed so nice that such thoughts were not necessary, Gavin being a priest, after all. Everyone she had met gave the impression they were quite pleased to be who they were, and it didn't matter what anyone thought; that was who they were. Nothing seemed to worry them. Above all, they treated each other with kindness, even if it didn't sound like it at times. It was hard to tell when they were kidding each other, as they had no fear of saying anything.

She caught her breath at the sudden thought of her own lack of courage and what they would think if they knew how timid and scared she had been, even of her own family. Funny, that all seemed so far away that she had to struggle to remember those humiliating times.

By noon, they had landed at Charters Towers. Ian explained

that giving places and things nicknames was typically Aussie. "They call this place Charley's Trousers," he said. "There's another twelve hours ahead of us, by ute, before we'll see the boundaries of Naringa."

Lindsay covered her mouth with her hand. "What's a ute?"

"A ute is Aussie for a utility truck – half-car, half-truck, really."

"Oh, thank God. I thought it might be a camel or something we had to ride."

"Don't worry, after twelve hours in the ute, you will have a sore bum, but not as sore as on a camel."

The small, treeless country town of one- and two-story wooden buildings, all in need of paint, reminded her of an old western movie set. The few people on the street seemed to be in no hurry, chatting and waving to people who drove by. "Is this the outback, Ian?"

"No not even nearly the outback. This is like New York compared to the outback."

Trying to joke, Lindsay quipped, "It's nice not to have parking meters, don't you think?"

"Yeah, but you really need them at rush hour."

They both laughed.

It only took them a five-minute drive to be out of the town and in the country again, where the roads consisted of rough red dirt. They stopped every couple of hours to stretch their legs and take a drink from the water bags that hung on the front bumper. What a shock it was for Lindsay to drink the water from the bags, so cold that she couldn't gulp it down without getting a brain freeze. It didn't make sense that in this 95-degree weather, the water could be just above freezing. Ian took his time explaining the principle of refrigeration – the condensation on the bag as the gas turned to water, and the air passing against the bag. Lindsay thought she got it.

After six hours, they came to a store in the middle of nowhere.

They stopped for a drink and a sandwich. Sitting on the veranda, they looked out into what looked like total sky. Lindsay had never seen such an expanse. It reminded her of early western movies she had seen, where a man on a horse looked out to a totally empty world that engulfed the entire screen.

Three caged parrots hung in the shade of the porch. One of the birds was making a heck of a racket, with loud screeches followed by streams of words.

Hearing the screeching words, Lindsay turned to Ian. "Did you hear that? That bird is talking Italian."

Ian laughed. "Come on, Lindsay, it's the swallows that return to Capistrano, not the bloody Aussie parrot."

But the bird kept it up. "Ciao, bambino, mumma," it squawked.

Finally, the storeowner came out and resolved the case. "The railway camp was in this area for the last three years," he explained, "and the migrant workers trained these birds from chicks. They couldn't take them, so they left them here. Between them, they speak three languages." Going to each cage, he pointed to the individual birds. "This is Shirley. She speaks English. This is Mickey, who speaks Italian. This is Jouvo, who speaks Portuguese. Unfortunately, no one around here can speak Portuguese, so Jouvo doesn't speak much at all anymore."

~~~

The country didn't change much, but the roads got worse, particularly where they had been washed away by a previous flood. The damage had not been repaired, and the road became whatever route the first vehicle had taken to get through the damaged area. Sometimes it didn't make sense to follow the track off the road and then cross, but that was what all the traffic had done since the flood, which may have occurred as much as two years earlier.
~~~

Six hours later, they came to a fence with a cattle stop grid at the gate. On a welcome sign next to the gate, Lindsay could just make out the word *Naringa* burnt into the wood, which had been badly splintered by gunshot holes.

"What does everyone do, shoot before they come and see you?" she asked.

"It must look like it, but the sign is years old, and all the hunters give it a little going-over for practice, I guess."

"How far to the house now?"

"About forty-one and five-tenths miles."

"Forty-one! Are you kidding?"

"No, that's it to the meter."

"My God, if that's the driveway, how big is the farm?"

"It's a station, not a farm, and it's 2,128,000 acres, about two hundred square miles, give or take a few yards."

Lindsay absorbed this. "It sounds bigger than a lot of countries in the world."

Smiling, Ian seemed to enjoy Lindsay's amazement. Suddenly, he pulled the car to a stop. "Lindsay, look – that's a Big Red." About twenty yards in front of the car, Lindsay saw the biggest kangaroo she could have imagined. Standing about eight feet tall, he sat on his haunches with his back in an upright position, looking very alert. No doubt this was his established territory, and he wasn't about to give any ground. To her amazement, the kangaroo's orange-red coat was long and thick. With brown button eyes, huge lashes, and large ears, he looked quite cuddly.

"Can I take a picture of him – or her?"

"Sure, it is a him, females don't get that tall."

"Can I just get out, or will he go for me?"

"You'll be lucky if he doesn't spring off before you can snap him."

It was almost as though he put on his best manners, because he waited while Lindsay pressed the button, only to find she hadn't advanced the film. She quickly did so and clicked a perfect photo.

"Oh, that's great!" she exclaimed. "I'm going to call him Mister Red, my official welcoming committee from the Way Out."

"Outback, I think you mean."

She looked around. "I must say, there doesn't look like there's a lot for Mr. Red to eat out here."

"You're right, there isn't. But they've learned to live in this climate and do well. Here's something for you. When it gets really tough out here, a pregnant female will extend her gestation period so she doesn't have to support a baby in a drought. The normal period is three months, and they've been known to delay it to a full nine months. The joey – that's a baby kangaroo – may be half-born in her pouch and will just remain there, not growing, until better times. They're the only animals in the world with that capability."

"My God, how did all that come about? It's amazing." Lindsay again looked around her in wonder. "Now the word 'outback' . . . it's funny they should call it that, don't you think?"

"Not really, especially when ninety-five percent of Australia lives within a hundred miles of the coast. It doesn't matter where you are; the middle of Aussie is always behind you. So 'outback' sounds about right."

"No doubt about it, sir. When it's explained so well, it couldn't mean anything else."

It was now 7:00 p.m., and the panoramic horizon behind them was deep red, with bright golden rays from the setting sun.

Ian pulled the car to a sudden halt at another cattle stop. "If we get out here, you can take your first glimpse of Naringa."

Standing at the fence, Ian gestured with a wide, sweeping introduction as he took a deep breath. "There she is, our oasis in the sand. No matter how long you live, Lindsay, I bet you a quid you will never forget this glorious sight."

The lighting was a soft glow, with dark shadows stretching behind each structure, outlining the yellow, low-setting sun reflecting off the front of the buildings, looking as though they were ablaze with fire. Compared to the surrounding barrenness, the sight was too much to take in with one glance. Without saying a word, they both stood staring at the beauty before them.

Ian was the first to speak as he pointed out each building within the group of buildings. The homestead stood very much alone, surrounded by tall, willowy trees. To the left of the homestead stood the windmill tower, a perfect touch to a perfect picture, representing independence. Lindsay heard the faint sound of dogs barking.

"You're right – I'll never forget this moment," Lindsay replied. "Beyond the buildings and the vibrant colors, the low horizon makes the outback different. The horizon appears to be only knee-high, which creates a tremendous sky."

"That's right. It's because of the flatness, of course. When you're alone in the hayfields, it appears as if the next blade of hay is the horizon."

"What are all those smaller buildings in the distance?"

"Those are the staff houses."

"There are lots of them."

"Yep, about eighty people live at the homestead."

Lindsay didn't say anything for a long moment, which caused Ian to ask, "Is something wrong?"

"No, but I imagined that a farm that raised cattle would have hundreds of pens and stockades for the herd. I can only see a few horse paddocks."

"Boy, you're quick for someone from the city. The reason why we only have a few house paddocks is because we never bring the herds in. Sometimes a herd will be eighty miles from here. We have maybe forty stockyards spread across the station. That way, we don't have to drive the herds so far. I'm really pleased you asked such a great question."

"Seeing such vivid contrasting colors, I wish I could paint."

"You'll soon meet someone who can paint. You know that Peggy is a famous artist, don't you?"

"Yes, Gavin mentioned it when we first met."

Though she dared not show it, the trip had been pretty hard for Lindsay. However, as they drove the last two miles and pulled up in front of the homestead, every thread of discomfort was replaced by the clarity of being totally conscious. For the first time in her life, she felt immersed in the moment. The last thirty-six hours had been life-changing, and she was aware of it now more than ever. Above all, she felt extremely special.

For Lindsay, meeting both Naringa and Peggy felt like love at first sight.

Peggy stood on the steps of the beautiful homestead waiting for the car to finally stop. She came running and was grabbing at Ian before he even had a chance to get out of the driver's seat. Lindsay realized that she hadn't seen Ian since her release from the hospital.

Ian seemed to have forgotten Lindsay, but just as Lindsay was starting to feel awkward, Peggy broke away from Ian and came to the passenger's side, opening the door for her.

Peggy hugged her excitedly. "Welcome to Naringa, Lindsay. I've already heard so much about you from Gavin. Oh, I am going to love having you here, and I'm sure you'll love it here, too. It's very special, you know. Ian, I'm going to take Lindsay to her room, as I know how she feels, believe me."

Lindsay hadn't said three words, but she knew she was going to love every minute she spent with Peggy. It was as if Peggy were talking so much so they didn't have to cover the fact that they had only just met. For Peggy, they were friends, and that was that. Lindsay did not to know that she would relive this time with Peggy a hundred times over.

Chapter 8

Over the next three weeks, Lindsay fell into the station way of life and loved every moment. Plus, she felt a special kinship to Mr. Pango and his mares, as they and she were all on the same curiosity level for the station staff. The staff was exceptionally friendly; they would go out of their way to introduce themselves and their families to Lindsay. The men were easygoing, but the ladies all seemed shy when meeting Lindsay. She didn't realize that her presence was special until Ian pointed out that most of the staff had put on their best clothes to meet her.

Lindsay wondered if they were dressing up for her or for Mr. Pango.

The general belief among the men was that Pango, such a small horse, was of no use in the Outback. There were those among the women who believed that Pango's breed, the Timor pony, was blessed with special spiritual powers and could accomplish amazing feats for such small creatures.

This belief could explain why Mr. Pango was doing so well the first few days, as the heat was severe. Pango didn't seem to notice the climate change. The mares were slower to adjust, but soon seemed to be doing okay. Mr. Pango's fabled skills made him the talk of the station, and he responded in a friendly, tame manner. Lindsay noticed that Mr. Pango reacted intuitively to Ian and respected him as his boss. It was strangely familiar, as she had seen the same reaction with her beloved dog Bitsy. No matter how much attention she personally paid to Bitsy, it was clear that Bitsy regarded her father as her boss. Both Pango and

Bitsy also displayed loyalty to their masters. She thought back to her friend John in New York, who believed that all children and animals reacted to the deepest voice. Since fathers always had the deepest voices, dogs naturally looked to them as their leaders. Ian's voice wasn't particularly deep, but it was obvious that he had command as the boss.

Ian clearly felt proud to see Mr. Pango react to his presence. When he showed up, Mr. Pango immediately whinnied and frolicked before nosing up to him.

On this particular day, Lindsay felt very close to Ian as they sat there together, looking at the Timor ponies. Ian seemed lost in thought as Lindsay tried to imagine what he was thinking. Neither had spoken for at least two minutes.

Finally, Ian spoke in a low voice, as though a thought had just occurred to him. "You know, Mr. Pango has a fight ahead of him, and it's one he may not live through."

The thought of a dead Pango made Lindsay's breath catch. "What kind of fight? Why can't you prevent it?"

"The fight will be with the leader of the station horses. No, I can't really prevent it, if I want this breeding idea of mine to be a success. It may be a different world out here, but it is the real world. If Pango is able to avoid the final confrontation, he would be very low on the totem pole as far as respect from the other horses, and they would all pick on him. In time, they would probably kick him to death."

She reflexively put a hand over her mouth. "That's ridiculous. You can just keep them apart, can't you?"

"No, that's not possible out here. There's not a job out there that's done by one man and one horse. Everything is done in groups, and each man and each animal must look out for the other. There have been times, few, I admit, but we have actually shot good, sound horses that couldn't work with the group. A troublesome horse can get the others riled up and cost men their lives."

Lindsay shook her head. "Honestly, I don't know if you're pulling my leg or not. Who is this king-of-the-castle horse that holds Pango's fate in his hooves?"

Ian shook his head. "No, I'm not kidding. The king of the castle you refer to is not a killer, but he is royalty. Do you want to meet him?"

"Sure, if he doesn't want to trample me to death."

"Okay, then." Ian rose and reached for Lindsay's hand. "Come on, he's over in the next paddock under the gums over there. He already knows you're here – he's been watching you walk with Karo. Believe me, we can only imagine what they really know, or sense."

As they sat on a bench, or a fallen log where someone had axed the top smooth and flat, a group of horses approached them. Ian just watched them approach, and all except one stopped more than ten feet from the fence. Lindsay could see that one stood out among the other horses, and he stopped two feet from the fence, fully alert but unafraid. Ian, Lindsay, and Radium all remained perfectly still, watching each other. Besides his air of aloofness, he was larger than the other horses, and his coat was shiny, compared to those of the other dust-covered horses. His eyes were bright, and his nostrils continually twitched with every movement of air.

In normal tones, as though he were speaking to another human, Ian addressed the horse: "Hello, Radium. You look good, but a little fat. I'm going to have work you."

Ian stood as Radium approached and pushed his nose against Ian's outstretched hand.

"This is my friend Lindsay." Ian withdrew his hand and invited Lindsay to meet Emperor Radium. "Just gently put your hand out and pat him. He won't bite. He's a real gentleman, I assure you."

Lindsay felt no fear as she tried to pat Radium's handsome head. Try as she did, it was impossible to touch the horse. He didn't appear to move a muscle, but when Lindsay moved her hand quickly, the horse raised his head, leaving Lindsay's hand waving in the air. It was a challenge, and the horse never took his gaze away from Lindsay.

Finally, she gave up. "What's the matter? Doesn't he like me?"

"Sure he does. Put your hand out again."

As Lindsay extended her hand this time, Ian commanded, "Stand." Obediently, Radium didn't move an inch and allowed Lindsay to scratch his forehead and rub his ears.

"Why wouldn't he let me do that before?"

"Because he was showing you that he really is the boss."

With a grin, Lindsay challenged, "That's ridiculous. You just gave him an order, and he obeyed. You don't really believe that, do you?"

"Why not? It worked, didn't it? I should tell you about Radium." He added as an afterthought, "That's *if* you want to hear about him. I get so carried away and forget that others may have no interest in him, and I bore them to death."

"Yes, I do want to learn about him."

"Well, first off, he's a 'waler.'" The name comes from New South Whales, where the breed was started. Australia was a tough place for horses to survive, as it took up to seven months at sea to transport them from Europe. The early English horses couldn't handle the heat and failed. Do you know that in 1798, there were only eighteen horses in all of Australia? Isn't that amazing? Eighteen in the whole country! To create this breed, special strains of English thoroughbreds, Arabians, and prized Cape thoroughbreds from South Africa were brought here and carefully bred."

Pleased to show her fascination, Lindsay interrupted. "What

about the Timor ponies?"

Ian grinned. "Bravo, Lindsay, you're quite right. Actually, there were two ponies to start, the Timor and the Welsh mountain pony. I don't know much about the Welsh pony, as the Timor pony became more prominent. Not only did the breed prove itself in Aussie, but in 1857 twenty-nine walers were sent to the British in Calcutta India and then the entire picture changed.

"There was an Indian mutiny, and the English were having trouble with their mounts due to the severe heat and challenging sands. Soft sand would cause the English horses' hooves to split. The whalers proved themselves to such an extent that the demand for horses went up, and they set up the first Australian industry of breeding and exporting walers world-wide."

Ian stopped and glanced at Lindsay to check that he still had her attention before continuing. "Heralded by history's greatest regiments, the Lancers, Royal Horse Artillery, Australian Mounted Light Horse Brigades, and New Zealand Mounted Rifles were all hugely famous. Thousands of horses were sent to Europe, and for the Boar War alone, from 1888 to 1902, over sixteen thousand horses were sent to South Africa. Now isn't that something in such a short period of time?"

"My God, Ian, that's a lot to remember, and it's a very impressive history."

"I'm glad you like it, but I don't have to remember it, as I believe I lived it in an earlier life, I love it so much. Let me tell you one more thing about Radium's lineage, and then I'll stop."

"Please go ahead. I love it."

"Well, imagine if you were a pioneer, stockman, bushranger, and you lived due to the reliability of your horse. You can imagine the importance of the country's horse championship events. You call it rodeo, we call it campdrafting. Careful and complete records were kept on all the events and the participation of famous horses, like Radium's grandfather. This wasn't just for history, but because the horses at the top of the breed would charge greater fees to stand for leading mares. Radium's great-grandfather, Cecil, was the greatest in history. As the story goes, he could gallop into a pair of dray shafts and turn within them. He was such a winner that he was even barred from some events. Bushmen came from hundreds of miles to compete against Cecil, but none had a horse that could beat him. My Radium Emperor is Cecil's grandson."

Ian held up his hands as if in surrender. "Truly, I will finish soon, but just one quick story about Radium's great-granddad. During the Second World War, at Dungog Bushman's Carnival, where only the nation's best could compete, the judge selected five horses for the final judging. Cecil received first place, and the four runners-up were all his sons."

Lindsay clapped her hands and laughed. "Ian, I loved every word. But if Radium is such a great horse, why would he hurt Mr. Pango?"

"He may not, but it depends on how Pango reacts to him as leader of the herd. Remember, Pango is also a leader of his heard."

"Is Radium a vicious horse?"

"Since the other horses don't challenge him, I don't know how he is with them, but he certainly isn't vicious with humans. Once, when Karo got hold of a bottle of whisky and passed out in the paddock, Radium stood over him until he woke up. He continued to guard him for half the morning and wouldn't move despite all the onlookers from the station."

"Like you said, Radium seems like a real gentleman."

As they walked back to the homestead for lunch, Lindsay felt decidedly better about Pango's safety.

"Mr. Pango has shown his good nature," Ian remarked, "but he still has to prove his courage and pluck, for which the Timor pony breed is famous. I'm sure he is one tough old fellow. I'm hoping I'm right, for his sake and mine."

Ian planned to take Mr. Pango on a week-long roundup, as soon as he was comfortable with the other station horses. Up to now, Mr. Pango had been separated from the station herd for his own safety. There was no real way to know how fierce the competition was among the station horses, but at least they could keep him safe while he got accustomed to the outback. This delayed the day Mr. Pango would have to fight for his place among the station horses. There was a chance that Mr. Pango would be severely beaten and injured for life, but that chance had to be taken. Only Mr. Pango could fight that fight.

"My main concern is that the entire herd might gang up on him if we interfere in their world," Ian explained. "Like humans, most animals have an order of ranking."

Every time Lindsay looked at Mr. Pango, she felt concern for him and wondered if he sensed, in some herd logic, that he would have to fight. She wondered if it was something all horses instinctively knew. Did he understand that neither she nor Ian could help him? Then, with a start, Lindsay thought, *My God, I'm getting as bad as Karo. Who do I think I am, Doctor Doolittle? I suppose we all have to fight our own fights.*

Her own fight for independence brought her father to mind, and she realized that she hadn't thought of him once since she had met Gavin and Ian. This was a dramatic turnaround, since she had once spent hours worrying about what her father thought or what he would say. *What do you know? Maybe I'm becoming my own person at last.*

~~~
~~~

Lindsay's meeting with Peggy that first night was an indication of the true openness Peggy felt for her. It was a good thing that Peggy made Lindsay sure of her feelings, because without it, she could have surely made Lindsay feel left out, for Peggy couldn't take her attention from Ian. Thrilled for Ian and Peggy, Lindsay felt sad that she would never know the natural true sibling love that they shared.

However, within days, Peggy and Lindsay did feel like sisters, and they started every day together over long, laughter-filled breakfasts. Lindsay was falling in love with Ian, and she suspected he felt deeply for her, too. Nevertheless, she was too shy to make the first move. At first, she thought Ian was on the timid side, but after seeing him deal so naturally with the station hands, this dispelled such a notion. He was straightforward, very firm, but absolutely fair. The station working staff numbered about sixty, and none of them showed any doubt regarding his judgment or authority.

On the second day, Ian had appointed Karo to be Lindsay's guide. "Personal helping hand" was the actual title they gave him. Lindsay was amazed when Ian came up with such a direct nickname, because Karo, in fact, had only one hand. His right arm was missing from the elbow.

I guess that's what the Aussies do, she thought.

This Aussie nicknaming style caused Lindsay to think back to the Surf Club party, when Gavin had introduced a man with a huge, round, shiny hairless head as "Curley."

She was unable to guess Karo's age, but suspected him to be in his mid-forties. Whenever Lindsay left the homestead, Karo's short, slight figure would magically appear, for he took his job to guard her seriously. Yet no matter what Lindsay asked him, he always answered with approving laughter. He reminded Lindsay of the African dwarf bushmen who would click their jaws as they talked to themselves all day.

She had been familiar with these aboriginals through her love of the National Geographic television show.

Lindsay quickly learned to listen carefully to him in order to decipher what he really meant. Karo didn't mean to mislead her, but one night at dinner, everyone had a great laugh at her expense when she asked about Father Gavin's graveyard. Karo had shown Lindsay around the homestead and pointed out two graveyards. Listening with half an ear, she understood Karo to say that Father Gavin had a good heart, but if one was ailing, Gavin would put them out of their misery.

That night, Lindsay seriously enquired, "How many people were buried in Father Gavin's graveyard?" The laughter was so uncontrollably hearty that Lindsay had to wait at least five minutes before anyone in the room could stop laughing to respond.

Ian was the first to recover. "There's no one buried there. It's just for Gavin's dead machines. Remember how I told you that my brother was the worst mechanic in Aussie? Well, that's where we put the machines he breaks, or screws up so badly we can't fix them."

Peggy cut in. "Sometimes Gav will spend a whole week in there, and he's yet to get anything to work. We haven't done it yet, but we keep saying that we're going to produce a working machine, with the hope that he thinks he got it going . . . just for his pride, mind you. He would love so much to be good with engines."

"It's the one area where he fails," said Ian, raising his glass. "Here's to Lindsay, for being a good sport and not minding our laughing at her. Hear, hear!"

Lindsay could imagine the delight that Gavin would feel in succeeding to fix an engine, and it made his image even more adorable.

Ian asked, "How is Karo doing with his new job?"

Lindsay smiled at the thought of Karo having a job. Right away, she had become aware that Karo saw life through the eyes of a child. She found that this child-like approach to life was contagious, and she had to remind herself that she was learning the station life through his imaginative eyes. *Maybe he and Gavin have something in common, by both appreciating the simple delights of life.* Later, when she and Karo watched a tree being trimmed, with the sap running out of the fresh saw cuts, she could not convince Karo that the tree was not actually crying. After empathizing with his child-like logic about pain and tears, it was Lindsay who suddenly felt that the tree was crying. Whether she truly believed it or not, she knew that she would never look at a tree the same way again. Karo introduced a kind of beauty into her thinking that related to the smallest of things.

"He is so nice," Lindsay replied to Ian, "and sometimes he quietly takes over. I have to be careful that I don't start talking baby talk, as well."

"He wasn't always like that, you know, Lindsay."

"Oh, I thought he was born simple."

"No, his real name is Trevor Brent. He was a bookkeeper here. A good one, too."

"Really? I can't believe it. What happened to him?"

"A sad, but common happening out here. I don't know if they're drink-crazy before they come out here, or if the outback brings it out in them, but some men go drink-crazy and will drink anything just to get high. Mentholated spirits, or kerosene, are eventually on the list, since they can get it in lamps and cooking stoves. It only takes a small amount before the brain starts to corrode, and once the hallucinations begin, the damage is permanent. Man can be such a desperate animal."

Lindsay's mouth dropped open in disbelief. "How did he lose his arm?"

Ian took a deep breath. "What I am going to tell you may sound humorous, but it did happen. Trevor Brent, and his friend Wallace Armstrong, had been drinking kerosene and started to hallucinate. Trevor thought he was a bird and climbed a tree. Wallace had a gun, and Trevor told him to shoot the bird out of the tree. Wally took aim and fired, shooting Trevor out of the tree and taking his arm clean off with the one shot. This happened in Charters Towers, so someone got him to the hospital quickly. Wallace died a short time after, but Trevor recovered and never remembered a thing, not even losing his arm."

Lindsay cupped her hand over her mouth in shock. "Surely he remembered having an arm?"

Peggy broke in. "I can answer that. A couple of weeks later, Gavin and I visited Trevor in the hospital. He was sitting up in the middle of the bed, as happy as Larry. When he saw us, he started to flap the remaining part of his arm, faster and faster. Then he asked us to guess what he was doing. When we couldn't guess, we both asked, 'What?'

"Beaming with pride, he bragged that he was cleaning his teeth.

"As sad as it was, Gav and I just stood there and laughed with him. It was then Gav gave the instructions that when the time was right, Trevor was to be escorted to live at Naringa. He has been here ever since and will die here, but with dignity and without worries. And that's how he got the name Karo, from Kerosene

"What happened to the other man, Wallace?"

"Now he was a real drinker, and died of the stuff a short while later. A great horseman, too. It's really hard for a man to be known as a great horseman out here, let me tell you."

"That is so sad," Lindsay remarked. "Does it happen out here a lot?"

Ian answered in a quiet voice, "Sadly, it does. If you have a crack in your character, the outback will break it wide open, especially if you let your guard down."

~~~

The next morning, over breakfast, Peggy teased Lindsay. "If Ian doesn't start to make a play for you, I would offer to give him lessons."

The more Lindsay's face burned with blushes, the more Peggy recited imaginary flirtatious conversation between her and Ian.

The subjects covered by the two girls varied, but usually returned to their sexual experiences. When they finished sharing stories, they honestly both agreed that they knew very little about sex. So far, neither girl had found the joys they had read about in books and seen in movies.

For the most part, Peggy and Lindsay spent hours upon hours planning Peggy's world trip. Lindsay had written to her parents asking them to inform the building management that Peggy would be staying in her Manhattan apartment for as long as she fancied. Because of this generous offer, Peggy planned to spend more time in New York and made it the first stop on her painting tour.

Peggy was convinced that her painting needed a new direction. She was famous in Australia, and her paintings fetched handsome prices, but they all featured life in the Australian outback. She questioned her ability to be as accomplished with other genres. Gavin always emphasized to Peggy that her talent came from her unique visual viewpoint. She reminded herself that Gavin was never wrong and she should trust his insightful opinion.

On this particular day, the girls were still chatting and laughing as usual when Ian came bursting into the room. "Listen, you two young, beautiful women, I have some good news and some bad news. If you invite me to sit and have coffee, I'll tell you of this news. Otherwise, it's back to work with me."
~~~

Both girls jumped up to grab Ian and push him down in the chair. "Careful, girls, you'll mess up my hair. Two sugars, please."

The girls were wide-eyed like a couple of school kids, and Ian purposefully took longer and longer to get around to breaking the news, slowly sipping his coffee with mock enthusiasm.

Finally, Peggy warned, "Ian Abernathy, if you don't hurry up and get it out, I will tip that hot coffee in your lap."

He set the coffee cup down. "Okay, the first good news is that Gavin has been honored by the Joint Churches of Australia for the work he has done for all faiths. It appears that his popularity on radio and the telly has increased church attendance across the board. Can you believe that his success has never been replicated in the history of Australia?"

The girls cheered and clapped as though Father Gavin were in the room. "Well done, Gav," Peggy cheered. "Come on, what's the rest of it?"

"The bad news is, because of the special service for Gav, he can't come up next week as he planned."

Peggy looked relieved. "That's not so bad, as bad news can go. Come on, Ian, what's the other good news?"

Both girls looked on in despair as Ian slowly rose from his seat and pretended to leave, without revealing the good news. Then, to their delight, he climbed up on a chair and barked, "Hear ye, hear ye, all in this room and in the sound of my voice, there will be a party at the Naringa Station this Saturday night for one and all. Phillipa and Max are back from England, and they're coming over for a farewell party for little Miss Peggy."

Peggy let out a delighted cry and turned to Lindsay. "He doesn't just mean Pip and Max. This means about thirty of their hands, and we all have a big party. You'll love it. The hands will go all night long, or as long as they can stand, and we'll have dinner station-style.

Phillip and Max are our closest neighbors and friends."

"How close?" Lindsay asked.

"Seventy-two miles. I know it exactly, as I used to go there for holidays and loved it."

"That sounds so exciting. I can't wait. How old are Phillipa and Max?"

"About thirty-six, wouldn't you think, Ian?"

"Yep, about that. Max was a year behind Gavin in school."

Peggy made Ian promise that she and Lindsay could make all of the arrangements and not to worry about her trip, as she had been packed for weeks. Ian accepted her terms and left the room.

"This is going to be the best party of your life, and you will love Pip and Max. You won't believe Phillipa – Pip, as we call her. If you've ever had the vision that farmers' wives, or women of the outback, are homely, with sun-baked, wrinkled skin, just wait until you see Pip. She could be a Parisian model. She and Max have been in Europe for the last six months – every two years, they take a world trip. Despite their worldly culture, they love the outback and call it their real home."

Lindsay felt growing excitement. "Is their station as big as Naringa?"

"No, but it has better land, so the herd of stock they run is pretty high. Their land has more permanent water than Naringa. The land to the north looks about the same, but in the south section, they actually farm sheep. Max is a very good manager, too."

"Sounds great. So when are they coming?"

"They'll be here on Saturday and will stay a couple of days."

Lindsay could hardly wait.

Chapter 9

The news of the party and of the upcoming visit of the entire staff from the Parkinson Station seemed to be airborne; even the ringers from the boundaries knew of the party. The entire station sprang to life as the various sites were made ready for the big day.

The wives and daughters of Naringa made every effort to dress up for the event. Party dresses could be seen on many porches as they were hung out to air, and many of the mothers wore scarves over huge mounds of hair rollers. Lindsay was no exception as she primped and pressed her own chiffon dress that she had bought in New York for her trip. She had tried it on at least three times since the news of the party.

She stood on her veranda as the trucks carrying the party guests drove through the yard in front of the homestead with much yelling and hoopla. A short while later, Lindsay saw Max and Phillipa's ute pull to a stop at the homestead entrance. Maybe because of Phillipa's heralded beauty, or because she was an unfamiliar guest, Lindsay felt shy and stayed in her room rather than running to meet the new arrivals. However, this didn't stop her from making every effort to catch a glimpse of the beautiful Phillipa. Lindsay couldn't imagine what to expect, but when she finally saw her, she was taken aback by the woman's casual but regal elegance. Her shoulder-length black hair was tied in a ponytail, accentuating her long, elegant neck. With large, round sunglasses and a tight-fitting white blouse, she could have stepped off the front of any fashion magazine.

"I can't imagine her being able to look so gracious if she really is an outback station wife," Lindsay murmured. Shocked by her own cynical thoughts, Lindsay turned her attention to Max. He was about the same height as Ian and boasted a large handle-bar mustache. His cultured voice gave him the air of English gentry. After seeing him express genuine joy at greeting his good friends, Lindsay immediately discerned that he was a strong, generous person with a great sense of humor.

Peggy answered the thoughts Lindsay had spoken aloud. "Oh, Lindsay, you couldn't be more wrong if you tried. Pip's story is well-known in the outback. Do you want to hear it? I've known it by heart since I was about nine years old."

Lindsay sat back in the soft chair. "Yes, of course I want to hear it. You make it sound so exciting."

"Well, here goes, and don't be surprised by the details I remember, as I wrote this exact story in my final year of university."

Peggy squinted her eyes as she concentrated. "Part of Phillipa's story is well-known in the area of Lake Mungada, or Spirit Lake, as it was called on the English maps. The Aborigine name translates as 'Sad Voice.' In 1915, Phillipa's mother Angela married Terrence Landaur in London and headed for Australia on the first available ship. The crossing was calm, which was most uncommon. Upon landing in Sydney, Angela came down with a fever and soon discovered that she was pregnant. Finding Sydney as tough as their home in Liverpool, they needed little persuasion to join Terrence's brother in the outback. Terrence was a gentle man and certainly not suited to the tough outback culture. Nevertheless, he was determined to succeed. By working harder and longer than others, and with some help from his brother, he was able to buy O'Burn, a neighboring station sixty-three miles west of his brother's Sherilee Station.

"Phillipa was two years old at the time. It was hard work, but after a year, O'Burn Station started to show good profit potential. The crop land had been more productive than anyone had expected, and the profits allowed Terrence to buy more cattle. Everything looked to be perfect, and Terrence expected to repay the loans ahead of schedule.

"Terrence was a kind, even-tempered man, but he couldn't stand having Aborigines on his property. Phillipa's nurse and a cook were the only natives allowed on the property, and he even scattered the wandering tribes when they camped at the water hole. Other folks favored having Abos on the property, as they would be used for seasonal labor, and they had an unbelievable way with all the animals. The Aboriginal belief was that earth represented their mother and father, and to be refused use of the water hole was like a personal strike against their family. Even though they obeyed without opposition, they knew actions against the earth would bring bad luck.

"Two years later, the wind storm started, noted historically as the Seven-Year Drought. It hadn't rained for a year, and the dry dirt just crumbled to the touch and turned to red sand. The livestock had to be moved and eventually sold as the sand slowly covered the ground. The wind was relentless, and as the sand piled up against any obstacle, it either buried it or knocked it down. Her father's dream became a nightmare, and his heart broke before his back. He'd never really liked the outback even in the good times, and now he hated and resented it. Overcome by desperation, he went out one morning and never returned.

"Phillipa's mother attempted to hang on for several weeks, clinging to vague hope. One morning, she told the nurse that, in a dream, she had seen her husband on the bank of the water hole. Hoping her dream was prophetic, at first light, she hurried to the scene of her dream, but she never returned. Two days later, a tribe of Aborigines on walkabout told the gin nurse that the mother would not return, as her spirit had spoken to them from the lake. Not questioning this mystical story, the gin nurse took Phillipa and joined the tribe on the walkabout.

“Three months later, the tribe camped at Sherilee, and within days, the story of the white child reached the ears of Phillipa’s aunt. Without knowing it was her own niece, she ordered the child to be brought to the house. Three days later, the gin nurse told the story of the Spirit Lake and the struggle Phillipa’s mother and father had undergone. Until that moment, the lady from Sherilee had no idea she was holding her own niece. It was only by sheer chance that Phillipa was saved, as the tribe cared little about death, but out of respect for nature and family, they would have cared for Phillipa as a tribal member.

“Phillipa’s uncle left for O’Burn the next day, accompanied by six aborigine trackers. They reached the O’Burn Station, to find the sand piled six feet high against any structure left standing, and erasing any evidence of the hard fight to save the station. Phillipa’s aunt expanded the search by sending an Aborigine search party to the lake. Upon their return, the search party reported that they had all heard the sad voice in the lake. The uncle’s station, Sherilee, had twice the amount of year-round water, and because it lay thirty-two miles to the east, it fortunately experienced no sign of drought.

“Her aunt and uncle showed the greatest love for Phillipa, but due to her early trauma, Phillipa developed a severe stutter. Since Phillipa had no other children to play with, other than her two older boy cousins who constantly made fun of her, in her loneliness she turned to reading. By the age of ten, she had read almost every word of Dickens. Her Aunt Mabel worked with Phillipa every day for four years with her own self-invented speech therapy method. After two years, Phillipa was able to read aloud with limited stuttering. This was considered a huge breakthrough, and after two more years of daily lessons, Phillipa’s stutter was completely gone.

“Her stutter had given her inspiration to read, and it had served her well. At the age of fourteen, she won a scholarship to the University of New South Wales, but once they discovered her young age, they advanced the scholarship to the following year. Three years later, she won a bursary to Oxford in England, where she met Max, though it was far from love at first sight. Only in their fourth year did they get together, and to their equal surprise, they fell desperately in love. The sad story of her parent's death was not uncommon in the early days of the outback, where dreams and lives were broken as though they never existed."

Peggy didn't smile, but looked at Lindsay as if trying to see if she felt as strongly about the story as Peggy did.

Lindsay spoke quietly, "I hate to think of those early people making every heart-stopping effort, only to be left with total failure and sometimes loss of life itself. We take so much for granted. I love the fact that Phillipa's reading served her so well, but I will always think of how close she came to being an Aborigine. Oh my God, can you imagine?"

Peggy got up to leave. "Well, there you have it, my dear, true stories to match those of the American Wild West. I'm going to leave you now so you can look pretty for the men at Naringa."

Phillipa's story made Lindsay feel that she was part of a grand adventure, filling her with even more excitement and anticipation. She took her dress out again to ensure her own elegance, now that she had determined the overall tone for the festivities and knew that the other women were making every effort to be as beautiful as possible.

Taking the remainder of the day to prepare was a joy for Lindsay, for she felt part of the celebration. As she dressed, she couldn't get Phillipa's beautiful image out of her mind. Phillipa moved like a slow piano melody, with grace and balance, appearing as if everything had gone right during her life. Above all, she had a mystique that made Lindsay want to be in her presence. Lindsay felt certain that this party would be the best time she had ever had. She reminded herself, *I must drink slowly and not too much. The last thing I need is to be sick.*

Around eight, Lindsay made her way through to the living room veranda. Standing alone, looking into the semi-darkness beyond the light from the house, Lindsay was overwhelmed with the sense of well-being. Her careful exposure to the harsh sun had added color to her complexion, which now glowed to set off her flowing Chiffon dress. Her love affair with the outback had been immediate, though completely subconscious until now. The thought of New York and her parents seemed as distant as another lifetime.

Ian's voice brought her back to the present. "Lindsay, you look absolutely radiant."

Lindsay turned to answer with a heartfelt smile. "Thank you, kind sir. But, Ian, you look very handsome yourself." *I hadn't thought of him in a tux, but, my God, what a beautiful man.*

Ian was about to say something more but was interrupted as Phillipa and Max entered.

Phillipa took Lindsay's hand before she spoke. "Oh, Lindsay, I am so happy to meet you, after all the good things Peggy has been telling me about you. But she didn't tell me that you were so beautiful."

Before Lindsay could respond, Max appeared face-to-face with Lindsay, looking directly into her eyes. "That compliment goes for me, too. I must say, we have fierce competition in the beauty department tonight, wouldn't you agree, Ian?"

Lindsay didn't listen to Ian's reply, captivated as she was by the attention from Phillipa and Max. Instead, she caught her breath to regroup.

Max continued, "Well, Lindsay, we will have a good time

tonight and do our best to show you that the Australian outback is not culturally bankrupt. And if we fail, we'll have a hell of a time trying. Now, our first round of drinks is a very fine champagne."

Max poured champagne into the hollow-stem glasses to all present. He was about to propose a toast when he realized Peggy hadn't arrived. "Wait a moment, please – glasses down. We can't start the evening without our famous ar-teest! Where is that little Peggy girl?"

At that moment, Peggy appeared at the far side of the room, making a theatrical entrance with her head cocked slightly to the side and her hand tucked under her chin. She queried with a mock accent, "Excuse me, kind sirs, is this where the party is tonight?"

Max bantered with an over-done English accent, "My beautiful girl, the party is wherever you are. You look stunning. No, I take that back, you look positively ravishing!"

Peggy curtsied. "Thank you, old boy, very nice of you to flatter me, especially when you have your own hot chick in the kitchen!"

Everyone clapped at Peggy's quick comeback.

Phillipa clinked her glass to offer the first toast of the evening. "I would like to accept Peggy's compliment, but didn't like the kitchen part. What do you say, girls? Let's just drink to our fine male companions for the evening."

"Hear, hear!" The cry of the evening was underway.

Lindsay was so impressed with the easy way these people enjoyed themselves. It wasn't just laughter; they truly had fun and couldn't get enough of each other. For Lindsay, she felt as if she were experiencing true friendship for the very first time. A big part of Aussie humor was making fun of each other. Even though there seemed to be a no-holds-barred rule about poking fun, Lindsay also sensed a respectful presence. Perhaps it was their feeling of equality, or just respect for their friendships. It didn't matter anyway; she felt thrilled to be counted as one of the special friends.

Everyone toasted in turn, and when it was Lindsay's turn, she considered her words seriously. Since she had never felt the need to discover her true inner feelings, let alone describe them out loud, this was a big first step for her. She realized the gravity of her expression and didn't want to fall short of her new friends' expectations.

"Ladies and gentlemen, before I toast our celebrity artist, it's important for me to speak from my heart by saying how special you have all made me feel. It's an honor and privilege to know you."

Max thumped the table, yelling, "Hear, hear."

Lindsay suddenly enjoyed being center stage. "If the gentleman to my right would refrain from making exuberant gestures and trying to break the table with his brute strength, I would like to continue."

At this, everybody began banging on the table, shouting, "Hear, hear!"

Lindsay threw up her hands, waiting for silence, before continuing. "I would like everyone to raise your glasses to drink to the health and happiness of the very beautiful and generous Peggy Elizabeth Abernathy. I personally wish her the best trip to my little old homeland, America."

Her toast was supported with a chorus of "Hear, hear!"

Max was the loudest, but Ian definitely howled the most. Lindsay was happy to sit down for dinner then, as the drinks were going straight to her head, but this respite didn't last long as the rounds of wine began with the first course. The dinner conversation quieted down somewhat, giving Lindsay a chance to converse with Phillipa, who insisted that Lindsay call her Pip. She was as nice as she was beautiful, and certainly showed every sign of holding her own against her loud, reveling husband.

After the third course, when coffee was being served, Ian

tapped his glass to get attention. "Lindsay, as we have to make our own fun out here, you can see how hard it is with this lot. We have a tradition where everyone must perform in front of the group. Past experience has proven that it is better to get this underway before the performer and the audience get too drunk. There are no rules, but we try to keep it moderately clean."

Before he could continue, Pip shouted, "That's emphasis on the *clean* and the *try*."

This brought a loud chorus of, "Hear, hear!" as they all raised their glasses.

Ian stood and called for silence. "Before my dear friend Max takes over the whole bloody show, as he usually does, I want to perform something of a serious nature." This was unexpected, and everyone sat quietly in anticipation as he produced an elaborate, official-looking scroll. Carefully unrolling it, he turned it so all could see. Clearing his throat in an exaggerated manner, he continued, "I would like to read this document and memorialize its contents as of this day, February twenty-fifth, 1953.

"'To Miss Lindsay Priscilla Graeme, because she has accepted me, in spite of my many cruel ways, because she has the depth of character to see my depth of beauty, and because she has shown patience and kindness to all, it is my pleasure to welcome her as my daughter. Signed, Mother Nature, Mother of the Great Outback.'"

The room grew loud with screams and shouts of endorsement as Ian looked admiringly at Lindsay. She couldn't stop the tears of joy and the feeling of embarrassment at the same time. Max thumped the table and burst out in song as the others quickly joined.

"For she's a jolly good fellow, for she's a jolly good fellow, for she's a jolly good fellow . . . and so say all of us, and so say all of us. Hip-hip-hurrah! Hip-hip-hurrah!"

Standing, Max held his glasses out in front of him and waited for everyone to do the same. All together, they cheered, "To Lindsay Priscilla Graeme." They drained their glasses in unison, shouting, "Speech! Speech!"

Lindsay wiped her eyes, stood quietly, and faced the group. The camaraderie of the group gave her complete confidence as she addressed her new friends in a theatrical voice. "I'm so overwhelmed by your exceedingly good judgment, and it is with great pride that I accept your kindness. I feel very privileged to be with you tonight. Even though I have been warned that I may have to sit through a couple of acts of Max's Shakespearian interpretations, may I raise my glass and drink to you all. Hear, hear!" Lindsay saluted mockingly. She drank along, thrilled by the attention, and drained her glass instantly.

Everyone was banging on the table and whistling and yelling. Surprised by her successful presentation, Lindsay was most aware of the love and appreciation from the group.

The wine was definitely having its effect on the group, as the noise level in the room increased in decibels. Ian and Peggy then started banging the table, shouting, "Max! Max! Max! We want Max! Shakespeare, please, Max!"

After two minutes, Max accepted and stepped to the head of the table.

"Before I begin, I would like to ask our American guest if she is familiar with Mr. Shakespeare."

Lindsay, feeling she was being set up, answered, "I'm not as familiar with old Bill as I should be, but I know who he was."

Max resumed his mocking English accent. "Splendid. I am always happy to convert people to the world of culture – and pretty young women are my specialty. Now, do you have any favorites, Lindsay, as I am master of them all?"

Before Lindsay could answer, the others were thumping the table demandingly. "'Stockton on Tees,' 'Stockton on Tees.'"

Raising his hands to beg silence, Max continued, "It seems my culture-starved fans have robbed you of your choice. Are you familiar with 'Stockton on Tees,' Lindsay?"

Lindsay shook her head no.

"Very well, 'Stockton on Tees' it is!" Going through his act, Max gargled some wine and cleared his throat, making all sorts of snorts and noises. Finally ready, he stood at the head of the table and waited a full minute in dead silence, apparently gathering his lines. Lindsay could see that he took this matter very seriously. Finally, he began.

"I will tell you a story
That is sure you to please
Of a grand farting contest
At Stockton on Tees."

Thinking she hadn't heard right, Lindsay held her breath.

"As the ladies lined up
For the signal to start,
Mrs. Jones won the toss
And was the first to fart."

Max held his serious pose and waited again for the shrieks of laughter to stop.

"In came Mrs. Dickboy
Who shyly appeared,

She bowed to the crowd
As they lustily cheered
And though it was thought
That her chances were small,
She stood on the floor
And out-farted them all.
With hands on her hips
She stood Farting alone
And the crowd was amazed
By the sweetness of tone.
Then the judges declared
Without hindrance or pause
First prize, Mrs. Dickboy!
She turned to the crowd
Who had started to sing
And farted the first verse
Of 'God Save the King.'"

Throughout the entire recital, Max showed mock impatience at the laughter and finished without a hint of a smile. For Lindsay, who had really expected some serious prose, this was hilarious. Even if the others had heard it before, it didn't stop their raucous laughter and screams of "Bravo! Bravo!"

After everyone had recovered from Max's recital, they agreed that coffee, brandy, and music on the veranda were now the order of the evening.

The evening air was cooler on the veranda, and Lindsay, feeling more radiant than ever, felt herself slip into a comfort zone as she sat in a huge overstuffed chair, letting classical music flow over her. Ian reached over and took her hand, but Lindsay didn't dare open her eyes for fear she would start to cry, or even worse, would simply climb on top of Ian right then and there. Everyone was enjoying the quiet time and the beautiful music.

They all jumped with a start as a loud knock brought them back from their dreams. Ian opened the door to speak to a man standing in the doorway. They moved down the hall out of earshot, but everybody stayed glued to the doorway, waiting to hear what news could be so important to interrupt the private party. Finally, Ian reappeared and called for Max to join him in the hall.

Lindsay asked the girls, "What do you think is the matter?"

Pip looked at her watch. "I bet there's a fight down at the barn. It's about that time. I brought plenty of supplies to patch them up."

"If it's that," Peggy said, "someone must have gotten really hurt, or else they wouldn't bother coming up here just for a fight. I'm sure there have been a few fights by now, anyway."

Lindsay was about to say something just as Ian and Max entered the room. Both men looked grim and showed no sign of the earlier festivities.

Ian spoke first. "That was Stewart, our radio operator. He received a call from a Sydney ham operator to report that a ham in New Zealand received an SOS from one of our boundary teams. It was a freak transmission and lasted only twenty-two seconds and couldn't be re-contacted. It appears there has been a cloud burst in blocks seven and eight, and the men have been caught in a flood. The group has been separated, which would mean the horses have fled."

"How do you know it's real?" Pip asked. "And how do you know they're from Naringa?"

Ian quickly fielded the question. "The operator said they heard the name 'Black,' and the foreman is named Blake. And we have blocks seven and eight, which, according to Stewart, is the approximate location called in last night. I'm calling a ten-and-twenty now. Max and a few of his best men will join us. Stewart has gone to get my men and supplies. We'll leave at five a.m."

Ignoring Lindsay, Ian left the room and returned with more instructions. "Peggy, you had better cancel your trip and get your things ready."

Lindsay jumped to her feet without thinking. "Ian, I don't even know what a ten-and-twenty is, but I can take Peggy's place, and she won't have to cancel her trip."

Not expecting a fight, Ian shot back impatiently, "Lindsay, sixteen men are stranded somewhere out there, and we have to go find them. This is tough stuff. We could be gone for two weeks. Lives are at stake, not your pride."

"Ian Abernathy, I will talk to you later about my pride. Right now I tell you that I am tough enough, and qualified with two years of nursing, to go on this trip. Is Phillipa going?"

"Yes," he said.

Lindsay turned to Phillipa. "Pip, would you feel confident working with me at your side?" Phillipa's eyes started to shift towards Ian, but Lindsay challenged, "Don't look at Ian. Would you?"

Phillipa smiled into Lindsay's eyes and answered, "Yes, I would."

Impatiently, Ian raised his voice. "Lindsay, you don't know how dangerous it is out there!"

"I have a fair idea that I will never speak to you again if I am not allowed to go. Were you just making fun of me in there tonight with that phony diploma? Were you?"

Ian had heard enough. "Okay, okay. There is work for six and room for two of you, so you work it out. You know what is expected, and nothing else will do. We leave at five a.m." Ian abruptly left to join

Max, who had been waiting at the base of the steps.

Peggy went to Lindsay's side. "Don't mind him, Lindsay. It's just that there is so much to be done. By the way you defended yourself tonight, I feel you would hate me if I didn't volunteer to let you go in my place."

Lindsay threw her arms around Peggy. "I could never hate you, Peggy, not even for a moment. Please forgive me for getting a little out of line there, but what was said tonight is what I want. 'The cruel and the kind' is the way Ian put it. I know it sounds self-promoting, but I do want to belong."

Peggy's expression changed to one of encouragement. "Well, if I was going, I would throw a few things together and try to get my head down for a couple of hours. Come with me, and I'll give you clothes and a couple of big hats. The sun will not be your friend on those long days on the wagon, believe me."

Chapter 10

At 4:50 a.m., Phillipa and Lindsay joined the party assembled by the main yard gate. There was little talk, and Lindsay could see no sign of Ian. Twelve men were mounted, each with a spare horse, plus two Aborigine trackers on horseback without an extra horse, and two Aborigine men on foot.

Minutes later, Ian appeared from behind the main barn, driving the bullock wagon. Max came alongside, trailing with the extra horses. Ian stopped the wagon thirty feet from the group, mounted his horse, and circled the group, stopping directly between them and the wagon. He seemed preoccupied and in no hurry to make an address. Finally, satisfied with what he saw, he pulled a leather book from his saddle bag, stood in the stirrups, and began giving the instructions. "As I call your name, proceed to the side of the wagon. Do not do so until I call your name."

The men quickly moved into position as soon as their names were called. Finally, Lindsay and Phillipa were the only two left, standing side by side, each with a small bag. Lindsay thought Ian was doing this to spite her, but next he called, "Okay, ladies, you can board the wagon now."

She could see no hint of any resentment, but she would not let her eyes meet his, in an effort to appear business-like.

Ian addressed the group once more. "All right, this is it. We must make block seven by nightfall tomorrow, and that's about forty-six miles. We'll only stop tonight for a partial camp, and make up more time before dawn tomorrow. I will lay out the ten-and-twenty tomorrow night. Remember, there are many lives to save, and be careful you're not on that list. Okay, Max, head them out."

Lindsay did not look back to the group standing at the chapel as the bell rang eighteen times, once for each lost man. Phillipa didn't speak, and Lindsay was careful not to make idle chatter. She didn't want anyone to think that she didn't understand the gravity of the situation and what was at stake.

About an hour out, one of the trackers brought his horse alongside Ian and pointed back over his shoulder. One of the riders yelled, "That's Smiley Blake's kid."

Looking back for herself, Lindsay saw a lone rider approaching the party. Ian waited until the rider was nearly alongside before he called both parties to halt.

Jimmy Blake was young, but not a kid. Lindsay thought him to be around sixteen, with blazing blue eyes and the frame of a man.

Moving his own horse squarely in front of Jimmy's, Ian asked, "Where are you going, Jimmy?"

"Where the bloody hell do you think?" Jimmy shot back. "To save my old man, that's where."

"That's what we're doing, so why don't you leave that to us?"

"Yeah, your lot, in that stupid wagon like a bunch of bloody Boy Scouts. My old man might die while you're sipping your tea over the bloody campfire. My dad will never say his kid let him down, that's for bloody sure."

Ian took the sternness out of his voice. "No, Jimmy, he won't say that, but your mother's heart would be broken forever if you get lost out there."

"Well, that's a chance I have to take, don't I?"

Seeing that this was not going to be easy, Ian dismounted to assume a friendly stance. "No, you don't have to take that chance. But, if you must, you know, I have to inspect everyone's gear before they go out there."

Thinking that he had convinced Ian, Jimmy also dismounted and stood beside his horse with his hands on his hips, as if to say, *Challenge me.* So intent at beating Ian, he didn't notice that Max had dismounted and was standing behind him.

"Now, how much water do you have?"

"Three gallons," came Jimmy's defiant reply.

Ian looked at the saddle. "This girth, any good?"

"Brand bloody new."

"Yeah, she looks like a beauty." In one quick movement, Ian slipped the buckle on the girth, and the saddle fell to the ground. "Max, put that saddle on the wagon," he shouted.

Before Ian could finish, Jimmy was running at him. Not seeing the flying fist, Ian didn't duck, and Jimmy hit him squarely on the temple. The punch knocked Ian down on one knee, and instinctively he ducked and weaved to avoid two other haymakers before he was able to get back on his feet.

Jimmy kept charging and swinging blindly, with tears of frustration filling eyes. "You can't stop me," he yelled. "My father needs me."

Lindsay watched it happening, but it was so fast that she didn't have time to understand the dynamics as Ian slammed his fist into Jimmy's forehead. Jimmy fell like a tree, and blood spewed across his face. He lay crumpled on the smoldering hot sand.

Ian stood over Jimmy with passionate concern as he motioned to Phillipa. "Pip, get the first-aid kit and patch that cut, just a patch, and they can sew it up back at the station."

Two men dragged Jimmy to the wagon, and in two minutes, Phillipa had the bleeding stopped.

As Ian remounted, he continued to give urgent instructions. "Lenny, tether his horse, take Jimmy and his gear back, and don't forget to tell someone to keep this wild bugger at the station. Then ride back to meet us."

Jimmy lay upon the wagon limp and semi-conscious as Phillipa dressed his cut and wiped the blood away from his eyes. His golden hair was thick with blood and globed across his forehead. Tears filled his blue eyes as he looked longingly towards Lindsay without really seeing her. Two men lifted him back onto his saddleless horse, and the wagon was underway.

All this happened in eight long minutes, and when Lindsay glanced over her shoulder, the two horses heading back to the station were already near the horizon.

Ian hadn't exaggerated about making an all-out push to make up time; they stopped only twice during the next sixteen hours. Phillipa and Lindsay didn't speak much, which was perfectly natural, as they were both concentrating on not falling prey to the relentless beating of the sun. The heat of the earth created heat shimmers, causing Lindsay's mind to drift back to the old-fashioned movies of Laurel and Hardy, with their ever-present mirages. She wouldn't have wanted anyone to know of these childish thoughts, but they did help to pass time. The alcohol from the night before was also taking its toll.

After fifteen hours, Ian ordered a "partial camp."

"Lie where you want," he said. "Bread and tea will be prepared. We're off at one a.m., only four hours from now." Lying on the bare ground, Lindsay needed no encouragement. She was asleep within three minutes of pulling the blanket over her head to escape the irritating black flies.

During the night, one of the trackers woke Ian and Max, informing them that a rider was circling the camp. They listened carefully as the tracker explained that the two horses were far off. Neither Ian nor Max doubted the tracker, or even wondered how he knew such a thing, as the horses could not be seen or heard. Over the years, white men in the outback had seen Aborigines perform feats that defied logic. The trackers always explained that the land was their mother and father, and because they belonged to the land, they only had to listen. They further explained that the logic of men paying money to own land was one of the biggest jokes to the Aborigines.

Max guessed that the only person who could be out there was that stupid little bastard, Jimmy Blake.

Ian agreed. "He might be stupid, but I hope my kid would have as much guts and desire to save me if I were out there."

"Yep, I only hope he has as much bush sense as he has guts. Better get some shut-eye, mate."

The next day was more of the same. Nobody spoke as they coped with their own fortitude to get through the unrelenting heat. Many times throughout the day, Lindsay felt faint and doubted whether she could make it. She worried that she would die before anyone saw her struggling. She longed for the coolness of the night that might revive her. Surely one would think that in a land so hot during the long days, the nights would at least be warm. How on earth could they be freezing?

Ian explained it to her. "The sky is perfectly cloudless, and at night all the heat of the land is drawn up into the atmosphere. If there was cloud cover like this on the coast, the clouds would block the hot air from rising." Somehow, hearing the answer didn't make it any easier to accept. It was just like the water bags staying cold on a hot car in this extreme heat.

Camp that night was a little more substantial. She and Phillipa cooked mutton shoulder chops and potatoes, with bread and tea making up the rest of the meal. Lindsay loved the tea. She couldn't get over how they spooned loose-leaf tea into a hanging pot called a "billy" and filled it full of water that boiled in just a few minutes. The tea flavor was perfect, with the bitter taste gone. It seemed that no matter how hot the temperature in the outback, it was never too hot for tea.

After the wagon boys cleaned up, Ian gathered everyone into a group to explain the 10-and-20 search system. Before he began, his eyes searched every face to ensure the serious commitment for the work at hand.

"You all know now about a ten-and-twenty, but I'm going to run through it again just in case you men from Heather Downs, Max's place, run things differently."

He took a stick to draw in the red clay sand. "We're here. Blocks seven and eight are each twenty-seven miles by twenty-seven miles. The wagon will proceed in a straight line west, covering five miles each day. We'll be in teams. Max's team will head north, and ours will cover the south." He drew four perfect diamond shapes, then ran a line through the center. "The search lines that we form are called 'the lifeline.'" Running his stick through half the diamond pattern, he continued, "The lifeline runs as long as we can make it, which is determined by how far apart you can get without losing sight of your mate. Each day, we cover ten miles and camp on the point for that night, and the next day we cover another ten miles. That will bring us back to the wagon base camp. As you can all see, there are acres of uncovered ground, but by using the grid system, we cover a greater percentage and will surely come across tracks or storm damage that will lead us to the men."

He stopped to double-check that they all understood. When assured, he continued, "Each search party will have radio contact with our wagon, but we have no radio contact between each of us, so always keep your mates in sight. As we spread out along the lifeline, don't go to the extreme. You can lose your mate in minutes, and your eyes will start playing tricks on you as you grow tired. If you lose your mate, you must notify the others immediately. If you're the one who is alone, stay put. Don't try to find the others. If you wander, you'll probably go in the wrong direction and then get really lost. Max and I will mark the map every hour, so the longest you can be lost is about two hours. I repeat, if you find yourself alone, stay where you are. Just stop.

"Now, here are the four golden rules not to be broken.

"One, stop the minute you know you're out of sight, as even the best of us dust-eaters can get lost, except for those black fellas."

The four Aborigines grinned with pride.

"Two, if you find an injured man, bring him in, even if you think he can't be moved. He has no chance of surviving out there.

"Three, God forbid, if you find a dead bloke, take his identity and don't stop to bury him. There isn't time. Remember, others might be alive.

"Four, above all, don't take chances of endangering your mates or yourself. Your team doesn't want to spend time looking for one of its own." He handed the list to Max. "Okay, that's about it. Max will call out the names for your team. We're off at four a.m."

Ian's leadership was beyond question, and Max totally supported him. If the search had been on Max's land, he would have assumed command.

For the first time since they left the station, Ian sat next to Lindsay. "G'day, eh. How are you doing?"

Happy to be spoken to, Lindsay replied, "Okay, mate."

He continued in a quiet voice, "I'm sorry I was a bit rough the other night. I'm really glad you're here, and I'm sure you'll make it okay."

She took his hand and held it to her mouth. "That kind of encouragement will get a girl through every time." She realized that she had never shown open affection to Ian. He responded by leaning over and kissing her gently on the lips.

As he got up to go to his bedroll, he looked longingly at her. "Tomorrow may bring happiness or loss of hope, or both, but one thing for sure – it will be a very long, hard day for everyone. Get some sleep, Lindsay Priscilla."

~~~

Next morning, when Lindsay and Phillipa awoke, the two wagon boys had the fires going and the billies boiling. The teams had saddled their horses and now surrounded the campfire in the cold pre-dawn, trying to finish their steaming hot tea before moving out.

Max was the one to give the go-ahead. "Okay, you jokers, my team, follow me and remember the rules. Ian's team follows Ian. Good luck."

What seemed like a large herd of horses and men were there one minute and gone the next. They quietly moved off and had evaporated into the darkness within minutes. Lindsay looked around, realizing that only four of them remained, two women and the two wagon boys.

Phillipa seemed to see the concern on Lindsay's face. "Come on, Lindsay, we can get back to sleep for another hour or two. We're in no hurry, since we only make five miles today. The waiting gets to be the worst part."

Lindsay didn't quite understand. "What exactly are we waiting for?"

"Until they find the men and bring them in, that's when our work starts. These blokes will be in pretty bad shape. I believe that many already have died, and some might die while we're treating them.
~~~

Dehydration and fear can kill you very quickly out here, and it's already been two nights."

Lindsay nodded. "Yes, I guess I hadn't thought it through. I was thinking we would take the wagon to the sick people, but they're bringing them to the wagon."

Phillipa pulled her bedroll under her chin and replied, "That's only if we find any of them. The flood waters could have washed them all miles away or covered them in sand. She's a bloody rough place, let me tell you. The next forty-eight hours will tell the tale."

Four hours later, they were on their way in the wagon. Somehow, it felt far more exciting to be out in the open flats alone without Ian and Max. The terrain hadn't changed, and Lindsay wondered how such a catastrophe could happen on this flat land.

By noon, she had her answer, as they came to the first gorge caused by the floodwaters. The gorge was dry, but strewn with large logs and bushes that had been torn from their roots. One of the wagon boys stood on the flood bed and held his hand up to his chin to indicate to the girls how high the water had been only a couple of days ago. Though there was no water now, the bottom of the gorge was soft and not traversable. The wagon had to travel a half-mile upstream before they came to a place where the sloped banks were more gentle and passable. Once back on the track, everything looked the same again.

Lindsay asked Phillipa, "How will we know when we've reached five miles?"

Phillipa gave a short laugh. "It may sound a little silly, but I guarantee these Abo fellas will take us to an inch of it. Please don't ask me how they know. They have special radar or something. Max says they never get lost because they have nowhere to be lost from. If they ever get found, that's when they'll be in trouble."

Lindsay tried not to look too concerned. "I suppose I shouldn't even think about it, but it does seem silly when you think we can fly across the Atlantic and land on a football field, and here we are relying on these two native boys."

"You're right. But it is the way of the outback, tried and proven, so don't worry."

Checking her watch, Phillipa yelled something to the wagon boys, then turned to Lindsay. "It's nearly ten, time for our first radio check." Pointing to the side of the wagon, she asked Lindsay to extend the antenna as far as possible.

The receiver was built into the underside of the wagon, and both women climbed under the wagon, into the welcome shade, and waited for a contact response. Precisely at ten o'clock, the speaker squeaked and whistled, and shortly Max's voice came through loud and clear.

"North party to base, over."

Phillipa spoke into the microphone, "Base to north party, hello, darling, how goes it?"

"Knock off the darling stuff," Max said. "All these blokes are listening."

Phillipa winked at Lindsay. "Okay, sweetheart, I understand. You don't want the men to see your feminine side."

"Very funny, Phillipa Parkinson, but I will still have to put you over my knee when we get back, just to show the men that I'm really the boss."

"Okay, north party, please state your condition and findings."

"Everything is fine with the party. We've crossed two small gorges, but see no signs of further damage. I think we're on the extreme perimeter of the flood, and by the next report, we should have something."

"Okay, north party, time check," said Phillipa. "It's now 10:04.

Next check at eighteen hundred hours. Over and out."

Phillipa had no sooner put the mike back when Ian called. "South party to base."

"Base to south party, state your condition and findings."

Ian's voice was loud and clear. "Hi, girls, everything okay with south party. We have nothing to report, no sign of any flooding. Has Max come up with anything? Over."

Phillipa answered, "Max has nothing, though he thinks he's on the perimeter the flood area, over."

"There's no telling which way the flood may have turned, but it looks like it's more south than north. Our next check-in should confirm that, over."

"That's affirmative. Time check 10:07. Next check-in at eighteen hundred hours. Lindsay sends her love. Over and out." Phillipa looked over to Lindsay and saw her blush. "Really, Lindsay, you have to show that guy how you feel about him. I know, because I can see your eyes light up at the sound of his voice."

Lindsay answered with a girlish smile, "Maybe you're right, but for me to do well out here is better than words right now."

"You're right, and I'm sure you'll do fine. Remember, we must keep an eye on each other, as I don't have a lock on success, either."

Lindsay waited until they were back on the wagon and underway before she answered Phillipa.

"Thanks for your honesty, Pip. I'm sure we will both make it no matter what comes up."

The going had been exceptionally easy, and they reached their five-mile mark before the next radio check-in. Phillipa and Lindsay took a nap under the wagon while they waited for the final radio contact of the day. The microphone hung only inches from Phillipa's head to ensure they didn't sleep through the vital last call.

It was Max's call that woke the girls from a sound sleep. He sounded a little alarmed at the sound of Phillipa's sleepy voice.

"Phillipa, are you all right? You sound dazed."

She took a deep breath and smiled at Lindsay before answering. "Yep, we're fine. Lindsay and I are just doing our aerobics, and I guess I got a little puffed."

"That's good. We've come across a lot of flood damage, but no signs of anything except the hoof prints of two horses. I think its Smiley Blake's kid."

"I hope that kid knows what he's doing. Did you make your ten today?"

"No, I think we're one mile short, but as the damage is to the south of us, I'm going to call it a day. Has Ian found anything?"

"No, nothing yet," Phillipa said. "Have a good night, and I'll hear from you at ten tomorrow. I have to go, Ian is calling now."

Ian's voice came booming in just as Phillipa hit the button. "South party to base."

"Reading you loud and clear, Ian. Have you found anything?"

"No, nothing. Has Max found anything?"

"Just some more damage and two horse tracks that he thinks belong to Jimmy Blake."

Ian paused. "That's almost impossible, because we picked them up, too. For those to be the same horses, Jimmy would have to be covering north and south ahead of us. If that's the case, I guarantee he'll be the body we recover. Well, tomorrow will tell. How's Lindsay doing?"

Phillipa handed Lindsay the mike. "Good, thanks," she said. "Phillipa is keeping me laughing."

"That's good. Enjoy it. I don't think we'll have much to laugh about soon. I thought we would have found them by now. You two sleep well, and I'll talk to you at the a.m. check-in."

"Okay, you be careful, too," said Lindsay. "Good night."

The wagon boys had the fire going and the camp set up for the night as the day finally started to cool off. This was to be the best night of the whole trip for the girls, since both had caught up on their sleep and were enjoying each other's company as they sat by the campfire. The two camp boys were always present, but could not be seen, sitting outside of the firelight. Lindsay couldn't get over how the boys would sit almost side by side for hours and not talk to each other; neither did she ever see one of them sleep. They seemed to be the most contented people she could imagine.

Neither Lindsay or Phillipa could sleep, so they sat by the fire, staring into the yellow flames. Lindsay broke the silence. "Phillipa, Peggy told me about your mom and dad and how they came to Australia. Did Max's family have such a tough time?"

"No, not everyone found hard times starting in the new Australian frontier. Remember, I know this stuff forward and backward. Max's family are very close and often talk about the early years of the family. They arrived about the same time as my parents. Their first disappointment turned out to be their luckiest break. They made a decision that was right, or they probably would have ended the same as my dad."

"What happened?" Lindsay blurted.

"Max's father and his two brothers emigrated from Dundee, Scotland, as soon as they were discharged from the army after the First World War. By the time they reached New South Whales, the Returned Servicemen's Land Grant had been in force for three years. The spread of population had already taken the best land, and all that was left was very marginal. Malcolm, the eldest brother, who was a well-decorated, high-ranking British officer, took charge. Because of his rank, he expected preference. He was shocked when the board told him in no uncertain terms that he was in Australia. They welcomed good men, and should he decide to stay, he should be aware that every man is treated the same. (At this point in the story, everyone in the family always yells, 'Next!') Malcolm was so upset, he considered returning to England. It was Max's dad, Teddy, who researched Queensland, which had just opened its land grant.

"It was the right decision, and in three months, the brothers had a thousand acres each, side by side. It is great, fertile land, and the money started to roll in. The brothers want to buy more land and stock, but Malcolm turned out to be the smart one. He made the brothers save the money, since cash is the only independence in the young land.

"Time proved Malcolm right, and the ability to ride out the drought of 1927 set them apart from every other struggling landowner. They helped their neighbors with money and labor and asked no return. Their families became the most respected in the land, and Malcolm became governor of the state."

Lindsay was enthralled. "It's a far cry from the luck your mom and dad had."

"They had good sense, but they also had good land, and that's the answer out here."

"So Max had a good life?"

Phillipa looked into the fire. "Yes, Max was very close to his uncles and didn't have a day's unhappiness, until he ran into two drunken boys from a sharing gang behind the barn. They had stolen the liquor from the main house. Max was twelve, and the bigger of the teenage boys, feeling the effects of the liquor and in fear of being caught, beat Max to a pulp. By the time Max's father found him, the gang had left the property."

"Is that the fight they asked Max about at the party?"

Surprised, Phillipa answered, “No, not at this stage, but it is what projected him into his boxing career.”

Lindsay was surprised. “I hadn’t heard about any boxing.”

“Oh, boxing was his life. From the age of twelve, he trained every day and became so good he almost turned pro. It was his boxing that got him a scholarship to Oxford, where we met. The fight you were referring to took place twenty years later. Max is a tough guy, and when we married, he refused his father’s land and insisted that we strike out on our own. Heather Downs was a very rundown station, but he believed in it, and now it’s one of the top producers in the area. Money really isn’t a huge thing for Max. His passion is to have a well-managed, well-staffed station.

“Max didn’t let the bitterness of his beating interfere with his life. He hadn’t spoken or thought of it for years, and then one day he came face-to-face with the man who delivered that vicious beating.

“Max studied the man before he came into the house and told me. He said the man’s name was Jim Fisher, and he had long, strong arms and stood six-foot-three. He wasn’t the boss of the shearing, but he certainly was the leader among the men. Max was sure he didn’t recognize Max, and there would be no way he would recognize the name, since only the property names are used.”

“How did Max hold his cool?”

“Well, Fisher was a big, strong man, and I’m sure Max knew he would certainly have his hands full, boxing or no boxing. Actually, we reasoned it out together. If there was a fight, the gang might leave, and we might not get another. The sheep had to be shorn before the wet season.

“The shearing run on Heather Downs takes about ten days, so Max had plenty of time to watch Mr. Jim Fisher. After a twelve-hour day of shearing, with temperatures up to a hundred and twenty degrees, all the men wanted to do was eat and sleep. Excitement mounted as they got down to the last day, when the manager organizes a party with food and nonstop beer.

"Max hadn't seen anything out of line with Fisher, and, in fact, he seemed to be the calm, driving force in the gang. You can imagine how happy I was to hear Max say that he would let the matter slide. We did go to the party, but left very early. About an hour after we left, a man came to the house saying that Fisher had hit two men with an axe handle, and he was holding all as hostage.

"Despite my cries, Max ran down to the wool shed. Bare-chested and covered in blood, Fisher was swinging an axe handle, taunting the gang with laughter and calling them cowards.

"I could see the unconscious men at Fisher's feet. It was obvious that the blood on him wasn't his own. We had to get them out of there."

Lindsay could hardly speak. "Didn't anyone help?"

"No, he had them scared stiff with that axe handle. Before Max could make a decision, Fisher called out, 'Here's the mighty station manager. Feel like another beating, Maxy boy?'

"Max and I couldn't believe that Fisher had the capacity to pretend not to recognize Max.

"Fisher expected Max to rush him, but Max knowingly did the opposite and addressed the group. He said, 'Men, I'm sorry you have to witness this cowardly behavior at Heather Downs, a man hiding behind an axe handle."

Fisher threw down the axe handle and said he didn't need anything to teach the high-and-mighty station owner another lesson.

"The crowd scattered. Fisher hadn't heard of Max's boxing success. His first surprise was when Max avoided Fisher's flailing attack with one small step, with his hands at his sides.

"I've seen Max break up some bad fights, and I've seen him in the ring, but I wasn't going to let this crazy bully beat up my man. I had a loaded shotgun. I relaxed a little when I saw Max's simple move, which meant he was fighting with his head, not anger.

"I heard myself say, 'That's it, darling. Calm down. Fight calm.'

"Fisher was no fool, nor was he as drunk as he tried to appear." She turned to look at Lindsay. "Do you want me to go on with the blow-by-blow?"

Lindsay almost shouted, "Yes, please don't stop."

"Well, Max saw by Fisher's next move that he wasn't so drunk. He tried to fool Max by repeating his first move, stopping halfway, and swinging a viscous roundhouse aimed at Max's head. Max knew he had to avoid wrestling.

"Fisher was smiling. He said, 'A little worried now, ah, Maxy boy?'

"Max decided he had to attack to take away Fisher's ability to think. At the moment Fisher took a step forward, Max took two short steps to his side. Max watched Fisher's mouth open wide with surprise and pain as Max put as much force as he could muster into two punches into Fisher's stomach. Fisher straightened up in pain, giving Max time for one more punch before he sprang out of reach. Max saw that Fisher was stunned, and without hesitation, he went in for the kill.

"Max hit him almost at will. When Fisher dropped his hands, Max could see Fisher's eyes filled with hate. Before Max could stop himself, he hit Fisher's face with at least six strong punches. The sound of Fisher's nose breaking could be heard on the third punch. No one had to stop the fight, because Fisher fell to the ground in a bloody mess, totally unconscious.

"I decided to take over right there. I ran into the circle and fired one shot from the shotgun. Max says I scared him more than Fisher. I had to get the crowd moving. I had the two injured men brought to the house. The manager asked, 'What about Fisher?'

"I said, 'Just elevate his head and leave him.'"

Phillipa sat back and folded her arms, indicating that the story was finished.

Lindsay blew out a sigh. "Whoa! That was the most exciting story I've ever heard."

She smiled at Lindsay's appreciation. "Well, the funny part of the story is when we hear about it today. The story grows every time it's told. Max and I have heard that the fight lasted over an hour, and no matter how the big fella tried, he couldn't lay a hand on Max. We laugh over the number of people who say they witnessed the fight. If that was the case, there would have been several hundred people there, not just twenty-two."

"Tell truly, would you have used the shotgun if Max was in trouble with the fight?"

Phillipa smiled. "You know I would, and I wouldn't think twice. But when I saw Max light on his feet and fighting with his head, I knew I wouldn't need any shotgun."

Rolling over and pulling the blankets up to her chin, Lindsay whispered, "That's a lovely thought of passion and love to go to sleep on. I'm so glad that Max won without getting hurt. Good night, you gun-toting mama."

"Yes, the sun will be up soon enough. Lindsay, it's nice being with you. I'm glad you fought to be here. Good night."

Chapter 11

Father Gavin was on the phone talking to the editor of *The Sydney Herald* about the day's headline that had appeared above Gavin's half-page picture: "Evangelist Catholic Priest Is a Phony."

The article went on to remind readers that all priests take a vow of poverty, but somehow that vow didn't apply to Catholic priest Father Gavin Abernathy.

> Not only does he own more land than 550 Australians put together, he also heads the wealthiest trust in Australasia. How could this man possibly know the plight of the common man, let alone guide him? Yet this is the man who appears on television telling us to believe. Believe in what? There doesn't seem to be a chance that we can't even believe him.

The story was signed, *J. Spencer*.

Gavin didn't raise his voice or show the deep anger he felt as he spoke to the paper's editor. "Okay, I think your man, J. Spencer, has made some very true statements, but from the wrong angle, and I want a chance to present the other side of the coin."

The editor assumed a quiet voice of concern, as if to show understanding for Father Gavin's plight. "I'm sorry about the harshness of the story, Father, but some of my young reporters are too eager. Are you sure you want to answer this? I could promise you not to print another word on the matter. We could just ignore the hundreds of phone calls we're getting."

Gavin could only imagine the smile on the editor's face as he mentioned the hundreds of calls. Playing along, Gavin replied, "That's very considerate of you, but I think I should address the issue."

"Why don't you and my reporter face off tonight on *Face the Globe*?

Gavin had only wanted to address the story in print, but quickly saw that TV would be even better. Shrewdly, he gave the impression of uncertainty. "Well, okay, but isn't the TV forum a little too open to hash this out?"

The editor answered in a tone of exaggerated surprise, "Surely, Father, you're not afraid to defend this report, are you?"

Smelling blood and looking for a controversy, the editor no doubt thought Gavin couldn't get himself out of this one. The man probably hadn't even expected Gavin to answer his call, let alone think that Gavin had the wits to challenge it.

Playing along, Gavin said, "That's very considerate of you, but I think we should address the issue."

The editor seemed eager to sign off, as if wanting to end the call before Gavin could re-think the situation and discover the dire predicament in which he was placing himself. "Okay, then, Father, the program starts at seven-thirty p.m. Please be there by seven for make-up. See you then."

Gavin pondered why a reporter would go out of his way to research his family's ownership of Naringa. Then he realized that once the SOS had been picked up by the ham operator, every operator would be on that band, hoping to hear another call. He also knew that a ham operator picking up an authentic SOS signal was like winning the radio ham sweepstakes. Most operators spent a lifetime just listening and hoping to play a part in some desperate SOS situation. He smiled and reminded himself that he had better get busy to prepare his case, if he was going to suck Mr. J. Spencer into his own trap on the nation's largest TV audience program.

Gavin was working diligently on his strategy when Mrs. Sweeny came running into the study without knocking. "Father Abernathy, I just heard a man call you names on the radio and say that you're going to fight him tonight on the telly!"

"You heard on the radio that I would be on the telly tonight?" Gavin replied without looking up.

"Yes, sir, that's what I heard with me own ears."

"My, they were quick to get the news out, which means they must be very confident, eh, Mrs. Sweeny?"

With her face showing signs of alarm, she threw up her arms in confusion. "I don't get it, Father. They're calling you a phony swindler, and you seem to be pleased about it."

Gavin laughed. "I'm sure it looks confusing, but if I play my cards right, they'll wish they never heard of me. But do you know what you could do to help me win?"

"No, Father, but just say it, and it'll be done."

"Well, I don't think anyone could lay a glove on us if I could have a cup of tea so I can prepare my attack eating one of your godly scones."

Backing out of the room, she said behind the half-closed door, "Right away, Father. But you make sure you get him good, won't cha?"

The speed of the announcement gave Gavin a feeling of dread, and he thought of what would happen if he was wrong. This doubt sharpened his instincts to the point where he was excited about the showdown.

~~~

Gavin had been to the TV station many times over the last two years and was usually treated like a celebrity, but tonight in the make-
~~~

up and waiting room, the greetings were in whispered voices, showing grave concern for him. The unspoken message was, *Doesn't he know these people are gunning for him?*

Gavin countered this reception by being more jovial than usual, which only caused them more concern that Gavin had no idea what was in store for him.

It wasn't a minute before the TV interview started that Gavin set eyes on Mr. J. Spencer. Gavin's resolve to teach this upstart a lesson doubled when Spencer refused to shake hands with him on air as the introductions were made to the audience.

Mr. Spencer was given the chance to make his claim, almost lounging in his chair, as though the game had already been played. He was trying to show off, but Gavin could detect uncertainty in his eyes as he blinked erratically.

Spencer started the straight-on attack without any pleasantries. "Father Gavin Abernathy, this won't take long, because I only have three questions for you."

Gavin never stopped smiling. "Fire away."

"Question one: Did you pledge a vow of poverty? Two: Do you own one million acres in Western Australia? Three: Do you own, and govern, the richest trust in Australasia?"

Still smiling, Gavin answered, "The answer to all three questions is yes, except that it's two million acres in Western Queensland."

Spencer looked to someone off-camera and grinned, as if thinking that this would be easier than he thought. "This being the case, Father Abernathy, I can't see why calling you a phony is out of order."

Careful not to change his cheerful appearance, Gavin replied, "I must say, Mr. Spencer, that you present a very strong case." A pause while Spencer preened to the camera. "But on the surface only. Perhaps we could take one point at a time?"

"I would be delighted, in fact." Spencer gave another you-are-wasting-my-time shrug to the camera.

"I will leave my vow of poverty to the last and start with the two-million-acre outback station called Naringa. "Mr. Spencer, I have the feeling that you think that is too much land for one man to own?"

"Too much is putting it bloody lightly. Yes, mate, this is Australia, where every bloke is meant to have a chance. But what chance does he have if people like you own two million bloody acres? I think it should be against the law for one man to own that much."

Gavin consciously tried not to appear smug. "Do you think, if the other bloke had twenty-five thousand acres, he would have a chance, Mr. Spencer?"

"You bet, and that's how you would make the outback grow for the working people of Aussie. We could develop the outback and really grow Aussie for everyone's benefit, not just a few rich guys. And certainly, one who has taken a vow of poverty couldn't chuckle at his vow-of-poverty remark."

Careful not to argue, Gavin continued to suck him in. "Okay, Mr. Spencer, I understand. But to prove your point in theory, why don't I give you 25,000 acres, which is the land mass of 127,000 football fields. We will call your 25,000-acre farm 'Spencerville.' That's if you agree that is enough land for the average bloke to make a start."

Spencer started to frown as he watched a large blackboard being wheeled onto the set. "Yeah, yeah, go ahead."

Spencer looked away with disinterest as Gavin walked over to the easel and wrote, *Spencerville Station 25,000 acres*.

"Now, Spencerville has average land that requires one hundred acres to each cow," Gavin continued, "so your herd would be 2,500 head of cattle."

Gavin turned to Spencer, who nodded reluctantly.

"At a cost of 170.00 dollars per cow, that would be 425,000 dollars for your herd." Gavin continued to write the numbers on the board as he spoke. "Now, if you wanted to ever see these cows again, you would need at least twenty-five in staff to find them. With housing and payroll, that's another 400,000 dollars. All together, that's 825,000 dollars per year that you have financed at seven percent, which is 58,000 dollars per year. Please note that no costs have been applied for the purchase of the 25,000 acres."

Spencer shifted in his seat, but still gave an air of disinterest.

Gavin continued, "Now, the bad news. Deduct twenty percent stock loss, due to drought, disease, etcetera. Your herd is now two thousand head. But with a sixty-percent birth rate, or a 1,200-calf yield, your holdings have increased. Unfortunately, however, five hundred of those have to go back into the herd for the twenty percent lost, so you now have 950 head to sell. At 63,000 per head, you will have received 59,850 dollars, or an annual loss of 87,000 dollars per year. And that's on a good year."

Spencer was smiling no more. "What do you take us for, fools? We know the economy of scale will make a difference on two million acres."

Gavin was now enjoying himself. "Yes, but what about the favor you just did for the 'working blokes of Aussie,' I think you called them? And sadly, Mr. Spencer, Naringa is no different from Spencerville. Over the last eleven years, we have averaged a loss of about 80,000 dollars per year, and our worst year's loss was 342,000 dollars."

Spencer was now shifting in his seat as though it was hot. "Really, Father Abernathy, you must think we are all mugs. Do you expect us to believe this bull? If that's the case, why would you want to own it?"

Knowing that he had gotten Spencer to go over the edge of civility, Gavin answered the question with such politeness that it became apparent he was dealing with an opportunist who no longer had the cards to win a single hand.

"Of course, Mr. Spencer, you may believe what you wish, but Naringa was saved by my father nearly fifteen years ago. He did so in an effort to save the great Australian outback heritage and the sixty-four families who have worked Naringa for two generations."

Mr. Spencer turned to someone off-stage for some direction and looked more and more embarrassed by the moment.

Gavin gladly asked, "Do you have any further questions, Mr. Spencer?"

"Yeah, what about your running the wealthiest trust in Aussie?"

"Yes, of course. You are speaking of my family's trust, created when my father staked the famous Mt. Kunba claim. I administrate the trust, mainly, to oversee the eleven to twenty million that we donate to charity every year."

While looking directly into the camera, Gavin watched out of the corner of his eyes as Mr. Spencer tore off his mike and walked off the set. Looking around to an empty chair, Gavin quipped to the audience, "Mr. Spencer seems to have lost interest in stating his case."

Then, as though he were speaking from the pulpit, Gavin simply asked everyone to bend their heads in prayer. "Tonight there are fourteen men from Naringa lost because of fierce floods in the outback. A rescue team is in the area, but has not yet made contact. Tomorrow will be the fourth day, and many miracles will be needed for these men to survive." He stood with head bowed and eyes closed for a full thirty seconds. "Thank you all. Your prayers are strong. Good night, and may God bless you."

Gavin did not wait to see the reception to his speech, but ducked out the back door of the studio. *I'm sure we won't see any more of Mr. Spencer, but I bet the morning papers will cover it.*

Gavin had no idea that he had caused such a rebellion. The morning papers covered his showdown with Spencer and spoke glowingly on Gavin's behalf. However, the afternoon papers carried the headline, "Reporter and Editor Fired for Undignified and Scandalous Reporting." Not only did the paper apologize to Father Abernathy, they also assigned a reporter to cover the rescue mission and started a charity fund for the families of the lost men. Mrs. Sweeny was highly pleased.

Chapter 12

It was Jimmy's third day out, and the harsh truths of the outback were coming to bear. Ian's words about breaking his mother's heart were ringing in his ears. Now, just the thought of the safety of his mother's arms seemed like a dream.

The first two days and nights had been like an adventure, but now he thought only of failure and the possibility of his own death. This was something he hadn't considered, because he was young and strong and his father had taught him how to survive in the outback. Jimmy vaguely realized that he was no longer practicing those lessons, as he had done during the first two days. Now, in a state of exhaustion, he kept no rules and maintained no discipline. He had lost his alertness, drifting in and out of consciousness during the heat of the day. The cold of the night brought the reminder of his fragile existence. Even though the cold made him more alert, being alone in the dark, empty space only increased his fear of failure.

The sun's rays were now growing hot, and the plains began to shimmer as the heat baked into the parched land. His station horse was not doing well, and Jimmy knew that if he didn't find water today, their chances of survival would disappear. The Timor pony looked about the same as when he had started, except for lowering his head. Jimmy determined that it was the water bottles weighing it down but, in fact, it was Pangos' attempt to shield his eyes from the constant glare of the bright sun as it reflected off the bleached earth.

This day was no different from the others. After the first hour in the full heat of sun, Jimmy had trouble staying conscious and began to hallucinate for minutes at a time. The horses made their own way and seemed to be heading south. Jimmy did little to control the direction, knowing the horses would fear for their own lives, and their survival instincts could be greater.

A noise jolted him into awareness. Other than the clop of the horses' hooves on the hard sand, this was the first sound he had heard in three days. At first the high-pitched whirling sounded like an engine of some kind, which immediately produced in his mind the image of a truck on the shimmering horizon. With great effort and excitement, he stood in his saddle to search the horizon in each direction. He saw nothing.

He waited with great expectation and raised himself in the stirrups again. Still nothing.

He spoke aloud for the first time in days. "They're here. They have to be here."

For the first time, he started to cry, knowing that it was his imagination again. The tears stung as they rolled down his dried, cracked cheeks and onto his lips. The tears tasted like pure salt, but they fell freely as he rested his head in his hands. Then, with a burst of energy, he sat up straight at the realization that the sound was still there and very real.

Trying to control his excitement, he slowly surveyed the land again. He still saw nothing, but the noise remained. The horses were headed for a distant, dark cloud. He could see the cloud, but had no idea what it was, having never seen anything like it before. As they drew closer, the noise became louder.

Twenty steps further, the sickening smell of decomposing flesh told him exactly what the sound was. Swarming black blowflies created a funnel-like vortex as they circled at high speed, none breaking away to bother Jimmy or the horses. He distantly remembered hearing about such a thing as a "fly vortex," although most considered it a figment of the imagination.

The vortex was the result of the black flies' survival instincts as they tried to propagate their species. Millions of eggs had been laid in the moist, rotting mess of the bodies. Then the race began, for the eggs had to hatch before the sun and heat dried them out and eliminated the entire hatch. By forming a vortex, the movement caused by millions of tiny beating wings quadrupled the air flow within the vortex to shorten the hatch cycle.

Jimmy knew that death was present, and he had to force himself to investigate the crater carved out of the flood-ravaged ground. Looking further ahead, he could see by the broken ground the direct path of the flood. He took firm control of his horse and moved it closer to the edge of the black cloud. At first, he couldn't make out what he was looking at, and then the shapes seemed to scream back at him. Two bodies were wrapped around each other, and one stared at Jimmy with a frozen, agonized expression. The features on the glaring face were hardly human, due to severe swelling.

After turning away in horror, Jimmy forced himself to look back again to study the grotesque face. A minute later, he identified the dead body as belonging to someone he had known all his life on the station: Allan Lawson, who had two children just a year younger than Jimmy. Their families had been very close, celebrating every joyous occasion together and supporting each other during life's tragedies.

The smell was so putrid that he had to get out of there fast. Just as he tried to pull away, he saw a third foot sticking out of the puddle of fetid water, buried in the murk. At that moment, he realized that his horse hadn't stopped, but was determinedly inching towards the small spot of water that remained at the bottom of the trench.

At least two of the bodies had exploded in the heat, making the water deadly poisonous. If the horses drank from that water, they would die, which would mean certain death for Jimmy. No man could walk very far alone in the outback. Pango seemed unsure and did not push forward, but the station horse wouldn't stop. Though weak, Jimmy was able to pull the horse's jaw close to his neck so the horse couldn't move its head. Despite his persistent effort, however, the horse continued forward down the first part of the bank and was now only a few feet from the gurgling floodwater. Unable to stop the thirst-crazed animal, Jimmy let the horse have his head, in fear of falling into the rotting bodies. Just as its nostrils flared to suck in the poisonous water, the flies broke from their vortex to swarm over the horse's face, causing it to blindly bolt up the bank, away from the hole. Jimmy let the reigns go and clung to the saddle with both hands as the horse panicked and bucked in an effort to escape the flies.

Once the majority of flies had dispersed, Jimmy calmed his animal to a stop. Not wanting to take the chance of losing the horse by dismounting, Jimmy remained in the saddle, using his hat to swat the remaining flies.

Now fully alert, Jimmy knew that if there was still some floodwater left in this hole, there must be some further up. Within ten minutes, they came to a large, shallow pool. The horse walked to the middle and started to drink. Convinced that the horses wouldn't leave the water, Jimmy dismounted to lie down in the lifesaving water. With the scene of the dead men still fresh in his mind, he was unable to drink any water from the pool. He still had two canteens of water. The horses drank, allowed the water to reach their stomachs, and then drank more.

After an hour's rest, Jimmy felt new anticipation. He was sure that he was in the flood path and closer to more men who might be alive.

Back on the search again, Jimmy felt renewed optimism. But before long, the agony of exhaustion and doubt returned. Allan Lawson's face kept appearing in his mind, and he couldn't escape the haunting image. He had only seen one dead body before, when his brother Brian had been hit by lightning in an open field not far from the station. Jimmy had been only ten when he saw ranch hands bringing his brother's limp body into the wool shed. His body was laid out on the wool fleecing table, while Jimmy's dad went to get wraps to cover the body. Jimmy, against his father's orders, sneaked in to see his brother Brian. Instead, he saw the charred outline of a mangled, shrunken body, the clothes, hair, and lips burnt off, leaving exposed teeth. The shock was so great that Jimmy sat in the middle of the floor, not even trying to avoid being seen by his father.

As soon as his father saw him shaking on the floor, his anger was replaced by understanding and sadness. He took Jimmy in his arms and carried him home, putting him in bed and staying at his side until Jimmy fell asleep. After Brian's death, the family grew much closer, and Jimmy's dad, Smiley, showed the open affection that he had been unable to express when Brian was alive.

These thoughts, and concern for his mother, brought Jimmy back to awareness. *I will find my Dad and the others,* he thought as he glanced to double-check that the water bottles were still safely fastened around the pony's neck.

~~~

Lindsay and Phillipa had a sound night's sleep after an hour of talking about any subject that came into their heads. They got underway early. Phillipa thought they may need extra time, since there would be more and more damaged terrain to avoid. The noon hour sun was hot, and the black flies swarmed fiercely.

As Lindsay held out her arm, twenty flies immediately landed. "That's one thing in the bush that I could never get used to . . . these bloody black flies."

"What do you think they live on?"

Lindsay looked at her arm. "By the looks of it, my arm. Isn't it
~~~

time for the radio check?"

Phillipa looked at her watch. "We have just fifteen minutes, so we might as well stop and set up."

Max was the first to report. He had found more damage and was heading into the heart of the storm area. The team had come across the two horse tracks again, and he was sure they were working a pattern. One of the shoes was marked with an *O*, which could even be a mule, since it was smaller than a regular horse. Ian called in on time and reported that he had found two station horses without saddles. With no sign of real damage, he was moving his search pattern more to the north. One of his men reported the two horse tracks, but Ian had not seen them himself and didn't think too much about them. He was sure they would have plenty to report at tonight's camp.

The wagon was now encountering even rougher storm-damaged terrain, and it was necessary to travel a mile south in order to cross the gouged-out ravine. An hour later the wagon came across a pool of fresh water.

Phillipa jumped with sudden excitement and called the wagon to a stop. "Come, Lindsay, let's take a bath. We won't get another chance for days. Come on, let's go."

Lindsay was not so thrilled, because of the two wagon boys who always seemed to have their eyes on the two women. "What about them?" she asked.

Phillipa waved a hand dismissively. "Oh, for God's sake, don't worry about them. They think we're just another animal, and an ugly white one, at that."

Lindsay suddenly felt resentment. "What cheek! Do they really?"

"Yes, they do."

Phillipa was stripped naked in minutes, with soap in hand, and headed for the water. Meanwhile, Lindsay stood in her underwear, trying to make up her mind.

Phillipa yelled, "Come on, Lindsay, don't be an old girl."

Stripped bare, Lindsay looked at her white torso and had to admit that the wagon boys might have a point.

Finally in the water, soaping her entire body, she didn't even notice the two boys sitting on their haunches watching from the far edge of the pool.

She giggled. "This feels so good, I wouldn't care if the whole tribe was watching. I've never felt anything like this in my life." Lindsay also mused that being stark naked in the middle of such a huge open space aroused her sexually. In an effort to hide her raised nipples and the pounding sensation in her breasts, she knelt in the water, letting the cool water lap against her chin.

As Lindsay let her mind wander in the perfect tranquility of the moment, one of the wagon boys stepped into the water with a deliberate, slow step.

Phillipa looked up in alarm and spoke in a deep voice. "Lindsay, be still. Don't move a muscle."

The black fellow held his spear above his shoulders and kept advancing. His eyes didn't move, and to Lindsay they looked like they were focused on her waist. He stood only ten feet away . . . and then five.

Without warning, he yelled and threw his spear directly at Lindsay. The spear entered the water two feet in front of her rigid, fear-filled body.

The boy triumphantly raised the spear tip as the water boiled. Lindsay closed her eyes against the splashing blood that covered her face as an impaled black snake fought for freedom. When she opened her eyes again, she saw the snake wriggling on the tip of the spear as the proud captor held it in front of Phillipa for her approval.

Lindsay and Phillipa looked at each other, rigidly standing in the nude, and began to laugh. Once Lindsay looked down and saw her blood-splattered body, laughter gave way to uncontrollable tears of hysteria.

The other wagon boy remained sitting on his haunches and had not moved a muscle through the entire event. Still nude, Phillipa held Lindsay in her arms until the shock subsided.

Finally, Lindsay recovered enough to ask, “Was it a poisonous snake?”

Phillipa nodded. “Yes, it was a black snake. But it may not have bitten us.”

Lindsay tried to be brave. “I didn’t see anything else to bite, did you?” Starting to sniffle again, she made Phillipa promise that she would not say a word of this to Ian or Max. Phillipa agreed and encouraged her to finish her bath. Lindsay was still covered in blood, and there was no chance of any more surprises.

~~~

After the snake scare, being back on the wagon felt comfortable and safe. They traveled for another two hours before stopping to set up camp. When they were settled, and a fine lamb stew was on the boil, the teams arrived. Ian’s team was the first.

Both Phillipa and Lindsay were relieved to see the men safely back, but the purpose of the search kept the mood somber. The men hardly spoke as they ate the welcome food. Ian’s team had eaten and were in their bedrolls by the time Max arrived in camp. His team ate in silence also and wasted no time bedding down for the short night ahead.

Max and Ian joined the girls by the fire with a cup of hot tea.

“Ian, what do you think finding the two station horses without saddles means?” Phillipa asked.

Ian shook his head slightly and looked at the ground, deep in thought. “It could mean many things. The horses may have wandered over thirty miles in the last couple of days, and the fact that they have no
~~~

saddles could mean that the men were holed up in a makeshift camp, or the flood caught them by surprise at night, and the horses bolted. Though normally, horses stay together, so I think it looks like the party got split up."

Max nodded. "These guys could have been washed apart, and some even buried in the sand. All we can do is search as much damaged area as quickly as we can before the elements get them. I bet tomorrow we'll find some of them, at least. By the way, Ian, what do you think of the two horse tracks we found? Do you think it was the kid?"

"No, there's no way."

"Oh, by the way, the second print almost looks like a mule hoof."

With those words, Ian jumped to his feet and started to curse. "That little bastard of a kid has taken Mr. Pango! That's what the small prints are. We don't have any mules on Naringa. The kid must know that Pango isn't used to the heat yet."

"I bet I know how that happened," Max continued. "When you sent the kid back, you told Lenny to tell them not to let the kid off the station. Well, the first thing they would lock up is the station horse paddock. Mr. Pango, and a couple of other mares, were probably the only horses he could get his hands on."

Ian nodded in agreement. "I think you're right, because we put a new lock on the home paddock after a few losses last year. But that still doesn't answer the question of how you found those tracks, and one of my men found the same tracks sixteen miles apart."

Max put his tea down and drew in the sand. "We found them yesterday, and again today, and you saw them over here, so the kid must be covering both sides of the center wagon line."

"Jesus Christ, that can't be possible. He would be traveling better than thirty miles a day. Even if he could last, the horse sure couldn't."

Max scratched his head. "It has to be him, and I'll wager he'll be the first body we bring in."

Lindsay sighed. "Oh, I hope you're wrong about that. What a beautiful boy he is."

Ian looked longingly at Lindsay's concerned face. "Yeah, he's a good boy, too," he said. "Both his parents grew up on Naringa. His brother was killed by lightning about six years ago, and I thought his mother was going to pass away from grief then. Now, both her husband and only remaining son are lost out here. I'm sure she couldn't take that." He added, "Lindsay, you know it's the kid's father who is in charge of the men, don't you?"

"My God," Phillipa interjected, "could you imagine belonging to the outback and giving your life and your whole family to the outback, just so you could struggle and then die of a broken heart? Sometimes this place makes no sense at all."

All four sat there deep in thought until Ian jumped up to go to the radio and call the station. Max put his arms around Lindsay and Phillipa as they leaned against him and stared into the fire. The sound of Ian's voice awakened them from their deep thoughts as he returned to the campfire.

"Gavin arrived at the station today with a reporter from *The Sydney Herald*," he said. "At first light, they're setting out to block six with the trucks, and will drag an airstrip."

"What's that?" Lindsay asked.

"They have to drag a big log, or something heavy, across the sand so that all the hidden holes are filled in. The water makes hollows, and the dust gets hard and covers them up. If a plane were to land on these holes, the undercarriage would just snap. So we drag it up and down for a few hours until it's safe. We need the strip for the Flying Doctor, who is on call for the moment we need him."

"That is, of course, if we get anyone back there alive," cautioned

Phillipa.

Max agreed. “By this time tomorrow night, we’ll know the extent of the loss, the good and bad fortunes of all, but now we all have to sleep.”

They all got into their sleeping rolls, and Lindsay fell asleep in moments, before she could even think about kissing Ian good night.

Chapter 13

The next day did not go as Max had predicted. The damage was everywhere, and it took the wagon a full day to make the five miles. By nightfall, neither team had found anything and had nothing to report. Because of time, Ian implemented changes to the search pattern, and both teams camped out for the night after making their ten miles. Ian's new plan called for everyone to move faster. Tomorrow, both teams would cover only five miles, then head three miles due west, and then return to the normal pattern. This plan would place them one day ahead of the planned 10-and-20. Phillipa pointed out that the teams would have to stay out on the point two nights, and only had water and rations for one night. Ian said they would just have to tough it out. Phillipa passed the plan onto Max, who agreed that something had to be done, as five days was too long out here. So, for the second night, the girls slept in an empty camp as the men stayed out on the points.

Phillipa explained the plan in detail to Lindsay. "There's no way of knowing if it's the right decision, since there could be some men in the uncovered ground, but the percentages were with the plan."

By 10:00 the next morning, Ian reported in. "We've found three men drowned and dead. They had a lifeline tying them together. Obviously, the flow carried them off, and they became entangled on a stump. We couldn't recognize any of the men, and it was too late to search for identification. The fresh horse tracks surrounding the bodies indicate the kid has been here, so he was still alive as of yesterday. I can confirm that the small prints are from Pango. Jimmy might kill himself, but he will kill Mr. Pango, for sure."

"I'm sorry, Ian," Phillipa replied. "Please be careful, and don't take any unnecessary risks. Over and out."

By 2:00 p.m., Ian had reported four more men alive but in bad shape. They were bringing them in slowly.

Max had also rescued six men, exhausted but unhurt. In spite of exhaustion, the success of finding the men kept spirits high, as each team arrived back at camp after dark.

Now Lindsay knew what Ian meant when he warned how hard it would be in the outback. For eighteen hours, she and Phillipa hadn't stopped for a moment. Lindsay was amazed how the flies laid their eggs in any open wound. The eggs hatched into maggots within hours and multiplied, creating a swarming mass of white larvae, moving maggots. Though the scene repulsed Lindsay, Phillipa explained how the maggots were a good thing, as they fed on bacteria to keep the wounds clean. The putrid stench suggested that nothing good could come from the writhing mess, but Lindsay kept her doubts to herself.

With the white canvas awnings opened from the top of the wagon, they looked like a moving building. The awning provided the necessary shade for the sick men.

Before sunup, the teams resumed their search, and Max was the first to call in. "We've found a camp with three men alive, but they're too weak to bring into the wagon. Phillipa, call Ian and get his okay to bring the wagon two miles north to pick them up. My idea is to leave one man with the group of sick men and take the others to continue their search as planned. I'll call back after you've talked to Ian. Darling, you know there is no time to waste. Over and out."

Phillipa turned to Lindsay. "Ian will call in about two minutes. Please take the mike and ask him about picking up the men. I have to finish the dressing I was doing."

Before Lindsay could answer, Ian's voice came booming through the small speaker. "Hi, Pip, have you had any news?"

Lindsay answered, "Hello, Ian, this is Lindsay, and I do have the following news. Max has found a camp with three injured men. Two are too sick to move, and Max wants you to okay bringing the wagon to them. They're two miles south of here. Over."

Ian's voice rose with excitement. "Yeah, take the wagon to them. I knew we would get lucky today. My area seems pretty much untouched, so I'm going to head south. We're too far from Max, so we'll stay out on the point tonight. We're running out of time. I'll have to make decisions by morning, no matter what. Talk to you at ten tomorrow. Oh, by the way, it's nice to talk to you, Lindsay, love. Over and out."

Lindsay stood there holding the mike to her lips, astounded that the single word "love" could transport her out of this world of heat, flies, and injured men. Then, with a click, he was gone. Phillipa's call for help brought her back to the present with a jolt.

~~~

Two tiers were set up on the wagon for the sick beds. Each man was washed and given an injection, and the weak were put on an intravenous drip. A young ringer had a broken leg and had rigged his own splint. As soon as Phillipa saw that the leg had not been set correctly, she rounded up four men who were making small talk. As she was changing the splint, Phillipa gave a signal, and the men pounced on the boy and held him down as Phillipa reset his leg. His cries of pain filled the camp, but only for a few seconds, until he passed out from the intense shock.

Several men had large, gaping cuts that needed to be sutured. Rubbing alcohol was the only pain reliever, but in most cases it didn't matter, as infections had numbed the area around the wound.

By midnight, all the sick men were clean and cared for, and the two women silently collapsed into their bedrolls.
~~~

The next morning, things had calmed down, except for the ringer with the broken leg, who was delirious with a high fever. Phillipa doubled his injection and kept him well sponged. Lindsay was amazed by the energy of the wagon boys, who never seemed to sleep and accomplished everything promptly, without being asked.

Ian called in first at the ten o'clock check-in. "Girls, we've searched all through the night and have found nothing. My men will be in danger if we try to go much further. We haven't found even a sign. I've decided to call the search to a halt. Tell Max that we're going to head back, and that he should make it back to camp by two p.m."

The girls doubled their efforts so they could have everything done and spend some time with Max and Ian when they returned.

Once back in camp, over bread and a cup of tea, Ian and Max planned the next step.

Ian said, "I take it you've asked everyone if they knew where Smiley and his team were when the storm hit?"

Phillipa quietly answered, "The only thing known for sure is because of the water, they couldn't get back together the night of the storm, so they made camp about three miles apart. About three a.m., the camps were hit by what they described as a tidal wave. The horses broke free at the first burst of displaced air caused by the wall of water, and the men held on for dear life. There were eight men in Smiley's camp."

"If Smiley was south of the others," Max said, "you'd think we would have found him first."

"Not if they were completely washed away," said Ian. "The dead men, O'Reilly, Stevens, and Stock, were with Smiley, and they were miles from where we found the others, so they must have been hit hard."

Lindsay spoke for the first time since they all sat down. "Even though I'm here and have seen the results, I still can't imagine waves of water in the hot, dry sand."

Max gave a little laugh. "I can certainly see why you find it hard to believe, but if you see a monsoon in full force, you'll think the other way."

Ian got to his feet and addressed the group. "Okay, we can't wait any longer. Otherwise, we'll lose some of the men we have found. We must head for block six and the airstrip, where Gavin has a full camp set up, waiting for us. Phillipa, how many men do we have in really bad shape?"

"Five men who are semi-conscious and need proper medical attention," she replied.

Ian turned to Lindsay. "How are our supplies, Lindsay?"

"We have about a third left," she said, pleased to be included.

"That's sounds about right. Max, how far to block six?"

Expecting the question, Max had already worked it out. "About thirty-six miles."

"Do you think we can make twelve miles a day?"

Max scratched his forehead. "Yes, once we get out of the damaged ground in about fifteen miles. I think we'll be lucky to get out of block eight the first day."

Ian nodded. "Okay, let's get going."

Lindsay was just about to speak when Phillipa asked with a tear in her eye, "What about Smiley's men and his son?"

Max stood behind Phillipa and draped his arm tightly around her.

Ian stated the obvious. "Believe me, Phillipa, I can see Mrs. Blake's face now as I deliver the news that will break her heart forever, but we can't risk the lives of the rescued men."

Tears flooded Lindsay's eyes. "Does that mean that Jimmy is dead, too?" she asked.

Phillipa held Lindsay as Ian tried to respond to her question.

"Dead, I can't say, but lost, yes. Both Max and I saw his tracks last night on block eight, which means he rode both sides of the home line. Max and I rode about eighty miles, and he would have ridden one hundred and fifty miles in the same amount of time. He had two horses up until block seven, but even with two horses, it couldn't be done in this heat. And if he has Mr. Pango, there's no way the poor little bugger could last out here."

"I hate to say this," Max added, "but I think Jimmy perished long ago, and the pony is just roaming."

Lindsay asked carefully through her tears, "You haven't given up, have you? That's not the end, is it?"

Patiently, Ian hung his head and waited for Lindsay to stop crying. "On the way home, I will have the teams ride in a flank formation, which will cover a mile and a half on either side of the wagon. We're still in block eight, and we still might find them. We won't give up, but we must move now. There has to be light for us to cross the broken ground, so we'll keep going until dark. While we get ready to move out, I'll call Gav and tell him that we're coming in."

Everyone on the wagon was pleased to hear Father Gavin's voice over the radio, confirming that they really were rescued and in touch with the mainland. Gavin was given the names of the missing and dead men. He confirmed that Jimmy had taken Mr. Pango. He reported that he would be with the truck at block six, and continued prayers went to all.

Hearing Gavin's voice, Lindsay was struck still with emotion. Finally, she said to Phillipa, "I can't tell you how soothed I feel hearing Gavin's voice. It gives me a kind of warmth."

Phillipa smiled wearily. "That's Gav, all right, on any occasion. He has that effect on all women sometime or another. Times like this, I can see why he is a priest, and other times, I can't bloody imagine it."

Lindsay nodded. "Yes, I agree." But her mind raced on, and she felt convinced that her thoughts of Gavin were her own and she was not like anyone else. At least, she hoped that was the truth.

~~~

Max organized the riders to cover the flanks before moving out of block eight, with five men on each side, at the quarter-of-a-mile system. Each team checked its radio and then headed out.

It was slow going. The wagon was in danger of tipping over several times. On the worst slopes, Ian and a couple of other horsemen tied ropes from the wagon to their saddles for steady security. The wagon was completely loaded, and the women had to squeeze together to make room for the wagon boy driving the oxen team. He spirited the team of horses, and when extra effort was needed, he prompted each animal gently by name.

At 8:15, the light was fading fast, so Ian called in the flankers to make camp. The two Aborigine trackers helped set up camp and brewed tea for the sick. Lindsay was impressed that no orders were needed to accomplish anything when everyone automatically pitched in. In other circumstances, the atmosphere would have seemed peaceful and enjoyable. Lindsay shuddered at the word *enjoyable*, for the near-dead men on the wagon were a vivid reminder of man's vulnerability against the elements. She felt guilty for thinking beyond the discomfort of these sick men. Every time she recognized these straying thoughts, she consciously sat straight to survey her surroundings and get back into the harsh moment. This technique always worked, as she would immediately pitch in with a task or a conversation with Phillipa.

There was little talk that night, except from the rescued men in the wagon, who were thanking their lucky stars with stories of their near-death encounters.

~~~

When the 10-and-20 directions were changed, Smiley Blake lay in the uncovered ground near the camp area, though he had no idea he was being bypassed. Awakened by the coldness of the night, Smiley was surprised to be alive, looking up at the starlit heavens one more time. His two mates had been unconscious for the last twenty-four hours, and Smiley had given up hope of seeing another morning.

Mumbling out loud, Smiley used all his strength to get on his knees and pray that his family would not be left behind. Prayer for Smiley was simply talking to God as though he were just another good mate.

"Well, God, I'm sure I'll meet you soon, as I've been a good bloke on earth . . . took care of my wife and kids, and helped anyone who needed a hand. Got drunk here and there, but not too much. I guess I could have played a bit too much poker, but really the only thing I can think I done wrong was hit that 'I-ty' fella with the bottle. But mind you, there was three of them. Anyway, I don't have any doubts that I'll be there soon to see my son, Brian. I would just like to ask ya, could you look after me wife Agnes, and be sure to let that mad little bugger son of mine, Jimmy, grow up to be the great man I know him to be. That's about it, really. Funny, though – this is the only place I feel at home, but I never thought I would die out here."

At that moment, Smiley was distracted by the sound of horse hooves out in the darkness. He sat still, trying to figure out if he was still on earth or already in some spiritual state. Then, from out of the darkness, a horse stood beside him. Without looking up, Smiley felt for the hooves of the horse, thinking this was his transport to the land beyond.

Grabbing the small hoof of the horse, he continued to pray. "My, they have little horses up there, don't they? Still, I suppose there are no hills."

Thinking that he had to mount this horse, he slowly moved his hand up the horse's leg, and then his arm hit something firm hanging from the horse. He drew back as he realized he was touching a human leg. The shock cleared his vision, and he tried to focus on this small horse. The horse stood still as Smiley searched for the strength to stand up almost at full height.

Then he came face-to-face with his son Jimmy, and he let out a scream. Jimmy was tied to the saddle, dead or unconscious, slumped over with his head hanging down the horse's side. Hanging to the side of Jimmy's head were the two water bottles, also tied to the saddle.

Looking into his son's face, Smiley began to cry like a baby. He held Jimmy's head in his hands, knowing that he didn't have the strength to get him down off the horse.

"Jimmy, my big boy, my big, beautiful boy, what have you done? I know what you've done – more than any father would ever ask of a son. If you're still in there, Jimmy, love, hang on, and I'll get us out of this somehow."

Smiley couldn't tell if Jimmy was breathing. He wiped the tears from his own eyes and tried to think. "First, I have to get this water for all of us." He unbuckled the strap, and to his joy, four bottles fell to the ground; he hadn't seen the two on the other side. The horse snorted as Smiley removed the cap from a bottle. Looking up at the small horse, he said, "Smell the water, do you, old girl? I guess you're the one who earned it the most. Just wait a minute."

Smiley took off his hat and spilled the water into it, then held the hat straight as the horse sucked the first hatful up with one breath. Now stamping his feet, the horse begged for more.

"Hang on, I'll give ya more."

After four full hats for the horse, Smiley put the bottle to his lips and drank. Hoping that the water would give him some strength, he just lay there, trying to work out what to do. The horse kept pushing at the hat that Smiley had replaced on his head.

"Well, I guess you're right. If we can find them, you're the one we need." He opened another bottle and gave the entire amount to the horse. Holding the horse's reign, he moved over to his mates and tried to get them to drink, but they didn't stir.

"I'll tell you what, I'll give you another bottle, and we'll try and find them out here. I've been on enough ten-and-twenties to know how it works, and they wouldn't have given up yet. If they haven't started back, we'll be found. But I haven't got a show of getting Jimmy down off ya. I know yer just a little bloke, but can ya carry both of us, just for a mile? I know I can find 'em. There's no hurry, 'cause they can't cross this stuff in the dark, so I'll give ya another bottle, and we'll rest a while, eh?"

After an hour or so, refreshed by the water and the excitement of hope, Smiley felt strong enough to walk a few steps without stopping. Looking at the little horse, he said, "Ya might be small, but I still can't get up on ya. If we can go down the bank a little ways, I'll find a high spot, and then I can make it."

Before starting off, he said good-bye to his mates, knowing that they couldn't hear him, but he still promised to be back for them.

Nearly an hour later, they had only gone a hundred yards, and Smiley feared that the dawn light was only an hour away. He knew if he wasn't farther south by daybreak, they would pass him, and all hope would be gone forever.

Having found a spot where the horse stood on low ground, Smiley slid onto the horse's back and clung to his son Jimmy.

At first, the horse just stood there, trying to adjust to the weight. Then, slowly, Mr. Pango managed to find his legs and walk forward, fighting for every step.

Smiley spoke words of encouragement into the horse's ear until he himself lost consciousness. He lay his head on Jimmy's back, and to stop himself from sliding off, he tucked his arms under his son.

Pango blindly plodded on.

~~~

Camp broke at first light, and Ian gave the okay to make tea and have a quick breakfast. There would be no stopping on this day. He and Max stood in the cold morning air planning the day, with their hands wrapped around hot mugs of tea, when a whistle from one of the trackers sounded the alarm.

Quickly, Max and Ian ran through the line of tethered horses to join an Aborigine tracker who silently extended his arm into the darkness. Neither Ian nor Max could see anything, but as they waited in anticipation, the shape of a horse emerged. A few minutes later, it was clear that it was a lone horse.

Ian was the first to speak. "It's probably one of the strays looking for water. When she gets here, check to see if she's one of ours, okay, Sammy?"

Sammy smiled back at Ian. "Okay, boss man, I check horse foot."

Satisfied, the two men went back to join the others, who were now cleaning up the camp and packing the wagon. Ian gave orders for the flankers to be sent ahead, out of block eight.

~~~

At that moment, Mr. Pango stumbled and fell, catching his right leg under him. Had anyone been near, they would have heard the loud crack of Pango's breaking bone as it pierced through the skin. Mr. Pango lay still and snorted to clear the sand from his nostrils, no longer able to raise his head. Jimmy and Smiley lay entangled, their right legs under the exhausted horse.

Chapter 14

The wagon was ready, and the flankers had left, so Ian gave the order to move out. Just enough light remained to pick their way over the broken ground. Lindsay and Phillipa had done what they could for the sick men, whose conditions hadn't improved much, except for the young ringer. The fever had left his body, and his breathing was relaxed as he slept. It seemed like daylight just appeared – one moment of darkness, and the next moment, bright light warning of the hot sun to follow.

After some time, Ian noticed that something was wrong with the wagon, which wasn't moving ahead in a straight line.

Ian called Sammy. "Why is the wagon going to one side and not the middle?"

Sammy looked at the team and didn't answer. At first he couldn't see the problem, so he rode forward and stopped the wagon. Much yelling and shouting took place, but no one moved, and the wagon remained stationary. Even if they had nothing to say, an Aborigine shouting match could not be stopped until each man had shouted his lungs out. Ian and Max just waited until the driver got down and went to the front to release the right bullock from its harness, while Sammy rode back to Ian with his piano-keyboard smile.

"She okay, boss man. When I watch for stray horse, boy put Shirley on wrong side. We change now, boss."

"The stray horse – was it a station horse?" Max asked.

Sammy answered somberly, "Me no see, boss. Horse fall down and not get up."

Max turned to Ian. "Bloody hell, we can't leave her there to die.

I'll go back and put her out of her misery."

Still concentrating on the changing of the team, Ian agreed. "Okay, you go back, and I'll get us moving again."

Max wheeled his horse around and trotted, without haste, back to the campsite. As he neared the spot where the horse had fallen, he heard choking sounds as the horse tried to clear blood from its nostrils. Max had his rifle drawn before he actually came upon Mr. Pango with his amazing cargo.

At first, the scene was too much for Max to grasp with one glance. Automatically, he fired two shots as a distress signal.

~~~

Ian heard the shots and called the wagon to a halt, while the other riders rushed back to aid Max. Since Max was out of sight, Ian's first thought was that he had fallen off his horse or been bitten by a snake. Giving Radiant his head, Ian galloped through the old campsite, leading the men in the general direction of the spot he had seen the horse coming out of the darkness. They found Max on his knees, trying to find breath from Smiley and Jimmy.

Ian jumped from his saddle before his horse had stopped. "Are they alive?"

"It's hard to be sure, since my own pulse is racing, but I think they both are. Call the wagon back. We can't carry them."

Ian fired two shots to signal the wagon, and then realized for the first time that he was looking at Mr. Pango's spent body. "Oh, no," he cried.

As he bent down in front of Pango's face, the pony gave a sign of recognition, trying to lift his head. The blood from his nostrils had completely dried to block his breathing, so that he could only breathe through his mouth. Kneeling beside him, Ian unbuckled Pango's bridle and brushed away the heavy mane from his eyes. Mr. Pango's head
~~~

showed signs that life was slowly draining away, but he had not lost his pride and struggled to keep his eyes open by looking longingly at Ian.

Max helped Ian to his feet and turned him away from the horse's gasping body. Shortly, a shot rang out. Ian stiffened, and tears ran down his face. He knew the shot was a mercy bullet for Mr. Pango. After a few moments, he forced himself back to the rescue scene to help cut Jimmy free from the tangled saddle. Dried blood had hardened the rope around Jimmy's hands, which had to be cut before they could pull him from under Pango's dead body.

The wagon arrived nearby, and Phillipa had boiling water and the tailboard cleared for the nearly-dead father and son.

Looking up from the hollow where Pango's body lay, Ian saw Lindsay standing by the wagon, looking down at them both. He was grateful that Lindsay said nothing and turned away to help Phillipa, knowing that someday she would have to deal with the image of brave little Pango lying dead on the hot sand.

Phillipa demanded of Ian, "Stay here until we've had time to give injections and attend to these cuts. We need an hour."

Ian nodded in agreement. "Take as much time as you need, but we're pulling out of here in twenty minutes."

Lindsay was insulted by Ian's cold reply, but Phillipa stopped her by cautioning, "Don't say a word, love. He's right. We need to move quickly now. You take care of Jimmy's wrists, and I'll inject them, and we'll be off."

Lindsay acknowledged her orders and concentrated on Jimmy's cuts. The thick rope had cut both wrists to the bone. Fortunately, because the rope had moved up the wrist towards the thumbs, the veins were still intact. Lindsay could see the bones on both hands, just as if a butcher had scraped away the meat. There was no bleeding, as the fly larva had done their job by keeping the cuts clean. Stitching would not work, so Lindsay simply washed the wounds, spread penicillin on sterile bandages, and wrapped them. The cut on Jimmy's face, from Ian's punch, had some festering under the scab, but looked good enough to leave uncovered. Jimmy seemed so totally lifeless that Lindsay couldn't imagine him having any will to fight for his life.

Smiley regained consciousness long enough to tell Phillipa of his two mates over in the hollow ground. Max and three men rode to the spot, only to find them dead, their bodies so bloated that it was impossible to search for any personal effects. The riders mounted their horses and left their friends, knowing that the bodies would soon explode in the hot sun. By the time they returned to make their report, the wagon was ready to roll.

While sitting on his horse, Ian took off his hat to say a few words of prayer for the two dead men. Everyone else bowed their heads, and in three minutes, they were off.

With all the men accounted for, Ian ordered the flankers to find the best path for the wagon. Phillipa and Lindsay crushed together on the driver's seat but hardly spoke. Lindsay reflected that this was, by far, the hardest day of her life.

~~~

The sun was relentless, and time dragged on slowly. By four o'clock, the wagon had stopped only twice in the last ten hours. Lindsay was pleased to walk away from the wagon with Phillipa for a bathroom stop. The land was sparse, with no cover, so each held a blanket for privacy while the other relieved herself. Lindsay laughingly confessed to Phillipa that in the beginning of the trip, the bathroom stop was her greatest humiliation, and now it was the highlight of her day. Intimately understanding Lindsay's feeling, Phillipa agreed, and they both chuckled as they returned to their perch.

Four hours later, the wagon stopped because of darkness. Fatigue
~~~

was taking its toll on everyone.

While Ian and Max worked out the distance to the airstrip, about twenty-six miles away, Lindsay approached Ian with an idea.

"Ian, I've been thinking of a way to get the very sick to the airstrip."

Both Ian and Max looked up with interest.

"Since they have to get help ASAP, why don't we leave those who can cope here with half the men? They can have a long camp and take an extra night if necessary, and we'll take the very sick and travel through the night. I think we're back on flat land, so we don't need the light. How much time could we save?"

Ian looked at Lindsay with pride. "That's a great idea. I think we could make it by noon tomorrow."

Max nodded his head in agreement.

Lindsay couldn't believe her idea had been accepted so enthusiastically. "Okay. Let's get going, then."

Ian distributed the remaining rations and spoke to every man before leaving with the wagon. Once they were underway, Ian and Max took two-hour shifts at riding in front of the wagon, while two other men did the same riding in the rear.

During Ian's break, he climbed up next to Lindsay, where she cuddled up to him. As tired as they both were, they couldn't sleep due to the excitement of seeing Gavin and the trucks that would assure them they were back in what represented civilization.

Lindsay couldn't get over the fact that when Ian wasn't riding out front, Radium would walk alongside the wagon. "Ian, do you think Radium walks with us so he can be with you? Or do you think he just doesn't want to be alone out here?"

Ian reached over and grabbed Radium's ear. "Because he wants to be part of us. He is a leader, we are leaders, but above all, he is a hundred and ten percent loyal through thick and thin. That's the bond men talk about. A man will die for his horse, and the other way around. It's been that way throughout the ages."

"I think he knows we're talking about him. Why don't you tell me more about his history?"

Pleased at Lindsay's interest, but doubting her sincerity, he asked, "Miss Graeme, are you humoring me, or do you really want to hear some true stories that might get a little long? You know, I get pretty wound up with this stuff."

Lindsay protested, "What do I have to do, pass a test or something?"

"No, no, nothing of the sort. How about the Battle of Beersheba?"

Nodding in agreement, she cuddled up to wait for Ian to begin his story.

"The Battle of Beersheba was the biggest turning point in the First World War. The 'ANZACs,' Australia and New Zealand forces, had just come from Gallipoli after sustaining horrific losses. It was estimated that one-third of New Zealand's male population was killed at Gallipoli. Beersheba, in Arabic, meaning 'the Given Word.' The history of this ancient place comes from Genesis chapter twenty-one, verses twenty-five through thirty-one. 'Then Abraham reproved Abimelech and pledged that he had dug the two wells for all. Because he gave his word to it, he named the place Beersheba.' These two wells were still the promised land of the time, as the desert was without water for over forty-six miles in any direction."

Ian caught himself going too deeply into his favorite pastime. "Sorry, Lindsay, that's probably a lot more than you wanted to know, and I haven't even gotten to the colorful history of the unique waler horse."

Lindsay confessed, "It's really interesting, but I'm a bit lost."

"Let me give it another try. It's October 1917. The enemy is Turkey, Germany's eastern ally. They held the high ground in towns such as Bir Saba and Tel El Saba in the Sinai Desert. The entire area today is referred to as Gaza. Besides having the only water, they held the line preventing the British forces from proceeding along the Hebron road. A battle plan was drawn up, where the British artillery would soften up the well-entrenched Turks, but because of the topography, a frontal attack was the only way to rout out the enemy.

"In order to get into position, the Desert Mounted Corps with a thousand walers rode forty-one kilometers through the night with fully-loaded packs. Smoking and talking were forbidden as they traversed the bare hills of the Sinai." Ian stopped to ask, "How are you doing with this picture?"

"I get it. But you're not going to tell me the same horses were used in the battle, are you?"

Ian was delighted at her interest. "That's a great question. I'll just set the scene before I answer that. After the full night's ride, the Light Horse Regiments approached the ridge with the crest of Beersheba in full view. The attack site was a long, swooping slope absolutely bare of cover. The entrenched enemy had the advantage of the high ground.

"Every man knew there would be only one chance to mount the charge. With bayonets in hand, they moved off in a trot, deploying an artillery formation with five meters between horses.

"General Chauvel, watching the battle develop, couldn't believe his eyes when he realized the soldiers couldn't contain their excited, prancing mounts. He shouted so that only his fellow officers could hear: 'Hold those horses, boys, or they'll never make it!' There was no way the horses could cover the last mile and a half, after traveling through the previous night. If they slowed down over the last half mile, they would be picked off like flies.

"Excitement was in the air, and seven hundred fifty horses quickened their pace to a full gallop. As there was no chance to hold the charge, the orders were given, and the light horsemen drove in their spurs and rode for victory and Australia.

"The Turkish riflemen fired, horses and men were hit, but the charge was not checked. The general's staff, watching the advance, could see that the distance was still too great for the horses to make it at such a pace. But the horses didn't slow. So fast was the advance that the bewildered enemy failed to adjust their sights soon enough, and their firepower was passing harmlessly overhead. Not only did the mighty walers carry their fighters to the enemy trenches, they leaped over them and surrounded them. There was a bitter fight, and in less than an hour, the enemy was beaten, and the walers' unique attributes had galloped into history. The generals maintain that this battle was won solely by the actions of the walers, as no man-made military plan could possibly include horses who courageously galloped such a distance, after traveling all night without water.

"A squadron, Third/Ninth South Australian Mounted Rifles, started in 1841 and began as the Redbeds Cavalry, who inherited the honors, history, and tradition of the Australian light horse."

Ian looked over to Lindsay for the first time since he had started to recite the battle. Lindsay had tears in her eyes, and she studied Radium with more insight as he walked alongside the wagon.

"Did you like that?" Ian asked.

"Oh, Ian, it's hard to imagine how brave people and animals have been. I feel that I truly understand Radium now. I'm sure, with his courage, he would have been the leader in that great charge."

Ian wiped his own eyes. "I'm sure he would be out in the front. Mr. Pango was also as brave as any horse we'll ever know."

No more words were spoken. Lindsay snuggled into Ian's arms, and soon they were watching the dawn creep slowly across the huge expanse of uninterrupted flat sand. She noticed that at dusk, red was the prominent color, while at dawn, golden shades made the landscape look warm and friendly. "Not so friendly," she remarked to herself, as she thought of the men they had left behind, dead from exposure.

~~~

At 10:30, Ian was the first to see the truck and Father Gavin's camp shimmering in the distance. Twenty minutes later, they were there. Four shiny silver single-engine planes waited on the newly-made landing strip. A medical tent had been set up for the doctors to examine the injured men. Father Gavin quietly greeted everyone and accompanied the doctor as he inspected Jimmy.

The doctor took one look and called the nurses to load Jimmy and Smiley into the very first plane. "For these two men," he said, "every minute will count if they are to have any chance at all."

As the men carried the stretcher to the plane, the reporter jumped up alongside the stretcher and took a picture of Jimmy's ashen face. The flash of the bulb caught Ian's attention. He immediately ran over and threw the photographer to the ground, preparing to punish him, but was stopped short by Father Gavin's iron-like grip.

Gavin spoke calmly and evenly. "Easy on him. He's on our side and was brought here by me."

Confused, Ian challenged, "What for? To take pictures of sadness and people dying?"

Gavin still had not let go. "I hope no one dies, but yes, he is."

Finally free, Ian turned and faced Gavin. "I can't bloody believe you said that. What the bloody hell is going on?"

Gavin was about to answer, but the plane engines started to run, covering everyone with sand as the plane began its takeoff. Not fifty
~~~

yards from the first-aid tent, both men held their breath until the plane was safely in the air.

Gavin was the first to speak. "Ian, there is a lot you don't know about how this story is being reported across the world, and how the people of Australia are following our every report. *The Sydney Herald* has started a nationwide fund for the lost families. And where do you think the extra planes came from?"

Father Gavin went over to the reporter, who was dusting himself off, and brought him over to Ian. "This is my hot-tempered little brother. He didn't understand that we were working together."

"Yeah, sorry, mate," Ian said. "I guess I got a little protective."

The man offered Ian his hand. "She's right, mate, no worries. Jim Engle, from the *Herald*."

"Okay, Jim. I guess we'll get a chance to talk later, but now I have to see to the others."

Ian found the doctor at the wagon, examining the young ringer whose fever had returned.

Once out of earshot, the doctor told the nurses that the boy's leg was now infected and was causing a new fever. "He must leave immediately. Had I known his condition, he would have been on the first plane. Take him now and put one of the other men with him. The other three can wait, get cleaned up, and go together in the last plane."

The doctor's orders were carried out, and within minutes, the second plane was lumbering down the red clay runway. As soon as the last three men were inspected and made more comfortable, they were packed into the small plane. The doctor climbed into the cockpit and waved as he gunned the engines down the runway.

~~~

As Lindsay watched the plane climb into the sky, she felt herself take a breath and exhaled slowly, enjoying the feelings of great tension
~~~

being lifted from her shoulders. The tension grew less and less as the plane climbed higher into the pale blue, cloudless sky.

Gavin's loud, cheerful voice jolted her from her thoughts as he announced that breakfast was ready. Lindsay had never heard such a beautiful word: *breakfast*. Her nose was immediately aware that the air was full of delicious-smelling bacon.

During the welcome-home meal, Gavin exclaimed, "I must say, Lindsay, I was surprised to hear that Ian let you out on the ten-and-twenty."

Ian spoke first. "It's not like I had any choice, Gav. She threw a bloody fit and scared the hell out me. I had to take her, and now I'm glad she came. Did a splendid job, didn't she, Phillipa?"

Phillipa was pleased to answer on Lindsay's behalf. "You couldn't ask more from anybody, and I think I had to work harder to keep up with her."

Lindsay could barely hold back the tears of pride that welled up at being accepted. Suddenly it occurred to her that it wasn't independence she was looking for all this time; she just wanted to belong. This new realization felt like the most important revelation in her life.

Max cleared his throat to get everyone's attention, bringing Lindsay back from her thoughts.

"Ladies and gentlemen," he said, "let's raise our teacups to Lindsay, a true 'daughter of the outback.'"

All of the people from the camp came under the tent and clapped for Lindsay. Led by Max, they sang,

> "For she's a jolly good fellow,
> For she's a jolly good fellow,
> And so say all of us,

And so say all of us.
Hip ra, hip ra, hip ra!"

With tears openly flowing, Lindsay proudly answered, "Thank you all. I am happy to be one of you, but sad that it took so much tragedy and sorrow to bring it about."

"That was well spoken, Lindsay," said Father Gavin. "Now I think we'll let you sleep the rest of the day, and we'll travel through the night to be back at the station tomorrow afternoon. The boys will keep the camp ready for the rest of the men, who should arrive tonight."

"That sounds great to me," Max added. "I think I could sleep for a week."

Gavin laid his hand on Max's shoulder. "I know it was tough. You and Phillipa were outstanding, and we can't thank you enough."

Phillipa spoke up. "No need for thanks, Gav. You would do the same for us, and everyone did their part as a team." Grabbing Max's arm and heading to a small tent, Phillipa bowed and said, "Good night, all. Wake us when we're ready to roll."

Ian and Lindsay bedded down under the wagon, which was far cooler than inside a tent. Feeling his warmth beside her, Lindsay intended to reveal her emotions to him, but fell into a deep sleep before she could decide what to say.

Chapter 15

Upon landing in New York City, Peggy's anxieties heightened somewhat, when she read the large sign on the main terminal: "Welcome to New York Airport at Anderson Field." She had been told she would be landing at Idlewild Airport. "I am sure these pilots know where they are going," she mused. The airport construction, had started ten years earlier in 1943, was still under, some construction. The sheer scope of the area was like nothing Peggy could imagine, "Surely, no city needs all this space." At Naringa she was familiar with huge expanses of space but they had always been empty, as vastness expanded from your feet to the horizon. What she witnessing now looked more like a busy ant colony.

At the ticket counter she asked the clerk about the name on the building. "Oh yes everybody gets a bit fussed when they think they have arrived at the wrong place. The real name is Anderson Field but everyone calls it Idlewild because it was built on the Idlewild golf course and the name has just stuck." Peggy thanked her, and made her way to the bus.

The first person she actually introduced herself to was Frank, the doorman at Lindsay's apartment. Dressed in his uniform and pecked hat, Frank Lindsay's doorman welcomed Peggy excitedly, saying that that he had been expecting her for the last two days. He was glad to hear the good news of Lindsay's love of Australia. While carrying her bags from the curb Frank chatted enthusiastically. "We all love Lindsay here, speaking of us all,

I mean the three doormen for this building.. She is one person who was always so nice to everyone, without any effort."

"Well, she will have her work cut out now, to be always nice, as she's on a rescue in the bush with my brother Ian. To say he is a bossy bugger is putting it mildly. They should be back at the homestead by now. They had to rescue some boundary riders who were hit in a flash flood.

Frank laughed at her description of her brother. "From my little spot on the universe it sounds really exciting. Just imagine, I know someone out there in the wild of Australia."

After thanking Frank Peggy brought up the tipping situation.

"Lindsay told me about how you men get tips, which is something we have never heard of in Aussie. Anyway, here's a hundred dollars which you can share. I hope that's okay."

As the usual tip was $10.00 a month, Frank tried not to show his amazement when he looked down at the hundred dollar note. "No, that will be just fine, thank you Miss Abernathy. I will share it with my two co-workers."

Peggy now anxious to get on, "That's fine, by the way you can call me Peggy."

As Frank ended his shift he happily informed his colleague of Peggy's arrival and that she was more than generous giving them $50.00.

New York City immediately felt like home to Peggy. For the first two days she walked the city from early morning until she chose a restaurant for dinner. The food and the choices were amazing, but nothing beat her joy of eating food from the street carts. Coffee was the other great thing. No matter where you were or what time you could always get good coffee.

Once Peggy saw the Plaza Hotel she just stood there in awe of sheer elegance and stature of the famous building. Even though she knew the history of the famous stars that stayed at the Plaza, only one stood out for

Peggy "Zelda" Scott Fitzgerald's wife. When she was a young girl Peggy would fantasize about those exciting days at the Plaza Hotel in New York City … beautiful women, with too much make-up, strikingly big brimmed hats, smoky rooms, immortal musicians whose melodies would last forever. She couldn't wait to start painting.

The days just flew by as Peggy enjoyed every minute. It seemed that she no sooner set up her easel than it was time to finish because of the failing light. Besides the excitement of this beautiful city, it was her sense of freedom. No one to tell her what she had to do or what she should be thinking. She was consciously aware that these were the happiest days of her life, "Oh, how good life is, I can actually feel the fresh air in my lungs. I am so happy that I will write to Naringa as soon as I get back to my apartment. I am so happy."

CHAPTER 16

Three days passed before all the rescue teams returned to the station. Funeral services for the lost men were held on the fourth day.

Lindsay sat on a folding chair on the cemetery grounds at the Naringa Station, watching sadly as the families of the station filed silently toward their seats. White crosses, one for each of the dead men, had been lined up in a row in front of the seating.

The widows who sat in the front row took their seats before Jimmy's mother entered. Stooped and draped in a bright blue dress, she was helped by two neighbors as she hobbled to a seat behind the line of widows. She dabbed a wet handkerchief at her face as tears fell from her eyes.

Lindsay gulped back her own tears, swallowing hard.

Word had been sent that Smiley was out of intensive care, but there was no word that Jimmy's condition had improved. Mrs. Blake had been given the chance to go to Sydney to be with her husband and son, but she had declined. "This is my place," she told Gavin. "I have faith that my men will fight hard enough to come home to me."

Lindsay had overheard someone say that, apart from two or three trips to the closest town, Mrs. Blake hadn't been off Naringa in twenty years, and the thought of it probably frightened her. Lindsay's heart went out to the woman as her bent, fragile body settled into a seat and she leaned forward, sobbing.

Father Gavin, dressed in his full black vestment with starched collar, stepped in front of the line of crosses to begin the services. He made a severe figure in contrast to the full array of colors worn by the staff and their families. Lindsay noticed that, no matter what the men wore, they all sported a tie. This seemed to be the ultimate sign of respect and consideration, getting "dressed up."

Gavin waited for complete silence. "This is a sad day for all the families and friends of these departed good men. It is now and forever that we must think of them in their best moment of life. I say this with emphasis on the word 'must.' I instruct you to do so, because I know in the deepness of my heart that when that moment of passing came, they thought only of you, not themselves. If you had only moments to think of your loved ones, wouldn't only the precious thoughts come to mind? These precious thoughts are what our deep love rests upon. Through hardships of daily living, deep love may lay dormant and out of reach, but it's always there and can never be erased. Be assured that, in the hour of death, it was you who was being eulogized by your loved one.

"I stand here before you with these solemn words, and many of you will ask me how I know there is a God when things like this happen. What proof is there? My answer to you is always the same. If you had proof, you would not need faith. Remember that faith means 'belief without proof.' I say that it is simple to believe something that can be proven. On the other hand, it is not simple to maintain faith, especially at times like these." He paused, as if pondering the depth of his own words. "I, too, like you, must make my choice, as I have no more proof than you. It is my heart that always reminds me that if I did have proof, I would be lost, without the need for faith.

"Today we speak remembrance and faith. Your memories will serve you well, and your faith can be supported by the many unexplainable miracles you see every day.

"Please bow your heads in silence as the bell tolls for each of our lost loved ones."

For Lindsay, Father Gavin's voice seemed far away as she tried to feel what he was feeling. She wanted to feel his suffering and be part of him. She didn't know how long she had blocked out the proceedings, but she was brought back with a shock by the first loud ring of the bell. The bell rang once for each of the dead men.

As the people left the graveyard, they were given a fresh red rose that had been flown in for the service, as it was the custom to place a rose in a Bible for a lost loved one. Gavin had to go back into the cemetery to help Mrs. Blake from her seat. Feeling guilty or foolish about her thoughts for Gavin, she hurried from her seat to leave the cemetery without having to speak to him.

~~~

Hours later, the mood of the people had changed, and the life of Naringa followed its tradition of honoring the dead with the best wake possible. It was also the custom to drink as much as they could during the rowdy wakes, and they soon resembled the best of parties. During the wake, Lindsay was treated as part of the family, and there was no question about her belonging in the future. Lindsay felt a contented sense that her life had traveled a full circle. She wanted the beauty and happiness, as well as the cruelty and sadness, of the outback to be part of her. It had awakened her soul. She was overcome by the realization that she felt very proud of herself. *Proud of myself, feeling pride for my achievements . . . that's a first, and it feels wonderful.* The feeling was so joyous, it was intoxicating.

The funerals were on Friday, so Ian pronounced a three-day holiday on the station. Everyone mostly spent their time sleeping or resting up, either from the 10-and-20 or from the wake. *Mostly the wake*, Lindsay thought. Either way, life on the station was quiet, and people didn't get together except for Father Gavin's church service on Sunday
~~~

morning.

Philipa and Max returned to their station right after the funeral services, and Lindsay felt very much alone without Phillipa. It wasn't until Phillipa had left that Lindsay realized the true meaning of close friendship. She now understood Phillipa's explanation of how the Aussies gave the greatest value to good mates as one of the most important elements in life. She had to admit that before coming to Australia, friendship was more of a word than a prized possession. In Phillipa's words, "What are you, if you don't have good mates?" That led Lindsay to reflect back to the girls at the swim meet, now understanding their openness and close friendships. At the time, it had been something she couldn't see, but after being in their company, she had come away with a feeling of cheer and goodness. That night, she fell asleep with a deep contentment previously unknown to her.

Ian and Lindsay spent the quiet days together, but she spotted Gavin only during his church service. Concerned, she asked Ian if something was wrong with him.

"Gavin gets like this over death and takes a while to heal," he explained. "I think it raises a conflict that gets in the way of his faith. Anyway, he always takes time to work it out. These times confirm for me that Gav's feelings are truly deep, because sometimes he is so easygoing, I wonder."

Lindsay was starting to worry about more than Gavin, as Ian had not paid much attention to her since returning. She hoped that the distance was because of the stressful duties he had on his plate. However, when alone in her room, she caught herself constantly looking at her reflection in the mirror, trying to imagine how she would appeal to Ian. She imagined that Ian was observing her while she slipped off her bra, and she posed theatrically in front of the mirror. Then the cloud of darkness would crash around her. *Maybe he doesn't find me attractive –*

the thought that made her feel rejected and vulnerable. Invariably, she would lie in her bed and comfort herself until this overwhelming fear passed.

They were alone at the table during Sunday lunch when, out of the blue, Ian reached for Lindsay's hand and asked if they could have drinks on her veranda that night. Lindsay was glad she was seated, because the look in Ian's eyes made her body flush with warmth, and the inside of her thighs felt as though they were being caressed by an invisible hand. Instead of simply replying with a "yes," she couldn't believe her ears as she heard her own voice say, "Oh yes, Ian. I've been waiting for this night."

After Ian left, she shook her head in amazement. *My God! What a thing to say. I either sound like a kid or a hussy. I'll be surprised if he shows up at all!*

~~~

Not wanting to face him before their rendezvous, Lindsay skipped the evening meal. Lindsay had taken two showers and tried on several combinations of the four dresses she had, as she wanted to look casual and at ease. She found that selecting the appropriate outfit wasn't easy, as it was warm now, but would be very cold soon. Giving up in frustration, she decided on a full skirt and a tight cotton blouse, with a light cardigan draped over her shoulders.

She set the table with glasses and fresh flowers. After double-checking that everything was in place, she clicked on the table lamp and tried to read, or to appear to be reading.

Finally, she heard the welcome knock, and she softly invited Ian to enter.

Ian entered with a tray of glasses in one hand and an ice bucket in the other. "Is this the right room? Good evening, Miss Graeme. May I come in and entertain you?"
~~~

Blushing with delight, Lindsay rose from the chair. "Certainly, kind sir. I believe you have found the right room, and more importantly, the right woman."

As Ian passed through her room to the veranda, she swept to him with a soft kiss on his cheek. Ian made a theatrical fuss about uncorking the champagne, which helped both of them relax. After raising their classes for a toast "to health," Ian took the floor in what sounded like a rehearsed speech. "You know, Lindsay, few women in the world could have done what you did during that rescue. Some of those days were very hard, even on the old station people, and you got through them without a whimper. That's not the only reason, but I love you for that."

Knowing Ian was on uncomfortable ground, Lindsay attempted to elicit an answer. "Do you mean you love me as a figure of speech, or do you really feel love for me?" After a pause, she added timidly, ". . . As I do for you?"

Hearing Lindsay's admission, Ian seemed relieved. "No, I mean I really love you, and it started that day in Bondi when I saw you on the hill with the girls."

Lindsay was about to reply when Ian leaned forward and kissed her lips, slowly at first. Then they stood and embraced, kissing passionately. Lindsay lost all of her inhibitions as she pulled Ian into the bedroom and pushed him on her bed. Bending over him and kissing him, she unbuttoned his shirt and kissed his shoulders and neck. Once his shirt was off, she swiftly peeled off her own blouse and bra. Nothing mattered to her now, except to satisfy the longing to have her skin touching his.

In all her life, she had never felt the sensitivity she now felt in her breasts as they stroked against Ian's hairless chest. Ian responded with heavy breathing and firmly drew Lindsay to him. She fell on the bed and pulled him on top of her as she fell. Ian made no further advances, and Lindsay, in a fever of desire, reached for Ian's manhood. As soon as

Ian felt her hand slipping below his belt, he moved out of reach. Without thinking, she reached for him again. Thinking that he was getting up to further undress, she began fumbling with her own clothes. Then, glancing up, she saw Ian's horrified face looking down at her while tears streamed down his checks.

He stood frozen there for a brief moment, gazing at Lindsay's bare breasts and her flimsy skirt pulled up to her waist, revealing white panties. As though the sight was too much for him, he wiped the tears from his face and bolted out the door.

Lindsay couldn't comprehend what had just taken place, but as she looked down at her bare breasts, she felt cheap and totally ashamed. The door had slammed closed, and she didn't make an attempt to get up and follow Ian. Rolling over on her side, she cried uncontrollably. She had never thrown herself at a man before, and now she was totally humiliated. He had been so disgusted with her that he had run away. Had she looked pathetic, common, or ugly? No matter what, it was enough to make him flee from her room. She cried for hours until sleep overtook her, and she didn't hear Ian reenter the room, quietly calling her name.

~~~

Lindsay woke several hours later at the touch of Ian's hand on her shoulder. She turned onto her side in the bed and faced him. His face looked deeply troubled, and his hand shook.

Before he could speak, Lindsay started crying again. Between sobs, she tried to explain her forward approach. "I've never done that before in my life, but I thought that's what you do when you love someone. You give yourself to them. I love you, but I didn't want to disgust you."

Ian remained silent as he stared at her, which only made her cry harder. She no longer felt self-pity, but sadness and overwhelming confusion.
~~~

Rolling over, Lindsay turned her back to him. Unexpectedly, Ian pulled back the bed sheet and lay down beside her. She did not reject him as he slid his arms around her.

Finally, Ian spoke into the darkness. “Please, Lindsay, don’t blame yourself. You are as beautiful as any man could imagine. I am the problem, and for the first time in my life, I have been forced to face the demons that have been haunting me since my teens.” His arms tightened around her as he seemed to search for words. His voice became desperate. “I’ve said this a thousand times in my own mind, but never to another living soul.” He paused. “I am a homosexual.”

This was the last thing that Lindsay expected to hear. Her breath stopped as the meaning of the words drifted slowly through her mixed-up mind. She was at a loss for words.

“Lindsay, did you hear me?” he asked, looking for confirmation. “I said, I’m a homo, a queer, a gay . . . a queen.”

Before he could continue, Lindsay turned over and gently put her hand to his lips. “That’s enough, Ian. Just lie still in my arms.”

Ian searched her face for some kind of reaction. “Aren’t you mortified or something?”

“No, Ian, I’m not. But you have to give me time. Whatever it is, it is a shock. Just lie in my arms and let me hold you.”

Ian’s body relaxed with welcomed silence in the quiet room. They lay so still that neither was sure the other was awake.

Finally, Lindsay asked, “How long have you known?”

Ian sighed. “I’ve never been completely sure, or perhaps completely honest with myself, but I’ve had concerns since I was fifteen. Only once before did I try to be with a woman, and the same thing happened. I thought it might be different for us, because I love you. It was my disappointment that made me run from you. You mustn’t blame yourself, as you are so beautiful inside and out, no man could want more.

And there lies the rub – I'm not a man."

"Please, Ian, don't flog yourself. You are a mighty man and always will be. If you were not a man, do you think the men on this station would follow you and obey you, when they rely upon you to keep them alive?"

Lindsay felt somewhat ashamed knowing she felt relief that it wasn't her half-naked body that had driven Ian from the room. She knew it should be Ian's problem that she should first be concerned with. She felt her power of reason return and sat upright, not bothering to cover her bare breasts, and looked directly into Ian's red eyes. "Now, Ian, this is something you are going to have to start dealing with, not hide from. It should feel better to have it out and have someone to share your inner feelings."

Ian let out a deep sigh. "I can't tell you what it will mean to me, but not tonight. I have no emotion left. Can we just go to sleep and look at this tomorrow?"

Lindsay turned her back to Ian and pulled his arms around her.

After a five-minute silence, Ian spoke clearly into the dark room, "Wilson, I always knew the roads you spoke of, and that we are on the same road. I hope you can handle yours better than I have. God bless you."

Lindsay heard him clearly, but not wanting to speak or hear another word, she pulled his arms tight around her and closed her eyes.

Chapter 17

The next morning, the early sun was streaming into her room when she was awakened by the screams of young children. She was alone in the room, and last night seemed like a bad dream, except for the glasses and champagne remaining on the table. Pulling on a robe, she went to the veranda to see what the commotion was about.

A large blue bus, with furniture and luggage strapped to the roof, was parked in the main yard. A young boy was being carried kicking and screaming from his pony. A collection of other animals stood behind the bus: several horses, goats, and what looked like a pack of dogs. Once the boy was in the bus, it pulled away, leaving the animals in the dust. Lindsay stood watching for five minutes as the bus made its way down the home road. She thought it was strange that no one waved good-bye.

Ian was seated, eating his breakfast, when Lindsay entered the dining room. He seemed at ease and welcomed Lindsay to the table. She, too, had a good feeling as she faced him, now that they had something special to share.

"What was that big bus doing here this morning?" she asked.

Ian seemed pleased to have a real subject to talk about. "That was the 'Widow Bus.'"

Lindsay couldn't believe her ears. "What?"

"Not a very nice name, is it? But that's what it has been called for years, and it's even mentioned in songs of the outback."

Lindsay was not impressed. "Lovely, I'm sure, but what does it mean?"

"There is a Naringa rule that does not allow single women to remain on the station when a man dies. His widow and family must be off the property within five days. We have many single men on the station, and history has taught us that it's better this way."

"But where do they go?"

"The company has a large boarding house in Townsville, and they stay there until they make more permanent plans. The kid's schooling is paid for, and the widows receive a pension. A mate of Gavin's, a retired priest, takes care of everything until they are established. It may sound tough, but it helps everyone get on with their lives. It never happened, but we were always told that if a widow continued to live at Naringa, it was plausible that someone could kill, or not save, his work mate so he could finish up with a widow, too."

Shocked, Lindsay replied, "You have to be kidding! All the people I've met look like they would die themselves in an effort to save their mates."

Before Ian could answer, Gavin walked into the breakfast room. "Good morning, all. I got all the papers off the bus this morning, and I have them set in the other room. I think you would like to see them."

Ian was surprised. "God, I nearly forgot about that reporter and the ham operators."

They followed Gavin into the den, where he had all the papers laid out in chronological order.

Gavin picked up the first paper. "Just reading the headlines tells the whole story. I made a list of the *Herald* and *The Morning Star*, as everyone in Aussie and every school kid have been following the rescue, but it has turned into Jimmy's story. One of our country's best, if you ask me."

Lindsay and Ian perused the list of headlines:

Search party making good pace, but young

son of lost man travels twice the distance alone.

Search party in flood area, but no men found.
Three bodies found by search party, but son of lost man Jimmy Blake beat them to it.

It's confirmed, the kid is riding both sides of the search. Pros say that unless the main party finds him, he can't make it.

Party speeds up the search and covers more ground as hopes fade. Lone kid still not found.

Party forced to call off search. Three men and the kid still missing, given up for dead.

Miracle horse saves men. Kid finds his father, and tiny horse carries them both to safety. Horse dies of exhaustion. Additional two dead found.

Kid and his father plus six men flown out to hospitals. Chances not good. Aussie holds its breath and prays.

Kid may not make it. Others all okay. Hundreds wait outside hospital. The Rescue

Fund breaks all records.

Kid still in coma. Father tells of kid and that horse.

Prayers answered as "Jimmy Blake, the hero kid" breaks out of coma. It is said that the mothers of the world willed boy's recovery.

Nation rejoices as Jimmy's recovery completes the greatest ride in Aussie history.

Ian laughed. "God, I thought it was just one big slog out there every day, but they make it sound so exciting, I can't believe it."

Gavin walked over to put his arms around Lindsay and Ian. "Well, you're both part of Aussie history now. What do you think of that, Lindsay?"

Lindsay laughed. "I don't know whether to laugh or cry, but I feel proud to be a part of it all."

Gavin, now back to his old self, held up a letter from Peggy. "You can both read it later, but the highlight so far is Lindsay's apartment. Peggy loves New York and has been painting for two days already. I think my prayers have been answered, because it sounds as though the real Peggy is back on track. Perhaps that's another intervention from our own Lindsay Graeme."

Both Gavin and Ian clapped and gave Lindsay big hugs of affection.

Proud tears filled Lindsay's eyes. "Come on, you two, you're getting too sentimental."

Gavin gathered the newspaper articles. “Lindsay, Ian and I have to go out and inspect some equipment, so we’ll see you at dinner tonight, okay?”

“That will be great, as I have to remember where America is and write some letters. It will be good to write to Peggy, too.”

“If you get them done by three, the mail will go out with the supply truck,” Ian advised.

“Thanks. That’s the incentive I need to get on with it. I’ll see you guys tonight.”

Gavin handed Lindsay Peggy’s letter as he left. “You may want to read this before you write your letter. Oh, by the way, she loves your doorman, Frank, who sends his regards.”

Lindsay laughed as she thought of Frank. “God, that seems twenty years ago.”

~~~

Dinner that night was very quiet. Afterward, they were all enjoying their coffee on the main veranda. Lindsay lay on the couch, and both Ian and Gavin sat with their feet up on foot stools. No one spoke as classical music filled the air. On this first evening since the return from the 10-and-20, an air of contentment, though not mentioned, was felt and enjoyed by all.

The stillness was shattered when a truck appeared out of the dark night and turned into the tight circle in front of the homestead, shining its bright lights across the veranda. Lindsay watched Gavin get to his feet, not knowing if he was alarmed or annoyed by the interruption.

A figure got out of the truck, but could not be identified against the truck lights. Lindsay’s heart jumped when she recognized the approaching figure as a police sergeant in full uniform. Obviously, this was not a social call.

Gavin went forward to intercept the officer, who wore an English
~~~

bobby helmet and white spates. “Good evening, Officer. There must be some great emergency to bring you out here in person.”

Without offering a handshake, the officer stood at attention in front of Gavin and Ian. Revealing a Scottish accent, the officer answered, “Aye, it is of a most grave nature.” He paused. “Under these circumstances, I think it best that I let you read directly from the communication we received at police headquarters today at oh three hundred, Australian time.”

He held out a yellow envelope for the two men. Neither Gavin nor Ian reached for the letter. Finally, Gavin took the envelope and feverishly ripped it open, reading the brief message printed on telegram tape.

A deep wail filled the air as Gavin’s legs buckled beneath him, and he collapsed. Ian and Lindsay remained motionless for a few seconds as they struggled to comprehend what they had just witnessed. Ian was the first to move. Looking at the officer standing at attention, Ian made a sudden swoop for the telegram held in Gavin’s lifeless hand.

Ian likewise screamed in agony as soon as his gaze met the paper. He ran from the room with the telegram still in his hand. Lindsay was left staring at the officer, who offered no comment.

Lindsay asked in a quiet, calm voice, “All right, Officer, what is in this telegram?”

Looking straight ahead as though he were on parade ground, the officer replied, “It reports the death of Miss Peggy Abernathy, miss.”

Lindsay’s heart pounded in such a manner that she was unable to catch her breath. Feeling weak, she fell back helplessly into the chair. She did not notice the officer turn and retreat from the veranda, leaving the grief-stricken bodies where they lay.

A short while later, Lindsay read the terrible telegram:

Body identified as Peggy Abernathy found
dead at the scene of a robbery break-in.
Request family to identify the body ASAP.
New York City Police Department,
Detective Jim Holly.

~~~

Five hours after the sergeant brought the news, Gavin was still in a trance, slumped in a chair and biting on his forefinger. Ian had tried to calm him from time to time while he worked with the radio operator.

Now, Ian knelt beside him. "Gav, I've got the Flying Doctor Service checking their flights tonight and in the morning. There's a Qantas flight leaving Sydney at two p.m. tomorrow. If I can get us out of here by air, we can make it. She's right, Gav. Just sit tight, mate."

Lindsay sat across from Gavin, but she could think of nothing to say or do. Gavin looked as though he couldn't care less if he died on the spot.

Two hours dragged by without anybody speaking. Finally, Ian entered the room carrying a map and a notepad, and he went to Gavin's side.

"Gav, you must listen. I've found a plane that will be at Brittle Creek Station at eight this morning. They haven't got enough fuel to come here and pick us up, but we can catch it if we can drive to Brittle Creek in the next seven hours. That's nearly a hundred miles, but I'm sure we can make it. They can fly us back to Sydney, with a stop at Charters Towers."

Gavin looked up and spoke surprisingly clearly. "Will that get us to Sydney in time to get the plane to New York?"

"Yes, but you'll have to call the vicarage from Charters Towers to get them to get your bag and passport to the airport. We won't have time for any stops."
~~~

Gavin closed his eyes and nodded. "Okay."

Ian took charge, naturally. "All settled, then. I'll get Jim from the radio room to get the ute up to the house. Lindsay, could you get a couple of things for Gav and give him a hand to get him up and ready? We'll leave in ten minutes."

Before Gavin got into the passenger's seat, he hugged Lindsay, leaving her cheek and collar wet with his tears. "We love you, Lindsay. Get back to Sydney as soon as you can, and we'll call."

His last words were swallowed as he tried to hold back his tears. Ian came around the car and closed Gavin's door.

Looking up, Ian took Lindsay in his arms. "God bless you, Lindsay. We'll call you, as Gav said. Jim will have a plane here for you later today or tomorrow."

Lindsay had never felt so alone. Her happiness of just a few hours ago had been shattered, and everyone she loved had left her standing alone in the dark. Watching the ute speed off into the darkness, she didn't bother to avoid the dust cloud it left behind.

Once inside, thoughts of herself quickly vanished as she picked up one of Peggy's letters lying on the big oak table, where only a short time ago, she and Peggy had shared all their girlish secrets.

Gavin had asked Lindsay to return to the vicarage in Sydney and wait to hear from them once they reached New York. Lindsay was so upset by the news about Peggy that she didn't mind leaving Naringa. However, at the same time, her heart told her that she would return someday, and Naringa would forever be part of her life.

Chapter 18

The flight to the U.S. was without incident. The first-class section was only half-full. Neither Ian nor Gavin could sleep. They found it impossible to speak to each other without going over and over the same unanswerable questions, so they sat in silence. They both shared the belief that it wasn't possible that their sister had been killed; surely it was a mistake.

The stewardess brought a telegram back to Gavin from the New York City police department. Detective Jim Holly would be meeting their flight and arranging all lodging and transport. Father Abernathy was certainly an Australian celebrity, but he had no idea why he would receive such courtesy from the New York police.

Gavin felt great foreboding as he heard the plane's wing flaps being positioned for landing. He closed his eyes to weep silently, barely feeling the big plane touch the ground.

Ian tapped him lightly on the shoulder and pointed at his watch. "Better reset your watch to New York time. It's now ten forty-five."

Without interest, Gavin replied, "Yes, I suppose we'd better. Did I tell you that a detective is going to meet us?"

"Yeah, I saw the telegram."

Finally, they walked into the Idlewild terminal, where another stewardess greeted them and asked if they would follow her to the VIP lounge to meet a detective who waited for them.

Jim Holly was a stocky powerhouse of a man. Dressed in an immaculate suit, he could have passed for the chairman of any company, or even a Hollywood type. Getting to his feet as Ian and Gavin entered the lounge, he extended his hand, showing no sign of any awkwardness due to the difficult situation.

"Hello, gentlemen," he said. "I'm Jim Holly, and I've been assigned to look after you during your stay in New York."

Both men shook hands with the detective and followed him down to the baggage claim area. Once outside with their two bags, the humidity of the New York summer surprised them. It felt like a heavy blanket. Detective Holly had parked his unmarked police car right outside the door.

"One of the few advantages of working for the police department," he said as he removed a red light from the roof. "It will be easier if you call me Jim. How would you like me to address you guys?"

"Thanks, Jim," said Gavin. "Gavin and Ian will be fine."

"Are you sure you don't want me to call you Father Gavin?" Holly asked as he pulled the car away from the curb.

Gavin had forgotten he was still wearing his clerical collar. "No, Gavin is fine, since I won't be wearing this collar in New York." Wanting to be past the awkward questions, he asked, "Are you taking us straight to the morgue?"

Without taking his eyes off the road, the detective nodded. "Yes, I thought it might be best if we face that first."

They rode in silence as the word "morgue" brought the reality of the trip to the scary present. Arriving at the hospital, Gavin felt his legs weaken as they walked up the stone steps and read the brass door plate: *New York City Morgue*.

Ian must have sensed his state, for he put his arm around his brother and quietly encouraged him. "She's right, Gav. No matter what, we have to do this."

Ian still had his arm around Gavin as they waited in a cold, empty room. After a moment, an attendant wearing a white gown and mask wheeled in a covered stretcher. Only half of a foot showed beneath the sheet. A tag had been attached to the big toe, which had turned blue.

Without ceremony, the attendant whipped the sheet from the body and casually asked, “Can you identify this woman?”

The seconds seemed like hours. Neither brother could speak as the sight of Peggy’s dead nude body dashed any of the secret hopes that they shared. Gavin picked up Peggy’s cold hand and held it to his lips.

He started to speak as if he were alone. “I speak to many of God’s plan, and I always say that it is something we can’t challenge. If I believe that, or have ever believed that, why can’t I believe that now?”

Ripping off his collar, he threw it across the room.

“I reject your plan,” he shouted. “All you have ever done is give me everything, while you take everyone from me. I reject your gifts and your plan.”

Slowly, he placed Peggy’s hand back on the stretcher and bent forward to kiss her lightly on the lips. Without tears, he made the sign of the cross over her, turned, and slowly left the room, leaving Ian staring at his sister.

~~~

Standing near Peggy’s body, Ian didn’t cry. He was too sad to cry. As hard as he tried, and as much as he knew it was so, he couldn’t come to believe that these were his last moments with his sister, with whom he had shared all of his life.

Seeing that Ian was in a trance, the detective signaled the attendant to cover the body.

The detective put his arm gently on Ian’s shoulder and tried to bring him back. “Ian . . . Ian, I think we can go now.” He turned Ian away from the covered stretcher and started to walk from the dark, icy room. The attendant handed Gavin’s collar to the detective as they left the room.

As they joined Gavin at the bottom of the steps, Jim Holly said,
~~~

"Why don't you two get some air, and I'll wait in the car. Take as long as you like. I'll be here."

An hour later, Gavin and Ian joined Jim in the car. Gavin patted Jim on the shoulder. "Thanks for helping us get through that, Jim. I think we'll be okay now."

Ian asked the detective, "Do you have the keys for Lindsay's apartment, where Peggy was living?"

Jim and Ian's eyes made contact as they both looked in the rear-vision mirror. "Yeah, and we're on our way there now."

Ian barely noticed New York City beyond the car windows, or the flow of thousands of people in the midday traffic.

Jim parked directly in front of the building, ignoring the irate doorman as he waved his arms and pointed at the *No Parking* sign. Flashing his badge as he got out of the car, the doorman quickly apologized and opened the car door for Ian and Gavin.

Ian observed that it was a handsome building, as these sorts of buildings go, but two things turned him off immediately: narrow hallways and the musty smell of cooked food. On the fifth floor outside 531, the detective inserted the key in the lock and stood back for the two brothers to enter.

Inside, Ian felt closer to Peggy when he saw her paint boxes and other familiar possessions. He suspected that Gavin felt the same, as he lovingly fingered each item. Apart from two dining chairs on their sides, the place was in very neat condition. Ian carefully observed every inch of the apartment, as if he, too, were a detective.

"Jim, I don't understand," he said. "Why would anybody break in to shoot a woman and not steal anything or attempt a sexual act?" Standing directly before Detective Holly, he loudly challenged, "Don't you think that's crazy?"

Not avoiding the challenge, Jim responded matter-of-factly.

"Well, it doesn't fit any profile we have, but we don't know the perpetrator's intentions. If he pushed his way in for a robbery or rape, we think your sister put up such a fight that he was surprised, the gun went off, and he ran. The gun was a small-caliber pistol, which is not the usual gun for a seasoned criminal. We suspect that the perpetrator was a novice and used the gun to scare the victim. But in this case, it didn't work, and your sister fought him. The profile of that type of man is generally a weak, frightened person, trying to use the gun to threaten his victim. When it doesn't work, he panics."

Quietly, Gavin asked, "Have there been any other reports in the building or other nearby buildings?"

"No, and no strangers have been seen hanging about, which brought us to suspect someone in the building. According to the doorman and the super, your sister hadn't befriended anyone in the building. We interviewed every tenant, and this was supported by all. As fare as we know, Peggy only made one contact in NY and that was Sam Gilmore from the Gilmore Gallery. He met her a couple of days after she arrived. Mr. Gilmore has been away and planned to have Peggy visit his beach house when he returned. The only other people were his nephew and his girlfriend. We spoke to the nephew who had nothing to add and his girl friend we still have to interview. They only met her for about 30 minutes, so I can't imagine anything there.

Satisfied for the moment, Ian asked Gavin what they should do with Peggy's things. Gavin suggested that they leave everything for Lindsay to sort out.

Ian nodded in agreement. "That's okay, but I'm going to look through everything first in case there's some clue."

The apartment was hot, and as Ian took off his jacket to throw over the arm of the sofa, the contents of his breast pocket emptied onto the couch. Bending to pick them up, he removed the cushion to check that nothing had been missed and found a roll of film tucked into the crevice of the couch. Holding it in the air for all to see, he asked Jim, "How come your boys didn't find this?"

Jim turned and shook his head in surprise. "I have no idea, but I'll have the lab develop it for you this afternoon. It could have been there for years and may not even belong to Peggy."

They found nothing else as they painfully went through Peggy's belongings. Ian's thoughts drifted back to childhood, when he would sneak into Peggy's room and secretly go through her belongings, looking for notes from boys or other secret things of great value. He couldn't believe that these few possessions represented everything left on earth of his dear sister.

Gavin said he would call Lindsay to fly to New York and take care of Peggy's things. Then they shut the door and left, leaving the upsetting scene behind. The walk to the street was one of the longest walks Ian had ever made, and he fought the temptation to run back to the empty apartment in hope of finding Peggy. The sight of daylight seemed to represent the finality of Peggy's last days on earth.

Jim Holly drove them through the city and parked the car in front of the Plaza Hotel. "Believe it or not," he said, "the department gets a thirty percent discount from this hotel, so I took the liberty of booking you here. Is this okay?"

Without enthusiasm, Ian answered, "Yeah, thanks, Jim."

Leaning into the back seat, Jim handed Gavin his card. "My home number is on the back, if it's needed. If you guys are still sure you want to leave tomorrow, I'll pick you up for the four p.m. flight."

Gavin sighed. "Only if you can assure us that you will have Peggy's ashes by then."

Jim nodded. "Because you're a priest, I was able to arrange everything, and I've been assured that it won't be a problem."

In the double room reserved under their names, Ian collapsed on the bed. Gavin recited the time aloud. “Four twenty-five p.m. I can’t take any more of this. I think I’ll have a long shower and try to sleep for a few hours.”

“I think I’ll try the same thing, if sleep is even possible.”

~~~

As per Gavin’s instructions, Lindsay left Naringa by plane the next day and now stood on the steps of the rectory with great trepidation, waiting for the gingham-draped skeleton of Mrs. Sweeny to come to the door. After ringing the bell three times, Lindsay imagined the housekeeper standing behind the closed door, showing her scorn for Lindsay by making her wait. Finally, as the door opened, Lindsay’s image of the blue gingham dress was confirmed, but she was unprepared for Mrs. Sweeny’s enthusiastic greeting.

“Hello, Miss Graeme,” the housekeeper said with a prim smile. “I am happy you to see you again.”

Surprised, Lindsay returned her smile. “Thank you, Mrs. Sweeny. Unfortunately, the circumstances don’t allow me to say that I am pleased to be here, but I certainly appreciate your kind words.”

Unaccustomed to making polite chatter, Mrs. Sweeny looked uncomfortable and stared at the floor. “I have made the same room ready for you, and if you would like a cup of tea, I will serve one for you in the study.”

Lindsay was taken aback. “Yes, thank you, Mrs. Sweeny. That would be very nice.”

Back in the study, after putting her things away, Lindsay was joined by Mrs. Sweeny with tea and scones. Having poured the tea, Mrs. Sweeny paced around, as though she couldn’t make up her mind over something. She looked childlike with her awkward gestures.

Suddenly, the thought of more bad news flashed through
~~~

Lindsay's mind. "Mrs. Sweeny, is there something you want to tell me?"

Working up her courage, Mrs. Sweeny just stood there in nervous silence, and then blurted out, "Will you tell me all about the rescue and the outback?"

Lindsay slowly let out her breath in relief. "Of course, Mrs. Sweeny, but I'm sure Father Gavin has told you about Naringa before."

"Yes, but I want to hear you tell me about the rescue. I read every word about you in both the papers every day. You and that Phillipa are famous. Don't you know that?"

In the rush of that last day at Naringa, Lindsay had done no more than read the headlines. "Really, Mrs. Sweeny, I never would have thought that our names would even be mentioned."

Now in an animated state, Mrs. Sweeny confirmed with a smile, "You and Phillipa were the main story, besides the dead, of course. You drove the wagon alone in the desert to control the search, and you saved the lives of the sick. The men said that if you were not there, they would have died."

Lindsay beamed to herself as she proudly remembered Gavin's words: *You're part of outback history now.* "Where would you like me to begin?"

"Back when Ian knocked the kid, Jimmy, off his horse with one punch."

Realizing that there was no way anyone could have reported seeing the start of the rescue, Lindsay realized that the story had been retold many times and grown each time. She didn't bother correcting Mrs. Sweeny, but instead asked her to sit. Lindsay quickly found that she enjoyed remembering the hours of hardship and the moments of joy, but above all, she savored her friendship with Phillipa.

An hour later, Lindsay stopped talking, and Mrs. Sweeny closed her mouth for the first time since the first sentence. She looked at

Lindsay as if she were royalty. Lindsay herself felt quite the star.

~~~

Later that night, Lindsay received a call from Gavin. She quickly picked up the phone as Mrs. Sweeny left the room. "Yes, Gavin, I'm here. What's going on?"

He cleared his throat and said in a sad, defeated tone, "You should come over now and take care of Peggy's things, bring them back to Australia."

Her heart went out to him. She wanted to say something, but words didn't come.

"There's no rush back," he continued. "I know you might want to spend some time with your parents. I told my travel agent to deliver your tickets, so you will arrive in New York the day after tomorrow."

"Thank you. I'll be there."

"We . . . Ian and I . . . feel such loss. We may leave before you arrive." He seemed to choke up at the end of his words.

Tears welled up in Lindsay's eyes. She gulped back her grief. "That's okay, Gavin. I understand."

As he hung up, Lindsay put her hand to her face and sobbed. *It hurts so much to see them in pain. And I miss Peggy, too. How am I going to get through this?*

A half-hour later, she lay awake on her bed. As she wiped the tears from her cheeks, she heard a loud thump from the room above. Listening carefully, she heard no further movement and became alarmed that something might have happened to Mrs. Sweeny. She got out of bed to investigate, hurrying up the stairs.

At the door, she knocked several times. "Mrs. Sweeny, are you there?" She knocked louder and called out, "Mrs. Sweeny, are you okay?" She cautiously opened the door.

Mrs. Sweeny, fully clothed, was sprawled face down next to the
~~~

table.

"Oh, no," Lindsay said, fearing a heart attack. She knelt beside the woman and gently turned her over.

A gin glass rolled from Mrs. Sweeny's hand to the floor, landing next to a gin bottle and a fallen table lamp.

Lindsay shook her head. "Oh, my dear Mrs. Sweeny, you certainly are full of surprises this trip, I must say. Do you think I'll be able to lift you? Well, I'm going to have to try."

Without too much trouble, and without so much as a peep from the limp housekeeper, Lindsay managed to get the woman onto the bed. The third-story room, still quite warm, didn't call for a blanket. Lindsay picked up the table lamp and placed the gin bottle and glass in the center, as if nothing had happened. She whispered as she closed the door, "Dear, lonely Mrs. Sweeny, this will be our little secret. Sleep tight, and may God bless you."

A little later, while lying awake and trying to clear away the circling thoughts of Peggy, Ian, and Gavin, Lindsay realized that Mrs. Sweeny's dilemma hadn't crossed her mind. She wondered what the timid Lindsay in New York would have done or felt. She knew what she felt. After seeing so much death and struggle for life in the outback, all she wanted to do now was help and protect any life she came into contact with. She thought back to her dislike when she first met Mrs. Sweeny, hiding behind her gingham uniform. Now, she thought of her fondly as a lonely soul, fighting any glimpse of happiness. Pleased that Mrs. Sweeny's secret was safe with her, Lindsay finally fell asleep.

Chapter 19

Trying to sleep was hopeless, even though Gavin's body needed it. He could not suppress the recurring thoughts that circled in the dark vacuum of his mind. As he stared at the ceiling, he could hear Ian rustling in the other bed.

Ian sat up. "I don't know about you, Gav, but I can't stay in this room a minute longer. I want to go out and have a couple of beers."

"I think that would be the best thing we can do." Gavin rose from the bed. "I have to take a quick shower before I go anywhere."

Ten minutes later, Gavin finished dressing in his street clothes as Ian came out of the shower. He stood at the doorway, waiting to leave.

Ian froze when he saw Gavin. "What's this? You're not wearing your collar?"

"No. I'm wrestling with my old mate up there at the moment, and besides, we'll be less conspicuous in street clothes."

Puzzled, Ian agreed. "Okay, then let's get going and try this American beer."

It was only eight o'clock when they left the hotel and made their way to the first open bar they could find. The name sign above the bar read, *Welcome to Flannigan's, Ireland's Finest*. It was a long bar with a dining area in the rear. The dining room had plenty of business, but there were only four other people drinking at the long bar. Every inch of wall space was filled with some item from Ireland.

Gavin turned to Ian. "What do you say we have a couple here, and then find another pub with a little more life?"

"Sounds good to me."

They drank the first three beers in silence and must have looked very solemn, as the bartender remarked when he brought refills, "You two lads look pretty serious. This one's on me. Hope it helps."

Gav looked up with a genuine smile. "Couldn't hurt. Thanks, mate."

They both held their glasses up to the bartender for a token toast. "To your health, mate."

That did it, and Mike the bartender kept the drinks coming, with every second or third one on him. Looking around, Ian was surprised to see that the bar was now completely full. The jukebox had been turned up, and Irish music filled the air. The music sounded good to the boys, and they knew all the songs by heart. During their younger years in Australia, the Sunday Request Session had been the highlight of the week. The only trouble for the kids was having to wade through two hours of the old songs before they would play the pop chart requests. Their mother always made sure they could leave the lunch table by two o'clock so they wouldn't miss a song. It seemed so long ago, like another world, and now it definitely was another world without their beloved sister Peggy. They didn't have to talk much, as they knew they were both feeling the same loss, trying to deal with it the best they could. It didn't seem real.

Because of fatigue or sadness, Gavin hadn't realized that the beer was taking its toll. Not thinking much about it, he got up from his stool, intending to go to the bathroom. But before he could stand, his foot shot out from under him, and he fell sideways into a group of drinking people. Attempting to regain his balance, he fell with outstretched arms. As he brushed by a man, he fell into a young woman. Knocking her to the ground, he fell on top of her. Her companion, now drenched in beer, threw his glass on the ground, grabbed Gavin by his hair, and slammed his fist into Gavin's head. The man was bent over with his punching arm drawn back again, when Ian slid from his stool. He punched the man in the ribs with perfect leverage and all his force. The man's intended punch stopped in mid-air as he fell to the ground in agony.

His three companions stepped over their fallen friend to get to Ian and could only mount a one-on-one charge. Ian managed to strike the first man twice before he even got close, and then a sudden jab shot out of left field, striking Ian squarely on his forehead.

There was no pain, but the noise was frightening, and he immediately felt hot blood rushing down his face into his eyes. Blinded, Ian did not see two more punches crashing into the side of his head. In self-defense, he lunged at the nearest body and grabbed on to his adversary.

In what turned out to be their biggest tactical error, the four men had forgotten that Gavin was even present. With a clear head and untouched, Gavin aimed his body at the three men, exploding across the four-foot distance. Catching the men at knee-height, they all crumbled into a tangled heap. As Gavin rose to his feet, two more bullies lunged at him. The first directed a throw into the air as Gavin grabbed his coat tail, pulling him down hard against his shoulder. Twisting his wrist, he flipped the man into the air. The next man lost his advantage as he hesitated at the sight of his buddy disappearing over Gavin's shoulder. Before he could recover, Gavin punched him twice in the face, and was about to slam his midriff when the bartender attacked Gavin with a baseball bat across his chest and pinned both arms from behind.

Just at that moment, ten policemen streamed into the bar, causing everyone to stop in their tracks.

"What happened here?" yelled the sergeant.

Everyone argued angrily at the top of their lungs.

The sergeant yelled for quiet and turned to the bartender. "You, and only you, can tell me what happened here."

The room fell silent as the bartender hesitated. "These two guys were drinking a little with no trouble," he said, "and then I looked up, and they were fighting these six guys. I dunno what happened."

The sergeant told his men to handcuff Ian and Gav and take them outside. Gavin and Ian didn't protest. Once they were outside, the sergeant questioned the other men. Gavin could still hear the sergeant questioning the people at the bar. "No matter who started it, you guys look like the losers. Now, one at a time, please." He pointed to the girl Gavin had fallen upon. "You first, miss."

Finally, the sergeant and his men joined Gavin and Ian outside. "Okay, you two. I'm going to book you down at Fifty-Seventh Precinct."

Nobody paid much attention to their story. Even when Gavin told them he was a priest, the unimpressed desk sergeant answered, "You'll be okay, then, as we booked the Pope a couple of hours earlier, and you're in the same cell."

Ian remembered Detective Holly. "Aren't we allowed one phone call?" he asked.

"Yep, one call for each of you," answered the desk sergeant without looking up from his forms.

"Well, then, I want to call Jim Holly, New York police detective. I have his phone numbers in my wallet, which you have taken from me."

With surprise, the sergeant's head snapped back, and he focused on Ian's face. "Jim Holly? How do you know him?"

Happy to see some reaction, Ian replied, "We spent the day together, and he was assigned to look after us during our stay in New York."

"Well, he didn't do a very good job, did he?"

"He did a fine job. If your citizens would stop trying to beat people up, there would have been no trouble. Now, if you would please pass me my wallet, I will retrieve his number."

Back to his habit of not looking up while speaking, the sergeant said, “There is no need.”

Hearing this reply, Gavin stepped up to the counter. “Now listen, you. There really is a need, and if you stop us from making that call, I will bring more trouble than you thought possible crashing down on your head.”

Still not looking up, the sergeant repeated, “I said there’s no need.”

As Gavin responded with more threats, the sergeant looked up and cut him off in mid-sentence. “When I say no need, I mean no need.” With a slight chuckle, he whispered, “No need to look up his number, ‘cause he’s my brother-in-law, and I know his number.”

It took quite a few seconds for this news to sink in, but once it had, Ian simply asked again, “Could you please call him?”

“I will, but after you two sit on that bench over there and be quiet, as by all rights, you should be waiting in the cell now.”

An hour later, Jim Holly walked out from behind the counter and sat with the men on the bench. “Gavin, are you sure you’re a priest and not a prize fighter? I just read the reports, and the three men have been taken to the hospital. That doesn’t make things any easier, in case you didn’t notice.”

Without smiling, Gavin answered, “Yeah, I’m sorry about the wounded men, mate, but things got a little rough in there. Six against two didn’t help the situation.”

“Okay. I got you out, anyway. Now go and sign yourselves out, and ask Scotty for your things.”

As they retrieved their personal things, Gavin addressed the desk sergeant. “I’m sorry if I tried to pull heavy guy with you, and thanks for your help.”

“That’s okay. I’ve never witnessed a priest fighting before, let alone one who actually won.”

With a sincere handshake, Gavin smiled back. "Thank goodness for that. We are meant to help God's children, not beat them up." Then, with his boyish smile and a wink to the sergeant, he added, "Let's hope we taught them to have a little tolerance."

The sergeant laughed. "Well, I'm sure they won't be in such a hurry to have a swing at you next time, if that's what you mean."

"I knew you were a religious man, Scotty."

Jim Holly led the men to the unmarked police car. "I'll take you to your hotel, and we'll pick you up tomorrow at noon. Your flight leaves at two p.m. After tonight, you had better be on it."

It was just after 1:00 a.m. when they pulled up in front of the hotel. Ian and Gavin thanked Jim and said good night. Curiously, Jim waited in the car.

After they were turned away by the doorman, they returned to the car.

"They won't let us back in this bloody hotel," Ian told Jim.

Jim grinned. "I didn't think they would. You guys have no idea what you look like, covered in blood, with torn clothes. Believe me, that is not the profile of the average Plaza Hotel guest." Jim got out of the car. "Come on, we'll try again and see if New York's finest can help."

By the time Jim climbed the steps, a security manager had arrived on the scene, and Jim could see that he was determined to block these two blood-covered ruffians from the hotel. His attitude changed abruptly as Jim flashed his detective badge and took out his notebook.

"Your name, please." Deaf to the security man's protest, Jim repeated his request three times, each time a little louder. "Your name, please."

Completely bullied by the detective, the man finally gave his name in a timid voice. "Alan Louis."

Jim barked, "Your position."

"Night security."

In a quieter voice, Jim continued, "Now, Alan, I'm sure part of your job is to prevent any bad publicity for your hotel, right?" The confused security guard nodded in agreement. "Well, let me give you a heads-up and ask your opinion. How would it read in tomorrow's papers, if these two men were cited by the mayor for bravery by coming to the aid of a young eighteen-year-old against great odds, and then 'Alan Louis from the Plaza' wouldn't let them back into their rooms?" Waving his notebook in front of Louis's face, Jim asked again, "Tell me, how would it look?"

Just wanting to get away from the detective, Louis turned to the doorman. "Okay, Harold, let them in."

Just before Ian followed Gavin through the door, Jim called out, "Hey, Ian, I got the photos back from the lab." He walked over and handed them to Ian.

Exhausted, Ian slipped the envelope of photographs into his pocket and forgot about it. The two men had no trouble sleeping the rest of the night, and in fact, they fell asleep only minutes after placing a wake-up call for 10:00 a.m.

~~~

The left side of Gavin's face was bruised, but there were no cuts. His rib cage was what really hurt, causing him to whimper if he took too deep a breath. He figured Jim Holly's story must have really impressed someone, for the management had sent up a very fancy breakfast to their two supposedly famous guests.

It was the first time the brothers had been able to smile since the news of Peggy. During that fine breakfast, Ian remembered the photos, and removed them from his jacket pocket.

"Gav, do you think we can bear to look at these pictures of Peggy?"
~~~

Unaware he was slipping into his priestly tones, Gavin answered, “It’s something we have to deal with. Peggy is in our heart, where we see her best. Not to talk about her or look at her pictures is a strike against our memory of her. For me, she will always be my beautiful Peg and with me until the day I die, so I will learn to love to talk of her and see her images. The thing I may have lost is my faith. Ian, do you realize how many people around us have died?”

Ian gazed at his brother. “You’ve had to work it out with him before. Remember when mom and dad died? It took you three weeks to get back to the vicarage. You’ll be right, mate. Thanks for your view on Peggy. It will help me, too.”

Ian opened the packet of photos and began to go through them. Watching from his bed, Gavin finally said, “Well, what are they?”

“They’re of nobody, just her painting sites and the time of the day. She didn’t get time to mark these.”

The boys had seen hundreds of shots like these. Peggy would always take photos of the subject she was painting and pencil in the comments by hand. The camera recorded and printed the time on the photo. As she painted large subjects, she often had to return to a site three or four times, and not always the next day. So when she missed a few days, she could match the weather and the time to set up the subject in the exact position and light.

The main person in the pictures was a Navy officer in uniform. He was kind of like a perfect image of what a man in uniform should look like. Very neat, but his features were too big for him to be handsome. There were three distinct pictures of him. One was full frame, with his hand held up and his lips parted, as if speaking. He carried a small briefcase in his other hand. Another man in a business suit, his face fuzzy and turned away from the camera, walked past the admiral in the background of the photo.

Ian smiled and said aloud, "It looks like the officer was joking with Peggy." He looked at the date on the prints. "This film is only five days old, and that means it was taken on the day of her death. We know what she was doing on her last day on earth, but we don't have a picture."

Gavin flipped through the photos, not paying too much attention until he came to the man in uniform. A strange foreboding feeling blanked out his mind when he looked at that image. The feeling brought him back to how he felt when he was walking off the plane. It disappeared as quickly as it had occurred, but it lodged an uneasy feeling. He handed the photos back to Ian.

Ian smiled and said, "Well, one thing we know, Peggy was doing what she loved to do best on her last day on earth. I think that's something for us to be thankful for."

Gavin gave it little thought. "I can't bring myself to say that I'm thankful for anything that has happened, but I know what you mean. Come on, better get ready. Jim will be here in twenty minutes."

As they left the hotel, the two day managers were at the door saying their farewells, expressing their hope that the two bruised heroes would return. Finally, in the car, Gavin spoke to Jim in his quiet holy-man's voice. "Jim, you're such a powerful liar, I'm going to have to get you a confession box, I'm afraid."

Jim laughed out loud heartily, but he cut his laughter short as he remembered the cause of their trip. "Sorry, got a little carried away there."

Ian knew what he meant. "Don't worry about it, Jim. We'll all laugh in time."

Relieved, Jim changed the subject. "What was in those photos?"

Ian was also pleased to change the subject. "They were of her painting sites. Peggy always took lots of shots of her subjects and recorded the times and weather, etcetera, so she could return to the same image. Going by the dates on the photos, she was painting on her last day on earth. There was no one in the pictures other than a naval officer who looked like he was having fun with her. Thanks for getting them done. Do we owe you any money?"

"No, I had the boys at the police lab do them."

At the curb outside the American terminal, Jim said good-bye, saying how he sincerely wished they had met under different circumstances. Both brothers felt warmth for Jim and shook his hand with a true feeling of friendship.

In the first-class lounge, after getting their tickets and seat numbers, the two men sat like lost souls, staring at the television. Their flight was still an hour and a half from takeoff. Ian sighed as he thought of how Jim had gotten them to the airport so early. He supposed that Jim wasn't taking any more chances of them getting into trouble.

With still more than an hour until boarding, Ian and Gavin continued to stare blindly at the television. The 12:30 news blared across the screen, changing quickly from subject to subject. Ian had no real idea what they were talking about, when out of the blue, the host introduced "Commander John Litchfield" to talk about America's new submarine fleet. It took a moment of intense staring before Ian recognized the man from Peggy's photos.

Jumping to his feet and grabbing Gavin's arm, Ian shouted, "Gavin, look, it's the guy in Peggy's photos."

As Gavin shot up in his chair to pay attention, Ian shuffled through the pictures and handed the admiral's picture to Gavin. "There, check it out. It's him, right?"

Gavin agreed. "There's no doubt about that. It's him, all right. What do you want to do about it?"

"I want to go to him and find out all he knows about Peggy's last day on earth. This is a chance in a million to find out who that guy is, so I have to ask him about Peggy. I'm not taking this flight. I'm going to Washington to see this guy."

Carefully, Gavin asked, "What makes you think a high-ranking admiral will even see you?"

"Just because he will. I will live on his doorstep until he sees me. I'll ring him as soon as I get to Washington."

"Why not ring him from here?"

Stumped for a moment, Ian thought about the question, searching his soul for a rational answer. "Because I might be told that it's impossible for me to talk to him. I won't accept that, so I'm going. I can't believe you're not as excited as I am, Gav. Don't you want to come?"

"Yes, I will come, but for me there's nothing much this man can say that will make it any easier to accept Peggy's death. Nor can he in any way further enhance Peggy's beautiful image that is forever deep in my soul."

"I understand that, but for me it means everything. I'll replay her last day in my mind for years to come."

Ian went off to change the tickets, and soon he returned with tickets for the Washington shuttle. His excitement was obvious as he picked up their bags and told Gavin that they had to change terminals. Gavin tagged along, not complaining or agreeing, as sadness paralyzed him.

Chapter 20

Sensing Gavin's silent struggle, Ian had not spoken since they left New York and now leaned over to the front seat, speaking to the taxi driver in an effort to avoid disturbing Gavin.

"Where do you think we should stay?" he asked.

"Depends on where you intend to stay," the driver replied without interrupting his gum-chewing.

"I'll be going to the Pentagon . . ." Ian caught himself about to add *hopefully*, and instead said, "Primarily."

"Then you should stay in the Congressional. It's a good old hotel, and there's always something going on. This time of year, you shouldn't have any trouble getting in, either."

"Thanks, that would do fine."

Ian felt guilty at his slight feeling of excitement about being in Washington, D.C. *It's a long way from Naringa.* The thought of Naringa brought the memory of Lindsay and the rescue to mind. It seemed years ago. Then he thought of what he had confessed to Lindsay about being gay. *Probably a good thing to have some time between that night and when we have to discuss it.*

The Washington Memorial faced them as they crossed the Potomac, heading for Ian's meeting with destiny.

After checking into the Congressional Hotel, they waited for at least twenty minutes for the bell captain to show them to their room. Ian couldn't get over how dark the American colonial architecture was. Other than the main foyer, all the ceilings seemed too low. All the main archways leading from the main foyer featured a door with beveled glass, with what looked like twenty panes to one door. For Ian, the poor light and the heavy red carpet throughout gave the place a dull, lifeless atmosphere, nothing like true English colonials that he knew so well. But they were all in tropical settings and were much more open. To his pleasant surprise, their room proved to be much brighter, with large windows overlooking a park.

Once the bellman

left, Gavin collapsed on one of the beds. "What are you going to do now?" he asked. "How are you going to get hold of this admiral of yours?"

Pleased to hear Gavin's calming voice, Ian shrugged and quipped, "I'm going to give him a call."

"Yep, I'm sure admirals pick up for all visiting tourists."

"Well, I won't tell him that I'm a tourist. How about the Wool Growers Association of Australia?"

Gavin let out a long sigh. "Do you want me to throw the old priestly image about and see if I can get to him?"

"No, I'll try by myself first, and then if I dip out, the Church can save us. They are in the business of saving, aren't they?"

"Truthfully, I don't know anymore. When you get to see the admiral, I'll go down to the closest church and do a little asking. I'll let you know when I come back."

"Come on, Gav. You've been in this spot before, and I bet you will be again."

"I have been angry before, yes, but now I feel nothing but doubt. That doubt, and my profession, hardly go together, you know."

Ian couldn't tell if Gav's agitation was just sadness, but he knew enough not to push further. "Okay, you go to church, and I'll go to see the admiral. Sounds good, but I have to get hold of him first."

Picking up the phone, Ian started his quest by calling the front desk. An hour later, after twenty tries, Ian had located the number for the admiralty in the Pentagon. His first try was rebuffed by a very sharp female, who recommended that Ian write to his congressman to apply for an appointment, which was always needed to see senior admiralty staff. Hoping that there was more than one operator on the switchboard, Ian immediately redialed the same number.

"Operator, Admiralty House."

With an air of familiarity, Ian said, "John Litchfield's secretary, please."

He could hardly hide his surprise when the operator replied, "One moment, please."

It was now happening so fast that Ian had no idea what to say when a woman's voice came over the phone. "Admiral Litchfield's office."

Without thinking, Ian spewed out, "Hello, my name Ian Abernathy from Australia. I'm the brother of the artist that the admiral was photographed with a few days ago in New York."

"The admiral is very busy, Mr. Abernathy. What is it that you want?"

Grasping at straws and trying not to sound like a naïve tourist, Ian pressed ahead. "That artist was my sister, and just hours after talking to the admiral, she was shot. So I know the admiral will want to see me."

Taken aback by the mysterious nature of the call, she simply said, "Please stay on the line."

Ian noticed that he was actually sweating, and next he heard the sound of a man clearing his throat.

"Hum, hum. Hello, Mr. In-Abernathy, this is Admiral Litchfield. How may I be of help to you?"

"Well, Admiral, since you talked to my sister on the last day of her life, I wanted to talk to you about her being . . . about her happiness on that day."

The admiral paused. "I would like to help you, Mr. In-Abernathy, but I don't recall talking to any young ladies when I was in New York."

"It's Ian Abernathy, not In-Abernathy, and I have photos of you that my sister took."

"Oh, you must mean the young lady painter."

Excited by the image of his sister sitting at her easel, he said, "Yes, that's her." Ian's mood quickly changed. "Peggy was her name."

"Well, we spoke very casually, about the weather, etcetera. What is it you want to know?"

"I've come all this way from New York to talk to the only person I know who saw my sister on her last day on earth. She had a few pictures of you, so I thought you had spent time together, rather than just exchanging a quick hello."

There was quite a pause before the admiral replied, "I'm sorry I can't be of more help. Since you've come so far on such a sad mission, a touch of Yankee hospitality would be in order. Would you like to join me for lunch at the Pentagon tomorrow?"

Ian was a little despondent after hearing that the admiral didn't really know his sister, but was grateful at his attempt to be kind. "Thank you, Admiral. That is very kind of you."

"Okay, then, noon tomorrow. I'll have a pass at security, and they will show you to the reception area. Where are you staying?"

"At the Congressional. Thanks once again, and I look forward to meeting tomorrow."

Gavin was lying on the bed, staring into space, when Ian entered the room.

"You're not going to guess what just happened up on the Hill, as it were," Ian announced.

Gavin didn't turn his head. "No, I don't know what happened on the Hill, as it were."

"Not only did I contact the admiral, we're having lunch tomorrow at the Pentagon. I'm sure you're invited, too."

Gavin didn't move a muscle at hearing the news. "That's good, Ian. As I said, you go there, and I'll go to church and try to sort myself out. Until then, I'm just going to lie in this bed and do nothing. Besides, my body is aching worse today than yesterday. The first two punches caught me completely by surprise. I'm sad, and I'm hurting. The rest will do me good."

Somewhat deflated by Gavin's lack of excitement, Ian nodded in agreement. "Yeah, that'll do me, too."

~~~

The next morning at 11:30, the two brothers went their separate ways. Gavin deliberately didn't ask directions for the nearest church, but chose to stride off in the direction he was facing. He had the feeling that something was going to happen on this day that would shape the rest of his life.

After three miles of solid walking, that feeling faded, as he hadn't come close to anything that looked like a church. He noticed that the neighborhood had changed and he was now in the poorer part of town. Just as he was about to turn back, he found himself in front of a whitewashed building crammed between two other buildings, with a cross in the center of the gable. The polished wood main door looked like any normal house door. To the right of the door hung a white wooden sign that read, *Church of Apostle*.

Without hesitation, Gavin entered the tiny church. After his eyes became accustomed to the semi-darkness, he could see the simple altar, a long, thin table draped in pure white cloth. In the center of the table was a statue of Christ with a shiny brass cross above it. On each side sat a
~~~

small, colorful flower arrangement. On the left, the altar stepped up to a platform. The platform had a single rail, with a carved wooden book rest in the center. Gavin looked around him and saw that there were no pews, only assorted chairs with no matching colors.

To his surprise, Gavin felt quite spiritual in the sparse surroundings. He knelt on the bare floor in the middle of the row nearest him. Blessing himself, he looked to the altar. With a shock, he found himself staring at a gold-framed picture of Christ that he had somehow not noticed before.

Gavin did not believe in beating around the bush. In his straightforward manner, he proclaimed out loud, "I'm glad you're here to sort this out. There are many things happening that just cannot be right. My efforts have been sincere and earnest and have brought thousands of people back to your side. I changed my life for you and expect nothing in return for myself. You gave me a lot, and now you take it away by surrounding me with death. I feel that I am cursed."

Gavin continued speaking to the picture on the altar, as if hypnotized. "I do question your ways – those poor devils drowning and being washed away to their deaths at Naringa, and now you take my poor, beautiful Peggy from us. What can any reasonable man think? I know that it's faith that takes one through times like this. Faith I have, but I see little value in that faith when sorrow is its fruit. My poor Peggy had a troubled beginning, and just as she was on her feet for the first time in her short life, you allowed someone to shoot her."

Despite his efforts to stay angry, the picture seemed to suck the stress and anger from his body. As he sat in silence looking at the face of Christ, his conversation seemed shallow and unimportant.

In somewhat of a trance, Gavin didn't react to the sound of a guitar being played in the back of the church. When Gavin did focus on the direction of the music, he recognized a single guitar being skillfully played Flamenco-style. He listened to the rhythmic music with its simple melody. It seemed almost like a child's song, and then, just as he expected it to repeat, it would wander off on a different melody related to the first.

Gavin didn't take his eyes off the picture until the music stopped. Then he turned to see the guitar player. He saw a slight man dressed in black, wearing a white Panama hat. Gavin guessed him to be in his forties. He tucked the pick in the strings and carefully set the instrument down before turning with a smile to greet Gavin's puzzled gaze. Casually, he walked down the narrow aisle and offered his hand.

"Hello, Father. My name is Octavio. I um de pastora."

Gavin was brought suddenly back to reality when he heard himself addressed as "Father." His hand immediately went to his neck to check for his collar. He had forgotten not to wear it and had put it on out of habit.

He stood and shook the man's hand. "How do you do, Octavio? My name is Gavin Abernathy from Australia."

"Oh, Gavin, from Australia. Yes, you have accent."

Gavin had to laugh, as he could only catch every second word from Octavio. In his best English, he said, "Yes, I do have an accent and sincerely hope you can understand me."

Gavin thought he had made a joke, but Octavio didn't seem to notice and answered in his thick South American accent, "No matter, I will understood. I hear you talk to God, I play guitar so I don't scare you. It sounds like you are pretty uneven up with him."

Gavin felt immediate caring for this kind man. "Yes. I am not sure if I like his ways at all. But most of all, I don't know how I can go on preaching his words if I don't feel them."

"How long have you been the priest?"

Meeting Octavio's stare and gentle smile made Gavin smile

back. “Nearly eleven years.”

Octavio shook his head and sighed. “In my country, Brazil, we don’t expect every man to give his life to the church forever. He can still have God, but maybe he doesn’t work for him. You look like you done plenty for God. But it is of no matter what you think. God will show you, for sure.”

Octavio put his arms around him in a hug. At first Gavin was alarmed, but to Octavio, it was clearly the most natural thing in the world.

Octavio then put both hands up in the air. “I have an idea. You pray, and I will play guitar for you.”

Before Gavin could comment or object, Octavio walked to the back of the church to retrieve his guitar. Sitting three chairs away from Gavin, he said, “You pray, and I sit here and play very beautiful music for you. I start now. You and God will get even together.”

“Before you start,” Gavin interrupted, “let me ask you . . . Have you been a professional musician?”

Octavio’s smile beamed. “Thank you for ask the question. Yes, it is the moneys from my recordings that allows me to be Pastora for this small church. These people have no moneys, and I give what I can, too. All this from my guitar. Is that not a God gift?”

Gavin felt good humor and warmth for the first time since the news about Peggy. “Yes, Octavio, that is . . . God’s gift for sure.”

Octavio started to play, and Gavin just listened to the beauty of the sound. He thought that Octavio must have surely been more than just a professional in his life. The music was so perfect in every way that it took away Gavin’s intention to pray, until his eyes caught sight of the picture of Jesus at the altar. As he began to pray, his bitterness vanished, and he felt complete freedom, not only from his anger but also from God.

Gavin didn’t notice when Octavio stopped playing and just sat there, happy to look at Gavin’s new illumination.

Chapter 21

Ian had studied the pictures so much, he could have picked the admiral out of a lineup of ten people wearing bathing suits. This man was suave, with lightly tanned skin and silver hair. His slightly oiled hair was brushed back in place, and looked as well trained as the man himself. Standing over six feet, he was indeed as impressive as he was confident. His handshake was firm, but Ian felt it was overdone, like that of a man accustomed to canvassing for votes. The picture was perfect, a powerful man in uniform without a hair out of place. Ian couldn't take his eyes off the admiral's large teeth, which reminded him of a picture in a book from his youth, depicting a whaling ship's captain who had wooden teeth. As a child, he always asked himself the same question: *If they were going to make false wooden teeth, why not make them the right size?*

So immersed in the admiral's teeth, Ian heard only the last part of the admiral's greeting. ". . . very pleased you could make it, and before you say a word, please let me say how sorry I am about your lovely sister."

"Thank you, Admiral. As I said on the phone, it's her death that brings me here, since you're the only person I know who saw Peggy on the day of her death. I want to be part of that last day, and I want to know if she was happy, sad, or whatever. I just want to feel that I was with her on that last day."

Still with the same smile, the admiral tried his best to sound sincere, but Ian thought he didn't really understand what Ian meant. The negative thoughts kept running through his head, so quickly that Ian scarcely had time to recognize them. *Perhaps the admiral is right, and I'm only trying to avoid facing up to Peggy's death.* These emotions mixed him up so much that he didn't hear what the admiral said as he led Ian to a table in the beautiful Art Deco dining room.

After they had sat down and ordered their meals, the admiral continued to try to make conversation. "Did you travel to the U.S. on your own, once you heard the sad news of your sister?"

Having to think for a moment, Ian answered, "No, my brother Gavin came with me."

The admiral seemed surprised. "Oh? Why didn't you bring Gavin with you today?"

"He had some personal things to sort out, so it was good for us to have a break from each other during this tough time."

"You know, I never really understood how you knew that I had seen your sister in New York last week."

Ian said slowly, "Well, as you know, Peggy was a painter. A perfect painter, I would say. Anyway, as most of her subjects were large and required her to return to the site several times, she always took pictures of the entire area. The camera recorded the date and time. She would then make set-up notes on the prints."

The admiral allowed the soup to be served before he replied, "How does that lead to you and me having this delightful lunch?"

"In her pictures, there were three shots of you. I know that doesn't answer your question. It wasn't until my brother and I were waiting for our flight back to Sydney in the Qantas lounge that I recognized you on a television interview."

The admiral stared at Ian with his fixed half-smile.

"As you see, it means everything to me to know about Peggy's last day on earth, so we came to see Washington to see you."

To Ian's surprise, the admiral showed no emotion over Peggy's death or Ian's plight. In a business-like tone, he finally said, "She seemed like a very nice girl, and though I only said a few words to her, she seemed very friendly."

Ian pushed the admiral to go further. "In one of the close-up pictures, you had your finger to your lips. What did you mean?"

The admiral leaned back in his chair and put his right hand under his chin. "As I remember, she said she would be able to paint many of the birds into the scene. I held that pose, as if to say I would be quiet and not scare them away. She seemed quite happy at the time. We only spoke a couple of words, so there's not much else I can say."

The admiral changed the subject and asked a few questions about Australia. Looking up from his soup, Ian recognized the admiral's smile as condescending, and his expression disinterested. Ian got to his feet and abruptly held out his hand, to the admiral's surprise.

"Thank you, Admiral, but I find I am not as free from Peggy's death as I thought. I must leave now."

Before the admiral could get to his feet, Ian was halfway across the dining room.

Once outside, Ian relished the fresh air and the smell of the trees. He now felt bad for Peggy. If she'd had to pick anyone with which to spend her last day, it certainly wouldn't have been that pompous bore. Feeling weak after the agitation of being with the admiral, Ian just wanted to go back to his room and lie down.

The taxi ride seemed only to take a few minutes, and after picking up his key and checking for messages, he went straight to his room. Halfway to his room, a thought stopped him in his tracks. *The admiral didn't ask how Peggy died. How could that be?* Slowly, he continued to his room. Just as he inserted the key into the lock, he heard the sounds of banging and men's voices coming from inside the room.

As careful as Ian was, the men heard the key being placed in the lock and fell silent. Angrily, Ian pushed the door wide open and saw that the room had been ransacked. A man stood by the window. Without thinking, Ian walked inside and demanded, "What the bloody hell are you doing in this room?"

Before the man could answer, the door slammed shut behind Ian. Alarmed, he turned to face another man just two paces behind him. He was a huge man, but moved slowly as he approached Ian with his closed fist raised, ready to strike. Without thinking, Ian assumed a fighting stance, and before the man could strike, Ian snapped his right arm out in a karate punch, leaving his two forefingers open to strike the man in the eyes. As he threw the punch, he realized that the huge man was not only slow, he was old and slow. He didn't even see Ian's punch coming and screamed in shock as Ian's fingers penetrated his eye sockets. Ian didn't have time to feel repulsed, but was sure his fingers went into the man's eyes up to his second knuckle.

As the man fell to the ground, screaming, the other man stood facing Ian, as if trying to make up his mind whether to rush him or get out of the room. Looking frightened, he pulled a revolver from his belt. Seeing the gun, Ian put his foot on the edge of the bed and pushed with all his might. The bed frame didn't move, but the mattress slid across the bed, pinning the man to the wall. As Ian jumped on the mattress to subdue the man further, the gun fired twice. Ian crumpled to the floor.

~~~

The room fell silent for a few seconds, and then panic set in. The man with the gun ran to the window and called for his friend to hurry.

"Come on, Eddie," he urged. "We got to get out of here."

Still crying, the man wailed, "I can't see. Help me, Jimmy."

"Okay, I'm coming."

Eddie was writhing on the floor, holding both hands over his eyes as bright red blood ran freely from each eye socket. Seeing the man was helpless, Jimmy raised the gun and fired into Eddie's temple. Once again, the loud explosion from the gun created a momentary silence, and
~~~

seemed to hold the gunman motionless as he stared down at the man he had just shot.

Hearing banging at the door, he turned and left the room through the window, taking time to slide the window closed behind him. The gunman reentered the hall a few rooms down and began pushing his way through the crowd outside Ian's room, which had gathered to wait for the house detective to open the door.

~~~

Three blocks away, Gavin could see the flashing lights from the police and emergency vehicles double-parked and blocking the road outside the hotel. The motorbike police had parked their motorcycles across the sidewalk and were continually pushing back the crowd of curious bystanders. In cases like this, Gavin's first thought was to be of service as a priest. His relationship with God had nothing to do with his reaction to life's tragedies, as his natural training over the years was there for all victims.

People obliged Gavin's request to let him through, and even called for others to make way as soon as they saw he was a priest. When he reached the steps of the hotel, the first police officer addressed him. "Hello, Father. There's nothing much you can do. The dead guy is still up there, and the other guy, who was shot, has already been taken to St. Joe's hospital."

Wincing at the news, Gavin replied, "I would like to go up and be of service to the dead man."

The words that followed were cannon shots going off in Gavin's head. "He's in room 360."

Afraid he had heard correctly, Gavin asked the officer to repeat the room number.

"Room 360. They say it was a break-in."

Gavin shuddered in disbelief. "That's my room."
~~~

Before the policeman could reply, Gavin was halfway up the steps. Whether it was his clergy collar or his clear sense of purpose, no one tried to stop him as he passed policemen at the head of each of the stairwells. Not even bothering to face the two policemen guarding the room, now classified as a crime scene, Gavin burst into the room and found a body covered by one of the bed sheets. Not giving his greatest fear time to take hold, he swiftly fell to one knee and pulled the sheet back from the victim's face.

There was no face. The bullet had entered the head directly at the bridge of the nose and shattered the entire face. Gavin was forced to turn away, but as he did so, his eyes traveled down the corpse, revealing a much heavier man dressed in drab clothing and wearing unpolished brown shoes.

Gavin remained on his knee for at least a minute, trying to collect his thoughts. He thanked God a thousand times that it was not his brother. Only after pulling the sheet back over the corpse did he turn and bless the dead man.

As Gavin stood, he found himself facing a tall man wearing a shiny police badge on the breast pocket of his jacket. His soft, personable voice did not match his tough image.

"You must be Father Abernathy, brother of Ian Abernathy? I'm Chief Detective Stanley O'Connor."

Before he could ask any further questions, Gavin interrupted in a frantic voice, "Yes, where is my brother?"

The big man replied cautiously, as though expecting to be punched. "Your brother was shot and taken to the hospital. He was alive when he left here. I will have one of my men drive you to the hospital, but I need to talk to you as soon as possible, okay?"

Gavin replied as he made his way out the door, "Okay, but I have to leave now."

With just a shake of his head, O'Connor gave the uniformed officer in the room the order to take care of the priest, adding, "Bring him to the station after the hospital."

At the hospital, Ian had been taken directly into surgery and was in the observation room by the time Gavin arrived. Sitting at his side, Gavin wept for joy that Ian was alive, though still unconscious. He hadn't yet spoken to the surgeon, but he surmised that everything must be okay if Ian was out of surgery in such a short time.

Distraught, Gavin sat by his brother's bed and spoke his thoughts aloud in a rambling fashion. "Really, Ian, if I lost you, I don't think I could go on. I think you can hear me, so don't mind your poor old mixed-up brother crying and talking like a kid who feels sorry for himself. I know you're the one who's hurt, but I can't stop thinking of myself and how everyone I love dies or gets hurt. I spent time today talking things over with my boss, as you call him, and thought he was on my side. At least, I felt I was on his side, and then this. What the bloody hell is it?

"Honestly, I feel cursed, when I think I should feel chosen. That's a bloody laugh, isn't it? Chosen to see all around me hurt or die. What are the chances of two people in the same family being shot by a robber in their own rooms? Ian, you have to get through this, not only for me, but think how proud you will make Peggy when she sees you fight for your life. Mum and Dad, too – they always said you were the tough, stubborn one.

"Even though I'm really pissed off, I'm going to pray for you now. I know I said I can't do this anymore, but I don't know what else to do."

Gavin took Ian's hand in his and knelt to pray, forgetting his doubt, since he had nowhere else to turn. He was in that position when he heard the door open and the doctor cough discreetly to announce his presence. After the second feigned cough, Gavin looked up at the young doctor.

"Sorry to interrupt you, Father, but I'm off in a couple of minutes, and I wanted to give you a report on your brother before I left."

Feeling insignificant, Gavin replied sarcastically, "Yes, I understand. Just because a man is shot and clinging to life is no reason to be late getting home."

The doctor seemed taken aback by such a remark coming from a priest. "I will put that remark down to your shock and sorrow, but Father, you of all people know that life goes on, no matter what happens in this hospital."

The doctor paused, but Gavin didn't make the slightest effort to acknowledge or apologize for his comment.

The doctor continued, "We had Ian on the operating table and found that the two bullets passed through his body, and Ian is in no danger of losing his life. The problem is, only a neurosurgeon can assess the damage. Both bullets undoubtedly caused nerve damage."

The mere sound of the words "nerve damage" made Gavin get to his feet and face the doctor. "Nerve damage? Does that mean he won't walk, or what?"

Not reacting to Gavin's challenging tone, the doctor calmly replied, "It could be one or the other, both, or none. You will have to wait a few days for the tests."

Gavin knew he was acting selfishly, but he didn't care. He went back to kneeling with his elbows on the edge of the bed. With his head down, he muttered, "Thank you, Doctor."

On the drive to the police station, as per O'Connor's orders, Gavin started to think about the impossibility of two people from the same family being shot in separate incidents and in separate locations. Trying to use logic, he asked himself over and over what could possibly be the connecting factor, besides Peggy and Ian being related.

It didn't take long. The two constants in each shooting were the photos and the admiral.

Before he could make any sense of it, the police officer tapped him on the shoulder to announce that Detective O'Connor was waiting for him. Gavin looked up. For the first time, he noticed that the car had stopped.

Quickly trying to collect his thoughts, Gavin jumped out of the squad car and put the officer at rest by claiming to have had a nap. "Excuse me, Officer. I was just getting a quick wink of sleep."

~~~

O'Connor's manner was friendly, yet authoritative. To him, this case was murder, and the fact that Gavin was a grieving brother and a priest made little difference. To Gavin, the efforts of O'Connor and the whole D.C. police force would make no difference, for he wasn't going to leave the finding of the killer to anybody but himself.

As he sat across the desk from O'Connor, it soon became clear that he would be forced to lie more in the next few minutes than he had done in the last twelve years.

O'Connor started simply enough. "Why did you come to D.C.?"

Not wanting to give O'Connor his suspected connection, Gavin made the decision to lie from that moment on. "Ian is a history buff, and he wanted to see the capital and other monuments."

"Do you know anyone here?"

"No, we don't know a soul."

"Did you and your brother get along?"

"Couldn't be any closer."

"Did you or your brother have a gun?"

"No."

"Do you know of any reason why two men would break into
~~~

your room?"

"Two men?" Gavin asked in surprise.

"Yes. If you didn't have a gun, who shot the man on the floor next to your brother?"

"Yes, I guess you're right. I never thought of that. You can tell I'm not much at working these things out."

"That's why we're here, Father Abernathy. Is your brother a fighter, karate or the likes?"

Gavin was surprised at the question and looked at the detective with new interest. "Yes, Ian went as far as a Black Belt, but I don't think he kept it up. Why do you ask?"

O'Conner watched Gavin's face as he spoke. "The dead man on the floor had is eyes poked out. He could no longer see and became a liability, so I believe his partner shot him and made his escape through the window."

"My brother has guts, I can tell you that, but he wouldn't hurt a man like that unless his life was threatened."

"I think you're right. Right now, we're questioning everyone, guest and staff at the hotel, and I'm sure we'll make the connection."

Getting to his feet, Gavin asked, "Is that about it, Detective? I have to get some sleep and be in shape to be with Ian. *I have a sense that you don't believe my story, Mr. Detective, but you are not going to stop me finding the man who shot Ian, and maybe even Peggy.* "I'll be at the hotel or the hospital if you need me," he added.

O'Connor rose to walk Gavin to the door, asking the same officer who had driven Gavin to take him to the hotel.

Pleased to be involved, the officer gave an enthusiastic, "Yes, sir."

~~~

When Gavin returned to the hotel, he was shown to a new room
~~~

on another floor. None of his belongings had been moved from the crime scene. In an effort to work out how to get the photos, he tried to remember exactly how they had gotten ready that morning. He could see Ian sitting at the desk, wearing his red dressing gown, going over the photos for the hundredth time. Gavin had still been in bed when Ian showered, but he couldn't remember if Ian had dressed in the bathroom or back in the room. If he dressed in the bathroom, he would have hung his robe behind the door, and with any luck, his scribbling and photos would still be in the pocket. Ian was tidy by nature and put things away, so if the photos weren't in the robe, they would have been on him – in which case the police would have them, or they were back in his suitcase. Gavin could see little chance of the police letting him shuffle through Ian's case, and he couldn't say it was his because of the nametags.

Gavin picked up the phone and spoke to the front desk. "Yes, good evening. This is Father Abernathy. I would like to speak to the officer in charge of room 360."

The operator sounded like a small child as she said, "Yes, Father, one minute please."

Seconds later, a stern voice came on the line. "Officer Starace."

Trying to sound matter-of-fact, Gavin said, "Yes, Officer Starace, this is Father Abernathy, the brother of the man shot today."

In a less officious voice, the officer replied, "Yes, Father, how may I help you?"

"Well, I'm in my new room, but I don't have any of my things. Could you please help me?"

"I'm afraid that's not possible. This room is an official crime scene. No one can enter, and nothing can be removed."

Gavin tried to sound supportive but needy. "I understand, but I had hoped to get my suitcase with my clothes. Surely they're not included, are they?"

"Yes, I'm afraid they are."

Gavin couldn't care less, but in his "holy voice," as Ian called it, he said, "Well, I understand a little, but that puts me in a real bind, since I can't just pop down to the lobby and buy a clerical collar, now, can I?"

"Sorry, Father. It will probably be another couple of days."

"Officer Starace, you are indeed making it hard for me, but maybe you could do me at least one favor."

"I can't promise anything. What is it?"

"If you can't give me my case, could you just go in and get my shaving kit and my red dressing gown hanging behind the bathroom door? You know, this has been a very tough day for me, you must know that. You should also consider that America has been very cruel to us thus far, as visitors."

"Okay, okay, Father, that's enough. I'll go in and get them, but you have to come up here and pick them up, since I can't leave my post."

"Thank you, Officer Starace. It's the black shaving kit and the red dressing gown behind the door. I'll be right up."

When Gavin arrived at the room, the officer was standing guard outside the door with his hands behind his back. Gavin was sure he had changed his mind or hadn't yet retrieved the goods.

Officer Starace spoke before Gavin could get his question out. "Father, the goods you asked for are two doors down." Gavin could see the red robe down the hall. "There's just one thing. If asked if anything has been removed from the room, my answer must be no."

Relieved, Gavin, replied, "Completely understood, and remember, a little white lie to aid a person in need is quite permissible, I would say. Thank you again, Officer Starace. Good night."

Gavin stooped to pick up the red silk dressing gown without stopping. Once he was in the elevator, he began to squeeze the bundle, hoping to feel the envelope with photos. He felt nothing, and by the time he got out of the elevator, his sense of achievement was again replaced by despair. However, this reversed itself once he rolled the dressing gown out on the bed and saw the photo package sticking out of the dressing gown pocket, just as he had seen it in his mind.

Quickly, he opened the envelope and carefully went through each photo. He found nothing out of the usual, just the admiral looking at the camera and some blurred businessman in the background. To his dismay, this blew the theory that the admiral was behind the two break-ins. What about the other man? He wasn't sure. He seemed innocuous in the picture, not paying attention to anyone. Gavin had no way to identify who he was. He put the photos back in the package and lay back on the bed, staring at the ceiling. The more he tried to think, the more overwhelming the circling thoughts became.

Getting up to turn off the light, he spoke aloud in the empty room, "This is hopeless. But I know there's something here, somewhere." Once in bed, he turned on his side and started to pray for Ian, falling asleep halfway through. He prayed only out of habit, for he still intended to hold a decision on his faith after being dealt such tragic blows.

Chapter 22

Next morning, while paying for two cotton sweatshirts in the hotel gift shop, Gavin asked the sales lady for directions to the nearest railway station. Her southern accent was so thick that Gavin had to ask her to repeat the instructions three times before he understood the words "Union Station."

Back in his room, he called Jim Holly in New York. It was still before seven, so Gavin called the home number that Jim had given them when they arrived in New York.

The phone rang once before Jim answered in a businesslike voice, "Yes, what is it?"

"Hello, Jim, this is Gavin Abernathy, Father Abernathy."

"Yes, I know who Gavin Abernathy is, but what bothers me is that I don't think this call is coming from Australia."

Surprised at the comment, Gavin cleared his throat with a small cough. "Well, no, I'm not in Australia, but actually in Washington."

"Shit. How come I know this is going to be one of those days, and it's not even seven yet? How come you didn't catch your plane?"

Not used to answering to anyone, Gavin felt like he was the child, and Jim the father. He ignored the question. "You know the photos you developed for us?"

"Yeah, the ones your sister took of her painting sites, right?"

"That's right. Well, I think there must be something in those photos besides her painting, because not only did she get shot, but now Ian has been shot by two guys who were searching his room, and I think they were after the photos. Where did you have them developed?"

"In the police lab. I got the prints for Ian, and the negatives were put back in the file. What about Ian? How badly hurt is he?"

"He's bad, and still in a coma. We won't know the full story until the neurologists get done. It's only been twenty-four hours, so we still hope for the best."

"Why do you think the photos have something to do with it?"

"Well, they're the reason we came here. Ian saw the same person, the admiral who was in Peggy's photos, being interviewed on TV, and he just had to speak with him about Peggy. So we came to Washington to meet him. Ian had lunch with him, and when he returned to his room, he interrupted two guys ransacking the place. Ian must have put up a fight and got shot."

Quick to the point, Jim asked, "How do you know there were two guys in the room?"

"Because one was found shot dead on the floor, and there was no gun, so someone had to do the shooting before they fled."

"Who's the detective on the case?"

Gavin didn't want to give O'Connor's name, in case Jim got to him before he could leave the hotel. "In all the commotion and stress, I can't remember his name. Look, I have a plan, and if I'm right, I can prove that he was after the photos. If you really check these negatives, maybe you can find out why."

"What are you going to do?"

"I have half a plan and I know the rest will come to me. But one thing I'm sure of is that it will take an individual effort to flush this guy out. The police will have their hands tied, but not me."

Now Jim changed his tone and tried to show more friendly concern. "Gavin, you should think this out further. You have no idea what you might be dealing with, if anything. Emotions and imagination can go crazy in times of grief like this."

"To tell you the truth, Jim, I don't give a stuff about any of that bullshit. This guy has taken away my desire to live, and if I don't go after him, I know I'll never have a chance of finding that desire again, no matter how long I live. Look, all I want you to do is look at those bloody prints and tell the Washington detective the answers."

Knowing that this conversation was ending, Jim tried to keep it going. "What about a Miss Lindsay Graeme who contacted me today about Peggy's ashes?"

Gavin stopped cold at the sound of Lindsay's name. All the scenes from Naringa flashed through his head, from meeting her in Sydney to that fateful night when the constable came to the station with the news of Peggy.

The long silence caused the New York detective to repeat, "Gavin, are you still there? Gavin, listen. We do have a lead of sorts. The gallery manager hasn't been found, but we do know she was using false name and security number. We are checking in London as the airlines have a record of under her phony name. Gavin, do you hear me? Stop and think man.

Gavin ignored the policeman and let his racing thoughts bring him up to date with his own feelings of the moment. Apart from Lindsay, he was alone in the world, his faith was torn apart, and the only two humans who were part of him had been shot. At that moment, he knew that nothing else mattered. He would find the man, or men, who had done this, and would kill them or die trying. Revenge may not be sweet, but for Gavin, it was life itself.

Jim raised his voice. "Gavin, listen to me. You can't do everything by yourself. If you expose this admiral alone, he will be forced to kill you. If he has gone to this trouble to hide his identity, he will have no trouble killing once more. Wait until I get the photos analyzed, and then you can work with the Washington detective."

"Just tell Lindsay to come to Ian's bed side and wait for me." Gavin replaced the receiver with a renewed sense of purpose, knowing now what he must do. He also knew that he had to be quick, since it would only take one call to O'Connor to have Gavin tailed, or worse, confined to the hotel. He threw the photos and some hotel stationery into a bag and left the room within minutes.

Once outside, he kept his head down and proceeded to find his way to Union Station. As he turned the first corner, he glanced back to see two black and white police cars pull to a screeching stop in front of the hotel.

~~~

Back at police headquarters, Detective Stanley O'Connor drummed his thick fingers repeatedly on the desktop as he spoke to his assistant, who was writing at the next desk. "Bronski, I don't like surprises like this on my watch. I knew when I saw this priest guy that he had some toughness in him, so it's not a total surprise. Do you hear me, Bronski?"

"Yes, sir, he didn't fool you completely."

"Not completely, but who the hell ever expected to have a rogue priest on the loose playing detective in the middle of a crime scene? This could get out of hand and quickly become an international mess."

"Yes, sir."

The detective's thoughts were interrupted by a buzz on the phone in front of him. He picked it up and barked, "O'Connor." He listened for a moment and then said, "I don't want to hear about that. He was there five minutes ago. You're a policeman, damn it. Find him."

~~~

Jim Holly didn't waste any time after receiving Gavin's call. Before he left home, he rang the police lab and ordered the Abernathy negatives to be rerun and enlarged. He also made a call to his boss, Brian

Stewart, who said he would leave for the station immediately upon hearing about Ian's shooting.

With large cups of coffee, they gathered in the lab with the photos projected onto a large screen. One by one, the photos filled the screen, and after an hour of sitting silently, they sat scrutinizing each shot. At the end of the session, no man knew more than when they had started.

Stewart was the first to speak. "I'm sorry, Jim, but if these photos are why two people have been shot, then it's beyond me as to why."

Sighing, Jim agreed. "But there has to be something. What are the odds of two people from the same family being shot in two different cities inside a week? Both in safe, upscale places, to boot. I say it's impossible for it to be random."

Stewart nodded as he spoke. "I agree, it seems impossible. This priest fellow seems to be on the right track when he points out that the only two common denominators in both cases are the films and the admiral. Beats the hell out of me; I can't see any connection. I think all you can do is call the lead detective in Washington and tell him what we think, and then suggest he interview the admiral."

"Okay, I'll call and also send him the photos, just to cover our asses."

Stewart looked up, as though he hadn't thought of that angle. "Yeah, good thinking. While you're at it, why not send them to the Feds and the CIA? You never know. If this does become some kind of international thing, I don't want us to be the only ones who don't know what the hell is going on." Stewart got to his feet. "I must go now, but be sure to use the official pouch when you send that stuff over, okay? I don't like the feel of this thing at all."

~~~
~~~

Lindsay checked her watch to find she had only a couple minutes before landing in New York. The letter from the travel agency instructed her to call Detective Jim Holly from the New York police department, supplying a main number and a department number. Her mind drifted to the two men in her life, and she felt sure that they would have left New York by now. The last time she had seen Gavin, he was in shock, being pushed into the ute at Naringa.

Dear Gavin, I hope you are coping with your sorrow over Peggy. God only knows what it must have been like identifying her body. The thought of Peggy's cold, lifeless body made Lindsay shudder and start to cry. *Ian, I hope you're still looking after Gavin. I know we haven't talked since you told me your secret, but you must know I still love you. Our love will be more like brother and sister. Oh, I don't mean I can take Peggy's place in your heart. Oh, poor, sweet Peggy, how I love you, too. If Gavin and Ian have left, I hope they take some time off on the way home. Maybe they will stay in Hawaii or some other great island. I'll see when I ring this Detective Holly.*

Lindsay dozed but did not escape all the thoughts that had been going round and round in her head since that night in Naringa.

Chapter 23

Gavin started his plan by renting two lockers side by side on the second level of Washington Union Station. Once he had placed the photos inside and locked the door, he headed in search of the messenger service advertised in the station lobby. *Only two blocks north on the left*, the poster said.

Gavin walked through the large glass door and approached the clerk at the counter. "Excuse me, how long would it take to get a package across town?"

The clerk didn't take his eyes off the form he was filling out. "About an hour or so."

Gavin looked around and spotted a couple of empty desks near the window. "That would be great. Do you think I could sit at one of those desks and prepare my mailing?"

The clerk still did not look up. "Be my guest. Take all day. No hurry."

As Gavin sat down, he placed Ian's notes and the hotel stationery and pen on the desk. He wrote the following letter.

> *Dear Admiral,*
>
> *My name is not important in this transaction, but I am an employee of the hotel, and I was the first to enter the room where two men were shot yesterday. I heard the police say that the robbers were looking for something, and I pocketed this envelope addressed to you. I know they are photos, and you are in them.*

If, by chance, these are of interest to you, they are in locker 378 at Union Station. The enclosed key is for that locker.

I want two thousand dollars for the photos. Just lock the locker and leave the money.

If you take the photos and don't leave the cash, I will tell the police that you have the photos.

If, by chance, the photos are of no interest to you, forward this letter to the police.

Thank you.

Rereading the letter, Gavin thought it sounded a little too pat, but he was sure that this bait would prove the admiral's involvement one way or another. He then took the locker key and traced both sides on a piece of paper, using a very sharp, pointed pencil. Satisfied, he enclosed the original key and sealed the envelope, using the address from Ian's notes.

The disinterested clerk guaranteed delivery by four o'clock. Gavin didn't think it likely that the admiral would have that much cash on hand and would not make his decision so quickly. This meant no action until the banks opened the next day. He didn't want to be questioned by O'Connor, which meant he couldn't go back to his hotel or the hospital. He decided to wait until noon and then check into another hotel. He thought about going to a church to pray, but quickly dismissed that notion. His desire for revenge may not have been merited, but it remained unchallenged, and he wanted to keep it that way.

~~~

Still in the office, Jim Holly took a call from Detective Stanley O'Connor.
~~~

"I got your communication and the photos today," said O'Connor. "You are aware, I suppose, that the damn priest lied to my face. He said he was here because his brother was a history buff. What do you think of that?"

Holly sighed. "There's not much that would surprise me about this man. He's a good man with a broken heart. You know his initial reason for coming to New York?"

"Yes, I do now. It seems I'm the last to know a lot of things on this case. I don't like it, Holly. I see you want me to interview this admiral about a murder in New York and some photos. Is that right?"

"Right," confirmed Holly.

"Well, either you don't know what clout these admiral types have, or you want me to lose my goddamn pension. I need written orders from your boss to mine, and then maybe I'll make the call for you, okay?"

"Okay, O'Connor, just take it easy. You would have been just as pissed off if we didn't keep you appraised, so cool it. Did you see anything in those photos?"

O'Connor spat back. "Nothing that I can link to the case. We're checking on the man in the background, but his face is fuzzy and turned away from the camera. We're working on seeing what we can do with our software, but, so far, we haven't been able to identify him. The admiral seems to be the main focus of the photos and remains the main object of our concern."

Wanting to finish the call, Jim replied in a friendly voice, "We gave them to the Feds and CIA, so if they come up with something, we'll call you." He hung up before O'Connor could say another word.

The click of the disconnect sent O'Connor into a shouting rage as he called the officers on watch into his office. "Has anyone found the priest yet?"

Two of the officers answered in unison, "No, sir."

"God damn it, he is a priest in our town. What do I have to do, paint the bastard blue? I want him found."

~~~

Gavin checked his watch, hoping that he had allowed enough time for Lindsay to travel from New York to Ian's hospital. It was only 4:15, and he decided to wait until early evening before making the call. Earlier in the day, he had moved into a room at Hotel Excelsior, definitely a hotel of the past, but it suited Gavin's needs for a couple of nights.

For the last two hours, he had been busy filing the second locker key to fit the pattern. At first he had no way to hold the key stable while filing, so he packed the bottom of the top drawer of the dresser with pages from the phone book. To test it, he slammed it shut without the key in between. The drawer jammed so tight that he had quite a job to open it.

Once open, he realigned the paper, inserted the key, and slammed it tight again. The key was held as tight as any vice, and Gavin was surprised how his mood changed when he achieved ultimate success with his improvisation. An hour or two later, he lay back on the bed, confident that the key was perfect.

His mind raced back over his plan and how his intentions were the exact opposite of his priestly duties. He knew that he was acting like a phony, and that exposure was the only difference between himself and the poor souls who came before him screaming for vengeance. Until now, Gavin hadn't been exposed to life's betrayals. The tragedies heaped upon good people brought them back to the true nature of man. Like any animal, he struck out to protect himself and his clan, survival being the most basic instinct. *Everything we have been taught, or made to believe, is our second nature that covers up our true nature*, he thought. *Is this*
~~~

what I've become? He didn't know what he had become, but he did know it wasn't priestly. *Whatever that means.*

To stop the circling excuses, he reached for the phone to start his search for Lindsay. *She must have reached the hospital by now. I can only imagine what a shock she must have gotten when Holly told her that Ian has been shot, too. My poor Lindsay.* After the third department at the hospital, he managed to get through to Ian's room.

Lindsay picked up the phone and burst into tears at the sound of Gavin's voice. "Oh Gav, where are you? Why aren't you here?"

In a soothing voice, he tried to comfort her. "Lindsay, I can't be there now because I have to find out who has done this to us. Believe me, I want to be there with you and Ian, but I must do this now. Is Ian any better?"

Lindsay commanded through her tears, "No, no, Gavin, you have to come here. You can't leave us alone. Nothing else matters now. You have to come here. We need your love."

Gavin didn't expect anyone or anything to put doubt in his mind about what he was determined to do, but Lindsay was shattering his conviction in his plan. "I'll be there as soon as I can," he said. "Is Ian any better?"

"No, there hasn't been any change since he came in, and the doctors have finished most of the tests. They haven't been able to locate the neurological damage, because they suspect it's in more than one part of his body."

Gavin had to wait while Lindsay tried to control her sobbing.

"Lindsay, if I don't return in three days, take Ian home and have the best doctors in the world come to see him. I've written to my attorneys in Sydney and have given you power-of-attorney for the entire foundation. Do what you think, and don't let money be an obstacle."

Gavin had to stop as Lindsay wailed into the phone, "Gavin, you can't go anywhere. Come here with us. You're all we have."

"Lindsay, I love you and Ian, and you are all I have, but I must finish what I've started, or I'll never be a man again."

"Gavin, do you know the police are looking for you?"

"Yes. That's why I'm not at your side now. I haven't done anything wrong, but they would surely stop me from doing what I must do. If they ask you what I said, tell them I told you I'm coming right over."

"Gavin, I'm strong, and I will look after Ian, but you can't leave us. We have to stay together. We need you. We need each other." Tears overcame her ability to speak, and Gavin quietly replaced the receiver.

He counted back over the time since he had met Lindsay. In all, he had only known her a little over seven weeks. Finding that impossible, he recounted the time, and it was indeed only seven weeks. Seven weeks, and she was as close as any family member. Seven weeks, and he had signed over the 200-million-dollar trust to her. He had loved her when he was a priest, and now he just plain loved her. It felt as though she was all that he had in the world.

~~~

The next morning, Gavin jumped as the alarm went off at 7:00. It took him several seconds to recognize his surroundings. He showered and hurried down to the station to begin his vigil of locker 378.

The lockers were against the main wall, with subway entrances on either side and rows of seats surrounded by a large open area in front of the lockers. He chose the seats facing the lockers, even though they were well back, which caused his back to face the entrance. He thought that if he had to sit there for hours, he didn't want to strain his neck looking sideways.

Few people were seated, but many stood waiting, and it would be impossible for him to spot anyone waiting for him. It was then that it
~~~

occurred to him that he didn't have to retrieve the money or even go near the locker. Once he saw someone open it and place a package there, that was all the proof he needed. Some lucky person would be two thousand dollars richer. *What about my beautiful key?* A smile came to his lips as he remembered his desire for success. *Pays to be mechanical, I guess.*

By ten o'clock, he had only seen one man use the lockers, and he was nowhere near 378. Around noon, the station became busy again. Gavin tried not to stare at the lockers, but instead kept them in the periphery of his vision.

A well-dressed lady began going through the crowd collecting money for some charity. Gavin counted how many people she approached actually gave money. The score for the first ten was seven, which he thought was pretty high. On the next ten, it was five, and then seven again. Gavin got three dollars out as she made her way down his row, and he held the money out for her.

Accepting the money, she said, "Thank you very much. You make my job for Sisters of Mercy very easy. I normally have to shame the men . . . shame them into giving."

Gavin found that he was pleased to talk to someone. "Maybe it's your good looks that make them shy away."

"Thank you, kind sir, but I think they just can't be bothered. Have you got a long wait?"

"Yes, I think about another hour or so."

As she went on her way, she wished Gavin a good day and thanked him again. Her British accent was very pleasing to hear, Gavin thought as he watched her walk away.

A few minutes later, Gavin's heart jumped as he saw a tall, well-dressed man approach the lockers and open 378. He took out the photos and placed a brown paper bag into the locker and locked the door. Gavin watched the tall man as he walked slowly to the right-hand side entrance.

As excited as he was, he decided not to approach the locker. His original plan was to follow the man, but after speaking to Lindsay, he realized that he didn't have to take the risk of opening the locker. He could just give the letter and the key to Detective O'Connor so he could check the locker and find the money. Bingo.

The thought of being with Lindsay and Ian made him hurry as he walked towards the main door. Once through the doors and on the footpath, he suddenly felt hands grip his arms like vises, and two big men hauled him into a waiting limo. It happened so quickly, Gavin was unable to protest. He found himself squeezed between two strange men in the back seat of a large limousine.

He was about to fight for his life, when he realized he was facing the attractive collection lady.

"Don't be alarmed," she said serenely. "The admiral just wants to speak with you." She then gave instructions to the driver, in what Gavin thought was Russian, as she instructed Gavin to remain still while they waited for another member of their party.

Moments later, the limo door swung open, and the tall, well-dressed man who had taken the photos from the locker climbed into the car. The car pulled away from the curb. Gavin shook his head, amazed at his own naiveté, when he found himself staring at the brown paper package the man had resting on his knee.

Incredulous, he turned to the lady. "You were checking for accents, weren't you?"

She did not answer, but offered a phony, disinterested smile.

There was no conversation or change in the bored facial expression they all shared. When he asked a question, he was told by the unfriendly lady to hold his questions for the admiral.

After an hour in the hot car, Gavin caught himself slipping off to sleep. He fought this urge by repeating to himself that it was his nerves and he wasn't tired. Plus, he had to watch every move and expression these people made, as any small thing could get him out of this situation. He heard Jim Holly's voice in his mind: *One more killing will be nothing to him.* For the first time, Gavin felt alone and desperate.

The gravel squeaked as the sleek limo slowly entered a long, manicured driveway, approaching a stately three-story stone mansion. The driver parked, and Gavin was ushered into an immense foyer, decorated with huge paintings and plush orange and gold Persian rugs. In this sudden predicament, the sheer opulence was shocking.

As he stood in the foyer at the threshold of the library, he could see a uniformed man seated behind a large mahogany desk. His head was down, and he seemed not to notice Gavin, his prisoner, waiting in front of him.

Finally, with a slight wave of the hand, the admiral ordered Gavin to be brought into the room.

The admiral, shuffling through the pictures, looked at Gavin with little interest.

"I hope you're the last of this Abernathy family that I will have the displeasure of meeting."

Gavin was so taken aback by the imperious coldness in reference to his Peggy's death that he was almost speechless. "Did you have my sister killed and my brother shot?"

The admiral shuffled some papers and cast his eyes downward, indicating the meeting was over, and then changed his mind as he addressed Gavin.

"Maybe in Australia you have a desire to sit and talk of how things were or how things are. Not here. I wanted these photos, and now I have them. That is that. Unfortunately, you have nothing else I want, so, for you, all that is left is a long, happy, drug-filled sleep."

At that precise moment, the two men restrained Gavin in the

chair, and the collection lady approached Gavin with a large syringe. Gavin tried to kick it out of her hand, but she moved to his side and continued to hold the needle to the light to ensure its function.

Gavin was now in a full panic and exerted every muscle trying to break free, but he couldn't get any leverage. Each man held him in a tight full Nelson.

Seeing the lady lower the needle, Gavin yelled, "Why? Tell me why!"

The admiral looked up impatiently. "That's not for you to know." With a simple wave of the wrist, he instructed the lady to proceed.

Gavin felt the pinprick, and in seconds, the room was spinning away from him into darkness.

Chapter 24

Jim Holly rode downtown in an unmarked police car with a blaring siren that helped cut through the busy midday traffic. Five minutes later, as the car entered the Federal Plaza, which housed most of the main municipal buildings, Jim jumped quickly out of the car before it pulled to a stop and bounded up the granite steps. Exiting the elevator on the thirty-sixth floor, he was escorted through a security check and asked to wait outside a closed door marked *OPERATIONS*.

Five minutes later, he was ushered into a room where five men sat around a large map table. The photograph of the admiral was projected on the far wall. The men all wore large red identification tags around their necks. The leader, a short, balding man with heavy glasses, stood to introduce himself as Don Brown and turned to introduce the other men.

He then took the floor and addressed Jim. "Well, Detective Holly, you may have handed us the most important lead we have had in this office in the last five years. If it pans out the way we think it will, it will be one of the turning points in America's fight against espionage."

Jim could hardly believe his ears. He stood there feeling very important. "Of course, I don't know what you mean, but I see the admiral's image on the wall, and it must be from those damn photos."

Turning to the screen, Brown confirmed, "You're absolutely right. And, as usual, the instinct of the man on the case paid off. Let us take you through this series of snapshots."

The photos jumped on the screen side by side, two at a time.

Brown continued, "Here is the poor victim's easel in the

foreground, with the admiral entering the picture from the left."

The next photo flashed on the screen.

"Here he is, opposite the easel." Brown stopped the slides to face Jim. "We'll take you through this and show you our findings without any games. Remember, we have a great advantage over you. We knew the name of the other man in the photo, which is the key."

Jim nodded in agreement, and the leader carried on. "If you'll look behind the easel, you will see the man in the shadows approaching the admiral. His alias is Jogan Dames. He carries a German passport, but he's really a top Russian operative, Vladimir Chinkoff of Moscow."

A new picture flipped onto the screen, where the two men stood opposite one another. The next showed the men passing each other without a sign of acknowledgement.

Brown asked Jim, "Did you see anything?"

Jim replied with a gesture of open hands. "Nothing that I haven't seen in the fifty times I've looked at these."

"You didn't spot it because you weren't looking for it, but your instincts, as I said before, are to be commended. Now look again as the men approach each other. Each is carrying a briefcase." The next set of images appeared on the screen. "Now they have passed each other, and they still have their respective briefcases, but something has changed. Can you spot it?"

At first, Jim could see nothing different. He was about to admit that he couldn't see any change, when it suddenly struck him like a lightning bolt. "The briefcases," he blurted out. "They're facing the other way, right?"

The men heartily clapped their hands.

Brown nodded. "The straps on the admiral's are facing away from him, and after he passes Chinkoff, the straps are facing into his leg. This proves the cases have been switched."

Jim sat upright in his chair, and with all eyes on him, asked the obvious question: “What’s in the case?”

The leader unsuccessfully tried to conceal an emerging grin. “Jim, I’m happy to report that a well-planned decoy is in the briefcase. You see, we’ve known for better than a year that there was a leak from the Pentagon. We’ve set traps before, but come up with nothing. We’re not that smart, though, because the admiral wasn’t even one of our suspects.”

“What are you going to do now?”

“Nothing. Absolutely nothing. We don’t want him to know. We can use him, because he now thinks that he has handed over the latest nuclear submarine location codes. This is too good to be true.”

Jim stood up and stared at the group. “I’m afraid it is too good to be true, because we don’t know where Father Gavin Abernathy is, and we know he plans on approaching the admiral.”

Brown’s one-word answer told Jim he was on dangerous ground. “So?”

“If he flushes out the admiral out, he’ll be killed.”

“Listen, Detective Holly, you have ten years in, so leave this to us. Sometimes the price of a few lives is not too much to pay for an entire country.”

“Maybe so, when it’s the victims’ country, and when I haven’t been given a job to protect these few lives you so fearlessly disregard. I tell you, the priest is in imminent danger.”

Brown jumped to his feet to make it clear there would be no more Mr. Nice Guy. “Holly, if you lift a finger, I will break you like a twig.”

Seeing no purpose in further exposing his hand, Jim pushed his chair into the table and asked if he could leave. As he passed through the door, Brown threatened again, “Like a twig, Holly, like a twig!”

Back in his office, Jim rang the angry Detective O'Connor. "Yeah, this is me," said O'Connor. "What would you like me to do now, have a chat with the President?"

Jim actually smiled. "No, I've got something much better. I'm going to take the next shuttle down and should be there in a couple of hours. Could you please have a car meet me and get the known addresses of the admiral?"

"Nothing else? No tea or coffee or anything?"

In a hurry to put the phone down, Jim snapped, "Listen, O'Connor, you're going to love this, trust me!"

~~~

Gavin's mind started to stir. Pain wracked his body, but he knew he had to make his mind search for some clarity. He pressed down on his eyelids as he tried to force his memory to return. *I know I was drugged, and I can remember being held down.* Then he had the sudden impulse to move, as if his life depended upon it. *I must move. I must move.* Without opening his eyes, he concentrated on sitting up. Slowly, his muscles responded, and he lifted his back two or three inches until he felt he had enough strength to sit up. With his eyes tightly closed, he combined his concentration with his limited strength and reached a sitting position, throwing out his arms for balance. His arms did not respond, and he fell sideways, banging his head on something hard. He screamed in pain.

My God, they have broken my arms. I must see, I must see. Slowly he opened his eyes and waited for them to adjust to the dim light. He discovered that he was in the hull of a small boat. He stopped searching the space and listened to the noises about him. He heard the sound of a small engine chugging and water lapping the outside of the boat. He sat still and could feel the slight rocking of the boat. His mind was racing now as he concluded that he was being taken out to sea to be dumped overboard. He let out another cry, but this was one of relief
~~~

when he saw that his arms and legs were tied and not broken as he had thought.

He was lying on rolls of fishing nets, and his head rested on a small, three-pronged lead anchor. The engine was only five feet away. He knew he had to do something to stop his inevitable murder. He maneuvered himself close enough to the engine to kick at it. *Maybe now my mechanical knowledge will save my life.* He aimed his two-legged kick at the fuel line again and again, but it was no use. He couldn't get enough leverage.

Just as he was looking for another possibility, he noticed a small stream of fuel escaping from the line. He tried harder, but it wouldn't give. *Okay, okay, don't panic. I need to free my arms and legs. Come on, think, mate.*

Giving up on the engine, he crawled to a small cabin door and began banging his head against it. Within seconds, the door slid open, and Gavin found himself face-to-face with a fat, hairy man, holding a gun inches from Gavin's head.

"Hello, Father, what can we do for you today?" The gunman turned to seek approval from his partner, a skinny man with stained teeth. They both laughed.

"Well, I'm sure you're taking me to my death, and all I ask is to spend my last minutes on earth in God's fresh air. For that, I would thank you very much."

"Well, if that doesn't take the fuckin' cake. We kill him, and he thanks us."

Gavin noticed that this time, the laughter was definitely forced and much shorter. He had no idea how to save himself, but he did know that he had to keep them talking and get out of the cabin.

"You can relax, gentlemen. I'm not in the least afraid of dying." Keeping his voice even and as priestly as he could imagine, he asked,

"Have either of you ever killed a priest before?"

They looked at each other and shook their heads, indicating that they hadn't. "Well, if you had, that priest would have asked to pray for you before you administered the final blow."

The fat, hairy man seemed more uneasy and was quick to retort, "Oh, yeah? Why wouldn't he ask his God to strike us down instead?"

The skinny man joined in, "Yeah, why not?"

"Because the blight will already be upon you. But more important, because his life was spent praying for sinners, and for his life's work to be worthy, he must do this when it takes great courage to do so."

With a quick, nervous laugh, the fat man asked, "What's this blight shit?"

"It's known as the 'Disciple Edict of Blight.' It translates from Latin as 'Instant Statue of Malformation and Blight for Six Generations.' They say most of the deformed beggars of the world are from the Edict of Blight. That means you, your kids, and their kids, and so on, will suffer blight."

The fat man laughed unconvincingly. "Oh, what a load of bullshit. Freddie, don't fall for the crap. He's only trying to mix you up."

Gavin looked directly at the skinny man, Freddie, and kept his voice forceful and clear as he challenged him. "You must be worried, because all I wanted to do was pray for you."

Trying to save face in front of his friend, Freddie shouted, "I'm not worried. You can pray as much as you fuckin' like."

Still with no ideas, Gavin pushed further. "Do either of you smoke?"

"Yeah, we both smoke."

"Well, believe it or not, I'm in the position to offer you guys a deal."

In a sing-song reply, the fat man said, “Oh, I don’t think so, ‘cause we already took the cash out of your pocket, if that’s it. And how come a priest is carryin’ fifteen hundred in cash, eh? Take care of the pot for the poor, did ya, father? But if ya got something else, let’s hear it.”

Gavin started to feel some hope, now that they were both hanging on his every word. “If you have orders to kill me and you’re not doing it from your own nature, I can lift the blight by offering the Prayer of Exculpation. This will ask forgiveness for you and place the Edict of Blight on the man, or men, who gave the orders. This was common in the concentration camps during the war. It’s also called the Nuremburg Defense.”

Freddie, the skinny man, moved a little closer to ask, “What does this ‘ex-culp-i-mantion’ mean?”

“It means absolution, or to be free of.”

“What kind of deal does that take?”

Gavin felt excitement as they started to take the bait. “I want two things only. One, to kneel unbound before my maker when I pray. The second thing is to have a cigarette. I know you will think that I’m weak and will laugh at me, but I gave up smoking about two years ago, and not a day has passed when I didn’t want one.”

The fat, hairy man looked a little easier and turned to Freddie. “What the fuck? Where’s he goin’ out here? Go ahead, cut him loose.”

Trying to dispel any suspicion or threat, Gavin said, “My only hope is that my arms still work enough to get the cigarette to my mouth.”

The fat man pushed Gavin on his side and pulled his knife upwards to cut the bindings.

Once Gavin was cut loose, he took his time to rise into a sitting position, and while he was checking for broken bones, he also noted that because of the thick fog, the boat was traveling at only three or four knots.

From his new sitting position, Gavin purposely spoke in sad tones, "Okay, guys, let's get this over with. Where's the cigarette?"

Gavin rose to sit on the transom as the fat man lit his cigarette. They both watched him as he took his first couple of puffs, and then laughed as he started to cough. Gavin continued to exaggerate his coughing fit as he worked his way directly in front of the open cabin door. Satisfied he could do it, he didn't think twice as he flicked the cigarette into the gasoline-soaked cabin and flipped backwards into the welcome sea.

Both men screamed at each other and leaned over the stern, trying to grab him. Gavin let himself sink as he saw the first flash of light from the cabin, and half a second later, the entire top of the boat exploded. Gavin surfaced in time to see the flaming shell disappear into the fog. The boat hadn't changed course, so Gavin was sure that if he turned and faced the opposite direction, he would be headed for land.

Everything was quiet, and the water was warm. Gavin felt on top of the world as he enthusiastically started to swim. He didn't think his journey would be more than four or five miles, as the boat had been going so slowly. That was nothing for him; it wasn't long ago that he had trained by swimming up to eight miles.

During the swim, Gavin had never felt so in touch with life. The water was like velvet, and he felt glorified in its familiarity. His thoughts returned to the two men he had just killed, and he realized that he felt no shame. Self-preservation was king, and he certainly didn't feel like a sad, guilty priest. To the contrary, as the proud victor, his spirits were high.

An hour later, he swam over a rope from a mooring. This meant that he was close to a harbor. He switched to breaststroke to take his time, and soon he was swimming between boats, swinging gently on their moorings. He could see a jetty and knew he was close to land. The fog dispersed at the shoreline, and he could clearly make out the slope of a boat ramp directly in front of him. It was colder out of the water, but he forced himself to sit and fix his clothing. He tipped the water out of his shoes and tucked his shirt into his trousers, trying to look halfway normal, since he would have to ask directions.

Apart from the one streetlight at the entrance, no light was on in any building. Starting to shake with exhaustion, Gavin sat down under the light. *It must be the effects of the drug*, he thought, *certainly not the swim.* He had almost dropped off to sleep when he heard a car. The lights appeared out of the fog, and Gavin stood aside, attempting to wave the car down.

The car increased speed at the sight of him staggering into the road, waving his hands. Gavin was still a little unsteady on his feet and just stood there watching the tail lights disappear into the fog. Strangely, though the fog was thick, Gavin could taste the dust that the car threw off as it sped away. The taste of dust made him realize how thirsty he was, and he instantly craved water. He had to have water.

Leaving the side of the road, he walked around the building, looking for a tap. Having no luck, he went over to the boat ramp and was happy to find a working hose. He let the water run into his hands and then drank from his palms. He sucked in the running water with such relish that he didn't think he could get enough. Finally, not able to drink another drop, he washed his face and ran his wet hands through his hair onto the back of his neck.

Feeling refreshed, but not very strong, he went back to stand under the light. Wondering what time it was, he checked his wrist for the time, but his watch was gone. Quickly he tapped all his pockets, then remembered that the boatmen had already claimed his money. That meant his watch and wallet, too. He had absolutely no sense of the time, so he sat down against the pole and waited.

Chapter 25

Jim Holly didn't expect to be personally met by Detective O'Connor himself, so he was surprised to see his big frame sitting in the back of the squad car.

Jim held out his hand and greeted O'Connor. "Hi. Jim Holly."

"Get in. There might be some things that escape us, but let me tell ya, we know the name of the guy when we go to the trouble to meet him at the airport. So I know who you are, and I know something else – the CIA don't want you here!"

"So they've contacted you already. Did you come to pick me up for my own good, as we say?"

O'Connor let out a deep sigh. "No, I haven't, but we would both be better off if I did. Let's say, I made it impossible for the CIA creeps to get a message to me. Someone told me that if they got the message to me, it would be, 'Stay clear of the admiral, and at all costs, keep the New York detective off the case.'"

Jim absorbed this surprising news. "And you're such a good guy, you wanted to warn me?"

"Not really."

"Then why aren't you taking me in?"

O'Connor didn't face Jim as he answered in a quiet voice, "Because no goddamn CIA dickhead tells me what to do in my sand pit. Plus, I met this Father Abernathy, and I think he's a good man. His brother showed a lot of guts, too. So why don't you fill me in, and then I can tell you what's what."

Jim started reporting from the time he had taken the brothers to the morgue to identify Peggy Abernathy. O'Connor was most impressed with the number of men they had taken on in the fight. Finally, he described the CIA briefing, where he had found out why the photos were worth killing for. "The CIA didn't care that Gavin would probably lose his life," he said. "And the chief told me he would 'break me like a twig' if I got involved. I believe he will, so I strongly suggest you don't get involved."

"Thanks, but how can I not get involved when I come across a murdering spy, and I haven't received word not to proceed?" He leaned over to the driver. "Sergeant, turn that radio off. It's obviously not working."

"Yes, sir."

O'Connor continued, "Do you think he's gone after the admiral?"

"I know he has. A family friend is now with Ian, and Gavin spoke to her and told her what to do if he didn't come back. She's frantic and says Gavin isn't scared of anything, not even getting himself killed."

O'Connor dropped the act. "When did she last hear from him?"

"At about eight last night."

"When did you meet with the CIA?"

"About three hours ago."

"The admiral has a pad in Georgetown, but he's not there, according to my men who are watching the place. He wouldn't be anywhere near the Pentagon. He has a villa thirty-five miles from here, so I think that would be our best bet."

As O'Connor gave the sergeant instructions, he noticed Jim looking behind them. "That's my car, with four plain-clothes men," he explained. "Their instructions are to follow us."

Jim couldn't get over how prepared and willing O'Connor was to help him like this.

Jim tried to thank the detective. "I want to tell you, you've blown me away with your cooperation. What's your first name? I can't keep calling you O'Connor."

"Stanley Albert, but if you want that cooperation you talk about, you'll forget the Stanley and the Albert, and call me Stan."

Jim smiled. For the next half hour, they rode in silence.

O'Connor didn't appear to be paying any attention, but he suddenly gave the driver directions. "Take the next right for about a mile, and then turn left and pull over."

A few minutes later, the cars pulled to a stop on what looked to Jim like a deserted country road.

"Sergeant, I don't want you to use the radio," O'Connor instructed, "so go back and tell the others that when we get out of the car. I want them to go around the back of the house and be ready to stop anyone making a getaway. These guys will have guns, so be smart cops, okay?" He turned to Jim. "Not much further now."

O'Connor was waiting for Jim's question. "Stan, how come you know this place? Do you know the admiral?"

"Never met him, but not because I didn't try. A year ago, a young girl was found dead out in the bay, badly beaten and raped. One of his staff had been seen with her, and a day or two later, he was found dead. Questioned all his staff, but couldn't get near him, which made me wonder at the time.

"Okay, Sergeant, pull up short of the house, and we'll wait and watch for a while."

~~~

Back under the streetlight at the boat dock, Gavin was thinking of finding a place to sleep for the night when he heard another car coming, this time from the other direction. He figured it didn't matter
~~~

which direction it was heading, since he had no idea where he was.

This time, he stood in the middle of the road with his arms above his head. Without any drama, the car pulled up short, and the driver got out before Gavin could get free of the strong headlights.

He heard a kind, natural voice say, "Hello, what's the trouble? Are you okay?"

As Gavin's eyes adjusted, he saw that the voice belonged to a young black man dressed in a uniform.

Gavin returned the greeting. "I'm fine, thanks, though I had a mishap with the dinghy." Noting the uniform, he asked, "Are you a policeman?"

The man laughed. "No, man, I'm a chauffeur. Can I give you a lift?"

Thinking that he might be in a small village, Gavin responded, "Yeah, that would be great." Do you know the admiral's place?"

"Sure, everybody around here knows the admiral's villa."

"Do they like him, generally?"

"Nobody seems to mind him, but he has some ugly, rough staff. They've beaten up a few young guys around here. They have accents, Russian or something." He gestured to the front passenger seat. "Get in. I'll drop you off."

"That would be great, but I have a problem. I just started as a cook, and I was meant to be there hours ago. I just want to sneak in unseen, if I can."

The man shrugged. "No problem. I'll do what the kids do on Saturday night when they want to piss them off. They drive up under the entrance, stop, blow the horn, and then peel rubber out of there. While I do that, you go in the back door. I did it lots of times myself, especially after the night the big guy beat up my friend's brother. Shit, we were only sixteen or seventeen, and he was thirty at the time. I'll drop you at the back gate."

A half-mile later, the limo pulled over. The driver wished Gavin luck and drove off slowly. Gavin was at the side of another driveway and couldn't see the house. There were no lights, so he stayed in the approximate center of the sealed service entrance. After three hundred yards, he came to a bend revealing the garages and the back of the villa. The rooms above the garage were ablaze with lights, but there was only a shadow of a light in the back of the house. Gavin crept up to the back porch and waited to see if he had been detected. Satisfied, he opened the door from a crouched position and slipped inside.

He was in a large commercial kitchen, with rows of pots and pans hanging over an enormous stove in the middle of the room. Still crouching, he made his way to the far door, thinking that it was a two-way swinging door. He was right. He slipped into the next room just as a loud horn blew three times, followed by the screeching of rubber.

~~~

Seeing the limo peel out of the driveway, O'Connor broke radio silence and instructed the back-up car to intercept and question the driver. He and Jim Holly sat in silence as they waited for the car to report in. Within minutes, the speakers crackled, and the detective's voice came over loud and clear.

"Chief, the driver was alone, and he claims to have picked up a cook from the villa. The guy was very late and wanted to get in the back way, so the driver said he would pull in the front, as a cover, by driving through."

"Okay, okay." O'Connor made no effort to hide his impatience and didn't let the detective finish. "Ask for a description of this cook?"

The limo driver could hear the request and answered directly into the mike. "He was under six feet, blond and sunburned, pretty fit looking, and he had an accent – English, I think?"
~~~

Jim Holly stated the obvious: “That’s him, all right.”

O’Connor looked at him. “No kidding. Are you sure you don’t need a photo?” He ordered the detective to let the guy go and get back into position behind the villa. “Orders are to stop and detain anyone found on the premises. We will go in by the front door five minutes from now.”

~~~

Inside the villa, the admiral didn’t bother to get up at the sound of the car but flicked a switch and barked an order into the intercom: “Come now.”

Gavin made his way out of the dining room and into the large foyer, which was dimly lit by two table lamps. Still in a crouching walk, he was making his way slowly to the office door when the overhead lights went on. A man rushed past him and stood guard at the front door. Gavin turned and saw another man behind him. Speaking to each other in Russian, both pointed revolvers at him. Helpless, Gavin stood rooted to the spot.

The man by the door reached over and opened the study, while the other armed man waved his revolver, indicating that Gavin should go into the study.

The admiral looked up and stared at Gavin with surprise when he saw him standing between the two bodyguards.

He folded his hands on the desk in front of him and said, “Well, Father Abernathy, it seems your god protected you for another day, but I assure you, the one day was all he had in mind.” He waved his hand and ordered, “Take him away.”

The men turned Gavin and prodded him to start walking.

After three steps, the admiral seemed to change his mind and yelled, “Stop.” He walked from behind his desk and faced Gavin. “What did you do to my men? Did you bribe them? I want to know.”
~~~

Gavin knew he had to do something, but the two men were so close to him, he didn't think he could get a punch off. He tried to sound casual as he made up a story. "The skinny one, I think his name was Freddie, I ground his head into the fly wheel of the motor until his face was gone and his brains ran out all over the cabin floor."

Seeing the three men trying to fathom this, Gavin continued, "The fat, hairy one, I didn't get his name. I overpowered him and cut his right hand off, then stuffed it in his mouth and choked him to death . . . by his own hand, as it were."

No one spoke, but Gavin guessed that each was deciding whether to believe this story, from a priest, no less. Before anyone could speak, the doorbell sounded in one long, continuous, impatient ring.

All four men jumped at the foreign sound. The admiral pointed at one of the men. "Get rid of those damn kids."

Gavin was watching the face of the admiral and the remaining bodyguard, and as soon as their faces turned to the door, he exploded with as much intensity and power as he had ever mustered in his life. He swung his right elbow back and aimed at the bodyguard's face. The blow struck the man's throat, causing him to fall back. Swinging around, Gavin put full force behind his right hand and struck the admiral squarely on his left cheek. Before the admiral straightened up, Gavin knocked him to the floor with a left punch to the bridge of the nose.

The admiral screamed in pain.

The bodyguard reached around Gavin and got him in a stranglehold. Gavin dropped his chin, preventing the hold from being fatal, but he still couldn't move.

Seeing that Gavin was being securely held, the other guard opened the door, expecting to see kids, and was dazed to see a man bigger than himself standing at the threshold of the door.

O'Connor held his badge above his head and lowered it as the man looked at it. The bodyguard's eyes followed the detective's hand downward. When the man's face was level with O'Connor's, with amazing force and speed, he head-butted the man, catching him directly above his nose. He cried out as he slid to the floor, unconscious. Thick blood from the gash in his forehead began running over the highly polished brass step.

Gavin was held motionless by the huge bodyguard, but made a last-ditch effort by pushing the man against the wall. As he did so, he managed to grab the man's pant cuff. He pulled as hard as he could with the man's leg between his, letting his full weight land on the man's knee. There was a snap and a scream, but the man still didn't let go. His hold was like a steel clamp.

Jim Holly followed O'Conner into the room in time to see the admiral aiming a gun at Gavin.

"Goddamn, you fucking priest!" the admiral yelled as he fired two shots.

Realizing that the bullet would pass straight through Gavin, the bodyguard pulled Gavin down to floor level just as the first shot slammed into the plaster wall three inches left of Gavin's head. The second shot was a little closer, but it was then that the admiral saw O'Connor and Jim for the first time. Jim warned O'Connor as the admiral swung the gun around and fired two more shots. One hit O'Connor, and his painful yell distracted the admiral long enough for Jim to squeeze to off two shots. Both struck the admiral in the chest, causing his gun to fly across the room as he threw out his hands and fell face down on the desk.

Jim ran to check on O'Connor, who was in enough pain and shock to accept help from Jim. Gavin and the bodyguard were still entwined, but neither was exerting pressure, as the events of the last thirty seconds had taken the wind out of both of them.

Once O'Connor was sitting up, Jim came to Gavin and put handcuffs on the bodyguard.

"I don't think they're necessary," Gavin gloated. "I definitely broke his leg."

He looked at Gavin with a smile. "Toughest fuckin' priest I ever met."

Gavin laughed grimly. "That's the second time in the last minute I've been called a fuckin' priest. Do you think I should get a new job?"

Before Jim could answer, O'Connor yelled and pointed at the admiral, "He has something in his hand!"

Jim was the closest, but he was not close enough to stop the admiral from taking the pill. Seconds later, he fell to the floor.

"There goes your pension, Jim," O'Connor said matter-of-factly.

Jim nodded. "Yes, Stanley, I think that last little pill will do it. Still, I think he would have killed all of us if he had the chance, so I had no option."

O'Connor was able to walk, but protocol called for him to travel to the hospital in an ambulance. He passed the CIA and the FBI agents as he left, knowing it would be hours before Jim and Gavin could leave the scene.

He was right. Five hours later, on the way back to Washington, Jim explained why the pictures had meant so much to the admiral. Gavin couldn't believe that Peggy and Ian had been shot because of Peggy's innocent picture-taking.

"God, what were the chances of that happening? I can't believe it." Gavin closed his eyes, but let the silent tears run down his checks. "She was so proud of herself for inventing her picture-taking method. She spoke of it often." The memory of Peggy joking and bragging about her picture system was too much for Gavin. He wept openly.

Jim drove and said nothing, but he put a comforting hand on

Gavin's shoulder.

Back at the hotel, Gavin rang the hospital, only to learn that Ian's condition had not changed. He left a message for Lindsay, saying that he would meet her at the hospital at noon. It was three o'clock in the morning. At Gavin's insistence, Jim used the other bed in his room.

~~~

Despite having little sleep, both men went down to breakfast at eight o'clock. Jim searched the newspapers, but there was not a word regarding the admiral.

"Because of the CIA," Jim said, "I doubt you'll ever see any mention of the admiral's death or his network."

"I suppose they have their reasons, but it seems like these agencies are always run by a few strong-willed guys with ideals which run too closely to their egos. O'Connor told me you're going to take some heat over this?"

"Let's just say that I won't be expecting any more promotions for a few years, but they can't fire me, which keeps my pension safe."

Gavin reached across the table with an open hand. "I certainly appreciate everything you've done, Jim."

Jim took Gavin's hand and looked him in the eye. "I don't want to say it was nothing, but on the other hand, I don't see how I could have done nothing. I think the only real good thing that came out of it is the fact that you're still alive."

Gavin smiled. "Both me and my inner voice agree that it beats the alternative. But I think a lot will become of our meeting."

"Good things, I hope." Jim stood up from the table and asked Gavin if he wanted a lift to hospital. Gavin declined, saying he had to make a visit to a friend first.

Out of the taxi window, from a block away, Gavin recognized Octavio contentedly sweeping the sidewalk outside his small white
~~~

church. He asked the driver to stop a block short of the church and wait for him.

Octavio, still wearing his well-worn Panama hat, was happily whistling while sweeping and didn't see Gavin approach until he was only a few feet away.

He stopped whistling as he looked up and recognized Gavin. "Gawin, my friend, you come back to see us. Thank you." He let the broom drop and gave Gavin a sincere hug of friendship that seemed so natural. "I hope time has made your argument with God more even for you."

Not answering right away, Gavin stood back, smiling at Octavio and taking joy in his contented demeanor. "No, Octavio, things haven't run smoothly since I saw you, but I have the feeling that nothing more can go wrong. Plus, I've also decided to end my fight with God."

Octavio raised his eyebrows as he spoke. "Ah, Gawin, this is good. You must be happy with God if you want things to go even."

"Well, I didn't say I was happy with him, but I have decided not to be a priest anymore."

Octavio nodded thoughtfully. "I think this is okay for you, and maybe timing is good. To be where you are and not sure where to be, makes everything very uneven. I think you have helped many people. So now, is good for your life."

Gavin put his hand on the priest's arm. "Thank you, Octavio. Your words are kind. I want to pray now, but I would like it a lot more if you could play music while I pray. Is this possible?"

"Gawin, this is more kind for me than possible. It would make me very happy."

Gavin knelt on the bare floor and looked up at the simple altar as Octavio's music drifted through the church from the back of the room. Gavin noticed that the gold-framed picture of Christ had been taken down.

Trying to finalize his feelings with God, he fumbled for words, and finally said, "I have been a priest for twelve years and have done my very best. Now I feel, and think that you feel, too, that it is time for me to leave that post. As I have said, I do have doubt, but that's not why I'm leaving the priesthood. If you ever wish to show me that my faith in you was justified, I'll always be on the lookout. Please watch over Peggy, who I know is at your side, and protect Ian. Thank you. Amen."

Gavin remained there, listening to Octavio's music, when he suddenly realized that a great burden had been lifted from him. The thought of freedom was something he had never considered not having. In spite of everything he had gone through, there were issues he still had to face, and he felt twenty years younger and eager to get on with it. This empowering feeling was completely new and exciting.

After Octavio had finished playing, they walked outside together. Gavin wanted to tell Octavio of his new zeal and feeling of freedom.

"Octavio, do you know I feel freer than I think I have ever felt in my life?"

The priest gazed out into the street. "This is not because you will be a priest no more. No, Gawin, this is because you deserve this way. I think so, and God must think so, too."

Gavin reached out and gave Octavio a warm embrace of true friendship. "I think we will be friends as long as we live."

"For this, I am very sure, and in time, I might not see your accent, Gawin."

Gavin laughed. "I must go now, but I will be in touch very soon." The taxi pulled up, and once he was inside, Gavin rolled the window down to say good-bye. "By the way," he said, "why did you take the gold picture of Christ down from the altar?"

Taking the question seriously, Octavio answered with a puzzled expression. “We have never had a gold picture, Gawin.”

Gavin could see that Octavio was in dead earnest. “I mean the picture of Jesus in the gold frame that hung on the altar wall.”

“Gavin, please, we are a poor church. I even know the number of not-broke chairs we have. Do you think I would not know about such a beautiful picture?”

They shook hands again, and the taxi rolled away. Gavin relived his prayers of anguish during his visit and how the picture of Christ had helped calm him. Without being aware of it, he had actually come back to pray to Christ’s picture, as this was his sign from God.

Alone in the back of the taxi, he spoke his thoughts out loud. “During all those years, when I acted with total conviction of your being, and influencing hundreds of lives, I asked for a sign, the smallest of signs, and you showed me nothing. Now that I have only myself to influence and I’m not in your service, you give me happiness and show me a sign. I thank you on both counts, but to say God works in strange ways is putting it mildly, that’s for bloody sure!”

When Gavin arrived at Ian’s bedside once more, he found Lindsay asleep in a chair next to the bed. As he gently woke her, she jumped out of the chair, wrapped her arms around him, and began to cry.

Chapter 26

A year after Ian had been shot, Lindsay and Gavin had taken him to the most famous doctors and hospitals in the world. His health was good, but he was still held deep in the coma, with no sign of change. There was no response from his nervous system. "Neurological electrical impulse disconnect" was the most feasible explanation the world's best specialists could offer.

Gavin spent as much time as he could at Naringa during that year. His resignation from the church had taken longer than he had planned, and he had taken a direct role in setting up the Foundation. The great news was that he was arriving at Naringa tomorrow afternoon and had a friend from the States with him.

In anticipation of seeing Gavin, Lindsay planned the first evening's dinner with great excitement. Phillipa and Max had just visited Ian and stayed over for three days. Unfortunately, because of the annual roundup, there was no way Max could spend more time away from his station, so there would be only three for dinner.

Lindsay yearned to see Gavin again, for he had become her soul mate. She loved him so much but understood that because of his loyalty to Ian, and the slim chance that he would recover, Gavin would never return her love. She was certain that if she shared Ian's secret with him, she risked losing his respect. Lindsay had convinced herself that Ian was too ashamed to revive because of his secret, and after fighting it for years, he now felt relief. Ian had been a sensitive soul in a rough man's world, forever blinded to his own success and faced with his own deceit.

So many times she sat in the darkness next to Ian's lifeless body, assuring him that he was more of a man than anyone she had ever met, and that he had nothing to hide. Over and over, she promised that their secret would never be revealed. Even at the cost of losing Gavin, she would never divulge Ian's secret.

Gavin treated Lindsay with such a loving attitude, yet she had no idea if he shared any of the same feelings for her. His strength of character would never allow the slightest innuendo. Gavin was a dedicated man, and loyalty ranked highest on his character scale.

Lindsay had hired a full-time nurse for Ian, but she still spent hours at his side, reading to him and playing music. Most afternoons, she would have Ian's bed brought out to the blue gum trees, where she spoke to Ian as though he could hear her. She realized that she might sound a little mad talking to herself, but she was willing to take the chance on the belief that Ian was aware but unable to speak for himself. The books she read on the subject reassured her that it wasn't just wishful thinking, and that there was better than a fifty-percent chance that a person could hear while in a coma. Though the doctors had tried everything from electric shock treatment to acupuncture, Lindsay believed that his care was in her hands, and she would do as much as possible.

The week before, remembering the bond shared between Ian and Radium, she had called the manager to find out what had become of Radium.

George Munck, the station manager, was a short man with bulging muscles and a booming voice that sounded too large for his frame. He was a tough man and performed his job well, according to Gavin. He had dark, slicked-back hair, and Lindsay couldn't get over the fact that he used oil in his hair. It always looked neatly combed, but she imagined that it must feel like concrete when mixed with the dry dust of the outback.

Lindsay was sitting beside Ian's bed, under the blue gums, as

George Munck approached.

Taking off his hat, he greeted Lindsay. "I was told you wanted to see me, Miss Lindsay."

"Yes, thank you for stopping by. You may have questioned my efforts to revive Ian, as I know others around here have, but I believe that as long as he is breathing, there's a chance we could still make contact with him. I know there must be something."

George cut in. "No, Miss Lindsay, I think you're courageous to have such faith, and I hope it is rewarded."

"Well, we will never know if we don't try. I have an idea that Ian would like to see his horse, Radium. Can you bring him over?"

George looked down and shuffled his feet. "Well, it's not quite that easy, ma'am. The horse has gone bush. No one could ride him, and because he was so wild, no one could get near him, so he was turned out to the bush."

"Does that mean you don't know where he is?"

"No, a lot of the boys report seeing him. He hangs around the station horses. He's still their boss, you know."

"Can you bring him in?"

"Yes, ma'am . . . Well, I think so. It would take at least fifteen men to bring him in. That horse is the cleverest animal I have ever come across. Certainly makes a great sire."

"Gavin is arriving tomorrow. Would it make it easier for you if I made my request through him?"

George smiled sincerely. "You know I'll do anything for you, Miss Lindsay. But that would make it easier, as it could take fifteen to twenty men to bring Radium back in his home paddock."

"I understand, George, and I appreciate your frankness."

As she watched George walk away, she wondered why he would apologize at having to get Gavin's okay. After all, she was only looking after Ian, and had no hand in the running the station. This reminded her that she had done little else than care for Ian for the last year. She hadn't given any thought to her own reliance, as Naringa had virtually taken over her life. Suddenly, the dreadful thought of life without Ian and Naringa scared her.

What will I do, she thought, *go back to Sydney and get a secretarial job, or go back to New York and be with my parents? What am I thinking? I have no intention of staying at Naringa for the rest of my life, and I'm not going to marry Ian, even if he gets well.* Then a new strange thought occurred to her. *Whatever is in store for me, I will look forward to the challenge.*

Thinking back to the girl who couldn't face her father, that girl now seemed like a character in a fictionalized book. Lindsay realized that she was no longer that weak-minded girl who let people walk over her. She felt like a woman, and her childish fears had vanished. Being involved with life-and-death issues had given new meaning to everything she saw and touched. Her success on the rescue team had created such strong confidence that she was sure she would never doubt herself again. Gavin's support, and her total inclusion on all matters of the station, had contributed to her confidence. It was her strong conviction that her opinions mattered. She believed that if Ian died, and she lost Gavin because of a promise made to a man who would never know would be extremely unfair. On the other hand, her silence would surely confirm to herself that she could be the strong principled women she wanted to be.

Constant circling thoughts confused her. She was frequently horrified by the thought of losing Gavin if Ian died. When these thoughts came and went, she assured herself that it was perfectly normal for the mind to race around in circles. These thoughts were meaningless, and she knew she would do anything to have Ian alive and well again.

For some reason, the image of Radium popped into her mind.

She wondered why she had forgotten him over the past year. She understood that Radium had a special understanding of people, especially Ian. She reflected back to the first time she had tried to touch the horse when she was only an arm's length away. What were the chances of retrieving him now as he ran freely in the outback? The thought of Radium brought back all the wonderful horse stories that Ian had told with such passion.

Who knows, maybe that strange bond between animal and human will bring Ian out of his coma or create a spark of change. Stranger things have happened, she told herself.

~~~

Gavin realized he was nervous as he walked around the Sydney airport, waiting with great anticipation to meet his friend Octavio. He hadn't seen Octavio since the day he had ridden off in a cab nearly a year ago. Gavin and Octavio had only corresponded twice during the year, but Gavin had a special feeling for this happy, charismatic man. He thought about the short time he had known Octavio. *It's really amazing what I intend to do for a man I've only met twice in my life. I could be wrong, but just the thought of it makes me feel really happy.*

He made his way down to the customs hall, where all the passengers would enter the airport through two large, shiny metal doors. Gavin wasn't the only excited one in the crowd. Many people waited there with children for parents and grandparents. Screams of joy rang out when loved ones appeared behind carts stacked with cases and packages. Gavin couldn't believe his own excitement as he strained forward, searching the line of arrivals for his friend.

Then, in the midst of the crowd, Gavin saw the old familiar Panama hat. Octavio, carrying his guitar case, moved more slowly than the mainstream of passengers, and kept looking behind him. Gavin moved to the front of the crowd and waited for Octavio to see him.
~~~

They hugged with great enthusiasm as they shared the pleasure of seeing each other again. Once in the car, Octavio sat up straight and addressed Gavin in a formal manner, convincing Gavin that he had practiced the speech that was about to come.

"Gawin, I am a man, not a boy, and I come across the world for some why that I do not know. Only a boy would do this thing with not knowing the why. So, I must now ask you the why."

Feeling empathy for his serious friend, Gavin tried to answer the question without telling him why. "Octavio, you have a very good point of view in your statement, but you will have to have a little more patience and trust for me, your friend. I am sure you will be pleased."

"No answer yet is okay for trust, but I would like to sleep for the nighttime again."

Gavin laughed. "All right, I will make you a promise. After tomorrow night's dinner at Naringa, you will sleep like a baby for the rest of your life."

"Gawin, this talk is very good, so why we have to catch another aircraft to farm? Why not tell me this here?"

Gavin almost laughed out loud at Octavio's simple charm and boyish nature. "If I could tell you now, Octavio, I would, but there is something I must have before I can tell you."

Octavio let out a large, exaggerated sigh and remained silent as they drove through the Sydney suburbs on the way to Gavin's new house in the city. The plane for Naringa didn't leave until 7:00 the next morning.

~~~

The plane circled the homestead with one wing almost vertical. Lindsay was excited to see Gavin and to meet Octavio, whom Gavin had described as the most grounded man he had ever met. Oh, how she loved the purring sound of the single-engine plane. To her, it meant excitement
~~~

and adventure.

She could see Gavin's excited expression as he pointed to her through the plane's tiny window. As the plane pulled to a stop and she waited for the two men to reach her, it was all she could do to stop herself from running and throwing her arms around Gavin.

Gavin hugged Lindsay before he introduced Octavio. The hug couldn't have lasted more than twenty seconds, but it was long enough for Lindsay to be excited by his manly smell of fresh perspiration and the taste of salt on his skin. *God, how I love this man*, she thought.

The sound of his smooth, enthusiastic voice jolted her back to the moment. "Lindsay, at last I can introduce you to my good friend, Octavio. Octavio, this is the lovely Miss Lindsay Graeme, coming from New York to become a prominent figure in Australian folklore."

Octavio put down his guitar case and lightly clapped his hands in appreciation.

In a fun-filled voice, Lindsay said, "Gavin, stop that. You're making fun of me. Octavio, I am very pleased to meet you, after all the good things Gavin has said about you. Welcome to Naringa."

In a formal gesture, Octavio took Lindsay's right hand and kissed it. "Yes, I am Octavio, and I am at your servicing, Lindsay."

Lindsay blushed. "Thank you, Octavio."

Gavin laughed and put his arms around them both. "Very nice English, Octavio, but I think the word is 'service,' not 'servicing.'"

Octavio didn't seem to notice the difference, but laughed heartily with Gavin and Lindsay as they got into the truck and headed to the homestead.

Because of the dust and the noise of the big truck, no one spoke until they pulled up in the driveway.

Octavio was the first to speak. "What a beautiful house. No one to think of such a beautiful building out here in the desert."

Gavin laughed. "Easy with the desert stuff. We do grow cattle and things out here, you know. But I know what you mean. I suppose I forget what a sight it must be, seeing it for the first time."

"I will never forget," Lindsay remarked. She remembered driving with Ian in his ute. Love was in the air for them both, and Ian was laughing as he proudly pulled the ute to a stop the moment the homestead came into full view. She still remembered his exact words: *I bet ya a quid you'll never forget this sight as long as you live.*

That love is still there, she thought. *But it's a new love, a secret love that Gavin must never know.*

Gavin looked at his watch. "Lindsay, could you show Octavio to his room? Dinner is at eight, and could you please dress for dinner, as I have a very special evening in store for both of you."

Octavio only understood half of Gavin's authoritative request. "I am very happy, but I have no understanding to be dressing. I always wear clothes."

Gavin took Octavo's arm. "Don't worry, old boy, I brought a suit for you, and I'll be over to help you. Tonight has to be just right, and your suit was one of the smallest items on the list."

Most of this went over Octavio's head, but he nodded in delighted acceptance.

Lindsay's curiosity was now getting the best of her. "What are all these surprises, Gavin?"

Gavin turned back to her with a boyish grin. "You'll find out. Now take me to Ian. Oh, by the way, I was talking to George yesterday, and he told me of your request to bring Ian's horse to him. I don't understand why, but I told them to go out and get him first thing this morning, so he should be here tomorrow."

~~~

Lindsay knew Gavin had given George instructions to bring
~~~

Radium in, as she had heard George giving instructions to the ringers. "Tomorrow morning, fifteen of us will ride out and see if we can get this bloody horse into the home paddocks. You all know this damn horse can outsmart us all, so there's no need to try and crowd him. We'll bring in a mob of station horses, and I'm sure he'll follow."

One of the men spoke up. "Yeah, there's sure to be a mare in season, and you know old Radium doesn't miss out. Not like all you jokers at home." The crowd laughed until George spoke again.

"Yeah, that's one thing, and the other is that Radium knows he can jump any fence on the station. He has no fear of us, I assure you. During my forty years with horses, he's the smartest damn horse by far that I've ever come across."

"You sound like you despise the horse," said one of the riders.

George gave a quick laugh. "Maybe 'despise' is too strong, but I don't like it when a horse is smarter than me, and certainly a lot smarter than you bunch of crazy buggers." The men all laughed.

George gave the orders. "Here's the plan. Tomorrow at seven a.m., we'll bring in the station mob. We won't bunch them or hurry them. I'm sure Radium will be there, but no man is to single him out. We'll try it like that, and if that doesn't work, I haven't got a bloody clue what to do next. Okay, at the gate at seven a.m."

~~~

Back at the homestead, Gavin sat by Ian's bed and looked around at the huge amount of medical equipment that made this part of the house look more like a hospital. Lindsay had left the room so Gavin could spend time alone with Ian. Though Ian hadn't changed since the last time he had seen him, Gavin couldn't get over the look of peace and contentment on his face.

"Why do you look that happy, mate?" Gavin asked. "It makes me think you don't want to come back. Of course, I'll never believe that,
~~~

and I still pray for your return. Ha, you might say! Leaving the church and still praying. Well, I still believe, but I think I've done as much for the church as my abilities allow.

"Listen, Ian, I have a plan for us. I think we could all be far more productive if we were to work together on the trust. Together means the three of us . . . you, me, and Lindsay. This would help another possibility that has been worrying me. You know, Lindsay has been here over a year without a break, and what would happen if she wanted to move on with her life? I can't imagine her not being with us. So anyway, I have a plan that I'll put in place for you tonight. If she agrees, she'll be here for you when you decide to wake up." Gavin's speech halted as he wiped a lone tear from his cheek. He suddenly felt tired and weak.

After a short silence, he continued, "Anyway, mate, you won't be alone, I promise you, but you must come back. Lindsay tells me she has had the nurse take you outside in the late afternoons, so tomorrow we'll have a picnic, and there's a friend of mine here I want you to meet. Sounds good, doesn't it? So look, Ian, just shrug this thing off and be with us, please."

Gavin closed his eyes in an effort to stop the tears.

Chapter 27

Gavin was already in the dining room when Lindsay entered to check the table setting and light the candles.

Making an effort to sound casual, Gavin said, “Miss Graeme, you look absolutely stunning.”

“And you, sir, should wear formal dinner attire at every occasion. It makes one think that your good looks have been taken for granted, as you look very handsome.”

Gavin took one step towards Lindsay, then halted and awkwardly changed the subject. “Did you hear that they managed to corral Radium?”

“No, was he very difficult?”

“Not according to George Munck. George is convinced that the darn horse wanted to come back to the station. George was very pleased, since there isn’t a ringer on the station who can get close to the wretched horse. Maybe being in the home paddock overnight will calm him down.”

Lindsay didn’t want to reveal her plan as she thought back on the things Ian had said about Radium. “No, Gavin, I don’t think Radium is upset or wild. I think the horse can think for himself and can control his effect on those around him. Ian thought so, anyway. Once, he told me to touch Radium’s head when I was standing within arm’s reach. He didn’t seem to move, but there was no way I could touch him.”

Gavin chuckled. “Unlike Ian, I’m not really into horses, but that sounds a little far-fetched to me. I bet it was just a trick Ian had taught him. God knows, he used to spend hours with that horse.” He walked over and took Lindsay’s arm. “Come on. We had better find Octavio and see how he looks in a tuxedo."

Drinks had been set out on the porch, and Octavio stood at the railing, looking out to the blue gums. At the sight of him, Gavin and Lindsay stopped in their tracks. Octavio had put oil in his hair and had it combed straight back, making him look sophisticated. He wore the tuxedo as though he wore one every night. His attire had not only changed his looks, but also his demeanor. Lindsay thought he looked and moved like a movie star.

Even his voice was deeper and richer as he greeted them. "Ah, my friend and beautiful hostess, good evening."

"Well, my dear Octavio, you look so glamorous," Lindsay gushed. "I hope you don't find us kindly old farm folk too dull for you."

"I'm not understanding all, but I say it is good, too, to be here with you and Gawin."

There was something else beside the clothes; he was a different person.

"How come you look so different?" Gavin asked.

"Ha ha, you forget, Gawin, I told you I was a music entertainer for all my life before America."

"That's right. You told me that you earned money for the church from your guitar, right?"

"That is the right. I will play for you after dinner maybe."

Gavin noticed that Octavio did not drink anything alcoholic and assumed that he had addressed drinking sometime in his life. This was to be one of the biggest nights of Gavin's life, and he didn't want to spoil it by drinking too much, either.

The dinner table was set for four, which both Lindsay and Octavio noticed. Both had been told of a surprise and thought that the missing person must appear. But all through dinner, nothing happened, and Gavin made no mention of what he had up his sleeve. Then, during dessert and coffee, Gavin told the wait-staff that their tasks were over for the evening and he didn't want to be interrupted. The business-like tone of his orders made Lindsay and Octavio sit up with some apprehension.

Gavin tapped his glass for attention, in spite of the fact that both Lindsay and Octavio were looking straight at him already.

He began, "I have looked forward to this night with such yearning because I know that your decisions tonight will affect millions of people. Octavio, when I saw how splendid you looked tonight, and you reminded me of your professional musical background, I realized that I didn't know very much about you. Then it occurred to me that you probably knew less about me. So, based on simple trust in me, you have traveled halfway around the world. For this, I thank you with all my heart.

"Now I will tell you my history. Several years ago, my father made a big mineral discovery, which was worth millions of dollars. Little changed in our family until both my mother and father were killed in a mining accident, and after their departure, the Abernathy Trust was formed."

Octavio blessed himself at the mention of the deaths.

"This was seven years ago, and with the royalties and interest, the trust has grown despite our charitable contributions." Gavin paused and asked Octavio if he understood.

Octavio nodded. "Yes, I know what interesting is, and it must be a big for so much money. What involve is this for me?"

Smiling, Gavin answered, "How does this involve you? A good question, because I now want to tell you, as I promised you, so you may sleep again.

"Octavio, from this trust, I want to donate four million English pounds to your church. This money will be spent totally at your discretion, though accounting for the spent funds must be submitted to the trust."

Lindsay sat spellbound as Gavin leaned back in his chair, enjoying the moment.

After a long silence, Octavio finally addressed Gavin. "Gawin, am I right that you give this four million pounds to my church?"

"Yes, my friend. The money is for you to build your church."

Octavio sat perfectly still, seeming bewildered. "Is that all? I mean, is it okay already?"

Knowing that question would come, Gavin got up from his chair and shook Octavio's hand. "No, that is not all." Gavin let the silence fill the room, and then he added with a huge smile, "Because you will probably enter a building program, there will be another million a year for five years made available to the church."

Octavio closed his eyes and thought of all his church members and the rows of unmatched wooden chairs and the makeshift altar. The delaminated plywood front door had been repaired many times.

Openly crying, Octavio stood and addressed Gavin. "Gawin, this is too many for me. I have to sit and say no words. Thank you, thank you."

So great were Octavio's tears that Lindsay rose from her chair and stood behind him, comforting him by rubbing his shoulders.

Gavin refilled his brandy and addressed them once again. "If you would both bear with me, I would like to explain that there is a selfish side of this that I want you to understand."

They both remained silent. Lindsay had no idea what could happen further, and Octavio dreaded to hear Gavin's next words, as they surely must say that there was a mistake and his dream would be gone.

"I presented Octavio's case first, so that I could demonstrate to Lindsay what good can be done through the trust and just what power it represents. The Australian trust laws call for a directive of no fewer than three members, and presently I am one of only two trustees. Therefore, to confirm the grant to Octavio's church, I would need another trustee to agree."

Lindsay didn't understand what Gavin was proposing.

"If Miss Lindsay Graeme were to accept the position of trustee, Octavio's church loan would be confirmed. The position is for a term of five years and covers all expenses and a generous salary." Gavin stopped and looked at Lindsay's worried face. He had expected joy but saw only concern.

The room became still, and Lindsay's shocked silence was frightening.

A dreaded sense of alarm overtook Gavin. "Lindsay, have I been too clumsy? What I thought would be a pleasure seems to be the opposite. Please tell me I haven't upset you."

This was the first time Lindsay had ever seen fear on Gavin's face. But there was no need for fear. Lindsay was overjoyed by Gavin's belief in her, and the proposal was far greater than she could have ever imagined. Scared that she might not be able to control her passion if she were to give Gavin a thank-you kiss, she just sat in her chair and looked longingly at him before answering. "No, Gavin, you haven't said the wrong thing. It is just so wonderful to believe you want to include me in your plans that I feel totally overwhelmed with happiness. Thank you."

Looking relieved, Gavin went to Lindsay and solemnly took her hand. "Lindsay Graeme, thank you. You gave me a terrible turn there for a minute, but now you have made me happy and made it all worthwhile."

Turning to Octavio, he said, "Now, can we raise our glasses to our very special Miss Lindsay Graeme?" The two men raised their glasses and toasted Lindsay.

Gavin laughed and asked Octavio to play something happy.

Octavio struggled to speak. "Before I play for you, please let us drink to Gawin's mother and father."

Gavin gave the toast. "In memory of Ralph and Clair Abernathy. May they forever rest in peace. Hear, hear!"

Lindsay took a deep breath and said, "Gavin, I'm scared to ask you this, as you may have another unbelievable surprise for us, but who is our other dinner guest?"

"No big surprise. It is for our third partner, whom I have already appointed, and he has accepted. Octavio, you don't know him yet, but he lives in the States. Lindsay, you do know him. Can you guess who he is?"

Lindsay smiled triumphantly. "Yes, I can."

Gavin raised his eyebrows in surprise. "Who is it?"

"Detective Jim Holly."

"My God, just how did you know that?"

"You two bonded somehow, even before he made the decision to risk his life and career for you. There was something there, and you both knew it, didn't you?"

From that moment on, Gavin knew that Lindsay possessed a special sense that would make her a lady that should never be underestimated. He also knew he loved her more than life itself. This realization wasn't new to Gav. He had fought the desire when he was a priest and when Lindsay was Ian's love. How would he ever be able to act on this love without being a traitor to his brother's memory? If he did, he was sure that Lindsay would lose all respect for him for having disregarded Ian. First, the collar had been his barrier to the intimate love that he always secretly craved, and now the brother he loved had somehow made it impossible for him to announce his love for this woman.

They progressed to the porch, where Octavio played the guitar into the early-morning hours. Lindsay longed to be in Gavin's arms, but had no conviction or indication that he felt the same way. Even at her door, he displayed no desire and simply gave her a peck on the cheek as they said good night.

If Lindsay had known he loved her, she would have crumpled into his arms and cried out her love for him. Instead, she cried herself to sleep, not giving any thought to the huge fortune she would control for the rest of her life.

~~~

The next morning, at breakfast, Octavio jokingly accused Gavin of being the death of him. In anticipation, he had not slept well before coming here, and now that he knew why he had come, he couldn't sleep because Gavin's kindness was more generous than he could have expected.

Lindsay waited until both men were present before she revealed her plan for the day. "Gavin, you know, I've been taking Ian out under the blue gums, where I usually read to him. Well, today I want to try something else, and I hope you don't laugh when I tell what it is."

"I wouldn't laugh at anything," he assured her, "since anything could be the magic trigger. Who knows – it may be your magical guitar, Octavio."

Octavio nodded. "I wish this could be so."

"Well, after Ian has settled in," Lindsay continued, "I'm going to bring Radium to him and let him see his old friend."

Gavin's eyes went wide. "That bloody horse has gone wild. He might kill us all. Anyway, George said no one can get near him. Are you sure about this?"

Lindsay smiled at Gavin's fears. "I know that Radium is a gentleman and we will all be safe. I also know someone who can bring him over without any trouble. Radium will be there around two, after we have had our picnic lunch."
~~~

"Okay with me," Gavin exclaimed. "Anything is worth a chance. God moves in the strangest ways. You never know, Octavio. This may be the day that you will tell your congregation about for years to come."

Immediately after breakfast, Lindsay went with George Munck to the home paddock to see Radium. The horse showed little interest in his visitors and stayed in the middle of the small paddock. George told Lindsay that he had never seen a horse in such good shape after being out in the bush so long.

As if he had heard the compliment, Radium held his head high. His coat was brilliantly shiny and clean.

George was polite in his approach. "You know, Miss Lindsay, I don't think it's a good idea to let that horse in the enclosure with you and Ian. Radium is a big horse who knows no rules, and how am I going to get him there without a fight?"

Lindsay replied confidently, "First, Radium knows all the rules, and the person to bring him to the enclosure is Karo."

George laughed. "Karo, with that wild thing?"

"George, there are things I know, and I know that Radium will allow Karo to lead him. Please bring him over at about two-thirty."

"Okay, if you say so, but don't expect too many miracles." George left scratching his head, likely wondering what Lindsay could possibly know about the horse.

Ian's bed was wheeled out to the blue gums around twelve. Octavio played, and Lindsay read aloud. Gavin kept saying that Ian looked so happy, either he could hear them all, or he chose not to recover.

The enclosure under the gums was fenced to about a half-acre. The gum trees were at least 150 feet high and provided much-welcomed day-long shade. The heavy smell of eucalyptus leaves made the enclosure the nicest place to be in the heat of the day.

At around 2:15, George called from the gate, "Miss Lindsay, Karo is bringing the horse over now."

"Thank you, George. How did Karo get on?"

"I don't know how you knew that, Miss Lindsay, but the horse was like a lamb."

Before she could answer, Karo approached the gate supporting a huge, proud smile and leading Radium as though he did it every day.

Thanking Karo, she unclipped the lead from the halter and let Radium roam in the enclosure.

Returning to her reading, Lindsay paid no attention to Radium. It took Gavin and Octavio an hour to stop watching the horse over their shoulders. Even though Gavin rode well, Lindsay knew he felt no great affection for horses, and Octavio seemed just plain scared of them.

Lindsay explained that she intended to move away from Ian's bed so that Radium could come over and smell Ian as he lay there.

"What is it that you expect to happen?" asked Octavio.

Lindsay shook her head. "I have no idea. Sometimes man bonds with an animal, and things happen that can only be classified as spiritual. I have read about such things, and we will try anything."

Casually, they moved their chairs and the one table twenty-five yards from the bed and tried to look like they weren't watching.

Radium, as usual, seemed to be running the place and showed no interest in Ian or the bed. After an hour, however, the horse started to move slowly toward him. Standing only feet from the bed, the horse froze as he stared at Ian's still body. Then he took one step closer and smelled Ian from head to toe. There was no reaction from Ian or Radium, and after a few minutes, Radium turned away from the bed and went back to the center of the enclosure.

Gavin got to his feet. "It was a good try, Lindsay, but I don't think the horse got the idea."

Lindsay looked at Octavio. "What did you think, Octavio?"

"Spiritual things did not appear, but maybe they did. We don't always know."

Lindsay smiled. "Thank you. I think you just said that to make me feel better. I guess I was hoping for too much."

Gavin walked back to Ian's bed. "I can't tell you how many hours Ian spent talking to me about that horse, so I think your idea had a lot of merit. Perhaps you can play for us, Octavio?"

Octavio played until the nurse wheeled Ian back inside. Gavin told George to leave the horse in the enclosure with the gate open. "If the horse wants to leave forever, it's okay with me. I don't want the horse put in any danger, but I don't like the damn animal. Let him go."

George hesitated before answering. "I understand, sir. I bet he heads for the bush. It's like he has no use for any of us anymore, either."

~~~

Everybody turned in early that night. Lindsay's hopeful experiment had somehow made everyone very much aware that they were simply wishing for miracles, and that Ian's condition was not going to improve. Lindsay knew she was grasping at straws, but she still felt a great disappointment and was pleased to escape to her room.

During the night, she was awoken by the loud neighing of a horse. She went out on the veranda and could tell that Radium was still in the enclosure. Not bothering to put on a gown, she ran out to the enclosure to find Radium sniffing and pushing at Ian's day bed. Radium saw Lindsay approach but did not cease pushing at the bed. Lindsay was unsure, and even afraid, of how Radium would react to her.

Rather than approach the horse, she sat down in the same chair where she had watched him earlier in the day. He kept sniffing and pushing at the bed until he finally knocked it over. As the bed hit the ground, Radium bucked high on his hind legs and began to gallop around
~~~

the small enclosure. He paid no attention to Lindsay and kept galloping, his hooves throwing grass and sand into the air. After a few minutes, he slowed down and stopped in the middle of the circle he had created. With his head held low, he just stood there panting.

After some time, Lindsay's mind started to wander, and she paid no more attention to Radium. Suddenly, she felt his hot breath on her neck and jumped with fright. Radium in turn jumped away, startled by her sudden movement. As they stood three feet apart, studying each other, Lindsay realized that she felt no fear. She began talking to Radium in her most soothing voice.

"Hello, Radium. You must remember me. Ian always told me that you were a fine gentleman. It would make me very happy if you would accept me as a friend. It would make Ian very happy to know we trusted each other."

Without fear, and without raising her hands, she took a step closer and stood with her face alongside his handsome head. With his lips, he pulled at her hair. It was a playful move, not causing any pain.

She talked to him again. "So, you have a sense of humor, do you? I wonder if you understand that Ian has been badly hurt, and he may not be able to be your friend again."

Radium dropped his head and brushed against Lindsay. She was thrilled by his obvious offer of acceptance, and spent hours with him before returning to her bed.

~~~

The next morning, she was frightened that her time with Radium had all been a dream. She ran to the veranda, looking for him in the enclosure. Tears came to her eyes when she saw him lying under the gum trees. Her first reaction was to get dressed and run to the horse, but she decided to wait and not tell Gavin of her new friend. She knew Gavin had it in for Radium for some reason, and reasoned that maybe he was
~~~

jealous of Ian's love for the horse. *That's crazy*, she thought. But something had certainly turned Gavin against Radium.

At breakfast, they discussed their plans for Octavio's last day at Naringa. Gavin would take him around the homestead on horseback, and then ride to the windmills. The windmills were about two miles away, next to a small lake surrounded by native bush. They would be back to have lunch under the gums with Ian.

Radium was grazing as Lindsay went to Ian's bedside. She didn't go over to him, but spoke to him as she passed. Octavio and Gavin returned for lunch at 2:30.

Napping under the trees after a fine lunch, all three of them were awakened by a cool breeze that rattled the eucalyptus leaves for more than a minute. Gavin was the first to run to Ian's bedside.

"That was Ian passing through the leaves on his way to God," Gavin announced as tears ran from his eyes. "His days on this earth are no more."

Lindsay and Octavio approached the bedside to see for themselves. Lindsay felt tears flood her own eyes as she fell over Ian's body.

Octavio said a prayer and finished by saying, "It is God's will."

At that moment, Radium neighed, rose up on his back legs, and galloped out of the enclosure.

Chapter 28

Octavio delayed his departure and fulfilled Gavin's request by performing the funeral service. Due to the heat, the funeral and burial had to take place the next day. Since many of the Naringa men couldn't get back to the homestead in time, the service was short and very sad. Ian was laid to rest next to his sister Peggy.

Octavio left three days later, and on the same day, without word to Lindsay, Gavin took off on his own sabbatical.

At first, Lindsay was hurt by Gavin's flight, but then she remembered his withdrawal after the funeral of the men lost in the flood. Gavin had told George Munck that he was going to the Spectacles, two small lakes side by side about thirty-two miles away, in the heart of the desert.

The first two nights after Gavin left, Lindsay didn't sleep at all. She knew that if she were to tell Gavin of her love for him, she would have to do it now. When he returned from the lakes, he surely wouldn't stay at Naringa one day longer than he had to. How could she confess her love and expect him to feel free to accept it, if she didn't tell him that she and Ian never intended to marry? To reveal that, she would have to explain why, and if she revealed Ian's secret, he would think less of her for revealing it. Not to mention how he might feel about Lindsay shattering Ian's image. For the first time since she could remember, she fell to her knees and prayed, asking God and Ian to show her the way to reveal her love to Gavin.

~~~

On the third day, Lindsay was in the enclosure when Radium returned. Without hesitation, he walked up to Lindsay and offered his
~~~

head.

Lindsay reached up with both arms around his neck and felt herself wracked by sobs. She cried harder than she had at Ian's death. When she couldn't hang on to Radium's neck any longer, she fell to her knees, weeping into her lap. Radium remained by her side. When she finally got to her feet, the idea came to her.

"Oh, Radium, I have to go to Gavin," she said. "Will you take me? Am I crazy, or why else are you here? I'm not an experienced rider. Will you look after me?"

The horse didn't move, but Lindsay began to believe in him. "I'm going to leave the gate open. I want you to take me to Gavin tomorrow morning. If you're still here, I will be sure of your spirit, and if you are not, I'll know my grief is simply misleading me. I will go now, but I believe in you, my mighty waler. Can you believe how happy this would make Ian?"

Lindsay's next act was to call for Karo and give him orders not to tell anyone of her request. She asked him to bring her saddle and four water bottles, and put them on her veranda. Then, in case some extra harnesses were needed, she decided to tell him that she planned to saddle Radium. He left the room laughing to himself with the pride of carrying Lindsay's secret.

Lindsay didn't think her next step would be quite so easy to achieve. George Munck arrived at her sitting room door.

She asked George to sit and then began her rehearsed story. "I don't know if you have been informed of my ownership of Naringa and all the Abernathy holdings?"

"No, ma'am, I have not."

"Well, before Ian's death, I accepted fifty-percent ownership of the Abernathy holdings, and I'm telling you this because I want to force you to do something you may not think wise. But I assure you, it would not be wise for you to refuse me. Need I say more? In fact, your cooperation will result in a fine bonus."

"What is your request, ma'am?"

"Gavin is at the Spectacles, and I want to go there in the morning."

Pleased to have such an easy task, he answered, "That's no problem, ma'am. I will have two boys take you there tomorrow."

In the most resolute voice she could muster, she said, "No, George. For reasons known only to me, I must go alone. I will ride Radium."

George crossed his arms as he gazed at her anew. "Please, Miss Lindsay, this isn't possible on two counts. First, no one can mount Radium, and second, it's thirty-two miles to the lakes."

"Only one of these facts is actually true, and that is the distance. You see, I have been riding Radium, bareback, for some time."

He stared at her. "I find that a hard to believe."

Her sense of authority shocked her, for it came without effort. "George, help or don't help me, but calling me a liar will not advance your course in any event, I assure you."

"Miss Lindsay, you know I never meant to imply that. It was my belief that no one could get near that horse. What you're asking me makes me responsible for your safety."

"If you don't help me, I will still go, but not as well-prepared and not sure of the direction, and certainly more likely to fail. That makes you more responsible should I fail."

George thought for a moment, then said, "It seems I have no option but to help you, Miss Lindsay. I will get you a compass and a map, and I will pack some saddle bags with food and water."

Lindsay smiled with satisfaction. "I appreciate your help, George, and don't worry. Thirty-two miles for Radium in one day is hardly getting started."

"It's not Radium I'm worried about. Thirty miles is a long way."

Not wanting to hear of the obstacles, Lindsay ended the discussion. "Thank you for your concern, George. I will be leaving at first light. And, for both our sakes, I think it would be better if we kept this strictly between us."

Having made up her mind allowed Lindsay to fall into bed and sleep a full nine hours, making up for the sleep she had lost the previous night.

~~~

Lindsay awoke at four o'clock and prayed that Radium was there. Fully packed for the journey, she left her room at half-past. Before she saw Radium, she was startled to find George sitting on the steps of the veranda.

"Morning, Miss Lindsay."

All of Lindsay's alarm bells went off. She suspected that he would try to stop her somehow. "George, what are you doing here?"

"Perhaps there are things I don't know, but I do know how to saddle a horse for a long bush trek. I have come to saddle Radium, if you will bring him to me."

Not quite convinced that he didn't have some other motive, Lindsay went along with his request. Then she realized that this was a test, as she had never tried to make Radium do anything. Now, in front of this man who could stop her, she had to control Radium. A fleeting thought of doubt momentarily took away her faith.

She found Radium as expected. As she gauged his size and strength, her inner voice said she must be crazy. But when she walked toward him, that voice was silenced and replaced by the joy of being close to him. She spoke to him as she approached.

"Radium, I have lied about riding you. Please don't let George
~~~

see that. I have never asked you to do anything before, if you are Ian's spirit please help me now."

To her relief, Radium lowered his head and took several steps forward to greet her. She reached around his neck with both hands and whispered, "Thank you." Sliding a finger under the halter, she proudly walked to where George was standing with the saddle. Reaching the spot, she withdrew her hand from the halter and told Radium to stand. He stood still as a statue.

George seemed astounded, and even more so when Radium took the bit on the bridle. "It must have been two years since he's had the bit between his teeth," he remarked. The animal hardly moved as George tightened the girth for the second time.

Once Radium was saddled, George went over the map and handed Lindsay the two saddle bags. "This horse walks faster than any horse on the station, so in this heat, he had better be kept at a walk. Be safe, and keep your eyes open for brown snakes, which are nesting this time of year. Good luck, and Godspeed."

Lindsay thanked him, gathered the reigns, put her left foot in the stirrup, and mounted Radium for the first time. Unhurried, she settled herself and thanked the station manager. She had heard Ian command Radium a thousand times, and without having to think, she clicked her tongue and commanded him, "Move away."

Radium immediately fell into his long-striding walk. Soon, they were well away from the enclosure and out in the open space of the semi-desert.

George Munck stood watching from the veranda until they were out of sight. He was not a betting man, but he would have bet his house that this couldn't happen. Lindsay didn't know anything about horses and was only just passable as a rider. Neither did he believe in spiritual happenings, but he was sure he had just witnessed one right before his own eyes. He wouldn't mention it to anyone, as the entire station would know of Lindsay's ride soon enough.

~~~

It was not yet full light, and the air was cool, making thc first two hours of the ride the most exciting experience Lindsay had ever had. Her experience on the rescue team with Ian had taught her just how hard the next eight hours were going to be, but she knew that if she trusted Radium, she could make it.

As she thought of Ian, she thought of Radium, and she started to wonder why this had happened. How had she known that Radium would accept her? On the day of Ian's passing, Radium had run from the enclosure within minutes of Gavin saying that Ian had passed.

"How did you know at that moment, Radium?" she asked him. "Or did you really know? If it was a coincidence, why did you let me befriend you? Is it Ian's will that you let me ride to Gavin's love? Whatever it is, I wish to think that's it. Ian knows his secret is safe with me, and he wants me to be with Gavin because he loves us both. I love you, too, Ian."

The sun was now up, and the shimmering of the hot earth had already begun. The black flies were up and buzzing for the day. *Always these black flies*, she thought.

By midday, she was having trouble keeping her focus. The constant, overbearing heat was taking its toll, and she started to hallucinate. Each time she thought she may not make it, Ian and Jimmy Blake would appear and tell her that she could do this. She saw images of Jimmy with his wrists cut through to the bone, and Ian stood out front in the shimmering distance, waving her on.

She had only dismounted twice since leaving the homestead, and now she was waiting to come to Ryan's Creek. According to the map, the lakes were only five miles from the creek. If she could make it to the
~~~

creek, she knew she could make the rest with ease, especially since the air would be cooler. Hour after hour, she searched the ever-present horizon for a sign of the trees that would indicate water. This territory was over seventy miles east of the rescue area, and the land was much more hospitable. It couldn't be called lush, but Lindsay had passed two water holes, and there was far more ground cover. Throughout the trek, kangaroos watched Lindsay as she and Radium passed within fifty feet. Radium's beautiful stride had not changed since the first step, and though he held his head low, this walk was no challenge.

Lindsay had fallen back into a semi-dazed state and listened to voices urging her on. When she next awoke, Radium had stopped and was casually drinking from the creek. The sun had sunk low, and the sky glowed bright red.

Revived by the cooler air and feeling the joy of success, she bent over and hugged Radium's neck. "You have been sent by God. I love you."

Lindsay worked her way out of the saddle and stretched before she went down to the water. Anticipating the meeting with Gavin, who was just five miles away, she was deliberate as she removed her hat and blouse. The water felt like golden oil as it cooled and lightly stung her sun- and wind-burnt skin. Retrieving a hair brush from the saddle bag, she rested her face on radium's forehead and told him how she loved him while brushing her hair. "Excuse me, brushing my hair in front of you. But after coming all this way, I have to look my best for Gavin, don't you think?"

It was only about four o'clock, so there was no hurry to cover the next five miles. She sat on the bank and enjoyed stretching her body and giving her bottom a welcome rest from the saddle. Radium seemed to be as fresh as when he had started and paid little attention to Lindsay.

Back on the trail, Lindsay's fatigue was replaced with the

anticipation of seeing Gavin. She also realized that she hadn't thought of what she would say to him.

At the sight of the trees ahead, she realized she had no idea where or on what side of the lakes Gavin would be camped. Leaning forward on Radium's neck, she said, "Please find him, Radium." As on most of the journey, she let the horse have his head and didn't bother holding the reigns.

Radium turned west at the bottom of the lake, and in ten minutes, their presence was known as Gavin's horses called out to Radium, who answered with a single loud neigh.

Gavin came out to greet his unseen guests. When Lindsay and Radium came into view, his mouth fell open.

He waited to see other riders, and when they didn't appear, he stared at Lindsay. "Don't tell me you came out here alone," he said.

Getting down from her horse, she replied, "No, I wasn't alone. Radium was with me."

He folded his arms. "You might be surprised, but I can see the damn horse."

"Gavin, you sound like you're sorry that I'm here."

"Come on, Lindsay, give me a break. I'm out here at the end of the world, and the most beautiful woman I know appears out of nowhere, riding a horse that no professional ringer can ride. I would say that's enough reason to be in shock and a little short, wouldn't you?"

Ignoring the question, she put her arms around him. "Gavin, I came here to tell you that I love you, and no matter what you think or do, I decided that I'm not going to let you take one more breath without knowing that I love you as much as any woman could love a man."

Gavin took a breath and started to speak, but she gently put her fingers on his lips to silence him.

"Wait – there's more. I've been in love with you since the day we went to the surf carnival. There, now you can speak."

He increased his grip on Lindsay and hid his head in her neck. He didn't make a sound, but Lindsay felt his tears running down her back.

It took a full two minutes before he spoke. "Lindsay, you can't understand that I have been here for three days trying to plan my life without you, and now you tell me that I don't have to. God could not have heard me more clearly. My heart is yours, until I take my last breath in this world." With a smile, he added, "And the world after, of course."

He let her go and skipped across the campsite like a teenager. "Why don't you sort the tent out for us, and I'll help poor old Radium get rid of that saddle. That's if he will let me near him . . ."

That night, in the immensity of the outback, they made love with passion that Lindsay hadn't thought could possibly exist. Not only did their climaxes reach to the heavens, they laughed together with such joy. Each knew, from this moment on, that they were one, never to be divided. Gavin mockingly apologized for taking out his ten years of chastity on her. She retorted that she was glad he had been a ladies' man before taking his vows. Lindsay's mind slipped back to her talks with Peggy, when she questioned if such sexual heights could even exist.

To herself, she addressed Peggy: *Peggy, my dear, I'm happy to say that I can confirm that these heights do exist. I am happy to be with Gavin, and I know you and Ian are also happy for us. I will always believe that you two made this happen. Radium knew he was carrying Ian's spirit to fulfill your heavenly plans for us. God bless you, my dear Peggy. You are ever in my heart.*

In that happy tent that night, Gavin made a vow that he would leave the cruel outback and never return.

Epilogue

Anna and Paul sat listening to Lindsay as the tapes whirled on.

"True to his vow," she concluded, "Gavin only returned to Naringa to be buried."

"Mrs. Abernathy, can you tell me what happened to the trust and Octavio's church?" Paul asked.

A broad smile came to her lips. "You know, it was only when I was telling the story about the night Gavin made me a trustee that I realized he only did that to keep me from leaving."

Paul had read of her fame as a businesswoman. "Maybe, but from what the papers say, it was probably the best business move he ever made."

"Thank you, Paul. I did sit on the boards of twenty-eight of the world's top Fortune 500 companies during those years. Who knew that the gutless girl who couldn't even face her father's wrath would become one of the most influential businesswomen in the world? As we sit here today, the fund has holdings of over one billion dollars, after distributing hundreds of millions of dollars over the years."

"And Octavio's church?"

"Dear old Octavio. His church, St. Barnaby's, was and still is a great success. Octavio is still playing his guitar. He has gone completely bald, but still wears his Panama hat. His church cost twice the amount Gavin started with, and he has remained our dearest friend, 'Gawin' could never say no to him."

"Did Jim Holly stay on as a director?"

"Yes. We are still the closest of friends and have spent most summers together all over the world. Some great memories, eh, Anna?"

Anna smiled and nodded.

"Did you and Gavin have a family?" Paul asked.

"Yes, a boy and a girl, who both became doctors and remained in England. They have never visited Naringa. As I said, neither Gavin nor I returned to Naringa during the next forty-seven years, but Naringa never left us. As much as we loved Naringa and the outback, we didn't speak of it much. So you could imagine my surprise when Gavin's last request was to be buried at Naringa. The family graveyard is almost complete and only awaits my arrival. Gavin's parents lie together. Peggy lies on one side of Ian, with Karo on the other. Gavin's and my grave plot is above them all, as I think he still would want to watch over all of us."

She looked up at Paul, who had a tear in his eye. "Don't look so sad, Paul. I'm not going to be up there for quite a while. Yes, I will be back, but not too soon, I hope. The day after tomorrow, I leave here for Italy, where I will summer with Max and Phillipa and all of our grandchildren.

"I'm afraid that's all I can do for today. Could you both leave me? Oh, by the way, Paul, please call me Lindsay."

Paul switched off the tape recorder and left everything in place. Once he and Anna had left the room, he asked Anna if she would sit and talk with him.

When they were seated, Anna spoke first. "I could feel your heart jump when Mrs. Abernathy, or Lindsay, as I call her, mentioned my remembering a certain time."

He nodded. "Yes, you're right. It was like cold water in the face. What a shock. How does this work out?"

Anna smiled, thinking that he might pass out if she didn't tell him who she was. "I'm Jim Holly's daughter."

"My God," exclaimed Paul. "It's like reading Dickens and

finding out I know one of the characters."

Anna laughed. "I can understand what you mean, but I do think Dickens is aging me a little, don't you?"

After sharing all those privileged hours with Mrs. Abernathy, Paul felt very close to Anna. "You told me you've been at Naringa for three years," he said. "How come?"

"Well, you were right when you called the outback 'the Foreign Legion of Down Under.' At least, I take that to mean people coming here to hide something or to work something out."

He nodded. "Yes. I wasn't referring in any way to you, but that's what I meant."

"Well, here it is. I met a wonderful man and fell deeply in love with him. He fell in love with me, too, but he was a good man and wouldn't cheat on his wife, whom he had married at a very young age and with whom he had very little in common. They had three beautiful young children. He was always worried about his wife's mental health and came to tell me that there was no way he could put his own life ahead of the lives of the children. We met and agreed not to see each other again.

"She must have followed him. She entered the restaurant, which was full of people, yelling that she would get even, and then ran outside and was run over by a bus. The papers had a field day, calling it a heart-breaking suicide, with catchy headlines like 'Harlot Kills Kids' Mom' and 'Betrayed Mother of Three Dies under a Bus.' It never stopped."

Paul reached for her hand. "I can image how hard that was to get through, but you can't hide away out here. You just can't."

"Paul, you really are a love, but I'm not going to. After the signing over of Naringa tomorrow, I'm going back with Lindsay. I said some people come out here to hide, but I should have added that some come to learn how to live with their secrets or with life's disappointments. I think I have, and I actually feel quite good about everything. Listening to Lindsay over the past few days also made me aware that life goes on no matter what." She met his gaze. "Are you shocked?"

"I'm shocked that you're a hero's daughter. Detective Jim Holly . . . I love him. Is he still alive?"

"Oh, sure, larger than life. And do you know, he's still good friends with that guy Stan? Look, I'm a little worn out, and I think I'll skip dinner tonight, so I'll see you in the morning for the signing. You also have one very big surprise in store, so sleep well."

"Yeah, I'm sure I'll sleep well now, trying to think what the surprise could be. Come on, tell me."

She shook her head. "If you're a reporter, you have to practice your craft. You will spot the surprise, I'm sure."

"Thanks."

~~~

The next morning, at 9:30, Paul was summoned to Mrs. Abernathy's veranda. She looked very awake and animated as she addressed him. "Now, Paul, there will be quite a number of people here this morning for the signing over of Naringa. A professional photographer will be here, and I want to record a photo with you at my side. I also want you to be in some of the group photos."

Paul's face went red, but he was delighted to be included. "Thank you. Thank you very much, Mrs. Abernathy. I feel so proud that you asked me."

"Paul, I'm happy to have asked you. Now, there will be a formal signing of papers, etcetera, and then I have drinks and some lunch for everyone. That is when you will meet everyone. Is that okay? Oh, Paul, I was hoping you would play for us."

"You know it would be my greatest pleasure."
~~~

Later in the morning, a shining two-engine plane buzzed past the house and landed on the 3,000-foot blacktop airstrip now located a mile away. Trucks transported nine people back to the homestead. Paul watched them from his room as they entered the main veranda. He had expected to recognize somebody after Anna's teasing comment: "If there is a surprise, it's not from the people who walked up these stairs, that's for sure."

Paul sat to play the piano as the party broke for lunch and drinks. As he played, he checked every person in the room, but got no clues to Anna's hidden surprise. Anna had refused to give him any hints, repeating that any good newspaper man would flush it out in a second.

Once the drinks were served, a few people came over to the piano and complimented his playing. Nothing new, nothing different. *What the hell could it be?* he thought.

After he had played for about a half hour, Mrs. Abernathy came over and asked Paul to come and meet her guests. The first people Paul met were from the farm association, now called the Naringa Foundation. He met three lawyers from the firm Blake, Pickles, Smith, and Hadley; one judge from Townsville; and *The Sydney Herald* photographer.

The photographer shook Paul's hand and told him that the whole paper knew of his scoop. "The bigwigs wanted to fly a senior writer out here, and the law firm told them no way."

Amazingly, Paul hadn't thought of the paper or his career since the day he had climbed the front steps of the homestead and looked into Anna's clear blue eyes. It all seemed so far away.

During lunch, one of the lawyers stood and asked if Mrs. Abernathy would stand for a photograph and say a few words. Everyone clapped as she rose.

"Thank you all for being here. As we all know, this will be the start of a foundation that will benefit, expand, and enrich the lives for hundreds of people for hundreds of years to come. To ensure just that, the Abernathy Family Foundation has donated another twenty-five million."

Lindsay had not told anyone of the gift, so the applause was loud and genuine.

She continued, "The foundation will protect and provide stability for families in harsh times, which is the nature of the outback. In this modern day, education is not only for the young. Many of the programs are especially for people who left school in their early years, or for those who didn't get a chance to go school at all. Education enriches all lives, and as living proof that Naringa's people are highly teachable, let me use myself as an example.

"Only days ago, a young man bumped his way up the homestead road in an old car that I fear may not make it out of here. This young man passionately explained to this old lady, who thought she knew everything, that the past has ownership beyond the personal involvement of the people in that past. It doesn't only belong to them, or Naringa, as Paul so eloquently put it. It belongs to Australia. The history of the outback is the heritage of Australia.

"So convincing was this earnest young man that I have spent the last few days recording the history of the Abernathy family and, of course, the people of Naringa." She looked at Paul. "Paul Bishop, will you please stand?"

There was light applause, and Paul sat back down like a new man. He grinned as Anna gave him a little wave of her fingers and an affectionate smile from her end of the table.

Lindsay continued, "Even a better example of how people from the outback can learn, let me introduce the most famous Naringain, the man who made the greatest ride in Australian history . . . chairman of Blake, Pickles, Smith, and Hadley, Mr. Jimmy Blake."

Upon seeing Jimmy Blake's deeply scared wrists beneath the starched French cuffs, Paul knew that this was Anna's surprise.

~~~

Paul didn't return to Naringa until eight years later, by an invitation written into Lindsay's will. Lindsay had died in her sleep in London, and her ashes had been shipped to Australia with instructions regarding her burial at Naringa. He was one of two people attending the solemn affair besides the Naringa staff.

He was given the same room he had used during his first trip. Sitting on that same Candlewick bedspread, his mind went back to the young, innocent kid who'd had no idea what would come of his naïve efforts eight years ago. The room still had the lovely smell of well-polished floors.

The reception wasn't until the following morning. Until he walked into the dining room for dinner that night, he didn't know who else had been invited.

Anna made her entrance dressed in an elegant, but simple black dress. She looked beautiful. Her skin was lightly tanned, and her blond hair sparkled with a healthy radiance.

She was the first to speak as she gave Paul an affectionate hug. "Paul, it's lovely to see you. You look very handsome."

Paul was surprised by his reaction to seeing her again. His legs nearly gave way under him as he inhaled her alluring scent. "Anna, you look so lovely that I am lost for words."

Putting Paul at ease, she said, "No, Paul, those are the right words a lady likes to hear. Hard to think that eight years have passed since we were in this room, isn't it? It appears Lindsay hasn't finished with us yet."

"What do you mean?"

"I am the executor of her will, and she has given us both a
~~~

position on the board of the Abernathy World Trust."

Paul couldn't believe his ears. "Why would she do that?"

"She told me that she liked seeing us together. But, of course, if you don't accept her offer, we wouldn't see much of each other. If being with me is not enough, it will sadden me to have to tell you the condition of the offer, to entice you further."

Paul smiled broadly. "No, you don't have to tell me to entice me more. But you might as well tell me, anyway."

"Let's just say it wouldn't matter if you never worked again."

After talking all night, Anna and Paul where still sitting on the veranda as the sun came up.

Later, after the burial of Lindsay's ashes, Paul held Anna's hand as they both looked out at the huge open space.

"I guess Gavin and Ian were right," Paul reflected. "Once you've come into contact with the outback, it will affect your life forever . . . one way or another."

THE END